THE MAGIC OF DISCOVERY

EMERALD LAKES BOOK ONE

BRITT ANDREWS

Copyright © 2020 Britt Andrews

All rights reserved. No part of this publication may be reproduced, distributed, or transmitted in any form or by any means, including photocopying, recording, or other electronic or mechanical methods, without the prior written permission of the publisher, except in the case of brief quotations in book reviews.

The unauthorized reproduction or distribution of a copyrighted work is illegal. Criminal copyright infringement, including infringement without monetary gain, is investigated by the FBI and is punishable by fines and federal imprisonment.

Please purchase only authorized electronic editions and do not participate in, or encourage, the electronic piracy of copyrighted materials. Your support of the author's rights is appreciated.

This book is a work of fiction. Names, characters, places, brands, and incidents are the products of the author's imagination or used fictitiously. Any resemblance to actual events, locales or persons, living or dead, is entirely coincidental.

Cover by: Jodielocks Designs
Formatting by: Inked Imagination Author Services
Editing By: Michelle Motyczka with Inked Imagination Author Services
Proofreading by: PollyAné Nichols
Photography by: TalkNerdy2me
Samantha La Mar www.thetalknerdy.com

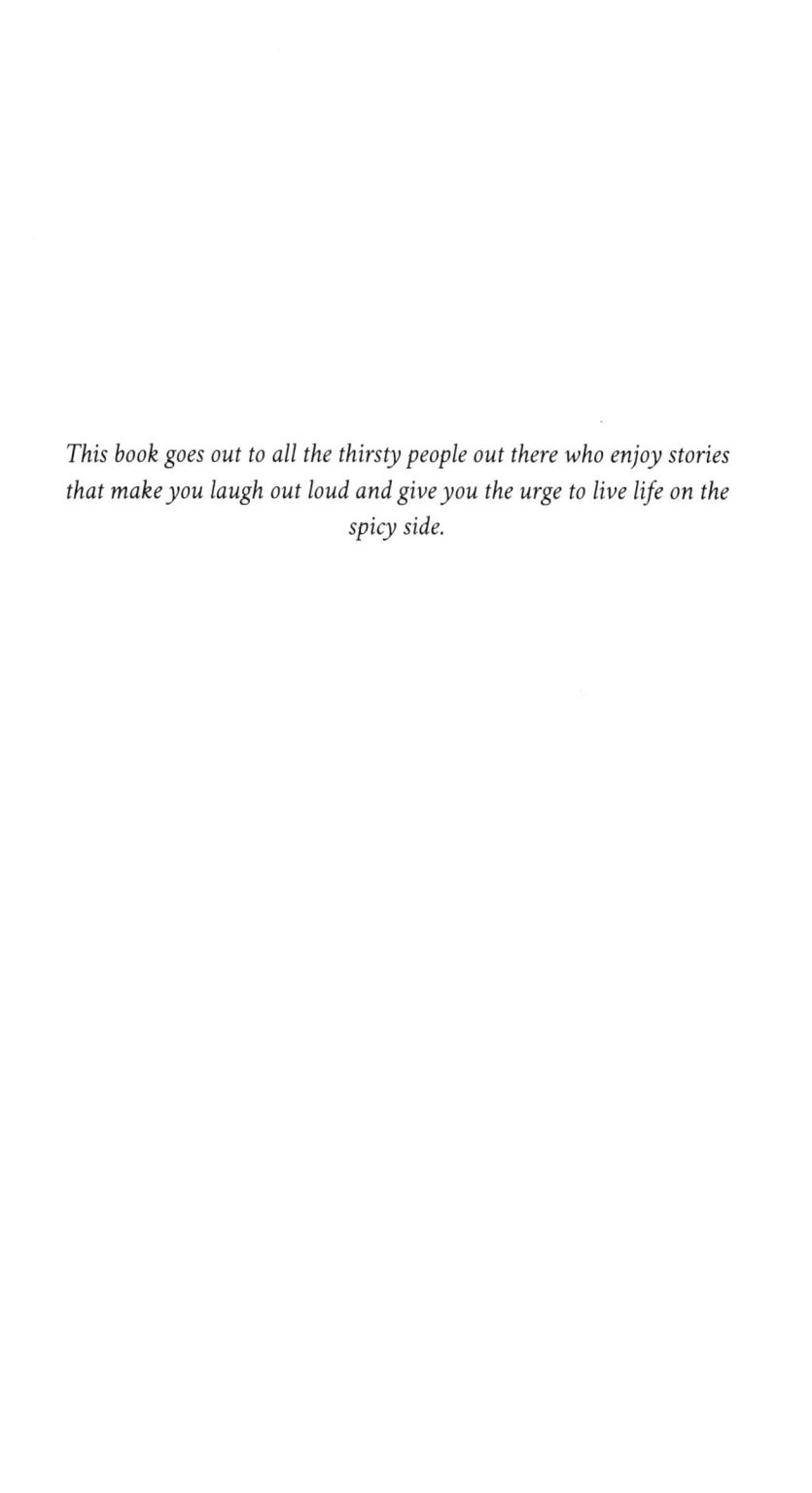

This book goes out to all the thirsty people out there who enjoy stories that make you laugh out loud and give you the urge to live life on the spicy side.

TRIGGER WARNING

This is a full-length RH romance, which includes MMFMM content. It ends on a cliffhanger and contains brief references to domestic violence and other themes that readers may find triggering.

This is the first book in a paranormal RH series.

Prologue
Khol Larson

It had been twenty-seven years, but the anger I experienced at Laura's betrayal felt like it had just happened yesterday. So help me, when I got my hands on her...

Love. Fucking pathetic. I should have known my black heart had no business delving into such pleasures. She had gotten under my skin, wormed her way into my veins, and given me hope for a future that I would never have. I was furious every single time her face flashed in my mind.

I'd told Cam's team that she'd stolen from me, and she had. She'd stolen whatever decency I'd had left in my body. When I met her, I'd had hope, something that I never would have given a second thought if she hadn't fucking pushed me. Then she humiliated me. *Broke me.* Now, I was going to find her and break her. The final conversation we had face to face constantly played over and over in my head, and I couldn't just banish it and move on with my life, my never-ending existence.

"Khol." Laura looked up at me when I entered our bedroom. She'd moved in with me only six months ago, but now a suitcase was open on the bed, almost full of her clothing and toiletries.

"Where are you going, darling?" Walking around the king-sized bed, I reached out for her, wrapping my arm around her waist and pulling her into me. She melted against me like butter, and my heart warmed. I loved this woman. I dropped a chaste kiss on the top of her strawberry blonde head.

"I have a business trip I have to take. My boss called, and while it's been fine working remotely for the last several months, I'm needed in

person for this job," she explained, running her fingernails down my back. "I wish I didn't have to go. I'll miss you. And I'll miss this." She cupped my erection with her palm and squeezed, summoning a moan from deep within my chest.

"How long will you be? Don't forget we have our engagement party in two weeks. It would be a bitch to have to reschedule at this point," I reminded her, my hands kneading her voluptuous ass. Gods, the woman was sculpted.

"I could never forget, Khol. It should take four to five days, tops," she reassured me as she closed the lid on her suitcase and zipped it up. I lifted it off the bed and put it on the floor for her.

"I've gotta get down to the airfield. My jet is waiting. I'll let you know when I land." She wrapped her lean arms around my neck, rose onto her toes, and planted her lips on mine.

That was the last time I saw her in person. The other five times had been through shitty camera snapshots using facial recognition software. I'd never come close to catching her slippery ass, but now I knew she was keeping secrets. Someone had put protection spells down to keep me out of that town. The guys had had no problem crossing that imaginary boundary, which just backed up my suspicions that this particular spell was keyed to me.

Or others like me. Now that's an interesting thought.

Sloane had texted me earlier to let me know they'd arrived, gotten settled, and were coming up with a game plan to tackle this mission. The kid was hardworking, one of the best I'd ever employed, but so was every single spy in my company. He was just easier to manipulate into doing this for me. He constantly sought approval, fame, and glory. He didn't do anything just to conquer it; he wanted to be the fucking legend. I'd read his file.

I knew everything there was to know about all of my elites.

Sloane Sullivan, thirty years old. Pyro mage. Top ten percent of his training class. Anger issues, loyal, broken family, only child. Master of wards.

Fischer Bahri, thirty years old. Cognitive mage. Interrogator, ability to not only read emotions but also push them, alter memories, hypnotize. Valedictorian of his training class. Loving family, one sister and two nieces.

Cameron Jacobs, thirty-one years old. Storm mage. Protector, fierce fighter, relentless. Can manipulate weather within a seventy-five mile radius with the ability to create more localized storms. Generates lightning from hands. Severe childhood trauma. Fear of loss.

Kaito Mori, twenty-nine years old. Shifter mage. Black panther: Bagheera. Heightened sense of smell, vision, and hearing. Oldest of five children. Struggled with depression in the past.

Pacing around my apartment, I swirled my glass of whiskey. Finding out about this town had me completely obsessed. I'd yet to have a lead this promising, and it was all I could think about. Once I found her, I could be free of this fucking weight.

Come out, come out wherever you are.

Saige

Chapter One

The Devil. I was staring down at the Devil. *Well, that's just a fantastic start to my Saturday.*

At least he's in tarot form and not an actual manifestation of the dark lord?

Gran had insisted she do a three card tarot reading for me this morning before I left for the shop, so I indulged her request as I finished drinking my coffee. Ah, sweet coffee, the root of every witch's power supply.

"I knew something was brewing! I felt it throughout my body from the moment these starry eyes opened this morning," Gran proclaimed. She slammed her tiny hand down on the table for emphasis, causing me and our filled to the brim coffee cups to jump.

I gave Gran a killer side-eye, but she was much too far down her own rabbit hole to pay any attention to my facial expressions. She started clapping her hands together, squealing like she did every time a man stepped foot on our property. *Any* man. Even her ex-husband who she momentarily forgets that she can't fucking stand. Gran has got mad love for the 'D.'

"Your emotional body is the Fool. Are you ready to take new chances? Experience change? Find a new man?" Gran's eyebrows rose up so high at the end of her question I thought they were going to blend right in with her wild and curly copper hair. Even her fine wrinkles seemed to be trembling with excitement. That's just how she was though, eccentric and unapologetically free. I wouldn't change her for the world.

"Gran! You know there isn't anyone in this town that I'm interested in. Even if there were, that piece of shit Bryce would do nothing but cause all kinds of drama just to make sure that I never got laid again so long as I live in Emerald Lakes," I retorted, stirring sugar into my liquid gold. My ex, Bryce, had been a two-year complete waste of time that I had only freed myself from six months ago. He was a total shithead. I'd taken my dear friends, Frank and Arlo, with me when I'd ended things, just in case.

"I'm so glad you're out of his clutches, but you don't need to kill the coffee mug, dear," Gran replied as she reached out and grabbed my hand to stop my violent cycloning motions. "And fuck Bryce, he's nothing but a limp dick noodle wand."

I laughed suddenly, startling my pet arctic fox, Maven. He released a low angry growl and lifted his head from his bed in the corner of the kitchen. I could always tell when he was pissed because his tail fluffed up to three times its size.

"Aww, don't be mad, Mave. Come over here, boy," I called out to him as I patted my thigh in encouragement. He hopped up and lazily meandered over to where Gran and I were sitting at the breakfast table. My long red hair spilled over my shoulders as I bent over to scoop him up. He nuzzled into my chest as I ran my fingers through his thick, silky, white and gray-streaked fur. Lifting my mug to my lips, I sipped the warm liquid and settled into the wave of contentment that burrowed deep in my heart. Gran, Mave, coffee... the three loves of my life.

"The Sun is lining up with your spiritual body. Positive outcomes, child. Success and optimism! Today is going to be a star-blessed day," Gran continued, moving down the line of cards, not fazed by Maven's antics at all. They didn't always see eye to eye anyway, so if they wanted to ignore one another, that was totally fine by me.

"And as for your... physical body..." She waggled her eyebrows and pinned me with her cornflower blue eyes. "We have the Devil. Sexual. Lust." Gran enunciated the last two words as she jammed her one hundred percent non-threatening index finger down onto the face of the card.

"Yeah, or materialism or envy or obsession and addiction. I highly doubt I'll be getting lusty over anybody, Gran." I stood up and took my empty mug to the sink to rinse it out.

"Dick addiction is a real affliction, Saige," Gran said in a serious voice.

By the stars, what is she? A rapper?

"You'd know since you're the Queen of Dick Addiction. If there was a figurehead for Dick Addiction, your face would be on it. The Twelve Steps of Dick Addiction with Bette Wildes," I bantered back at her, chuckling as I continued cleaning up breakfast.

"More like," Gran paused, already laughing her ass off at her coming joke, "The Twelve *Inches* of Dick Addiction, heyoooo!"

We both were dying now, and I felt fortunate that I had such a witty and fun grandma in my life. Wiping my eyes, I scolded her, "Gran. You're going to make me late to the shop. No more dick jokes."

"Awwww, man. You're no fun. But fine, I'll put a lid on it," she gave in with an eye roll, standing up from her chair. "But only until I see you for dinner."

She had raised me and was truly more of a mother to me than my actual birth mother, who had last blessed us with her presence about two months ago. It was the first visit in two years, but that wasn't unusual at all since she worked for a big magical firm on the other side of the country. Regardless of the physical distance, we'd just never had the typical mother-daughter relationship. My birth mother had only been nineteen years old when she'd gotten pregnant with me. My biological father was your stereotypical deadbeat, a one night stand. Laurie (yes, I call her Laurie) always told me that she didn't know who he was. They'd hooked up at a party, and she'd had no way of contacting him after that night. Lucky for me, my gran was an out of this world person, and I never found myself lacking when it came to feeling loved or taken care of.

I turned to put my mug back in the cupboard and caught my reflection in the glass of the large window that ran the length of my countertop. High cheekbones, full lips, and a slight upward turn on the end of my nose... those were all *my* features. Not Laurie's and not some sperm donor I'd never met. I'd always been relieved that I wasn't a carbon copy of Laurie, looks or otherwise. I mean, sure, we shared some things like our red hair, the arch of our eyebrows, and the shape of our faces, but that was where the similarities ended.

Movement outside broke me from my thoughts, and I watched a handful of baby bunnies hopping and playing in the yard. Scanning our wide property, I took in all of the different gardens that covered most of the acreage, ending with the large flowerbed closer to the house. That was when I noticed a row of my tulips had wilted, the blooms sagging so low they were brushing the dirt. *What the hell?* Those were in absolutely perfect condition last evening! I'd been planning to give them a couple more days to grow before I cut them to sell at my magic shop, The Mystical Piglet or The Pig, as the locals had so lovingly shortened it. *I'll have to remember to check on them when I get home from work later.*

Hearing Gran shuffling away since she knew I would be taking off soon for work, I continued to maneuver around my eat-in kitchen, grabbing some snacks to bring with me. Fishing my phone out, I checked the weather forecast for the day. *Perfect. Seventy degrees and sunny.*

"Oh, damn it." The sound of Gran's exasperated voice drew my attention as I walked around the kitchen table and took a right, intending to meet her on the back porch where she always entered and exited my cottage. She had her own sweet set-up along the back tree line. "I completely forgot that I got a phone call yesterday after dinner from a man who wants to rent the apartment above the shop. He already paid the first three months' rent and the security deposit. He's due to arrive at The Pig at ten. Here, take these herbs with you." Gran picked up an overflowing bag that was sitting on the countertop and shoved it at me. Fresh greenery peeked over the top of the bag, the scents of basil, sage, and oregano mixing together.

"A heads up would've been nice, Gran. I'm going to have to rush now," I huffed with fake annoyance, heading back to gather the rest of my things.

Following me, she chuckled. "Just keeping you on your toes, child." Her phone started ringing, and she silenced it with a curse. "I've got to get home. Had a bit of a rager last night, so there are streamers all over the living room and that lightweight Randy Roger passed out in my bathtub. This is the third time! No more tequila for him. I'm the umpire of drinking and questionable decisions, and I call them like I see them. Three strikes, you're out!"

The dude's name was *not* Randy Roger. It was Roger, and I'll let you guess why she threw the other name in there. In any case, Gran had bequeathed that name unto the man, and thus, he was now Randy Roger to everyone in town.

Throwing everything I needed into my backpack, I slipped it onto my shoulders. Glancing at the black cat clock that was ticking happily along on my kitchen wall, I groaned when I realized I really was going to have to rush.

"It's already 9:45! I'll be back later, and I'll call if there are any questions," I called out as I slipped my feet into my favorite pair of shoes. "Come on, Maven! We gotta hurry," I yelled to my little furry friend as I ran out the old screen door.

I COULD HEAR GRAN CACKLING AS THE SCREEN DOOR SLAMMED shut behind us. *Sick woman laughing at how much I'm going to be sweating by the time I get down there.* Shaking my head, I hopped on my pastel blue bicycle while Maven leapt into the large wicker basket attached to the handlebars. He never missed an opportunity to freeload, and my gods, he looked cute doing it.

"Maven, don't crush those herbs! Watch your tail, son!" He gave a chirp in response and then squirmed down into the basket, that damn tail now pulsating like a pissed off squirrel. *Sometimes he can be such a moody little bastard.* I pushed off of the brick pathway that led to the main road in front of my cottage. It was a beautiful day for gardening and witching, which happened to be two of my top five favorite things. Frank and Arlo, my two handymen who hauled our items down to our shop, had already been by and picked up today's fresh supplies. We typically left a clipboard on the side of the shed and marked things that needed to be loaded up and taken into town each day. It was mid-May, so most of our produce wouldn't be ready for several weeks yet. Good thing we had more than just your usual vegetable fanfare at The Pig.

A grocery store, we were not. I carried everything from smudge sticks, to moonstones, crystals, bulk spell supplies, tonics, elixirs, and I did tarot readings here and there. Selling in-season produce was just a little extra income for me, and it always sold extremely well. Fresh-cut flowers were also a hot commodity, and in a couple of months, I would be up to my tits in blooms.

The bicycle tires bumped along our rocky stone driveway, a path I had walked down a million times. Riding into town was just easier, and it usually only took about ten minutes. I just might make it in time, which would be a good first impression.

Whoever this guy was, we were going to be seeing each other a lot, and starting out on the right foot would set the stage going forward.

Thankfully, most of the ride was a straight shot, so I didn't need to worry about going uphill. *This body is not about that type of life.* I was curvier than your average woman, but that was just my build. I was in shape since gardening outside and doing most of my own home improvement projects kept me fit enough. Squats were something I had a love-hate relationship with, but with squatting being a near-constant gardening maneuver, my ass and thighs were thicccc. *Yes, with four c's.*

I assumed the renter was coming in from Portage Falls, one of the closest areas with more business opportunities than my small town of Emerald Lakes. It was about ten hours south, and I'd only ever heard of the place. I had never actually set foot more than twenty miles outside of Emerald Lakes. In fact, I'd never felt the need or the urge to. When I'd taken my mastery classes, I attended a university that was only ten miles from the cottage. I'd also commuted to save money and so I'd be able to help Gran with the upkeep around our sizable property.

The wind picked up then, blowing my hair off of my neck and breathing life into my body. I loved everything about being outside; I was a green witch, after all. Deriving my power from the earth and the sunlight, I was able to create vegetation and other natural growing items, like crystals and moonstones. The sun's rays hit my skin, sinking down to my bones, and I groaned. The feeling of my muscles being energized by the glorious golden orb was intoxicating. Nothing like that first blast of vitamin D in the morning to set you up for a fantastic day. My mind thought back to Gran's tarot reading. It seemed the stars felt I might be getting some of the more fun vitamin 'D' soon. *I fucking wish.*

Entering the downtown area, the road gave way to a designated bike path. Moving my bicycle onto the smoother asphalt, the ding of a bike bell drew my attention to the opposite side of the road.

"Hi, Saige! Hi, Maven!" a cute, tiny voice squealed, and Mr. Grumpy Fluff let out a low growl, not bothering to raise his head in acknowledgment. Ignoring him, I slowed to a stop and greeted the seven-year-old blonde across the street.

"Hi, Annie!" I called back, waving to her and her mother before adding, "Come by the shop later. We have a fresh batch of basil and the moonstones that you asked about last week, Miranda."

"Sure thing, girl. There's a reason you're everyone's favorite magic shop owner in Emerald Lakes!" Miranda gave me a wink and a smile as she began walking again with Annie pedaling in front of her.

Ha. I'm the only *magic shop owner in Emerald Lakes. But yeah, I'm pretty awesome. All the asspats for me.*

Miranda was my only friend who still lived in town; everyone else had left for one reason or another: schooling, careers, marriage, or just craving a change of scenery. She and I had grown up together, and it never mattered how many days went in between us texting or seeing one another. It always felt like we could pick right up where we had left off. I didn't know what it was like to have a sibling, but I'd imagine it would be like my bond with Miranda.

A loud rumble came from behind me, and I swiveled on my seat to see who would be driving so loudly through downtown. Oh hell, a moving truck with the words 'Get Your Move On' sprawled across the side barreled past me. A colorful tattooed arm was hanging out of the window, and I glanced up, my gaze connecting with a pair of emerald eyes. It was like time slowed to a crawl, and I couldn't bring myself to look away. *Who the hell is that guy?* The truck passed me, and I sped up, curiosity taking over. *Is that my tenant?*

My shop was sandwiched in between two other businesses.

To the left was Mr. Vladescu's crystal shop, and to the right was a bookstore that was owned by Madame Winston. I lifted my hand in greeting toward Mr. Vladescu who was just opening up for the day. Being such a small town, we were able to keep pretty cushy hours, most businesses opening between 9:30am and 10:00am.

Slowing to a stop, I hopped off my bike in a practiced move and walked it the rest of the way to the bike rack, no need for a chain since crime was basically nonexistent here. It was hard to get away with anything illegal when the town's residents had likely watched you grow up and knew where you lived. Maven leapt fluidly out of the basket and into my waiting arms. Frank and Arlo were already at work, stocking the produce stands in front of the large picture window that looked into The Pig. Green ivy climbed to the roof and blended beautifully with the deep red bricks that housed my livelihood. A continuous beeping alerted me that the moving truck was backing into the alley beside our row of shops, and I quickly ran inside to grab the keys for the upstairs apartment.

The dark hardwood floors creaked as my favorite flats quickly flew across the boards, my left hand trailing along the smooth twenty-foot-long wooden bar that I used as my sales counter. Floor to ceiling shelves lined the entire wall behind the bar. Having such a perfect setting for it, I'd enlisted Frank and Arlo's help to set up a mixing station so that I could whip up different elixirs, tonics, and potions for customers as needed. Once a month, I hosted 'Witching Hour,' an event that nearly the whole town attended. I ran specials on different items and mixed up magic shots, always a big hit.

With a quiet yip and eager squirm, Maven jumped from my arms, running straight to the back of the shop where I kept his food and water bowls. Figuring the keys were likely in the spelled safe we kept under the counter, I ducked down and unlocked it with a flick of magic, the safe recognizing me and popping open. The bell that was attached to the front door began to chime, announcing a customer, or in this case, a tenant. Sensing their magic immediately, the hair on my arms stood straight up. It felt like fingers reaching out to me, seeking, caressing, and I hadn't even seen these people yet. *They must be really fucking powerful.*

"Just one minute! Grabbing the keys..." My hands wrapped around the keyring, and I'd just spelled the lock when a thump sounded from the bar top, jerking my head up. When a face appeared right above me, I startled, releasing a shriek and falling backward onto my ass. A smiling man stared down at me, his almond-shaped eyes sparkling like onyx. Jet black hair fell playfully over his eyes, and his mischievous grin only served to spotlight his defined high cheekbones. *Beautiful.*

"Kaito, don't scare the poor girl," a deep voice chastised.

The man above me, who I assumed was Kaito, gave me a sheepish look. He still had a playful glint in his eye as he said, "Sorry, didn't mean to spook you. This is a really cool shop." Disappearing momentarily and just as quickly reappearing beside me, he held out his hand to pull me up. I grasped it and was instantly propelled upward, the momentum had me putting my palms out and catching myself on his chest.

"Hi, I'm Kaito, but you can call me Kai." He looked down at me and canted his head to the left, a move that instantly struck me as animalistic in nature, reminding me so much of Maven when he was studying something. His hands were wrapped around my wrists, barely an inch of space between our bodies. I knew I should back up, but my brain felt like sludge and my feet wouldn't listen. My heart was pounding so hard I wondered if he could hear it. Kai exhaled.

"Actually, you can call me whatever you want..." My eyes rounded when his grip tightened on my arms as he leaned in slightly, effectively destroying the inch of space that had been between us, his nostrils flaring as he inhaled deeply.

"Kai." That baritone voice from before broke the spell like a splash of cold water in my face. I pulled my hands from his grasp and took a step back, smoothing the front of my shirt down just to make sure I wasn't showing any skin.

We both looked to the front of the store, but the morning sun was shining brightly through the window, and all I could make out was a large, dark silhouette that was illuminated with golden rays. Turning back to Kai, I stuck my hand out to him. "Welcome to Emerald Lakes, I'm Saige. I'm not usually this clumsy, but I've only had one cup of coffee this morning, and my gran only let me know about your arrival approximately twenty minutes ago. She owns the apartment, but she's old and really fucking nuts, and I'm rambling, so can you just shake my hand now?" My mouth was going a mile a minute, but he just grinned at me with a blindingly perfect smile.

Now that I was no longer pressed against him, his eyes rapidly dropped from mine to my feet and then back. I wore a black shirt that said *I hope thistle cheer you up* and a pair of skinny jeans. A laugh broke free from his throat as he took my hand and pulled me close to him once again. I swear to gods, I stopped breathing.

"I love your shirt," he said as he leaned down to put his mouth next to my ear. "The answer is yes, by the way," he added softly, which caused my brows to furrow in confusion. With another flash of that blinding grin, he explained, "It did cheer me up."

It appeared that we had a Grade A flirt here.

Back away, Saige. Red alert. No, vagina, do not do that zingy thing. Looks like another night of digging around in my nightstand to see which electric weapon, I mean TOY, will be pleasuring me.

Problem was that everyone in this town knew everyone, and it was no secret how my old relationship had fared. Most had been extremely supportive, but you always had *those people*, the ones who made excuses for men who got off on preying on women. At this point, there honestly wasn't anyone in town I was interested in, so my toys and I were quite well acquainted.

A deep throat clearing made me jump, breaking the intense

eye contact between myself and Kaito. He held onto my hand, gently tugging me around the corner of the bar and up to the front of the shop.

"Saige, this is my best friend, Cam. Cam, this is Saige," Kai sing-songed.

I pulled my hand out of Kaito's and giggled. *What the fuck was that?* Taking Cam's offered hand, I tilted my head up to look at him. *By the moon, this one is a giant of a man.* Light brown hair with glittering strands of gold was twisted up into a topknot on his head. The arm that was extended toward me was covered in colorful rune tattoos. *This is moving van man.* My stomach bottomed out when our hands connected; it felt like an electric current was moving through my bloodstream, tethering me to him. His piercing emerald green eyes were staring at me so intensely I could feel my blush darken at least seven shades. I probably looked like a fucking strawberry. *Be cool, Saige.* I pulled my hand back, flipped my hair over my right shoulder, and put my hand on my hip. *No, do the other hip. This feels off, switch back. Yes. That's the pose of power. Now hit him with the scrutinizing stare from hell.*

"Hello, Saige," he rumbled. A delicious shiver worked its way through my body. "Do you have the lease agreement and keys so we can start moving in as soon as possible? I'm feeling a storm coming in later this afternoon, and this hair cannot handle that type of abuse." He winked at me when he said this, and I nodded at him like a bobblehead doll.

Laughter came from beside me, and my brain caught up with what I was doing. *Gods dammit! There goes my authoritative stance.*

"Oh! Yes, forgive me. So, my gran was um... not forthcoming at all regarding who was going to be renting, so which one of you is our new tenant?" I drew out the question while pointing between the two men.

My inner witch was jumping up and down, rolling around on

the floor, laughing maniacally, and doing hip thrusts. *Please just let it be one of them, please just let it be one of them.*

"Actually, it's me, Cam, Sloane, and Fischer." Kai smirked, the cocky twist of his lips saying he knew exactly what I'd been repeating in my head.

Well, poop sticks. I'm fucked.

Sloane

Chapter Two

"What the fuck are they doing in there?" Fischer groaned, clearly ready to get settled in the apartment upstairs.

"Did you not see that curvy redhead that ran into the shop right before we parked the van?" I raised an eyebrow as he looked at me, realization dawning on his face.

He shook his head and a grin tugged at the corner of his mouth. "Goddammit, Kai."

Goddammit, Kai was right. Dude would flirt with a toad if it so much as glanced in his direction.

I stretched down to touch my toes and then reached up to the sky as far as I could to really stretch my muscles. "I'm just glad to be out of that metal box for more than a piss and a Slim Jim at some shitty gas station."

We had driven for ten hours straight from Portage Falls. Thankfully, we were used to being constantly on the move, and this apartment came furnished, so we wouldn't need to put down any real roots. The moving truck was mainly a cover; the only things we were hauling in it were our duffel bags and four motorcycles that we'd use to get around this country ass town.

Fish hummed in agreement as he reached into his back pocket and pulled out his phone. His thumbs flew across the screen, likely texting Larson to let him know we had arrived.

Studying the picturesque town I was going to have to live in for the foreseeable future, my mind wandered back to our team's discussion with the CEO of Radical Incorporation, Khol Larson. We had been working for his company for about ten years now. They were a prestigious conglomerate in the magical world, offering first-class training to any witch or mage, no matter their affinity. You could enter their training program straight out of high school, and two years later, you were considered a badass in your specific area of magic. Most trainees opted to accept employment with Radical since it meant they'd get first dibs on new positions.

On the surface, Radical Inc. looked like any other mega company that raked in millions, except we catered to the magic community. If you needed specific marketing for your business? Radical had you covered. Your mage wand wasn't making the magic happen in the bedroom anymore? Radical had a fully functioning and extensive magical hospital facility. You were being a fuck head and caught the attention of Khol Larson? Well, that was where we came into the picture.

My team moved in the darkness, silent and deadly. Confidentiality and secrets were our specialties. We were spies, assassins, operatives; we did it all. Whatever you wanted to call us, one simple fact remained: you did *not* want to see us showing up in your bedroom in the dead of night or cornering you in a dark alley on your walk home from the office. My face was the last thing so many scumbags had seen before they left this sad plane of existence.

We were the elite, and after ten years, our group was the alpha team. The biggest, baddest, most-qualified team that Radical had ever seen. We were the top-rated team in everything from dispatching rogue demons to rescuing kidnapped humans from the hands of sick fucks involved in the skin trade. Our success rate was higher than any two units combined; every day was an adventure and another opportunity for me to be the best. So yeah, looking around at this fucking Sleepy Hollow-looking place, my blood was not pumping. *The fuck had Larson been thinking by sending us here?*

Yesterday, when he'd tasked us with this mission, I'd crossed all of my fingers and toes, hoping that something exciting would happen here.

"Gentlemen." *Larson's deep voice boomed across the conference room as he swept through the doorway. Our spines immediately straightened, all of us focusing intensely on the dominating man who was our boss. He was sharply dressed in an expensive as fuck, hand-tailored, three-piece navy suit. His dark hair was slicked back and combed to the left side, leaving his soul-penetrating gaze to make you feel like you were a ten-year-old shithead again.*

"Thank you for agreeing to meet with me on such short notice. I trust you're all rested up after the flight back from China?"

We each gave a short nod, not bothering to speak. Larson wasn't interested in our answer; this was just for show.

"Have a seat," *he offered after taking his place at the head of the conference table, his hard expression making the sharp lines of his features even more intense.*

Cam took the seat to Larson's right, and Fischer sat beside Cam. Moving to the other side of the table, I took a seat to Larson's left with Kai plopping down beside me. We always sat like this, even at a restaurant or eating dinner at home. Routine and structure, that was what our lives were. Plus, this particular arrangement left our dominant hands available to pull a gun or knife with the highest probability of hitting a threat.

"I called you all here to brief you on your next assignment," *he began. I looked across the table to Cam and saw his brow crease before he smoothed out his expression. We had never once gotten an assignment from anyone other than Johnny. He had been our handler since day one, and his lack of involvement had me even more on edge. What the fuck was going on?*

"This is a covert mission. The only people aware of the details are the five of us sitting in this room, and I expect it to remain that way. As

THE MAGIC OF DISCOVERY

far as Johnny is concerned, I'm sending you all on a well-deserved vacation." He paused a moment, jaw ticking and fingers strumming on the smooth, shiny surface before him. Larson wasn't a man prone to misgivings, so the fact that we were witnessing this hesitancy in a man who could effortlessly lock his emotions down told me that whatever he was going to say was of great importance. My heart began galloping in my chest, adrenaline already firing throughout my body at the mere thought of an exciting assignment. This was the kind of shit I lived for. The thrill of the hunt, the high of solving puzzles and mysteries, the glory of it all... balm to my black soul.

The tapping ceased, and his shoulders squared. *"For twenty-seven years, I've been searching for a ghost. Or she might as well be. I can count on one hand the number of times I've had her location pinned down through CCTV. An ATM camera here, a traffic camera there. She stole something from me all of those years ago, and it is imperative that I find this woman. Details of what was taken are not important at this time, just that you locate and detain her until you can bring her to me. She has things she needs to answer for, and I will not stop until she is tied down to a chair in our containment center, and I've bled the truth from her evil fucking body."* Larson took a moment to stare down each of us, vehemency rising with every word that spilled from his mouth. Whoever this bitch was, she was in for a world of fucking pain. Goddamn.

"Permission to speak, sir?" Cam asked.

Larson nodded once in encouragement.

"Forgive me, sir, but is this woman a witch or human? Is she dangerous?"

Larson stood from his chair and turned his back on us to walk over to the minibar that was stationed in the corner of the large room. Kaito quickly slapped the back of his hand against my bicep, drawing my attention. He raised his eyebrows up to his hairline as if saying *what the actual fuck?* I shook my head quickly just as a deep sigh pulled my focus from Kai to Larson. He plucked a crystal decanter off of the gold bar top, removing the half moon-shaped crystal topper. Selecting a tumbler, *he poured a healthy amount of the amber liquid into the glass, placing the decanter back in its rightful spot. His shoulders tensed, and I swore to the gods it looked like his entire body just expanded. He was one scary motherfucker. Spinning back around, his green eyes had darkened. Evidently, the more he thought about this woman, the further enraged he became, the fuse on a bomb getting shorter and shorter. Interesting. He swirled the scotch before raising the glass to his lips and taking a generous drink.*

"She's a green witch, and she's extremely dangerous. Once you do locate her, don't believe a word that comes out of her mouth. She's captivating. For years, I've wondered if she shared blood with a siren. I knew her as Laura Walker, but that was obviously an alias. We were romantically involved for about a year, and then she just vanished. I've used every available resource to track her down, but they only helped me discover that she was a lying bitch."

Christ, his anger pulsed through the room, spilling off of his body in waves. I didn't need to be a fucking empath to feel that level of hatred and loathing. I didn't think any of us had dared to blink since we realized how personally invested our boss was in this assignment. This woman must be talented to have pulled one over on Khol Larson. Dude was a beast. People had disappeared for much less than fucking with him.

"About two months ago, facial recognition picked her up on camera at a bank that's ten hours north of here." *He slid a photo to Cam who glanced down at it.* "She was wearing a disguise, but I know damn well it's her." *He slid another photo over, I'm guessing one of her with more detail. When the photos made it to me, I stared at the grainy ATM camera image. A woman with short, dark brown hair was smirking with her eyes downcast, likely grabbing her cash. She looked as though someone had just told her a joke and the smirk was as much emotion she was capable of giving when the punchline was delivered. K slid the second photo to me. This woman was younger, looked happier, and had long, strawberry blonde hair that was pin straight. Holding a glass of alcohol, her focus was on something out of the frame of the shot.*

THE MAGIC OF DISCOVERY

"I took it upon myself to fly up to this town, Emerald Lakes. The closest airfield is about sixty miles outside of the city limits. I wanted to deal with this on my own, but trying to get into the town itself was impossible. I was about fifteen miles from Emerald Lakes and physically could not take one step further without feeling like my skull was about to split open. My mind screamed at me to turn around, and I had to pull over to be sick before I could do so. I've never encountered anything like it in my life." He stopped to take another drink from his glass, just in time for Fischer to chime in.

"A warding spell?" he mused, pursing his lips in thought. *"Smart. But to also layer that with a revulsion spell? Someone very determined and talented did that."* Fish leaned forward in his seat, resting his bronzed forearms on the table as he spun a pen around his fingers.

"Emerald Lakes is the key to this mystery. You four will move there, get to know the locals, and investigate the perimeter to see what kind of fuckery is going on. Make up a cover story, I don't care what you go with. We need intel. Seems like a one horse, one stoplight kind of place. The town's website is from the stone ages and mostly has tourist information listed. Luckily, there was a classifieds section, and I was able to find a furnished apartment in the downtown area; I already set up everything for you to move in tomorrow. Get packed and get your asses to this shit hole town. Stay sharp and use your skills. I know this is a vague mission, but for now, it's really all about information. Contact me directly if needed."

Understanding the dismissal for what it was, we all rose from our chairs at the same time, ready to head out. Before we could leave, he spoke again.

"I'll text you all the information regarding the town and the apartment. Cam, Fischer, and Kaito, Johnny is waiting in his office for a debrief from your last assignment. He's expecting you. Sullivan, a word." His olive green eyes locked on my icy blues. What the fresh hell was this about?

Fish glanced my way with his eyebrow raised, and I gave a subtle nod. Kai clapped his hand on my back a couple of times in a 'sucks to be *you' kind of way before he walked around my chair and headed to the door. Cam just nodded at me and followed Kai out of the large double doors, leaving the two of us alone.*

"Sir?" I prompted as I lowered myself back down into my seat.

"Sloane, I heard about your trip to Beijing. Thanks to you, we were able to save millions of dollars by extracting that scientist. Their research is unfounded, and your quick wit and professional skills single handedly made that mission a huge success," Larson praised, sticking out his hand for me to shake.

"Thank you, sir," I replied, grasping his hand. "But it really was a team effort. I don't deserve all of the glory."

"See, Sloane, that's where we disagree. I've been kept apprised of all of your team's missions. There's a pattern developing, time and time again, and it's you that's stepping up and making the tough calls - the kind of calls a true leader makes. Cam is a solid lead, but sometimes his reserved decisions cost time, and time equals money. You have serious potential to move up in the ranks to a more prestigious role. When you're done with the spy world, you're going to want a job that you've earned. One that is kinder to your body and really stocks your bank account. With that being said, I would like to offer you a solo assignment, and if you're able to get this information for me, that will solidify my decision to give you this promotion. When you get to this town, there may be people who can lead us to Laura. I want you to figure out who these people are and milk them for any details you can get. Someone in that town knows something. I'll check in with you periodically to get updates on your progress." He stood up, clapping his large hand against my shoulder. "Keep up the great work, son."

The sound of laughter broke my flashback. *Real* laughter. Not that fake shit girls do to try and look sexy or coy. I cleared my throat and side-eyed Fischer, but he was already studying the redheaded goddess as she made her way down the few steps out of the magic shop.

Observant fucker.

Kai was guiding this girl over to our moving truck, and I

spied the keys dangling off of her finger. *Oh shit, this is the landlady?* Cam was a few steps behind them, looming like the huge stoic motherfucker he was.

The threesome reached us and came to a stop just in time for Kai to say, "Saige, these are our brothers, Sloane and Fischer." He nodded to each of us respectively. Saige's eyes widened slightly before she schooled her reaction, a smile lighting up her heart-shaped face.

Oh yeah, I saw that, baby. You can't hide from me.

Fischer stepped forward and held out his hand. "Hi, Saige. Thanks for meeting us so early. I'm Fischer, and it's nice to meet you."

Gods, he was always so damn pleasant. I watched Saige with interest, not that you could tell by the bored as fuck look I was broadcasting. *I'm good at that, not giving a fuck.* She was wearing a t-shirt with an awful pun scrawled across her chest and a pair of faded skinny jeans with cheetah print flats on her feet. I knew she was aware of my eyes trailing down her body because the longer I stared, the more pronounced the flush became on the creamy skin of her neck. Cam cleared his throat.

I realized everyone was awkwardly shuffling around, obviously waiting for me to take this opportunity to introduce myself to her too. Quickly deciding that I didn't have time for this shit or this woman, I raised an eyebrow at her and smirked. A blush instantly bloomed on her cheeks, and she quickly cast her eyes toward the ground.

And now my cock has a pulse.

I lifted my chin, giving her a bro nod like a royal douchebag, and walked off to the back of the truck, adjusting myself before my dick gave me away.

"Don't mind him. He's just... well, he's a dickhead," Kai reassured Saige.

"Okay, well, let me show you where the entrance is for the apartment, and I can give you a quick tour. Then I'll have to get back to The Pig since I'm the only one working today." Her sweet voice carried to me, and I noticed the strain, no doubt a product of my less than polite attitude. A pleased grin stretched across my face. *It truly is the little things in life.*

I enjoyed that. Getting under people's skin. It made my black heart dance in my chest like a virgin about to get laid for the first time. That rush, it fueled me. From the corner of my eye, I watched her as she led the guys away, the way her hips swayed seductively. Damn, the woman was packing hella junk in the trunk, and those jeans were sinful in the way they hugged her lush hips and cupped her ass cheeks. Saige stopped about ten feet short of the entrance of the magic shop and raised the key in her hand to unlock another tan-colored door that must lead up to the apartment.

As sexy as this witch was, we were here on a mission, and I wanted to stay on point so we could limit the amount of time we spent here. I'd already spotted six elderly couples, all walking fluffy dogs, and they all looked like talkers. *I fucking hate socializing.*

I must avoid those wrinkly fossils at all costs... but on second thought, they probably have a ton of information, and they'll just love to tell whoever will listen. The sooner we solve this mystery, the sooner we're out of this boring hell hole and back to doing big boy missions. I'm going to infiltrate their little old chit chat circle. Phase one begins tomorrow.

Saige

Chapter Three

What a freaking buttlord. A hot as hell buttlord with a smile that was fucking criminal. My face was still burning as I climbed the stairs to the apartment. *I mean, honestly, what a jerk.* The days of letting smug assholes walk all over me were done. He might be devastatingly sexy, but that was the only pass he was going to get from me. Sloane could kiss my big ass.

Each of them was incredibly powerful. Their magic swirled around them without any effort on their part, invisible waves that felt like pulses of strength. I'd only ever met a handful of magical people who gave off that kind of palpable power. My gran and Laurie were two of them. Shit-lick ex-boyfriend was another. Some people used that to their advantage, giving off a 'don't-fuck-with-me' vibe, and while I clearly knew these men weren't to be fucked with, I wasn't afraid of them. The way their energy coiled around me, colliding with my own power like ocean waves seeking out the sandy beach, felt natural and unstoppable. I was having trouble processing exactly where all of these hot mages had come from and why they were renting an apartment in this completely predictable little town. At least Kai was funny, and Cam and Fischer seemed nice enough. My hand trailed along the banister at the top of the stairs as the room opened up into a large open floor plan set up. Gran had hired a contractor a couple of years ago to spruce this place up, and it really was a beautiful apartment. The living room and eat-in kitchen were immediately to the left of the landing. Then there were three small bedrooms, a pull-out sofa bed, one and a half baths, and a large deck with a grilling area and hot tub. Not a bad place to live at all.

"This will be perfect," Fischer said.

"The kitchen is stocked with essentials. We usually rent on short-term leases, people looking to escape the city for a week or a weekend. Linens and towels are in the closet in the bathroom." I pointed to the right, down the hallway. "There are only three bedrooms, but this sofa does pull out into a bed," I explained as I walked around the room. The screen door slammed, and footsteps thudded on the stairs, so I braced myself for Mr. Sunshine to make his entrance.

"Everything looks great, Saige," Cam assured me as he sat down in one of the navy blue armchairs.

The whole place was decorated in a color scheme of blues, whites, and grays with small pops of yellow sprinkled here and there throughout the place. Kaito plopped down in the other armchair and picked up the remote control, the television kicking on a moment later.

Fischer disappeared down the hallway with his duffel bag, probably to investigate the bedrooms. Sloane looked in all of the cupboards in the kitchen before opening up the refrigerator. I could hear him grumbling about there being no food or drinks under his breath. *Jackass.*

"There's the diner next door if you guys are hungry, and then there's Dinner Thyme, our grocery store, over on Oak Street. It's a couple of minutes walk from here. They're open until eight tonight. I do have to get back downstairs to work, so if you have any other questions, just pop on into the shop. I'll leave the lease agreement here on the island for you guys to review and sign. Drop it off when you're done, and I'll make sure it gets to Gran." I started to make my way back over to the stairs, suddenly feeling overwhelmed being in an enclosed space with the four of them.

THE MAGIC OF DISCOVERY

"Don't you think we should exchange phone numbers?" Kai proposed as he turned his body in the chair to look at me. When I raised an eyebrow, he put his hands up with his palms out, trying to convey his innocence. "I simply meant that we're your renters, and say something were to happen here while the shop was closed. How would we contact you?"

"Hmm. Well, that *does* make sense. Here, give me your phone." He stood to meet me halfway, and I held my palm out. Placing the phone in my hand, his fingers brushed along mine, my stomach flipping at the contact.

Quickly typing my name and number into his contacts, I shoved the phone back toward him and spun around to get out of there, Kai's eyes widening at my haste. My foot had just hit the top step when I heard Sloane. "What about me, Red? You going to come back over here and give me that number, too?"

His smooth voice was patronizing and dark. *This fucking guy.* I stopped my descent down the stairs and turned my head to look at his smug face as he rested his arms on the kitchen island. He was blasting me with that megawatt smile, but it wasn't kind. It was arrogant and assholish and... sexy as fuck. *Ugh! Alright, Saige, time to let this dude know that you're not a pushover. Do not let him intimidate you.*

"Oh, I'm *so* sorry about that, Sloane," I began with so much sweetness in my voice it was practically dripping with honey. His smile somehow grew even more, probably thinking he'd one upped me, so I continued, "But I don't give my contact information to dickheads. I learned my lesson a long time ago. If you'd like to adjust your crappy attitude, I may reconsider in the future. If not, you can just go eat a bag of bat dicks."

Fischer had just turned the corner coming back into the living room to hear my final comment, and all three of the other guys busted out laughing. Kai bent forward, holding his stomach, while Cam called out, "Ooooooh, burrrrrn!" Meanwhile, Fischer just chuckled and shook his head, his beautiful, thick curls bouncing slightly with the movement.

I turned my focus back to Sloane, registering his shocked expression and mentally fist bumping myself. His index finger began tapping on the countertop, the only sound in the room besides the low murmur of the television in the background. A moment later, the corner of Sloane's lips lifted slightly, and his blue eyes focused on me even more so, like he'd found prey and the hunt was on. *Oh, fucking hell, he needs to stop looking at me like that.*

"This town might not be so bad after all," Sloane quipped despite the other guys still making fun of him. Saying nothing else, he turned his back to me and walked out of the room. *Why do I feel like I just whacked a bear in the nose with a stick?*

"So, I'll see you guys later!" I squeaked and sprinted down the steps, my pace not slowing until I was back inside The Pig, the sounds of masculine laughter chasing me with every step.

THE GUYS DIDN'T HAVE MUCH AT ALL TO MOVE IN, AND I TRIED TO ignore them as much as possible throughout the day. It was *hard*. The rest of the town was taking notice of them, too. A couple of hours after they'd arrived, the shop was packed full of customers. I hadn't had a day with this many sales in ages. People here were nosy as fuck, not that I could blame them; there was definitely something worth looking at.

Miranda and her daughter showed up around three. Annie was licking a vanilla ice cream cone with sprinkles, losing the battle to the warm air. Snapping into action, I snagged a few paper towels and handed them to my friend. She sighed in relief. "Thanks. She insisted on having a double scoop, like usual, but she can never eat it fast enough." Miranda bent down and wrapped the cone in the paper towels before handing it back to a smiling Annie.

"Like I always say, double or nothing. It applies to both shots of alcohol and ice cream cones." Miranda laughed and nodded her agreement.

"Speaking of self-indulgence... where in the stars did those four dudes come from? Did you see the one with all the tattoos?" She raised a hand and fanned her face dramatically. *Haha, ohhhh, I saw.* A flash of white from the corner of my eye drew my gaze to the back of the store, finding Maven scampering out of the tarot room.

Annie spotted him immediately. "Mom, can I go play with Maven? Please?"

"Sure, but don't touch anything with your dirty hands. I'll stay right up here." Annie squealed and took off down the aisle toward Mave. His ears perked up, and I caught his desire to run away from the little girl, but once he saw what she had in her hand, that disappeared. He was always willing to put up with her fussing over him if there was a chance he'd get some ice cream out of it.

With little ears out of hearing distance, I leaned in and answered, "Do I have eyes in my head? They're all gorgeous. The broody bad boy one is a jerk, though. They drove up from Portage Falls, but I'm not exactly sure why they're here. I didn't want to seem too nosy, and I'm sure someone will get that information out of them before the day is up."

Miranda nodded. "I saw the broody one talking to Mr. Phipps. He looked like he was enjoying their conversation though..."

"Well, I put him in his place, so I hope he cuts the shit. Anyway, let me grab your moonstone."

Turning around, I grabbed a hold of one of the drawers that lined the lower wall behind the sales counter. Think old time convenience stores, long wooden bars, wooden shelves lining the wall, drawers, and cupboards underneath a countertop. That's what I was working with. Pulling open the drawer, I grabbed the small purple velvet cinch top bag.

"This one has matured a lot in the past six months. It's been charged under eleven moon cycles, including a super moon and a blood moon. It should really help you get more restful sleep and keep your stress levels under control. Just set it on your nightstand with your other herbs and crystals. On full moon nights, I would leave it somewhere that it'll get direct light so it can recharge. Bring it in every so often when you think of it, and I can do a cleanse."

She held her hand out, and I dropped the bag into her palm. Pulling apart the cinched top, she retrieved the faintly glowing milky stone. Running her fingertips over the smooth surface, she let out a breath, and when she met my eyes, hers were brimming with tears. "Oh, no. Honey, what's wrong?" I whispered, not wanting to alert Annie to our conversation.

My oldest friend looked to the ceiling and took a few moments to get herself under control. "It's been a rough couple of months, girl. Thanks for this. Annie is such a great kid, but single-momming is not for the faint of heart, let me tell you. I don't know what I'd do with myself if she was anything like I was at her age. I'm just thankful my parents have been helping me out as much as they've been able."

Miranda was one of the strongest women I had ever known. Her ex-husband had up and left both her and Annie a couple of years ago. He'd been having affairs the entire time they'd been together, and one day he just took off and never contacted either of them again. His loss, in my opinion, because my best friend was *stunning*. Shoulder-length brown hair, beautiful chocolate eyes, and a tall, toned body? What kind of man just walks away from that? The tears welling in her eyes let me know just how hard of a time she had been having, and I felt like shit for not realizing how difficult things had been.

"Oh, honey." I reached out and took her hand in mine. "You'll get through this. Let me stop over one day next week, and I can hang out with Annie if you want to catch up on cleaning, or I can bring Maven to occupy her so I can help you with whatever. I'll bring wine?"

"That actually sounds like exactly what I need. I'll text you and let you know what our week looks like." She slipped the stone back into the bag and called out for Annie. The little blonde bounded around the corner from the back of the store and skipped her way up to us, sans ice cream cone.

"Maven!" I scolded. His little face peeked out from behind the same corner Annie had just emerged from, my frisky fox desperately trying to lick away the sprinkles all over his face.

"I hope that you offered that to him and he didn't just take liberties and help himself?" I questioned, crossing my arms over my chest and trying not to laugh.

"He said he'd help me finish it before it all melted and made a huge mess." She shrugged her little shoulder. She'd always said Maven talked to her, so that wasn't anything new. Imagination was a serious thing for kids.

"He did, huh? Well, so long as he didn't just steal it from you."

"Alright, baby. Let's get out of here. Saige is coming over next week to hang out with us, so you'll see her then."

"Yep, and I can't wait! See you guys soon. Just let me know what day works." I lifted my hand in a wave as they walked out, calling their goodbyes as the door swung shut.

The rest of the afternoon passed quickly with lots of gossip and chatter. New members to the community always brought everyone out of the comfort of their homes. It was nice though. I got to see a lot of people I hadn't seen in a while. As I counted out the deposit after closing up shop, I couldn't complain. Maybe these new guys would keep boosting my sales, and I could continue checking them out along with the rest of the town.

When Maven and I got back to the cottage, the temperature was still pretty nice, which was perfect because I needed to do some fixing to that poor flowerbed that looked near death's door. Mave scampered into the cottage through his little fox door, no doubt on the hunt for his dinner. After I walked my bike over to the garage, I took the clipboard off of the gardening shed for Frank and Arlo and checked off a few things that customers had requested.

All of our spring tree blooms were in their full glory right now, the fragrant aroma swirling through the air with each burst of wind. I made my way through the loose pea gravel pathways that separated our many gardens and flowerbeds. Stopping in front of the wilted flowers, I knelt down and brushed my hand over one of the drooping plants.

Gold and green wisps began sparking to life out of my fingertips until I looked like I was holding a sparkler in each hand. The twinkling tendrils gently caressed the stem from the ground, all the way to each leaf and each droopy petal. I closed my eyes, letting the connection I had with the earth search for the problem. The bed was well fertilized and watered, and I could sense the earthworms beneath my knees doing their part to keep the soil fresh. Pushing further into the connection, a sense of distress hit me. *Maybe some kind of pest?* I would have to talk to Gran about it later, see what she thought.

The gold swirls vanished, and I shoved both of my hands, palms down, into the dirt. I released a little bit of magic, the gentle brush of it sliding down my arms and into the soil, deep enough to get to the roots of the plants. I was aiming to give them just a little boost until I could figure out what exactly was going on. Using too much magic could kill these babies and give me one hell of a headache, and I was not game for either one of those outcomes. Satisfied when they started to perk up, I withdrew my hands and stood up, dusting my palms off on my jeans.

Walking back toward the cottage, a whiff of garlic and butter hit me, and my stomach gave a rumble. I pulled the screen door open, the hinges creaking with age, and slipped inside. Striding into the bathroom, I stepped up to the sink and set the water to warm. I mindlessly scrubbed my hands together, the apple cinnamon scent of the soap filling the air. Unbidden, my mind drifted back to those delicious mages above my shop. Their lease agreement was just a month to month deal, so who knew how long they'd be staying? And was I really lonely enough that I actually cared?

Once my hands were rinsed and dried, I found Gran rapping along with ASAP Rocky while she shook her little ass and stirred a pot of spaghetti sauce. I didn't even try to stop my laughter when she belted out that she loved bad bitches and that was her fuckin' problem.

"Welcome back, child. Dinner will be ready in a few. I trust that the renter arrived and everything was good to go?" she inquired as she took the boiling pot of pasta to the sink to strain.

"Yep. All four of them..." I mumbled, but I should've known Gran's bat ears would hear the tail end of that reply.

"Did you say *four*?"

"Yeah, four guys showed up. I've got the signed lease agreement in my backpack for you. I showed them where everything was and that..." I was cut off as she dropped the whole pot of spaghetti in the sink, noodles bouncing up and sticking to her shirt and arms. She sprinted over to me and before I could step back from her craziness, she put her hands on my arms.

"When do I get to meet them? What are they like? Are they mages or humans? How old?" She machine gun questioned me at a rapid-fire pace that would make an auctioneer jealous.

I grabbed her hands and pulled them back down to her sides.

"Alright, alright, you thirsty bitch. Let's set the table, and I'll tell you all about them. How's that?" I proposed, and she squealed and ran back over to the stove.

Well, this was going to be a really fun dinner.

Gran and I enjoyed a delicious feast of salad, spaghetti, and sexual innuendos with a side of red wine. Just how we liked it. I filled her in on the four men, and she was already hungry to set her eyes on these new specimens. Her words, not mine.

I was pretty exhausted from the excitement of the day, so I quickly picked Gran's brain about the flowerbeds. She seemed as puzzled as I was, but Gran was an extremely knowledgeable and powerful green witch. She was my mentor, and if anyone could figure out a plant problem, it was her.

Reassured we'd get to the bottom of this, I headed up to my bedroom, Maven keeping pace with me as I climbed the stairs. He always slept in bed, pressed against my side, and sleeping was his favorite thing to do. I pushed the door open, and he effortlessly jumped onto the mattress before curling into a ball on top of my boho-inspired multi-colored quilt, draping his tail across his eyes. *Good night to you too, sir.*

My room was full of bright colors - pinks, oranges, greens, blues. Wicker and dark wood accents were spread throughout. The master bedroom was pretty large, and I had a huge wall of windows that allowed the sun to shine in all day on the plants that dangled out of macrame plant pot holders. I dropped my backpack onto the bright pink loveseat in the corner of the room. Eyeing the pile of clothes on top of my inviting bed, I decided I better hang them up in the closet. Otherwise, they'd just get moved to the love seat for days and get wrinkled to hell.

My phone pinged in my back pocket as I opened up a dresser drawer to pull out a clean nightgown to wear to bed. *Do not even judge me for that; nightgowns were created by a saint of a woman who liked to catch a breeze, and they're comfy as fuck.*

I held my phone up in front of my face and saw a text message alert from a number I didn't recognize. Pressing my thumb on the little chat bubble icon, a smile started to grow as I read the message.

Hey, this is Kai. Would you be willing to give us a tour of the town tomorrow?

Hmm. Well, tomorrow was Sunday, so the shop was closed. Other than checking out that flowerbed problem with Gran, my schedule was pretty much wide open. I typed out a response, debating on sending it. *Fuck it,* I thought. Kai was a jokester and a serious flirt, so I pressed my thumb down on the send button.

Me: What's in it for me?

I held my breath as the message went from delivered to seen, and the three little dots danced as Kai responded to my message. While I waited, I quickly stripped down and slipped my nightgown over my head. A moment later, his reply came through. Flopping down on my back, I picked my phone back up, laughter tumbling out of my chest as I read the first line.

Kai: Aside from the pleasure of being in my direct vicinity for a couple of hours, we're thinking of doing a barbeque picnic down at the park for dinner. We'll probably head down there around 3 to enjoy the weather and hang out. Would you like to join us? I'm an excellent griller, one of my many talents.

Me: That actually sounds really fun. I can meet you guys at the apartment at two. An hour will be plenty of time to show you

around, and then we can walk down to the park. We can discuss those other talents in more detail tomorrow ;)

I was grinning so hard I thought my face was going to freeze like this.

Kai: I can't wait. See you at two.

Feeling like a sixteen-year-old girl, I set my phone down on my nightstand and trailed my fingers along Maven's fur for a few moments before I made my way to the master bathroom. While I went through my bedtime routine, I couldn't stop grinning to myself and hoping that these guys could be new friends... *and Kai might be a little more?*

Kai

Chapter Four

"I love eggs, I love toast, I love bacon, but I love Fish's mom the most. Rise and shine, my sleepy friends, I don't wanna hear Sloane bitch and moan. We're here in Emerald Lakes, get up bitch, I made pancakes!" I bellowed out my improvised song as I ran from room to room slapping all of their lazy asses with my spatula. Ignoring the groaning and cuss words, I danced back out to the kitchen.

Breakfast cooked, yoga done, shower time. Crushing it. I flexed my right arm and mentally high fived myself. Running a hand through my dark hair to swipe it back and out of my eyes, I stepped into the bathroom and turned on the shower to heat up.

I had just stepped under the stream of hot water when I heard the door open. Cam called out, "Sorry, bro. Fish is in the other one, and I have to piss like a racehorse."

"That's fine, but don't you dare shit while I'm in the shower. Not. Cool," I said sternly, receiving a deep chuckle in reply from the other side of the shower curtain. I got to work washing my body and asked, "Did Sloane come out yet?"

"I heard some movement coming from that room, but I haven't seen him yet." Cam put the toilet seat down, and a moment later, the sound of running water filtered through the bathroom as he washed his hands.

An icy spray poured from the showerhead, I yelped and jumped back as Cam's laughter and choked apology echoed throughout the room.

"Brooooo, my nuts just abandoned their happy dangly nest and moved into my stomach!"

"I'm sorry, dude. I didn't realize that would happen. I thought that was like a myth or something."

Myth, my ass. "Let's go over the plan for the day during breakfast. Everything is cooked, and I'll be out in a few." The door clicked closed, and I finished rinsing off in the now lukewarm water.

Stepping out onto the soft yellow bath mat, I grabbed my towel from the hook next to the shower and roughly rubbed it over my head, soaking up most of the water before quickly wiping the rest of myself dry and securing the towel around my hips. I mindlessly went through the motions of getting ready, a routine I'd gotten down to about three minutes. Spy life will quickly make you into a time-efficient machine. All the while, long red hair, green eyes, and an ass that wouldn't quit kept cycling through my brain in rapid fire flashes. Just as my dick started to respond, a loud voice from right outside of the door yelled, "Quit jacking off and get your ass out here, K."

That grumpy fucker.

"I was just thinking about you, Sloaney baby. You know I can't stop once that happens," I called out as I pulled the door open so fast that Sloane fell through the doorframe and right into me. I laughed as he pushed me back into the bathroom, the smile on his face letting me know he wasn't really upset. The grump only ever smiled around us, and we'd been a part of each other's lives for so long now that I knew him nearly as well as I knew myself.

I wrapped my arms around his waist, returning his smile. Sloane leaned in and whispered, "Are you hungry, K?"

His face was so close to mine that our lips were damn near touching, our breath mingling. I swallowed roughly, the air suddenly feeling turbocharged. *Damn this libido!*

"Starving," I breathed.

Sloane's hand dropped down to rest on my ass before he

roughly gripped me, pulling me into his body. "Good," he said softly, but there was nothing soft about the hardness pressed against me, or his personality. "Because some cheery asshole made breakfast."

His grip tightened briefly, and I struggled to contain the groan that wanted to come out of my throat before he released me and headed to the kitchen. It had been a while since we had fucked around.

Adjusting the towel, I sped into my room to get dressed. My dick was rock hard after that shit with Sloane, and I had every intention of dropping my towel and rubbing one out. Then I heard the voices of my friends and the clanging of plates and silverware. *I always make them amazing meals, and they don't even have the decency to wait on the fucking chef? You never take another man's kill; the hunter gets the first bite!*

Those bitches are not going to start eating without me. Rolling my shoulders back, I commanded my cock, *wilt, you beautiful steel sculpture. There's no time for shenanigans.* It didn't work. Rifling around in my dresser, I snatched some gray sweats and stepped into them. Sloane's voice carried into my room, saying something about delicious pancakes that sank my boner like it'd been hit with an enemy torpedo. Pulling the door open, a feline growl rumbled out of my chest, the sound easy to hear despite the guys' laughter.

"Chill, K. We're waiting. You know we love how you take care of your pack," Cam cooed when I stalked into the dining room, my eyes flashing yellow.

Storming over to the plate of pancakes, I stacked three of them up and ripped a huge bite out of them as I flopped down into a chair. Now that I'd had first dibs, my body calmed, so I nodded to signal the rest of the idiots could go ahead.

My thoughts drifted once again to Saige, the way she effortlessly bantered and flirted with me through text, how she made me smile. Something told me that she would be different from any other witch we'd ever met, and I couldn't wait until the guys figured out that she'd be coming to hang out with us today. *Gods, I really am so damn smart sometimes. Most of the time. Yeah.*

"What are we going with for a cover story, Cam?" Fischer asked as he carried the plates to the sink.

"Last night I was checking out properties in Kingstown since that's where Larson got stopped by that revulsion spell. There's a warehouse there that has been vacant for about a year. If they ask, we can tell the townspeople here that we're from Radical, and we were sent on a scouting mission for a possible business expansion. It's believable because Rad did just acquire that mega complex in Texas. We can say we wanted to stay here because we didn't want to deal with seeing any competing firms or giving away that we're looking at the property." As he talked, Cam scrolled through his phone, handing it to me after he'd pulled up the listing.

Joining us at the table, Fish grabbed the phone next, Sloane leaning forward to also take a look. "Yeah, I think that's about as solid as it's going to get, and the excuse of corporate secrecy might deter people from prying too much," I agreed.

"Sounds like a plan. We should reach out to the listing agent just to cover all bases," Sloane chimed in. "Send me the link to this, and I'll give the dude a call later this evening."

"This town is like Sleepy Hollow. It's a great place to hide anything. Why would anyone think to look here? The population is what? A thousand? Fifteen hundred?" Fischer spun a pen between his fingers, his eyes locked on it despite his focus wholly being on us. The man was *always* fidgeting. Being a cognitive mage, he had the ability to feel what everyone around him was feeling, and getting a glimpse into others' heads wasn't always the best for his own.

Mental distraction was the only way Fish was able to stay sane: fidgeting, tapping, bouncing his leg, anything to keep himself from getting overwhelmed. After being a part of his life for so many years, we all were able to effectively keep our mental shields up, but the habit was just a part of him now. Radical Training Academy had been amazing in teaching us how to fortify our shields, and not just for his benefit. In our line of work, it was just safer to keep that shit on lock. You never know who could be watching or listening in.

Cam hummed in agreement with Fischer's thought process. "Larson was vague about what we're supposed to be looking for here, but that's what we do best. If there's something here, we'll find it. It's only a matter of time."

Cam's fingers flew over the screen of his phone, and a moment later, all of ours went off. We opened the messages, finding the images of Laura that Khol had shown us. There was something about her causing a niggling in the back of my head, but when I mentioned it to the guys, nobody seemed to get the same sensation I did. I stared at it a bit longer, tilting my head as though there was some magic angle that would reveal the secret to me, but it seemed I was shit out of luck for the moment. *Maybe it'll come to me later.*

The others had already moved on, and I focused back on them in time to catch Sloane's question. "Did you guys get a look at the elderly couples mulling around the town square yesterday? I plan to start there; old people love to gossip. If someone's shady or hiding something, they'll be a great source of information. I'm going to be good boy Sloane and schmooze the fuck out of these villagers." He laughed, his face lighting up at the thought.

"I hope you've got some solid acting skills. You have to work harder than the average person to achieve good boy status," I countered; everyone laughed because it was true.

"I'll open up my walls when we're out and about today. If

anyone feels off, we can keep an eye on them. Saige will also be an asset for information," Fischer said as he looked to Cam.

"Agreed. This location is actually perfect for this assignment." Cam nodded as he went to stand from his chair.

Okay, now is probably the best time, so best to just rip the bandaid off...

"So, you know how we're going to explore the town today and have a barbeque at the park later?" I asked sheepishly, and instantly, I had three gazes burning through me. Thank the stars none of these feral bastards had the power to shoot freaking laser beams out of their eyes. I'd be one sliced up son of a bitch.

"Yes, Kaito. We all remember the conversation we had about that nine hours ago," Cam deadpanned.

"Well, I invited Saige," I blurted out.

Sloane snorted. "Of course you did."

"Don't be a dick, Sloane. She's nice, and we all just agreed that she'll be useful." I leveled a stare at him from across the table, the animal inside of me sending pulsing waves of warning to everyone in the room.

"Fine." Sloane raised his hands in mock surrender, looking to Cam as he said, "But we all know that she can't become a distraction. I don't care if you guys want to mess around with her, but we're not here for sex. We're supposed to be working."

"Nobody said anything about screwing her," Fischer spoke up, running a hand through his curly hair.

"Nobody said anything about *not* screwing her, either. She's sexy as fuck, and you all know I have these urges." A huge grin spread across my face, and they all rolled their eyes and groaned.

"Don't get distracted. This town may seem sleepy and boring, but Larson is a thorough bastard, and he wouldn't have sent us here if there was nothing to be found. It's not a vacation," Cam said, taking his coffee mug to the island to get a refill.

"What's the plan then, lover boy?" Sloane asked me, holding his coffee cup in the air and waving it around until Cam saw him

THE MAGIC OF DISCOVERY

and grumbled about 'the nerve of some people' before bringing the whole pot to the table.

"I texted her last night and asked if she would be willing to meet us here at two to show us around town. Then we'll head to the park to chill and grill. That gives us a couple of hours to finish unpacking our clothes, make a list of anything we need to grab from the grocery store, and you guys can work out. I already did my yoga this morning."

With nods and grunts of agreement, they all began shuffling out of the room, preparing for the adventure to come. Meanwhile, I got to work on a list of what we'd need to buy or bring to the park later, determined not to let Sloane's grumpiness ruin the mood. *This is going to be a fun fucking day. I can feel it.*

I WAS WALKING BESIDE SAIGE AS SHE TALKED, POINTING OUT different landmarks and businesses. She had shown up a few minutes after two, her little fox in tow. Her hair was styled into two french braids, and she looked so fucking innocent and sassy that I kept getting distracted every time I looked at her face. I was just glad I was walking beside her and not behind her like the other guys because her ass in those high-waisted shorts was straight fucking sin, and I was no angel.

"Over there is our single grocery store, Dinner Thyme," she said loud enough for us all to hear, lifting her left arm to point across the street.

"For fuck's sake, are you people obsessed with terrible puns?" Sloane grumbled.

Saige wisely ignored him. Maven, however, must've seen a kindred spirit in Sloane because he trotted alongside the broody ass, staying close to him throughout the tour. They looked like two peas in a pod. But Sloane had already been warned to be on his best behavior, especially since he was going to try to pull off the biggest scam of this decade: be a good boy. The thought alone almost had me shaking in silent laughter. It wasn't that Sloane was a bad dude, far from it. He loved big. He hated big. He had big feelings, much to his disgust, and often just didn't know what to do with all of them, so emotional explosions were fairly common with him. We loved him anyway. He was fiercely loyal and would do anything for someone in need. I just wasn't understanding why he was having such a fun time poking at Saige every damn moment.

I heard a muffled 'oomph,' and then I did let out a chuckle because I knew Cam had likely just punched him. *Good. Keep him in line.*

"Actually, could we run into the grocery store? I need to grab a couple of things for the picnic," I asked her. Not waiting for an answer, I grabbed her hand and bounded across the street. Her laughter was music to my ears.

"We'll just stay out here. Make sure you grab some beer, too. It's been a minute since we got to relax for an afternoon like this," Cam said to me, but his gaze bounced back and forth between myself and Saige. He smiled when he looked at her before turning to walk over to Sloane and Fish who were sitting on a bench a little ways down.

Oh, I see you, Big Man.

"What all do you have on your list? I know this store like the back of my hand, so let's see what we're looking at here." She grabbed a shopping cart, and I stepped up right beside her, making her scoot over so we could both push it. She smelled like sunshine, coconuts, and straight up sass.

I grabbed the list of supplies from my back pocket and handed it to her. Just then, her phone pinged. Pulling it out, she glanced at it and rolled her eyes before stuffing it back in her pocket. It wasn't the first time today I'd heard her phone blowing up, and she had ignored each and every message. Raising my eyebrow, I silently asked the question, but she waved her hand.

"Just a douche. Let me look at your list." Opening it up, she scanned it quickly. The guys and I were planning to come back, either this afternoon or tomorrow morning, to do a large shop to stock up on everything, so we only needed a few things now.

"Oh, I love sweet corn! And burgers? I'm glad I agreed to come to this cookout; the food sounds like it's going to be amazing." Her whole face lit up when she got excited. It was contagious, and I wanted to make it happen as often as possible.

"The food will be spectacular, the company will be superb, and dessert... well, that is to be determined." I flashed a wolfish grin at her, and her cheeks immediately went rosy.

"You're an animal," she whispered.

"You have no idea," I growled, forcing myself to take a step forward, away from her. In my head, the pacing of four big paws, an agitated flicking of a long furry tail, and the words, *'Mine, mine, mine, mine,'* played on repeat.

Saige

Chapter Five

*M*other of Saturn, we finally made it to Peridot Park. It was only a ten-minute walk from the downtown area, but I was overwhelmed by the hotness surrounding me. Kai had been looking at me like he wanted to devour me, and I was here for it. Fucking hell.

So far, all of the guys had been chatty with me today, even Sloane. After Cam had punched him for his snark, he had really changed his tune. Thank the stars, because I honestly just wanted to have a fun afternoon with these guys. Cam gave off some serious I'm-always-in-control alpha type vibes. He observed every little detail around him and silently eyed his friends as if he could see their thoughts and would know if there was anything amiss. Yeah, Cam was a protector. *He's definitely the dad of the group,* I concluded, and while the other guys had large personalities and their own ideas, it seemed to me that they had enough respect for Cam to indulge his alpha behavior.

It had taken us longer than I'd anticipated to get through our little tour, but that was due to all of the nosy as hell neighbors of mine. They actually had the gumption to approach the group of new guys now that I was with them, instead of just peeking out of their windows and attempting to look like they weren't interested. *Yeah, you know the type.*

When you lived in a small town where the tiniest of things were turned into major news, you got used to this behavior. One year, we had a boy who had gotten arrested for performing some dark magic. Everyone had already suspected that he was dabbling in it, but when the cop cars pulled up outside of his parents' house, you would've thought it was a ten car pile up on the I-95. Everyone was on their porches, not even trying to hide their rubbernecking. Phones in hands, snapping pictures, calling their grandmas and twice-removed cousins to let them know that little old Jacky boy was finally going to be locked up, and yes, of course, his mama was crying!

Didn't faze me anymore. That was just Emerald Lakes. That small town charm that drew in tourists who wanted to escape the bustle of the cities? We had it in spades.

"Is there more than one lake in town?" Cam asked as we all trudged along the paved walkway that wound through thickly wooded areas.

"Yeah, there are a few, but Emerald Lake is the largest, and it's at the heart of this park. People tend to use the smaller ones for fishing, and the town made some beachy areas that get pretty busy in the summer." He nodded as I continued. "There are seven pavilions here at Peridot, and they get rented out sometimes for private events like parties or company picnics. My favorite one is where I'm taking you now. It's within one hundred yards of the lake but tucked away from the playground equipment so it's also nice and tranquil."

"Do you get a lot of tourists then?" Fischer spoke up. Suddenly, he was right beside me, and I turned my head to the left to smile at him.

"I mean, a pretty decent amount. We're a ninety percent magical population here, only ten percent human. Humans do like coming for long weekends and holidays, so that's where we make most of our money. They get to visit, ohh and ahh over everyday magic, spend some money, then they head back home. Emerald Lakes hosts some large festivals, as well. Halloween is obviously a popular holiday for the magical community, and humans go ape shit for spooky stuff. Who does spooky better than witches?" I raised an eyebrow at him and wiggled my fingers while making "ooooooo" sounds.

Fish laughed and then asked, "How's the crime rate?"

"Pretty much non-existent, honestly. We all know each other, so if anyone's in a rough spot, we all tend to step up and take care of our own. Nobody feels the need to steal or vandalize property. It's really nice feeling so safe," I confessed.

As we walked around the curve in the sidewalk that ran alongside the expansive lake, I smiled to myself when I saw the old oak tree, her gnarled branches reaching out, riddled with knots that reminded me of an old woman with severe arthritis. Parts of her massive branches dipped underwater before rising out again, reaching for the sun. All of the kids and teens loved this tree, climbing up as high as they could go. There were even some ropes tied to the limbs so you could swing far out into the lake, letting yourself fly for a few moments before you crashed into the beautiful green water.

"Guys, this is my favorite tree in the whole world," I told them as I broke from the pack and walked up to the giant.

Kai whistled, holding his hand over his brow to block the sun while he peered towards the sky. "Wow. That thing's gotta be eighty to one hundred feet tall, easy."

"She's eighty-eight feet tall and still growing. A few years ago, she'd been pretty sickly with something called oak wilt. I spent days trying different spells until I was finally able to stop further damage from occurring, and if you look over here, you can barely see where the worst parts were." I motioned for them to follow.

The dark spots that I'd healed years ago had been nearly invisible, so you could imagine my surprise when around the edges of those scars, the color was darkening from a healthy brown to a darker shade. Not black, but still, this was different than the last time I'd checked on her. To anyone else, this wouldn't raise concerns, but I suddenly felt antsy with the need to push some power into the twisted giant.

The guys walked around the base of the tree, showing a genuine interest in what I was talking about, and that made me smile softly. My smile only grew when Kai began to climb over the branches with the grace of a cat. They all began messing around, typical bro behavior, so I seized the opportunity to press my palm to the troublesome areas on the trunk and pushed some magic, the spots fading instantly. Satisfied, I stepped back and raised my voice to make sure all of the guys would hear me when I pointed to the pavilion that was just down the way.

Walking toward the destination, I explained, "This is it. There's a charcoal grill over here, and you guys can just toss your stuff down on the picnic tables. It'll be safe. Like I said, no thieves to be found." I walked over to the closest table and set my backpack down before climbing onto the tabletop and sitting with my feet on the bench.

"Awesome location, Sprout," Kai murmured while he began unloading his backpack and the groceries.

"Sprout? You've given her a pet name already?" Sloane's exasperation at the nickname was obvious, especially when he ran a hand through his dark hair and then facepalmed. Maven snorted his agreement, and I shot the little traitor a dirty look.

"I mean, it kind of suits me. I *am* a green witch." I walked out from under the pavilion toward a small flowerbed, and sparks of gold lit up along my fingers before I flicked them at the barely blooming flowers. Little flower sprouts began to rise to the glorious sun before opening up. *Grow, little babies.* Stooping down, I gathered a few of them all into my hand, letting my magic dissipate. Gathering up the stems, I handed the little bouquet to Kai, watching as he held them up to his face and inhaled deeply. A giggle escaped me at his antics and then full out laughter when he'd tried to toss me a saucy wink and instead started sneezing seconds later.

"That was so cool. I've never actually been around a green witch long enough to experience their magical abilities. You'll have to show me what else you're capable of some time," Fischer exclaimed, genuine fascination shining through his voice.

I smiled at him. "Anytime, Fish."

An expression I couldn't decipher flitted across his features, and I blushed furiously at my boldness. "Oh my moons, is it okay if I call you Fish? I've just heard everyone else saying it. I'm sorry-"

Holding up a hand, he cut me off from apologizing further. "It's okay. You can call me Fish. It's my nickname, so don't give it a second thought." He smiled in reassurance.

Whew.

He really was a beautiful man. Dark bronze skin, with light, oak-colored eyes that looked like they were glowing. The best way I could describe his body was beefcake. A deliciously yummy, beefy cake. With broad shoulders and big arms, he was seriously edible. His dark hair was longer, not quite to his shoulders, and it had thick bouncy curls that any woman would be jealous of. Before I could process what I was doing, I ran my hand through his hair.

Girl, you do not belong in the public eye. What are you doing? But oh, so soft. Can I rub my body on it?

Surprisingly, it was Cam's deep as fuck rumbling laughter that had my eyes widening before I snatched my hand back. Fischer was staring at me with an expression I couldn't place, but if a dude had done that to me, I would be thinking of an escape plan right the fuck now. *Why am I so fucking weird?*

"Oh, moon maidens! I am so, so sorry. I don't know what came over me just then. I was just thinking about how you're the definition of a beefcake, then I got focused on that glorious mane of curls..." Fischer, bless him, was smiling and nodding despite his cheeks reddening. He was taking my forwardness really well, thank goodness. *Best not to have them thinking I'm going to be some kind of creeper that lurks and waits for the best moment to feel up their hair. That would be awkward.* All four of the guys were now staring at me with varying degrees of amusement, Sloane laughing the loudest.

"It's okay, Saige. I like your hair too." He reached out and tugged on one of my braids before slightly running his fingertips along my neck, the touch so soft I wondered if I'd imagined it. "Now we're even." Winking, he walked over to the grill to throw in some charcoal bricks, and Kai slid in beside him to light it up.

Have you ever felt a rapid cycle of emotions, two of which included embarrassment and arousal? It was a vicious circle. I just went from gazing at the object of said arousal, being embarrassed that I outed my own damn self for being aroused, and then back to being ready to get dicked down all in the span of a minute. *I need a drink.*

"Anyone else ready for a beer?" I asked, sounding chipper as fuck as I hopped off the table, beelining for the cooler on wheels.

Everyone was down to clown with some booze, so I was happy to play bartender for a moment and pass them out.

I sat with Kai while he grilled, passing the time drinking and laughing. The other three guys were all throwing a football around in the open meadow beside the lake.

"So, for real, what brings four guys to Emerald Lakes on such short notice?" I questioned, keeping my eyes locked on the others. They looked so carefree. Sloane was sprinting across the grass, heading right for Cam, attempting to intercept the football that Fischer had launched toward them. Just as it looked like he might actually pull it off, a white blur shot into my line of sight out of nowhere and collided with Sloane, knocking him off balance. Maven rolled fluidly and shook himself out when he stood upright again, and Cam and Fish were losing it. My smile widened as Sloane stood up and mock disciplined the white fox, pointing his finger at him and saying something about, 'supposed to be friends' and 'we're the president and vice-president of the Grumpy Guys Club.' *That's almost... adorable.* Kaito's voice pulled my attention back to him.

"We work for Radical Inc." He looked at me as he flipped a burger, and when I nodded to show I knew the company, he continued. "Our boss sent us here to scout a property that's in Kingstown. It's an old factory warehouse that's been vacant for a little while now, and Rad is always looking to expand into new areas. We're in Emerald Lakes because, first of all, it was the only town that was close and had an immediate vacancy for an apartment large enough for the four of us. Second, we don't want to run into any competitors in Kingstown and set off alarms that we're in the market to buy."

Kingstown was the biggest city I had ever been in, and it was only fifteen miles from here.

"Emerald Lakes is for sure the right choice if you're trying to be discreet. We don't get a lot of businessmen." I paused to think. "Actually, I don't think I've ever seen any businessmen come through here, so your secret is safe."

"This place kind of reminds me of where the guys and I are from. We all grew up in the same town. It had a bit larger of a population, but it was a tight knit community," Kai replied, still focused on his task, but his face had softened, and I just knew he was reliving something from his past. *Whatever it was, I'm glad it was positive.* While he had his moment, I eyed the waiting food. The corn husks were already starting to get some char on them, and the burgers smelled so damn good. He picked up his beer and downed about half of it, my gaze hungrily fixed on his throat as he drank the cool liquid. *Why is that so hot?*

I squirmed in my seat, searching for a way to distract my hormones. "So what's your affinity?"

Kai's eyes snapped up from the grill, and he gave me a smile that was bordering on predatory. For such a lighthearted and funny man, I had already seen his eyes flash several times with the kind of darkness that promised bite marks and adrenaline. The kind of darkness I wanted to dive into.

THE MAGIC OF DISCOVERY

"I'm a shifter mage," he growled. Legit *growled* like a jungle cat. I clamped my thighs together even harder.

"Wow, that's so cool. I can't even imagine how amazing that must be to shift into another creature. What's your animal?"

"I'm a black panther. He awakened when I was thirteen. That was a bitch, being a teenage boy in the height of puberty and then also having to contend with a literal beast taking up part of my psyche. I named him Bagheera, just like *The Jungle Book*." The look on Kai's face when he was talking about Bagheera was the cutest shit ever. He was like a proud papa, eyes shining with love.

The two of us worked seamlessly to finish up the food as I asked him questions. "Do you call him Baggie? Or would he get pissed about that? Because I think Baggie is super cute." I smiled widely at him.

A loud purr came from Kai, and his eyes widened in shock. "I do not call him Baggie, but judging by the purr that he just unleashed, I think he's okay with *you* calling him that. Typically, he's not big on new people, but right now he's rolling around on his back like a kitten."

"Oh my gosh, he's so loud!" Thinking about a big cat like Baggie rolling around like a little baby, I could hardly contain my glee. Just then, Maven jumped up on the table and knocked my beer over. Thankfully, it was almost empty, but by the stars, he was a jealous little thing.

"Mave! What's wrong with you? Unless we're snuggling in bed, you act like you're too good for me, but now you're getting all possessive." I grabbed his little white snout and pushed his ears forward so he had a scrunchy face going on.

He raised his right paw and placed it on my forearm before giving my nose a speedy lick.

"Yes, you're a good boy and also the cutest. You'll *always* be my favorite," I reassured the sensitive fox, and just to get back into his good graces, I grabbed a slice of cheese and held it out for him. He chittered at me, grabbed the offering, and then ran off to eat his earnings. Taking note that Kai was almost done with taking everything off the grill, I scooted off the table and started taking out the plates and napkins.

"Damn. You just got played by a fox," Sloane chuckled.

I hadn't seen the guys approaching, but here they were. *Shirtless*, except for Cam, and my brain just melted. I was looking like such a thirsty ass bitch, but I accepted that. *It's been too long, and these dudes... Eek!* Kai came up behind me, setting the platters of burgers and corn down in the middle of the table.

"Let's eat, boys!" Cam proclaimed. Then he looked at me and added, "And Saige."

I giggled. *Why does he make me giggle so much? What the hell is happening to me?*

Everyone grabbed a paper plate and started dishing up food. Dancing in my seat, I took a huge bite of my cheeseburger, my eyes fluttering closed as a moan escaped my mouth *Damn, Kai can really cook. I should thank him for inviting me.*

I looked up to do just that and found four sets of eyes staring at me. Cam cleared his throat and set his burger down before his hand disappeared under the table as he shifted around in his spot a little bit.

"What? Do I have mustard on my face or something?" I picked up my napkin and hastily wiped my mouth and chin.

"No, Red. The sounds coming out of you are bordering on sexual." Sloane's ice blue eyes looked nearly black with how blown his pupils were. My face probably looked like a tomato.

"Well, take it up with Kai. These are amazing," I retorted with a shrug, trying to feign nonchalance.

Fish reached across the table and put his hand over mine. "You don't have to apologize. We should always express how we feel, however we choose to." I looked up and gave him a small smile, grateful for his calming words.

"I was just about to thank you, Kai." When he gave me a confused expression, I explained, "For inviting me to hang out with you guys, for cooking the best burger I've eaten in my life, all of the above."

"You're most welcome, Sprout. We appreciate you showing us around and telling us all about your sleepy little town." Kai smiled at me and then proceeded to take a big bite of his corn.

"What were you guys talking about over here while we were throwing the ball around? Anything exciting?" Cam asked us.

"Ah, well, Kai was telling me about his affinity," I told him, suddenly feeling shy. Affinities could be a very personal subject for some witches and mages, but I'd felt so comfortable with Kai that the question had just come up naturally, and he'd reacted just as I thought he would. But I had to remember that just because I didn't feel weird talking about mine, that didn't mean that these guys would want to share theirs with me. We barely knew one another.

Cam's eyes snapped to Kai's and then back to mine, his emerald gaze holding me captive for a few seconds, though it felt like much longer. I wanted to ask him what he could do, and he must've seen the curiosity on my face. Smiling, he began to speak, saving me from the embarrassment of asking and being shut down.

"I'm a storm mage. I can generate electrical currents and manipulate the weather, to an extent. Best part is, I can make that all happen with just a thought." He tapped his finger on his temple.

"Wow, I didn't even know that was an affinity! It must be pretty rare," I replied, fascinated. I enjoyed researching and learning about other magical properties and powers, but I honestly had never heard of his. My curiosity was running rampant, my mind going a mile a minute just thinking about everything he could probably do.

"It's incredibly rare. There are only a handful of families with powers like mine," he said, confirming my thoughts.

"I bet that was fun growing up with a family like that," I blurted out, taking a swig of my beer.

Cam visibly stiffened in his seat. In fact, all of the guys did. *Gods damnit, Saige. Cam's family is clearly a no go.* Cam cleared his throat and nodded his answer to my question, but there was something more there, and that was none of my business. When Fischer spoke up, drawing my attention, I was more than eager to give it to him.

"I'm a cognitive mage, and I can sense people's emotions and intentions," he explained.

"Like an empath, yeah?" I questioned.

"Yes, but one that's been given a huge boost." His gaze left my face and swept out over the park before resting on a group that was walking our way on the path, probably about a quarter mile from us. "See the teen boy in the blue shirt? He's smiling, but he's not throwing off happiness vibes. The depression pouring off of him is so thick I can taste it from here." His nose scrunched up, and his eyes narrowed, giving him the appearance he'd gotten a whiff of something rotten.

"You can pick all of that up from this far away?" I was impressed but also alarmed. The teen was Sam Campbell, a talented sixteen-year-old high school football player. This past year he'd run for more yards than any player in the history of the Emerald Lakes Sirens. Blond hair and big blue eyes, he had the boy next door look down pat, and I rarely saw him without a girl on his arm or his buddies at his back. Sometimes, he would stop by the shop and ask if I needed help with anything. He was saving up for college and everything, so I'd let him deep clean the place to make some cash. Sam was a good kid, and if he was hurting that badly and concealing it so well, I'd definitely be reaching out to him.

"I can pick up even more than that from a greater distance. Especially if I've met the person before. Even better if I get the chance to make physical contact through a handshake. If I'm away from the guys, I can picture them in my head, and I can feel exactly what they're feeling. As a general courtesy, I don't go lurking around in my friends' headspace unless it's an emergency," he explained.

"So wait. You feel everyone around you constantly? Can you turn that off? I hope you can turn it off." I couldn't imagine what it would feel like to be aware of so many feelings twenty-four seven. It would be hard enough to be in a room with a group of people, but with his range, he could probably sense the entire Emerald Lakes population! *Fuck, that would drive me to insanity.*

Fischer tapped his fingers in a rhythm on the wooden plank of the picnic table as he responded, "Yeah, pretty much. I can't ever turn it off completely, but people who I'm around often enough know how to put walls up so it's not as potent. It's just what I'm used to, but yes, it can get overwhelming." He murmured the last part of his explanation, and my heart felt a little sad for Fish.

"What a tremendous power to possess. Are you able to pick up on my emotions?" *Oh, fuck a duck! I hope he can't see lust because it would look like four dicks floating around my head.*

"I've picked up on a few." He smirked at me, but luckily, before we could explore what was behind it, Sloane butted in.

"I'm a pyro mage, so I bring the heat." He opened his palm, and a little baby flame came to life.

"Damn, you guys all have awesome powers. I'm so excited. Can I see you all in action sometime?" I raised my eyebrows, hope shining through my eyes.

"Fuck me, you look like a puppy with eyes like that. How are we supposed to say no?" Kai chuckled. I looked to Cam next and gave him the eyes as he tried and failed to look away.

"Look right here, big man. You can't hide," I teased, and he lifted his green eyes back to mine before glancing at Sloane and huffing a breath.

"I dare say we've got a brat on our hands, boys," Cam stated.

"You just now figured that out, boss?" Fischer laughed, punching Cam lightly on the shoulder.

"Okay, so I got two out of four now. Don't leave me hanging here." I rapidly looked between Fish and Sloane, giving a cheesy smile and nodding my head.

"Sure, Red. I'd be happy to fire you up. Just say when." The smug fuck winked at me then flashed that megawatt smile. I'd be a lying son of a bee sting if I said I didn't get a jolt right to the lady biscuit. *Damn him.*

I fist pumped the air just as Fish added his yes.

"Four for four. I love getting what I want." I stood up and started grabbing everyone's plates to throw in the trash, singing a song about victory, and shaking my ass around.

Laughing, I walked over to start packing up the rest of the supplies the guys had brought, and I could've sworn to the sun and stars, I heard four distinct growls coming from behind me. I didn't think I'd ever smiled so hard in my whole damn existence.

Fischer

Chapter Six

It had been after five when we got back to the apartment. Everyone was in good spirits, and it was likely the most relaxed I'd seen my brothers in a very long time. I slipped off to the shower immediately, needing some time to myself after the sensory overload at the lake. My mind drifted back to Saige, the way she interacted with us so easily, like it was completely natural. The conversation had flowed seamlessly, and the little jabs we made at each other had Saige rolling with laughter. She'd even gotten under Sloane's skin a few times, which was hilarious.

No, I wasn't worried about her hanging out with our group. I found her to be very sweet and caring. The way she pulled me aside to ask more about the depressed teen, getting as much information as possible, showed a genuine concern that was refreshing.

So what was it about her that had me on edge? For the second time in my life, I couldn't get a single fucking emotion off of someone. Nothing. Not happiness when she was tearing her cheeseburger apart, not amusement when we were dicking around and teasing each other, not lust when she'd caught any one of us studying her pretty face or delicious curves. Not a fucking thing, and I was confused, and really, really intrigued. After obsessing over her long enough, I finished my shower, figuring I'd just chill out and read a book in my room for a while. The guys knew I needed alone time after spending so long around a bunch of people, so no one would begrudge me the privacy.

Hanging the towel back up to dry on the rack, I silently moved through the hallway and slipped into my room without any interruptions. Peace and quiet. *Sigh.*

Once night fell, we all headed out to different cardinal points within the town limits. With warding *and* revulsion spells in place, the caster would've needed to layer the magic. If they were sloppy, which I highly doubted, then their magical signature could still be lingering. In our line of work you never assumed anything; you double and triple checked *everything* before accepting it as fact.

I headed east, and the town was so damn small, it only took me three minutes to drive my bike there. We had all brought our motorcycles since they easily fit in the back of the moving truck, and it eliminated the need to find a car right away. Kai and I both had souped up crotch rockets, Cam had a big fucking Harley Davidson, not surprising, and Sloane drove a vintage Indian.

Pulling over to the side of the road, I walked the bike up to the tree line to keep it out of sight, an easy feat since the whole town was surrounded by forest. My boots crunched on twigs and rocks as I scanned my surroundings. This place really did remind me of home. It had been a year or so since we had all been back; I should give my parents and sister a call soon to check in. We were all close and had a solid and loving family dynamic, but my team's workload had been fucking intense the past year. This was the first 'break' we were getting, and it wasn't even a real one.

Leaving the bike, I headed into the trees, muttering the incantation for some fairy light. The small lights wouldn't be enough to draw attention, just enough to keep me from tripping over a fucking tree trunk and face planting.

"Mediocris lumina."

Little swirling dots flared to life, moving with me through the thick forest. All witches and mages had the ability to cast general spells and magic, though each of us also had a specific affinity, an area that we excelled in, a "gift" from the stars. *Not that I'd say never being alone in your own head is much of a gift.* Each magical person came into their affinity during their teens, though the *exact* time varied by the individual.

Since age thirteen, I'd been surrounded by emotion, so many fucking emotions. Sometimes a man just needed to be alone with his thoughts, and the only time I could ever manage such a feat was when I isolated myself in a very secluded area, like I was right now. I took a deep, shuddering breath. *Fuck. That felt good.* With a second deep lungful of fresh, crisp air, I pushed myself, holding it in my lungs until they were screaming for more, my heartbeat starting to race with the need for more oxygen. Depriving myself until I started to see black dots dancing in my vision, I finally let the air out and quickly sucked in another huge breath.

I am my own man. My feelings are my own. I am an individual.

My mind quickly flashed back to the teen at the lake. I hoped he found someone to confide in soon because his depression had damn near smothered me. I couldn't imagine what living day to day with that blanket of absolute blackness must feel like. If he didn't find some respite soon, I was concerned for his safety. I could check in with Saige in a few days to see what she'd done with the information I'd given her.

Damnit, Fish. Stop. You're out here on your own, which never happens. Don't think about that shit. You're free... for now.

Grunting, I hiked my pack up on my shoulders and picked up my pace. Allowing my senses to spread out, I tested the boundaries of the town lines. There was a presence, but it wasn't stronger than any other basic witch spell. It didn't even feel like a warding spell - just raw magical power. That might just be the town's potency though. A lot of magical people in one location could definitely let out power this palpable.

I pulled out my cell and quickly typed out a message to the guys.

Me: Out on the East line. Normal energy levels, nothing of notice. Heading back.

Shoving my phone back into my pocket, I turned around and started to hike back to where I'd left the bike. The moon was full in the sky tonight, but not bright enough to break through the thicket, so I was thankful for my fairy lights. *Guess I won't be sleeping.* Something about full moon vibes just set me on edge. *I might need a session soon.*

Pushing my bike back to the road, I hopped on and revved the engine, the smell of burnt rubber quickly invading my nose as my tires burned out. Yanking up on the handle bars, I rode a wheelie before slamming back down to earth and speeding down the road away from town. If I had time to myself, I was going to enjoy it for a little bit longer. Who knew when it would happen again.

WE WERE ALL SITTING IN THE LIVING ROOM WITH THE TELEVISION on, but everyone was distracted. Cam was hunched over in one of the armchairs, looking through some paperwork, Kai was lying back on the couch typing on his phone, and Sloane was draped across the other armchair, snacking on some popcorn, looking deep in thought.

"So what was the outcome tonight? Same for all of us?" I inquired, crossing my legs underneath me, my hand rubbing over the rough patterned rug I was sitting on.

Kai put his phone down on his chest and looked over to me.

"Yeah, I felt like there was something there, but nothing that would be strong enough to keep anybody out of the town, ya know? I wondered if that was just the town's pulse I was picking up on."

"I think you're right. We would have felt something more if the spellcaster had done the same level of magic they completed around the border in Kingstown. Speaking of, a couple of us should head over there and check out that perimeter and the warehouse, just for an alibi. If shit does start up, at least we'll have a rock solid cover," Cam said.

"I'll go," Sloane volunteered, which did not surprise me one bit. That mage was the worst at relaxing. He was constantly looking for work, a project, anything to give him purpose. He knew no level of chill.

His eyes flicked to me and held my gaze for a beat too long before looking back to the other guys.

Hmm, he might need a session soon, too. Fuck, I hope so.

"I'll go with him. I can get a read on the people in that area, too. See if anything feels off."

"Okay, Fischer and Sloane, head out there tomorrow. Not like we have any other leads to chase down right this second," Cam ordered, looking back to his notes.

Kai started chuckling, his gaze locked on his phone again.

"Goddamnit, Kai. Are you texting that woman?" Sloane asked, a hint of snark laced in his tone.

"Bet your white ass I am. Gods, did you see her today? She's a goddess. She's funny, and she ate my food with so much enthusiasm I thought my cock was going to hit the underside of the picnic table. And that ass." He groaned and ran his palm from his forehead down to his chin.

Cam laughed and shook his head; we were all used to Kai and his love of women.

"Bro, even Bagheera was all about her. He's lowkey obsessing right now!" Kai exclaimed, throwing his hands in the air.

"She *is* a beautiful woman. I won't deny that, but there's something about her that's throwing me off. I noticed it yesterday when she showed us the apartment, but I figured it was just because I was off my game and exhausted from China and the road trip."

All of the guys sat up and looked at me now. I wasn't the kind of dude to cry wolf over anything, so they always listened if I had concerns.

"Don't keep us in suspense, Fish," Sloane practically growled, and I raised an eyebrow at him. *Not the time or the place, asshole.*

"I can't get a read on her. I got nothing. Zero emotions, no feelings, no colors coming off of her. She's like a ghost. So either she's actually some sort of zombie, or she has mental shields on the same level as our boss and Johnny," I explained, dragging my hand through my hair. I couldn't get shit off Larson or our handler, either. The training we'd gone through taught us all how to build our mental shields, but those two were masters. Very frustrating.

"Seriously?" Cam leaned forward, resting his elbows on his knees. "Well, that certainly is interesting. What could she be hiding though? You can read what she's thinking clear as day on her face."

"Or she'll just tell you to your face after she runs her fingers through your luscious locks." Kai's laughter boomed, and everyone joined in for several moments before the mood got serious again.

"I'm serious. A corpse might have more emotions to read," I shrugged. "So, yeah... she's a puzzle. And I fucking love solving puzzles." I grinned at nobody in particular.

"What all do we know about Saige?" Sloane asked the room.

"She's twenty-seven. Owns The Mystical Piglet magic shop. Has lived in Emerald Lakes her entire life. Biggest town she's been to is Kingstown. Lives just outside of downtown on family property in a cottage. Her grandma lives in a smaller cottage on the back of the property, and they're very close. Her phone was buzzing today, and she ignored all of the messages. I'm guessing an ex. She's a green witch, loves all things earth connected. Pet arctic fox, male, named Maven. He's lazy and cranky, but they love each other. She hasn't referred to him as her familiar, so I believe he is truly just a pet." Kai spilled out so much information we all looked at him like he was the Saige Whisperer.

"What?" he asked us when nobody spoke up.

"When the fuck did you find out all of that?" Sloane barked.

"What the hell did you think we were doing when I was grilling, you dickhead? I was getting to know our girl." He smiled, pleased with himself.

"*Our* girl? K, do you even know how to have one girl?" Cam lifted an eyebrow, crossing his arms across his barrel chest.

Kai just flashed an animalistic grin, popping his shoulder in a lazy shrug as if to say, 'challenge accepted.'

Smooth, smooth shifter. Leave it to K. Our girl does sound nice, though. I shook my head and smiled softly. We hadn't talked about potentially sharing a woman for several years, and when it did come up, we were typically drunk off our asses. I'd given up hope on that dream a very long time ago, right around the time I realized I would never be able to have a normal relationship thanks to my affinity.

Cam's deep voice pulled me from my internal thoughts, and I was grateful for it. That kind of thinking could lead me into a dark spiral.

"Okay, enough. Watch her. Fischer, see if anything changes in the next few days. Keep us posted." Cam stood up from his chair. "I'm heading to bed."

Everyone slowly started heading the same direction. It was late, and I just hoped my brain would be able to shut off so I could actually get some fucking sleep.

The morning sun was shining through my bedroom window as I changed clothes, getting ready to head downstairs to talk to Saige and see if I could get a read on her this morning. I'd already heard her laughter drifting up, bringing a smile to my face. She seemed like such a sweet and pure soul. I just couldn't see her as having any nefarious plans swirling around in that head of hers.

Sloane had already left for the morning, something about 'Operation Oldies.' When he got a plan in his head, that was the end of the discussion. Sloane did what Sloane wanted, and that was why Cam was our team lead. Cam had a protective streak that could rival a fucking pit bull, but he also had a calm, cool way of processing decisions and scenarios. He never jumped before thinking, and it had saved all of our asses so many times. Thinking ahead, he planned for every possible outcome, and the guy was rock solid. While he certainly had his reasons, he struggled to let go of that level of control and live in the moment. Like Sloane, he had his faults, but I loved them both, well, loved them all, just as much as my blood-related family.

The love I had for my brothers powered my overwhelmed and desensitized heart, keeping me going when everything was dark. Hell, it was what saved me from the dark.

Women, now, they were problematic. Beautiful, no doubt, but also vindictive and fake, and I didn't want anything to do with relationships. How the fuck could I ever connect with somebody if I could sense every damn feeling that crossed their psyche in a day? I couldn't, and with me in the picture it made it hard for the others to find that connection, too. Cam once had a girlfriend for about a year, but she wasn't good for him. I think he just liked the idea of having that kind of intimate connection, and in any case, that was during our training at Radical. Nikki had been another recruit, and they'd hit it off right away. Until she started getting increasingly more frustrated with Cam for not expressing himself enough, not giving enough to her on a spiritual level. That's when she started fucking around on him.

My best friend had beat himself up trying to be something he wasn't for that girl, and she hadn't deserved his efforts. I'd picked up on the cheating pretty quickly; every time she hung out with us, she had guilt swirling around her entire body like a tornado. Then Kai shut the whole thing down when she'd shown up one night without having showered, and he smelled Jack all over her. Cam was devastated, to say the least. Since Nikki, he had thrown up his mental walls so high you'd need full mountain climbing gear to crest them. Not that any woman had had the chance to even try since then. Cam fucked, and that was it. One and done.

I was similar to Cam in that sense, except I tended to find sexual release with men. It wasn't that I preferred men over women. I liked both pretty equally, but men were generally more straightforward. You wanted your dick sucked? Then you got your fucking dick sucked. No games, no bullshit. Just a mouth, and your cock slamming in and out until your demons were banished for too short of a time.

Fuck. Now I want my dick sucked.

I HAD JUST WALKED INTO THE STORE WHEN I HEARD A MAN'S VOICE; something about his tone immediately had my hackles up. Keeping my steps quiet, I walked further into the little space, discreetly eavesdropping on his conversation with Saige.

"Listen to me. I just want to talk to you, baby. You haven't been returning my calls or texts."

Who the fuck is this guy?

Saige was standing behind her bar with her arms crossed while a blond dude leaned over the counter, talking to her. Hidden behind a display that held different spell books and tarot cards, I started analyzing this guy's aura. Anger, lust, manipulation, more anger.

Yeah, this isn't going to work.

"I told you, Bryce. You need to get the fuck out of my store. I haven't returned your calls or texts because we are done. The end, it's over, and that is not going to change. Get. OUT!" Saige yelled at him.

Nothing. She was clearly feeling a multitude of things, but she wasn't projecting a single one of them. Her eyes were spitting daggers, but her expression also betrayed another emotion: fear. *What the fuck is going on?*

Growling started, and I realized Maven must have been back there with her, and he sounded pissed off. Animals were great readers of people, and this piece of shit was *not* a good person. Still, I didn't think I should interfere. *Yet, anyway.* I'd be here if anything escalated, but I wanted her to be able to do whatever she needed for her own sake. She was a grown ass woman, not a damsel in distress, and I was no brown knight in shining armor.

"Do not raise your voice at me, or have you forgotten how the fuck to behave?" the bastard hissed at her, standing up to his full height. Shrinking away from him, it was as if a switch had been flipped, turning off Saige's nerve.

"Ah, so you do remember. You were always such a quick learner. That's what I love about you, baby."

Mother of the moon.

"Come here. Do not make me repeat myself, Saige."

His aura was nothing but darkness, rage simmering under the false cover of calm. When she flinched as he reached his hand out, lust shot out of his body so strong it almost made me gag.

Oh, hell no, fuck face.

"Saige," I called in a low voice, "could you come over here and help me pick out a few things?"

Her beautiful green eyes filled with relief when she saw me there, giving her an out. I smiled at her, hopefully letting her know she was safe so long as I was here with her.

"Fischer, hi. Yes, of course I can help you out." Walking out through the open end of the bar, she made her way over to where I was standing.

"I'll be here when you're done, Saige," the idiot piped up, and I saw her back stiffen.

Douchebag Blondie was staring at me so hard his eyes were in jeopardy of popping out of his skull. *I'll happily remove them from his face if he wants to push his fucking luck.* Saige came up to me, angled slightly away from the threat, but she kept him in her periphery, clearly not wanting to have her back to the enemy. *Smart.* Her face was red, showing her embarrassment, but she had no need to be. That pissed me off.

"Thank you," she silently mouthed.

"I'm looking for some stuff to make a potion that might convince someone to be inclined to go out on a date with me." I smirked, breathing in that potent smell of brimstone that told me Douchebag was about to erupt.

Try it, motherfucker. I'm banking on it at this point.

"Oh? Did you find someone in town already? We do have quite a few single people around our age. But Fischer," she playfully teased, slapping my shoulder, "you know that isn't how potions work. We never make or cast spells to take away someone's consent." She flicked her eyes toward the idiot behind her.

I grabbed her hand, giving it a light squeeze. She looked back to me immediately, then down to our joined hands.

Not understanding how she was able to completely shield from me, I studied her face. Did I dare to even hope that I might have found someone I could have a normal relationship with? Not even romantically, not that I wouldn't jump on the opportunity. I'd be happy with anything at this point. Suddenly, I felt the need to get close to this woman. Opening my mouth, the words just spilled out.

"Saige, would you like to go out to dinner with me?" I smiled and watched her emotions play across her beautiful face. Shock, happiness, and excitement danced across her round cheeks and plump lips. *I wonder what those taste like?* Emotions weren't so bad if I could watch them like this instead of being pulverized. *How is this possible?* I couldn't tear my gaze away from her, wanting to study every movement she made. Standing there, I stared at her like a fool as she lifted her lips in a shy smile.

"Excuse me, asshole. She's not single." Douche had reached his boiling point; I could practically see the fury blowing out of his ears.

Ignoring him, I kept my eyes on the woman in front of me.

"Say yes."

"I would love to go out with you, Fischer." She smiled so big, her perfect grin made my stomach flip and my dick start to wake up.

Why am I doing this? What is it about her?

"Like FUCK you will," Douchebag roared, taking three big steps to grab her around the upper arm, attempting to yank her away from me.

I saw red. Swinging my left fist at his head, I was so fast he didn't have time to try and block me, and there was an audible crunch as his cheekbone cracked. He stumbled backward, and I immediately advanced. Rallying, he tried to land a punch, but I grabbed his fist and punched him right in the fucking throat. Dropping like a sack of shit, he started choking and wheezing for air he didn't deserve to breathe.

Ah, there it is. Fear.

I inhaled deeply, my eyes fluttering shut, then a tired sigh puffed out of my mouth, like I was really bored as shit and being put out by this waste of creation. Reaching down blindly, I grabbed him by his hair and pulled his sorry ass back up.

"You motherfuc-" Nope. My hold on his hair tightened forcefully enough to get him to shut his poisonous trap, and I waited until he looked me in my eyes. He was still pissed, but once his pathetic brain caught up with what he was looking at, I saw the realization in his eyes. He withered.

There's a fucking reason why I was the best at what I did. I was the king at switching my humanity on and off, and right now, I could only imagine what my face must look like. If I had to guess, my eyes were probably solid black. When I shut myself off like this, things... changed. My eyes go blacker than the sky on a starless night, and it's like the fear that people feel when they cower in front of me fuels me. With a lot of practice, I learned how to control myself, how to keep the beast at bay, and that really was in everyone's best interest.

I don't play games. I am the fucking monster in this room. All *of the rooms. I'm the nightmare you don't want dipping into your mind, and I want to fuck up this sick bastard's brain so badly he won't be able to close his eyes again without pissing his pants. But that will have to wait. I don't want to reveal everything I'm capable of, not yet.*

"Do not ever come in here again. Do not ever look at Saige again. Do not talk to her, do not think about her, and definitely do not fucking touch your sad little penis while imagining her beautiful body. So help me gods, if you ever think about touching her again, I will get my three brothers down here. We will fucking dance, and it will be your last, you shit stain. Now get the fuck out of here." My voice was so deep and rumbling I almost didn't recognize it as my own.

He ran out of the shop and didn't look back.

Saige

Chapter Seven

No, no, no!

I raced outside, abandoning my coffee by the kitchen sink, disbelief overriding all of my senses. Throwing myself down on my knees, I swiveled my head around to fully take in what I was seeing. The brightness of the new day was too much of a contrast with the shock and sheer outrage that hit me.

What the hell is happening?

"Gran! Come out here!" I yelled, loud enough for her to hear me from her cottage behind mine.

My magic was vibrating with the need to heal these plants. *This shouldn't be possible. Who ever heard of the gardens of a green witch shriveling up and dying for no reason?*

"What is it, child?" Gran called out, but when she rounded the corner and saw for herself, she stopped in her tracks. *I guess the old girl is still capable of being shocked speechless.* "Merciful moons," she gasped, her tone betraying how confused she was. *That's not good. She's supposed to know everything about this shit!*

Maven was sniffing around like a fox possessed, frantically digging his paws into the dirt, high-pitched whines escaping his mouth. He lifted his head to look at me, dirt clinging to his whiskers.

I don't fucking think so. This is my gods damn garden.

I called my powers to the surface, gold cyclone-like swirls sparked out of my palms. Snapping my hand out to the right, I started calling out incantations. Now that I was an older, more practiced witch, I didn't actually need to say the words aloud. As long as I visualized the outcome, I was golden. For me, witchcraft was honestly eighty percent mental, ten percent repetition, and ten percent stubbornness. I could picture what I wanted the earth to give me, and it gave. But when you needed a little extra dramatic *oomph*, there was nothing like yelling out the words.

"Crescere! Cresco!" *Grow! Rise!* A strip of St. John's Wort exploded from the ground. "Excresco!" *Enlarge!* It grew larger and larger. *Perfect, because I'm going to need all of this to unfuck my life. Fuck, I feel powerful right now.* It'd been too long since I'd let my magic flow so unrestrained, and I smiled to myself. I couldn't recall a time that casting magic had felt this satisfying, and I was drowning in the sudden hunger to let more power race through my body. *This feels so fucking good. More, I need more.*

"Crescere, adulesco!" *Grow, more!* Valerian root. *Yep. Gonna need that to chill my stressed out ass later.*

Focusing on the sick flowerbeds, I had held out both hands, preparing to cure the fuck out of these poor babies. I jumped when I felt a hand on my shoulder, snapping me out of my magical rush. I was breathing hard. *My power still works. Thank fuck. If it's not me, then what?*

"Let it go, Flower Elsa. You'll have the whole damn property covered in random shit that we don't need. I don't want you to blast the sick ones yet. I need to analyze them myself," Gran told me matter-of-factly.

"When the hell did you watch *Frozen*?" I questioned.

"It came out in 2016, Saige. I saw it in theaters, and I went and saw *Frozen 2* when it released a couple of months ago. I'm convinced now, more than ever, that Sven is actually a shifter, and he and Kristoff are both giving it to-" I shut that shit down.

"Okay! Gran. Focus, we have a serious fucking problem here."

"Then quit bitchin' and get to witchin'." She huffed at me like *I* was the one delaying this investigation. Turning her back on me, she stalked off to the sick flowerbeds, her bright floral print mumu billowing out behind her.

I'D LEFT GRAN ELBOWS DEEP IN SOME SERIOUS DIRT AND FUCKERY. She was working up a sweat but assured me that she would be fine and I should get to work. Gathering up my stuff didn't take long, but I did make sure to touch up my makeup before leaving the house, something I wouldn't have bothered with before. Now? I was texting non-stop with a sexy shifter and had a date tomorrow night with an equally sexy, dark, and mysterious mind master. *Mmmmm. Happy Birthday to ME! Well, almost. My twenty-eighth birthday is next month. Maybe I'll actually have a little get together this year? I hope the guys want to hang out. If they're still in town that is...*

Riding down into town, Maven looked majestic as a king, paws up on the front of the basket with the wind whipping through his thick white fur. Sometimes the cranky thing liked to enjoy the small pleasures.

Fischer rescuing me from Bryce had been playing in my head on repeat since yesterday. As satisfying as the memory was, I was concerned about retaliation. Bryce was a water mage with the temper of a fucking hothead. He liked to play the good guy, but behind closed doors, he was an abuser. Psychologically, physically, even sexually at times. He was an awful person all around.

I was so pissed that he thought he could come into the shop like that and threaten me just because he'd thought no one was listening. Initially, I wasn't going to put up with his shit, but then, he'd triggered me and, fuck- I had been about to give in. Flashbacks of everything he'd done to me had me wanting to submit in an attempt to appease him. A part of me still believed that if I could just make him happy, he wouldn't hurt me again. The trouble with abusers, though, was that they never meant what they said. Even if you listened, always answered your phone, and had sex with them any time they demanded it, it would never be good enough. It had taken me a while to learn this lesson, that you should never have to fucking obey a person to deserve their love or be spared their wrath.

When I saw Fischer there, witnessing the whole scene, my cheeks had flamed in shame. I didn't want him to see me as a victim or weak. I couldn't even imagine what readings he was getting from me, but then he'd asked me out on a date!

After Bryce had scrambled out the front door, Fischer turned back around to face me, his normally light brown eyes entirely pitch black. He stood there, eerily calm, and we just stared at each other until his eyes lightened a couple of shades. After a huge breath, he said, "I'll pick you up at six on Friday night. Here," he held his hand out to me, "let me see your cell."

I pulled it out of my back pocket and slipped it into his large palm. His thumbs moved over the screen quickly before he handed it back to me.

"I added my information. I have to run, but call me if you ever need anything. And if that fucker comes near you again, I want you to call me immediately." His tone commanded me to follow his request, and I had no desire to challenge him on this. Unlike Bryce's orders, there was nothing threatening about Fish. Instead, I just felt safe for the first time in a long while.

"Okay, I promise. To be honest, I'm expecting blowback from that encounter. Before you even stepped in, there were going to be consequences." I whispered the last part, humiliated once again.

"Hey, look at me." His black boots come into my line of sight since I was staring at the ground. A gentle hand went under my chin, tilting my head up so I could see his concerned face. His hardened features from moments ago had given way to something much softer, but it

wasn't pity. Thank the stars. I didn't ever want anybody's pity. I could take care of my damn self.

"You deserve respect from a partner. I know we've just met, but I can already tell you're stubborn as hell, powerful, and your confidence is beautiful. You're *beautiful*. You got away from him already, and that tells me how strong you are. You stood up to him when you thought you were alone, and that shows me how fearless you are. If he retaliates, you don't have to face him alone. There is no shame in owning our pasts and rising from them, and especially not in asking for help when we need it. Having people to lean on makes us formidable, not weak." All I could do was stare into his eyes, captivated by his words. He gave my shoulder a quick squeeze before spinning on his heel and heading for the door.

Without turning back, he called out, "I meant what I said. Call me if there's the slightest hint of trouble."

As I pulled up to The Pig, Roberta Miller and Matilda Graber were sitting on one of the benches alongside the front of the building, rising to their feet when they saw me approach. These two were as eccentric as they came. Bright colors, long beaded necklaces, loud eye makeup, they looked every part the fortune teller stereotype. I mean, they did have 'the Sight,' so the look was perfect for them.

"Good morning, sweetie. We were waiting for you. We must talk, but inside would be best, in private," Roberta requested as her partner in crime bounced up and down on her toes. *This ought to be good...*

"Sure, let me just get in here and set my things down." I extended my hand to push the door open before stepping out of the way for my visitors.

Frank and Arlo were inside when we filed through the door, and I saw they'd already finished updating the indoor and outdoor displays with new stock. They worked here a few days a week so I wasn't overwhelmed trying to do everything myself.

"Thanks, guys," I said to them as I set my bag down on the bar.

THE MAGIC OF DISCOVERY

Making my way around the sales counter, I trailed my fingertips over the deep stained wood.

"Hey, honey. Everything's good here; you could've taken your time. We restocked the dried bulk supplies and put away the shipment that came in yesterday from the book supplier," Frank said, patting my back before releasing me. Frank was in his late fifties. He had a round belly and a deep, contagious laugh. The evidence of how often he indulged in humor was engraved into his face. I'd never seen anyone with such adorable laugh lines. With twinkling blue eyes and graying hair, I found him enchanting.

"You guys are too good to me. I'd be drowning without you." I made sure to look at Arlo to let him know that I wasn't just speaking about his partner, and he gave me a soft smile in return. Where Frank was boisterous and loud, Arlo was his silent sentinel. Thin as a bean pole and ten years younger than Frank, he had every bit as big a heart as his lover. He had shaggy blond hair and sincere brown eyes that sucked you in; not one for talking a lot, the man could listen. They had been together for twenty years now, and they were planning a binding ceremony for early fall. It would be one hell of a party. Everyone in town would be invited because we all loved these two, and it made me happy just to think about it.

"It's just as well I came when I did since these two lovely ladies were lying in wait for me." I winked at the two witches behind me who were growing more and more impatient.

"Child, this is important." Matilda started shooing me toward the back of the shop, to the room that we used for tarot and palm readings. I threw up my arm in a hasty wave, hearing Frank's deep chuckle in response.

With a thought, the dangling stars and moon string lights that concealed the small room separated, so we could enter without having to dig them out of each other's hair later. Stepping through, hues of purples, blues, and pink enveloped us. I sighed. I loved this room. So chill and calming. Since this was an addition to the original building, I had skylights installed so I could have plenty of plants in here. The skylights had retractable shades, so if I was in here with a customer, one press of a button on the remote would close them and allow better mood lighting.

We approached the round table in the center of the room, each of us taking a seat. I looked between the two ladies, waiting for someone to start talking. And waited. *Alright, looks like it's going to be me.*

"What can I do for you ladies? What's this about?" I inquired, reaching out to the little cactus that was in the middle of the table. I flicked a spark of gold at it, and tiny pink flowers started blooming. *So pretty.*

"Yesterday afternoon, we saw your Sloane." My mouth opened, but her raised hand cut me off, their news apparently more important than my desire to tell them that he was not *my* anything. "He was strolling down the sidewalk with Judy and Harry while they walked little Potato. The moment we laid eyes on him, the Sight slammed into each of us so hard it nearly took our breath away. I cannot recall another time that we had such a strong vision. It was as though the stars themselves had manifested, and their sweet yet cautioning voices spoke the words in our minds: a prophecy."

I couldn't keep my mouth shut. "First of all, I didn't know that Potato was still able to walk." He was Judy and Harry's supersized pug who looked like a forty-pound tan watermelon. "Secondly, just to clarify, Sloane is not mine. Yes, he's pretty, but he's a dickhead."

The two women just smiled and nodded at me despite my narrowed eyes. *I don't think Sloane will ever be anyone's.*

"Potato has started hanging out at the Cosmos gym. The poor pup is vying for the affections of a female pug who skateboards and does other athletic feats there. The CovenFit crew took him under their wing, and now he wears these adorable little tank tops that say 'Cosmos CovenFit.' The gym coaches have started calling him Baked Potato, something about reverse psychology and baked potatoes being the healthiest option where potatoes are in question. Honestly, child, do you live under a rock these days?" *This fucking town is so weird sometimes...*

Chuckling, I agreed that I must indeed be living under a rock, but in all honesty, my mind just wasn't focused on anything other than my damn plants dying and the sexy mages who were probably upstairs right now, naked, working out, flexing...

The ceiling creaked overhead. *See? Cam probably flexed his gigantic biceps, and the floor groaned in appreciation.*

Needing to get all of us, myself definitely included, back on track, I decided to just ask and put them out of their misery.

"What did the stars show you?" I leaned in conspiratorially, a serious expression on my face. At least I hope it looked serious and not like I was regretting eating that pound of cheese last night.

Roberta turned her tapping hand over and slid it toward her friend as Matilda inhaled deeply and laid her palm on the waiting hand. The moment their hands clasped, the lights in my shop went out, and the candles I had strewn throughout the room ignited, flames shooting upward immediately. I shrieked and leaned back in my chair.

Looking at the women's faces, I gasped. Four solid black eyes blankly stared at me, the hair on their heads slowly beginning to stand on end. *Okay, this is scary as fuck.* I wanted to call for Frank and Arlo, but before I could open my mouth to cry for help, both of their free hands shot forward across the table, grabbing mine.

A feeling that I can only describe as electric jolted my body and my head bent back involuntarily. The tingling of my scalp left no doubt that my hair was rising to the ceiling too. *I bet my eyes are black.* I sucked in a wild breath of air as I felt something sinking through my veins, crawling, seeking. If a shadow were a living thing, it was inside me right now. What it was looking for?

I had no idea. The darkness started to settle into my bones, bringing with it a deep ache. The kind of ache that makes you question your existence and wonder what piece of yourself you're missing.

I was frozen in place, forced to allow this magic to complete its mission, its invasion. A sigh from a high-pitched voice sounded, and my head snapped forward. I could see again, but everything was in shades of green and black.

"She is the oneeeee. King will be pleased," something hissed, its creepy voice making me shudder. Unable to move or talk yet, I was forced to sit and listen, but I did scan the room with my eyes, unsuccessful in my attempt to find the source of the voice. The two women before me were just as still as they'd been before they snatched my hands.

Movement brought my attention to the doorway when an extremely tall shadow moved into the room, a slightly shorter figure following. *What in the fuck? I didn't sign up for ghost bullshit, if that's what they were.*

"Yes, so beautiful. Pure and selfless." The figures were drifting toward me now, my heart pounding so hard in my chest I thought it might explode. Now that these beings were closer, I could see that they had a humanoid shape, and it appeared they were wearing robes of some kind, but the fine details were lost in the shadows that made up their ethereal forms. My eyes widened when I realized there were protrusions coming out of their heads, like... horns?

"The others are near. It won't be much longer now. Come, let us go to King and tell him we have found her."

No, I don't want anyone knowing those things found me. What the fuck? Why are they even looking for me?

The room began to lighten with each step the creatures took toward the door, and once they stepped through, the candles extinguished and the lights came back. The room had returned to normal, and the witches across from me now had glazed over white eyes. Releasing my hands, they began to recite the prophecy, their voices distorted and scary as hell.

> A witch, a mix of green and red,
> Save a race before they're dead.
> Hurry, witch, find your five,
> If there is hope to survive.

> Change, rise, manifest,
> A soul so pure soon possessed.
> Before the year of two and eight
> The chosen one must find her mates.

> If she should fail to meet her task,
> To another the role will pass.
> Evil will consume her heart,
> Her soul captured by the dark.

For the first two parts, they alternated lines, their rhythm eerily in sync and voices never losing their haunting melody. The final third was said in unison, their volume increasing with each new line until the prophecy echoed throughout the room, its presence overwhelming. As soon as the last word left their lips, their eyes flashed back to their usual colors. Thank fuck, because I was never going to lose the memory of their fogged over eyes. *Shadow figures and black eyes? Scary, yeah, but those white eyes? I'll never get over that. Nightmares, here I come!*

"Are you two okay? For the love of the moon, that was the most intense and creepiest thing I have ever experienced. I'm sweating." I used my hand to fan my face.

"It was by far the most intense vision we have ever had. It truly is like being possessed by the stars to relay their wishes." Matilda took a small napkin out of her purse, dabbing at her damp face and wiping her thin nose.

"So bizarre how the stars were able to manifest their forms into ethereal beings like that. They were a thousand times more disturbing than I would have ever dreamed. If I'm being honest, I thought they'd be sparkling and radiating light." I was talking so fast, my mouth expelling thoughts quicker than my mind had time to process them.

"By the stars, child. What are you going on about?" Roberta's exasperation had my brain coming to a screeching halt. Both women were now staring at me like I had lost my mind. *Maybe I had.*

"Uh... those figures that were in here?" My hands moved to mimic the shape of the shadows as they watched me incredulously. "You didn't see them or hear them?" I questioned, feeling more and more alarmed with each second they continued to look at me with wariness and another emotion I couldn't place.

"No, Saige. It was just us here." The two women exchanged a glance with eyebrows cocked. *Better start to backpedal now...*

"I must have dozed off then. I haven't been sleeping the greatest the past couple of weeks." That wasn't completely a lie; I *was* having restless sleep. My dreams had started becoming darker, and I was remembering more of the details than ever before. *Maybe I should mix up a batch of Dreamless Drops and see if that helps.*

"Well, dear girl, do you understand now why it was paramount we share this information with you as soon as possible?" Matilda asked me, her face serious.

"Yes, but what about this makes you think it's referring to *me*? Prophecies are notorious for being misunderstood and in some cases, completely made up," I queried. The vision had unsettled me, and I needed to know what had pointed them in my direction.

Matilda scoffed, seemingly frustrated at my skepticism. Roberta laid a hand on her friend's shoulder in a calming gesture before explaining, "The fact that this information came to us when we ran into your boyfriend, Sloane, is one the largest clues. It speaks of a witch and five mates. Four of them are here, and all four are interested in you, if word on the street is any good these days. You're twenty-seven, and the prophecy speaks of the year two and eight. Your birthday is approaching, isn't it? Next month, right?"

"Yes, yes, her birthday is June twenty-fourth. I could never forget it! My little Poopsie shares the same glorious date of birth," Matilda giggled.

My life is now complete. I share a birthday with a giant cat named Poopsie. Will the blessings never cease?

Holding up a finger, I set out to correct their misconceptions over my non-relationship with all of the men. "Ladies, I don't have any boyfriends, zero. I'm not involved with any of the men staying above the shop, and even if I were, the prophecy speaks of *five* mates, not four. So unless one of them is hiding a sexy identical twin upstairs, you're grasping at straws."

"Saige, you're being far too nonchalant about all of this. The urge we feel pushing us to be here, telling you this information, is incredibly forceful. Just be on guard, okay? Relay the information to Bette, and perhaps she will have thoughts on it." *There's definitely no convincing them.* I might disagree with their concerns, but I saw no reason to upset them. Making some placating noises, I assured them as best I could.

Rising out of our chairs, I escorted them to the front of the store, giving each of them a small bag of different herbs as a thank you for their time. I'd known them my entire life, and they truly were sweet women, so I thanked them repeatedly and gave a few hugs to smooth out any ruffled feathers.

The door closed behind them, and I let out the biggest exhale before proclaiming to the empty store, "What the FUCK?"

There had been moving shadows, *talking* moving shadows, in my store, and despite the fact that I'd just downplayed the whole prophecy bullshit, a small part of me was on edge. *Losing my soul to the darkness? No, thank you.* Why did they say *I* was the one, and what King was going to be pleased that they'd found me? Now I had to figure out what was going on with the plants in this town, what the hell this prophecy was all about, and find a subtle way to ask Gran about shadow creatures, *with motherfucking horns. Great.*

Sloane
Chapter Eight

Fischer and I were tearing down the winding country roads that would lead us to Kingstown. His adrenaline-loving ass had just let off the throttle and dropped the clutch, his bike screaming out a roar as he blew past me, dirt clouds flying up in his wake. Fish's whoop of excitement brought a smile to my lips. Dude was wound so tightly ninety percent of the time that any activity he could find to give him a reprieve was more than welcomed.

The warehouse was located on the outskirts of the city, but after ten years in our line of work, you learned really fucking fast that you never knew who was watching. We'd arranged to meet the real estate agent at seven to ensure there weren't a ton of people out and about.

Keeping a leisurely pace behind him, I let my mind drift to the mission. It was hard to believe we had been in Emerald Lakes for just about a week. Operation Oldies was in full swing, and it was going swimmingly. Old people love good old Sloaney. I'd learned a shit ton of information about the town. I still wasn't sure that everything was pertinent, like how Alfred Tillerson was moonlighting in the next town over as a drag witch every other weekend, or how the two seers, who I swear to the gods looked like the sisters from *Coraline*, told me that they were working on decoding a prophecy from the stars. They'd said their last key piece of information could only be found on my abs. *Bet your ass I showed those old broads my muscles.*

Perhaps my most useful informant was a man named Randy. Randy Roger, seventy-three years old and one very interesting man. His fashion sense was straight out of the nineteen seventies, and his hair matched. He could talk for days, and he seemed to have almost a compulsion to touch you at any opportunity. I would've been more skeeved about that, but I'd followed him around town the other day, and he did it to everybody. Not being singled out on the man's people-I-must-touch list was perfectly fine with me, especially after seeing him thoroughly inspecting the cucumber and zucchini selection at the grocery store. When he saw me looking, he winked and made a lewd gesture with the veggies. As I shook my head in exasperation, he'd lifted his hands, a foot-long cucumber in each one, and began wielding them like they were weapons.

Now, I'd like to say that I did *not* engage this lunatic in an epic battle of vegetable weapons in the middle of a grocery store. I'd also like to say that we weren't both covered in a slew of exploded produce and that I didn't have a red mark across my cheek that oddly resembled a cock thanks to underestimating the stealth of that Randy asshole, but those would all be lies. I did what I had to do, and now that I had earned the respect and admiration of the mage, he was in my pocket. After our fight, he'd laughed like a madman, snapped his fingers, and the store went right back to how it was before. *That* was a cool as shit power. Maybe if I stay on his good side, I can get him to teach me how to do that.

It was frustrating that we hadn't made more progress on the assignment. I'd reached out to Larson, letting him know the little details that we'd discovered so far—which wasn't a whole hell of a lot. I was worried that he'd be disappointed, especially since this case was clearly a personal one. I couldn't wait to find this bitch for him. I could see it playing out now: Larson gets his hands on this woman, our team gets praised, and I line myself up nicely for a hell of a promotion. *Maybe I could request a personal assignment so that we could help Cam...*

It felt like hardly any time had passed before I was pulling my Indian up next to Fischer's bike. He was already standing on the sidewalk, hands in his dark jean pockets. He was wearing a dark red t-shirt with a design that looked like one of those palmistry hands you'd see in the window of a fake ass fortune telling shop, but instead of having all four fingers up, only the middle one was raised. Underneath the hand it said, 'Fuck the stars, own your own destiny.' One of his usual thick black fabric headbands was wrapped around his head. He always wore them when he was working out or riding his bike, keeping his curly ass hair out of his eyes.

We stood beside each other taking in what we could see of the massive industrial property. The metal siding was the most boring color of gray. *Well, it certainly wouldn't draw any unwanted attention, that's for damn sure.* Weeds shot up through the cracks in the sidewalk, completely unkempt.

Within a minute, a sleek white car pulled into the parking lot and a lean woman stepped out. She headed toward us, red heels clicking on the walkway, making her legs look miles long. A black pencil skirt hit right at her waist, her sheer white blouse tucked in and unbuttoned just enough to straddle the line of professionalism. She carried a binder full of paperwork, and her blonde hair was wrapped up in a bun on the top of her head, the picture of a polished and ready-to-sell realtor. I watched as she took us in, eyes slightly widening behind her black-framed glasses, appreciation clear on her face. She was pretty, but I wasn't interested, not tonight.

"Hi, you must be Mr. Sullivan and Mr. Bahri. I'm Sarah Cooper. I'm glad you reached out, welcome to the area." She held out her hand for us to shake, and Fischer spoke up first.

"Please, you can call me Fischer. This is my business partner, Sloane. As he told you on the phone, we're looking into this investment for our boss. We don't have the final say so on whether or not an offer is made, but he *does* value our opinion."

"Of course. Feel free to take videos or photos while I show you around." Sarah stepped up to the double glass doors, entering a series of numbers into the lockbox. "This is the vestibule, and just inside this door is the main entrance. Everything is original, as you can see. Some serious updating will need to happen to get this more up with the times. The company left nearly everything behind, and the property does come as-is, so the buyer is responsible for all of the contents." She flashed a seductive smile in our direction. *Sorry, honey, not happening.*

"Sarah, would it be alright if my colleague and I wandered around for a while? This is mostly just a fact finding visit, so we'll just be snapping pictures and possibly a video call with our boss, though we won't be able to do that if he knows you're listening in. He is very big on confidentiality," I bit out in response. I honestly didn't even try *not* to come off as an asshole.

She bit her bottom lip, no doubt debating telling me no and remaining professional or giving in to my request and possibly making a hefty commission. "Oh, um, well, I'm not technically supposed to leave clients unattended at showings." I stared her down, capitalizing on her discomfort. "I could wait outside?"

Before I could unleash my irritation on her further, Fischer cut in. He was always better at this stuff than me. Fuck, most people were better at this stuff than me. *Whatever.* I didn't hide what I wanted, didn't beat around the bush. Feelings? *Eww.* My skin actually crawled just thinking about the f-word.

"If you'd like to come back in a couple of hours to ensure that everything is in order, that would give us plenty of time to investigate and be out of your hair. Our boss appreciates your cooperation," Fischer told her in a soothing tone, his calming vibes mingling with his words. Her shoulders relaxed, all hesitation no longer a concern. Fish was able to project feelings onto others, so I'd imagine Sarah was feeling all sorts of chilled the hell out and

THE MAGIC OF DISCOVERY

ready to be compliant with our wishes. His power was cool as fuck and definitely useful when paired up with an asshole like me.

"Sure thing! You can call or text me if you have any questions. I live about ten minutes away, so I can always come back." She took a couple of steps toward Fischer, hope shining in her big blue eyes.

"Thank you, Sarah," Fischer said in a low tone that had my hot blood heating up further. "Let me walk you out." He took her arm and walked her back through the door with her looking at him like he'd hung the moon and every star in the damn sky. He'd no doubt continue blasting her with his power just to ensure that we got privacy.

While I waited, I took in the large reception area; the whole vibe screamed early nineties, pale pinks and blues in watercolor geometric designs. I felt like I was ten years old again, sitting in one of the many hospitals I'd frequented as a child. *Fuck that shit. Shut it down. Now.* I was just about to walk down the hall to get away from the horrid decor when I heard Fischer coming back into the building. Knowing him, he'd gotten the lock code from her, too. *That will come in handy later.*

Leaning against the wall at the beginning of the hallway, I waited. His eyes flashed when they met mine. *Hmmm, showtime.*

"This is a one hundred thousand square foot facility, Fischer. Where do you want to explore first?" I questioned, giving nothing away in my expression. *We're here to play a game, and he can play coy all he wants, but he* will *make the first move. We've both known what he really wants since the moment he stared me down in the living room.*

"Let's check out the manufacturing plant. This actually isn't too bad of a building if Larson ever did want to seriously consider expanding up here." Fischer pivoted away from me, and I narrowed my eyes at his retreating back, his muscles rippling as he tapped his fingers against his thighs. Kicking off the wall, I moved silently behind him down a long, musty-smelling hallway, my eyes flicking to the sign hanging above, an arrow straight ahead with the words 'The Plant.' That sign looked as pathetic as the rest of this place. I didn't even know what the fuck they made in here, and I didn't give a shit either. There was only one thing that I wanted right now.

Taking a left, we entered a new room through a set of metal double doors. Stepping onto a concrete platform that was covered in a layer of dust, we found ourselves about thirty feet above the manufacturing floor. Cobwebs and dust coated every fucking surface, draping off of the old machinery that had been abandoned like some hardcore Halloween decor. Fish passed behind me, and I swore I felt his fingertips trail over my shoulder, but when I snapped my head to the right, he was already heading down the stairs to the ground level. My hands balled at my sides, excitement flaring with the promise of things to come. *Where the hell is the breakroom in this place?*

"Damn, this place is huge. Deceptively so. I never would have thought this was in here!" Fischer exclaimed, his footsteps echoing in the cavernous space.

"Yeah, this is partly underground, too, but you'd never know from the outside. Larson might actually want to see this place. You know how he likes underground facilities for training and affinity testing." They contained the mayhem better, especially from nosy humans and any supernaturals who had no business knowing about the dark work Radical was involved in.

Fischer led the way, wandering in and out of offices and rooms that lined the perimeter of the work floor. Content to let him think he could take the lead, I prowled behind him with my hands gripping the straps of my backpack. *Gods damn, I'm on edge.*

He took a left, and we found ourselves in a large room with high glass windows. There were six tables with chairs scattered throughout the space. A couple of couches were arranged in the back section of the room, a tv hanging on the wall. *Bingo.*

I stepped up beside Fischer, swinging my backpack off my shoulders and letting it drop onto the table with a thud. *This room is perfect.*

Fischer set his own backpack down on the table before grabbing his water bottle from the side pocket. "So, where do you think I should take Saige on our date tomorrow night?" he asked, his tone teasing as he watched for my reaction. He tried to maintain his cool composure as his eyes met mine, but his fucking smirk gave him away. Breaking eye contact first, *like he fucking should*, he quickly unscrewed the lid and lifted the bottle to his lips to try to hide his grin, his throat working as he swallowed. *Okay, enough of this shit.*

Instinctively, my hand snapped out and wrapped around his throat, causing him to sputter. Water spilled down his chin, cascading down my forearm. His smirk turned into a full blown smile as I squeezed tighter.

Cocking my head to the side, I walked him backward until his ass hit the counter of the kitchenette. "Is that what you want to talk about? *Saige?*" I fucking growled at him. "Is she why you've been walking around with this all day?" Still gripping his throat, I grabbed his hard cock with my other hand. "Or are you just trying to taunt me? Wind me up?" With each question, I squeezed his dick, his groans igniting sparks of fire throughout my bloodstream.

His pupils were blown the fuck out, the tension between us palpable. Moving my hand from his erection to his face, I grasped his jaw. The rough stubble that adorned his face scratched my palm as I squeezed, forcing his mouth open. I liked him like this, at my mercy.

Leaning in, our lips almost touching, I released his throat. Sliding my hand to the back of his head, I sank my fingers into his soft curly hair, then, without warning, I yanked his head back. Fischer licked his lips as I stared down at him, and I felt his palms land on my pecs, grazing my nipples.

"Haven't you learned yet, pet? We've done this song and dance for years, and still, you like to taunt the beast inside of me. You know I always give you what you need, but sometimes... sometimes I think that you need *more*. What is it? A firmer hand? A harder fuck?" His breathing was coming out in short pants now, and I knew he was close to begging me at this point. Crowding him more, I forced his mouth open a little further before leaning down and swiping my tongue straight inside, sliding up against his. Fire licked down my spine, sending a shot of white hot heat straight to my cock. *How dare he taunt me with her.*

"Answer me, pet. Tell me. Is my dick not enough for you anymore? You need a wet pussy to sink yourself into? Or is it her sexy ass that you want to fuck?" I was growling at him at this point, but I gave absolutely zero shits about it.

"You know I love your dick," he breathed, pinching my nipples lightly. "And I love your nipples, and your shoulders," he soothed me, his hands moving up over my chest to my shoulders to demonstrate. My hands fell to rest at my side, and he took the opening to touch me without hesitation.

"And I love your big hands, especially when they're on my body." His hands trailed down my arms to my hands, guiding them to his ass, which I palmed as I leaned down and ran my nose up the side of his throat.

"And I love your lips," he murmured, turning his face and planting a chaste kiss against them. Breaking the kiss, he stared into my eyes; as much as feelings made my insides want to shrivel up and die, I could handle physical appreciation. Fucking right I was going to stand here and let him worship me. I didn't know that I ever felt as powerful as I did when Fischer and I were involved like this.

I had never met another person who could flip their humanity switch off and on like he could. It was both fascinating and fucking terrifying. He was the interrogator for our team, and he could infest your brain with all kinds of trauma or convince you that you were married to a freaking chihuahua. I'd seen him do both. His alpha male called out to mine, and he could fight me if he wanted to, but that wasn't what this was about. This was the absolute only place that he would ever submit to me, or anyone else for that matter. Fish gave me his obedience because he knew I craved that, and I gave him sweet oblivion.

I shivered with need as he tugged on the waistband of my jeans, the silky warmth of his tongue sliding up the side of my throat sending a tingle straight to my fucking balls. The need to claim, to possess, to dominate was pumping through my veins with every beat of my heart.

"Can I show you, Master?" Fischer asked, desire burning him up from the inside.

"No. Not yet," I bit out even though I wanted to feel him sucking me off. First, I had to know what the fuck was so special about this woman that she'd already captivated two members of my team with no effort at all.

"What is it about her? Tell me the truth." He withdrew his hands from the button on my jeans with a sigh.

"I like the fact that I don't feel like I'm drowning when I'm around her. There's nothing, no emotions fucking bombarding me... It's refreshing." He whispered the last two words, pain lacing his voice. Leaning in, I put my forehead against his.

"I thought I did that for you?" I whispered back. I sounded vulnerable, and I didn't like that shit. The last time I'd shown any sort of vulnerability, I'd been taught real quick that it was a weakness. Exposing myself emotionally wouldn't get me anything, except my ass on a hospital bed in an emergency room.

"You do. I just, I don't know— She's just different."

Inhaling deeply, I counted to ten. I needed to get my fucking head on straight. *Less talking, more fucking.*

"Well, Fischer. Get ready, because I'm about to take you so far outside of your own head you won't know any name except mine, and I expect to hear it while I'm fucking you. Follow me."

I released him then grabbed my bag from the table and headed to the back of the room where the couches were. I didn't look behind me to make sure my pet was following; I could hear his footsteps and feel his eyes on my body. Just knowing that had my dick straining against my jeans, begging to be released. *Not yet.*

His hand trailed down my spine, and just before he reached my ass, I turned around and grabbed his wrist. Pulling him flush against my chest, I rumbled, "Ah, ah, ah. You know the rules, pet. Do I need to remind you, or are you going to be good and obedient?" Raising an eyebrow, I saw the reflection of my eyes in his, red and orange flickers starting to take over the cool blue.

"I'm sorry," he replied, dropping his eyes to my feet. My cock pulsed.

"I'm sorry, *what?*" I bit out, gripping his chin and squeezing.

"Master. I'm sorry, Master."

"Hmm. I don't know if you mean that. You can't keep your hands to yourself, can you?" Releasing his chin, I dropped down onto the couch, my thighs spreading wide to accommodate the swelling that was becoming uncomfortable. Fischer's eyes locked on me as I smirked and palmed my erection while lazily pulling my phone from my pocket. Continuing my attention to my dick, I didn't glance at him as I scrolled slowly through my playlists. A sharp exhale from his lips let me know how badly he wanted this, how much he craved me, and the escape I could provide for him. Just as he was about to start begging, I hit play, and rock music drifted from my phone, hard and angry, just like me.

"Strip," I commanded. "Do it slowly."

Fischer grabbed the hem of his shirt, dragging it up over his ripped torso, his flushed cheeks disappearing as the clothing blocked his face from my view. He didn't have as much definition as myself or Cam, but he was still a brick house. *Fitting, because I'm the big bad wolf, and he's going to let me in.* Fish dropped his shirt, the red fabric bright against the pale linoleum. Flicking my gaze back to his chest, I admired the expanse of his shoulders and the inked design that painted his beautiful skin. Huge dragon wings, dripping in vivid colors, spread wide across his chest from shoulder to shoulder, his expression of ultimate freedom.

His hands ran down his chest and stomach, following the trail of dark hair that disappeared underneath his waistband, his hips rolling slowly to the beat of the song that I could no longer hear. *Fuck, he is so damn sexy.* My mouth was watering as I thought of dragging my tongue over the same paths his hands were taking, my fists balled hard when he began working the button of his jeans, his gaze practically setting me on fire. Hooking his thumbs in the band of his boxers, he slid them down his thighs, right along with his jeans, his thick cock bobbing with the motion.

Shit, I want my hands wrapped around his length, squeezing hard enough for him to squirm. But not yet. As much as I wanted the sexual release, I needed him to obey me, and I had to take care of his needs. He trusted me with this exchange, and we both benefited from these sessions.

"You look good, pet, so hard for your master." My dick was hard as fucking steel and begging for some attention, but I liked to deny myself as it made the pay off so much sweeter. Letting my arms fall back across the couch, I got comfortable.

"I need you, Master." His plea filled the air, and his hand reached for his dick.

"Stop."

He froze, a whimper escaping his plump lips, and the urge to bite them rose in me like a tidal wave.

"Turn around. Let me see that ass," I grunted, deep and husky.

He turned, obeying me immediately, keeping a wide stance. I couldn't tear my eyes away from his ass, couldn't wait to leave my handprints all over his brown skin. He was blessed with a bubble butt, and no other ass had ever come close to his. A low groan escaped my lips as Fish bent forward, no doubt trying to tempt me into action. *Motherfucker...*

"Pet!" I barked. "What the fuck is that?" I stood up and approached him. With my question, he'd frozen, still as a statue. I ran my hand up the back of his thigh and over the curve of his ass cheek, pushing him forward so his palms were flat on the ground.

"It's a surprise for you, Master," he replied, like it was no big deal. *He fucking knows how I feel about surprises. No thank you. I fucking swear he's just living to taunt me tonight.*

Squatting down behind him, I spread his cheeks apart further, finding a red and orange plug buried deep in his ass. *Fuck. Me.*

"When did you put this in, pet? I know you didn't do it here. Did you ride your bike here with this in your ass?" I asked as I pressed on it, pushing it further into him. He exhaled sharply, groaning as I continued applying pressure.

"Mmm, I put it in a few hours before we left. I wanted to be ready for this, and I thought you would appreciate it, Master."

"It does look nice, and knowing that you were clearly anticipating this..." I sighed and stood up. I dragged my fingers over his back before stepping away from him. "You are a greedy little thing, aren't you? Finish taking those clothes off then stand up straight."

He'd known what he was doing. He stretched himself out to prepare for my cock, and by the fucking stars, I am going to give it to him. A shiver worked its way down my body, and I ripped my black t-shirt off and threw it on the couch. Undoing my jeans, I stepped out of my boots and socks. My pants dropped to the floor just as Fischer turned around to face me, taking in the tight ass pair of black boxer briefs that were pulled snugly across the tops of my thighs, my cock straining for freedom.

Fischer's eyes scanned my body, his breath hitching. "Fuck, Master. *Please*."

"Begging already, pet? We're just getting started. Come over here and climb on the couch facing the back cushions. Rest your arms on the top."

THE MAGIC OF DISCOVERY

Gliding toward me, he was a gods damned vision. The muscles in his thighs rippling, his dark cock swaying, his need for me displayed proudly by the way the tip of him glistened with evidence of his desire. Might as well have been gasoline, the way my internal flames flared, heating my blood to boiling temperatures. Coming to a stop when his body was pressed against mine, I flashed him a wolfish grin, and he returned a smirk.

"I love when you look at me like that, pet. Now get your tight ass up on that couch. Don't make me ask again," I warned him. Climbing into the position I had requested, he spread his legs wide with his back to me, putting his ass on display, exactly how I liked. Turning his head to see what I was planning, I reached down and pulled his headband over his eyes. Sensory deprivation was a huge turn on for my pet, and since he was always in sensory overload, the mission of every session was to make sure the only thing he was overloaded with was me. My hands, my fingers, my paddle, my binds, my lips, my cock... only me.

"Hmm, you look delicious, pet. Put your arms behind your back and press your face into the cushion."

I picked up my bag and unzipped it, rifling through the shit I'd packed earlier. Fish wasn't the only one of us who'd prepared. I had handcuffs, zip ties, five different types of lube packets, ten feet of rope, and a paddle. *Yeah, I'm a dirty bastard.* Grabbing a zip tie, I set out the lube on the end table.

"I'm going to bind your hands with a zip tie, then I'm going to punish you for doing my job for me. I was looking forward to stretching your ass out. After you're sufficiently reminded that your ass belongs to me, I will have a closer look at this surprise."

A moan was the only response I got, and I smothered the chuckle that bubbled up from the dark and depraved depths of my black soul. I pulled off my boxers and stood behind him for a moment, admiring the view. Fisting my cock, I pumped it a few times, swiping my palm over the tip to spread my pre cum down my length. Pulling his wrists together, I leaned in and quickly fastened the zip tie just enough to take another sensation away from him.

"This body was made to be mastered by me. You will let go. You will give me your mind and your body." I brought my hand down fast over his ass. The smack echoed, and Fish mumbled something that was muffled by the cushions.

"While that plug does look hot as fuck wedged in your tight ass, I'm not happy that you didn't tell me about it. You know I don't like surprises, pet, and you sure as fuck knew that I was going to work you over tonight. Had you come to me beforehand and asked if it were okay, this might be a very different discussion."

Another slap. And another. More moans. *Gods, yes.*

"I'm going to give you twenty more just because I want you to feel the sting I'm going to leave behind on your skin with every vibration of your bike on the drive home. I bet your dick was hard the entire drive, wasn't it?" *Slap. Slap. Slap. Slap.* "You're such a little slut, and you love this dick, don't you?" Each question was punctuated with a harsh slap.

"Yes, yes! Fuuuuuck." Fischer's head was shaking back and forth, his thighs trembling. This was for his own good; he needed this to get out of his own head.

"You." *Smack.* "Are." *Smack.* "Mine." *Smack.* "SAY IT."

"Yours, Master. I'm yours. Please, oh gods," he panted, sweat starting to glisten on his beautiful bronzed skin.

Flames danced behind my eyelids, licking the mental shield I trapped them behind. Without another thought, I kicked that bitch down, and my magic surged. Fire exploded, warming my body to impossible temperatures as I directed it to my palms and threw my head back, reveling in the power.

"Hold on tight, we're finishing this," I gritted out between my clenched jaw.

I brought my palms down in rapid succession, the flames extinguishing with the force I exerted. The last slap sounded, my palm having landed right over his asshole, driving that toy higher into him, and I was rewarded with him yelling out. Smoke billowed off of my hands and his ass, and I inhaled deeply, savoring the scent that was all me. *My power.*

I rubbed my hands over his skin, soothing the tender spots that were a now captivating shade of red. Reaching between his cheeks, I grabbed hold of the butt plug. *Fuck, this is so hot...*

"Push," I commanded, and as he obeyed, I pulled the toy out of him.

"Do you like it, Master?" Fish asked me breathlessly. Looking down at the plug, a deep chuckle rumbled out of my chest. Conjuring a small flame between my thumb and index finger, I pressed it to the zip tie to free his hands.

"Stand up and turn around."

Spinning to face me, I pressed into his body, my arms wrapping around his waist, encouraging him to get closer. I uncovered his eyes, and he smiled, his hands moving down my back to palm my ass.

"Where the fuck did you find a flame-shaped butt plug?" Amusement laced my tone as I tossed the little ass flame onto a table, where it bounced a couple of times before coming to a rest. *Note to self, probably should wipe these bitches down when we're done.* Lowering my mouth to his neck, I ran my tongue up his warm skin, his cock jerking as it pressed against my own.

"I just wanted to get you something, and you're always saying how you have to light a fire under my ass to get me motivated sometimes..." He trailed off, suddenly looking vulnerable, like maybe this had been a stupid idea.

"I fucking love it, Fischer." Gripping his jaw, I pulled his mouth to mine. He groaned deeply, and I knew we were both going to burn. His tongue slipped into my mouth, strong and seeking, the motion almost frenzied. I loved when he let go. *That's right, pet. I've got you.* His hand wrapped around my length, his grip tight and sure, as he began walking me back toward one of the lunch tables. When we bumped into the edge of the surface, I spun us around so that the backs of his thighs were against it. He slid onto the top of the table, and I pressed forward, pushing him so that he was forced to break the kiss and lay back. My eyes trailed down his chest, my hand following their path as my fingertips swirled through the black, coarse hair of his chest and lower, to my favorite pathway, one that led me right between his legs. Mmm.

My deliciously dark prince sprawled out and waiting for me to be his even darker king.

"Touch yourself. I want to see you pump your fist up and down." A moan was his only answer as he wrapped his hand around his cock and slowly began moving it up. Legs spread wide and feet flat on the table top, he was a sight to behold. I fucking growled.

Turning, I dashed quickly to grab the lube I'd set out earlier. Stalking back toward my prey, I felt every bit the apex predator that I fucking was. Shit. I ran my hand through my dark hair, pushing back the strands that had fallen forward into my face. I knew an inferno would be raging in my eyes, my power still peeking out. Sometimes I didn't think the Devil himself burned this fucking hot.

Fischer jerked himself faster now, his hips starting to grind with the movements. I put my hands on his knees, letting my finger run down the insides of each thigh. Goosebumps erupted on his skin, and another moan reverberated in the air.

"Do you want my mouth? Do you want me to suck this dick?" I asked him, gravel coating my voice as I gripped his balls.

"Yes, fuck. Please. I need it, Master." He panted beneath me, and fuck if it didn't make me feel like a damned sex god.

I lowered my head, running my tongue from base to tip, circling around the head of his cock like he was the finest ice cream cone in the whole world. The sounds that came out of him spurred me on, and I fisted my own dick as I wrapped my mouth around him and sucked. Taking him deep into my throat, the salty taste and his spicy scent had my eyes rolling back in my head. Keeping him locked against my tongue, I blindly reached beside me for the little packet of lube, easily locating it. I made quick work of ripping the corner off of the packaging, squeezing the contents onto my fingers, the primal urge to be inside of him possessing me completely. His cock popped out of my mouth as I swirled two fingers around his ass, pushing in with little resistance. He squeezed me tightly, and I groaned as I rubbed my throbbing dick with my other hand, making myself nice and slick. Adding another finger, I heard my pet cursing then begging for more. His prep work was paying off in spades.

His hips lifted off the table, desperately trying to fuck my fingers, but this would happen at *my* pace. Not his. I stilled, and he whimpered. *Whimpered.* Begging like a little puppy.

"Tell me, pet. Tell me what you need." I pushed my fingers all the way in, leaning over to take him into my mouth once more.

"Fuck me, fuck me hard. I don't want to think. I just need to feel. Shit. Yes, like that."

I'd begun relentlessly ramming my fingers into him. Pulling them out suddenly, I hooked my arms around his thighs and yanked him to the very edge of the table.

"Legs up. Hold them."

Fish hooked his palms underneath his knees to open himself up to me, and I swirled my fingers into him, dipping them in and out so easily. Seeing his asshole wide open made my head fucking spin. Sparing a glance at his face, I'd expected to see him looking at the ceiling, but his eyes were pitch black as he watched what I was doing to him. Pulling my fingers out of him, I slapped his ass, and his gaze locked on mine. With a smirk, I gathered saliva in my mouth and let it drop right into his hole, the thought of my spit coating his insides leaving my balls motherfucking boiling.

"Fucking shit, Master. Fuck me."

I lined up and thrust into him balls deep. If cocks could groan in relief, mine was doing that right now. Not that anyone would hear with it being buried eight inches into Fish's tight ass. His groan joined my growl as his eyelids slammed closed, his body squeezing my dick for all it was worth. Grunting, I leaned in and put my palms on either side of his hips, starting to really fuck him.

"Is this what you need? You needed to take my cock like a good little bitch? What do you feel?"

"You. I feel *you*. Oh fuck." His legs began trembling, his ass gripping me like a vise.

My pace was relentless. The best part of our sessions was that I could shut my pet down completely. He would never have to worry about my emotions bombarding him, neither of us would, for that matter. Sweat dripped down my chest and back as my core temp rose, causing steam to radiate from the droplets covering my flesh. *Was he taking my dick like a pro? Yes. Did I want him to know exactly how much I enjoyed fucking him? No.* I essentially put a gods damn choke chain around my feelings and yanked the leash any time they needed grounding.

The increase in my temperature was indication enough for him to read me, and he took the bait.

"You fuck me so good." Groaning out the last part, he reached between us and took himself into his hand.

"Are you ready to feel my cum? I'm going to fill this ass up, pet. My cum will be dripping out of you for hours. Look at me."

Fish's eyes snapped open and locked right into my gaze. *Fuck, this is intense.* He wrapped his legs around my hips and clasped his hands around my forearms.

"Give me your cum, fuck me. Fill me up. Please, make me come." The beast inside of me purred in satisfaction with each of his pleas. Leaning back, the change in position allowed my dick to hit at a different angle, and I knew right when I hit that magical spot inside of his body because his ass started constricting so fucking hard.

"Fuck! Do it, now. Come for me, pet."

He grabbed his dick and pumped it in time with my wild thrusting, spurts of cum shooting out of him to decorate his stomach and the dragon wings on his chest. Just as I'd told him earlier, my name spilled from his throat as he worked every last drop from himself.

"So. Fucking. Tight. Milk me, pet. Squeeze. This. Dick," I gritted out, my jaw clenched so tight it was bordering on painful. His hips were frantically meeting mine, and I only lasted another moment before I fucking exploded, shooting ropes of hot cum in his ass. A roar left my throat, my head thrown back, letting the stars know what the hell had just happened here.

Saige

Chapter Nine

It was just after seven when I finished up the few things that Frank and Arlo hadn't gotten to before they took off. I had already locked the shop up an hour earlier, and my stomach gave a rumble, signaling that it was time to head back home. Before leaving this morning, I had thrown a bunch of ingredients into my cauldron, so I would have some soup ready when I got home. Just thinking about it had my stomach growling again.

"Off lumine," I commanded, the lights in the building obeying and turning off. Snagging my backpack off of the counter, I swung it around onto my back as I walked out of the front door, Maven hot on my heels. Pulling the door closed, I stuck the ancient skeleton key into the lock and twisted, making sure everything was locked up for the night. The key itself was spelled, so while it physically locked the mechanism, it also activated the security spell I'd designed. Satisfied, I hopped down the steps and on to the sidewalk, walking over to my bicycle. Maven was already in the basket, paws on my handlebars, ears wiggling.

"You're such a cute boy, Mave," I cooed, scratching the top of his fluffy head with my fingernails. "Let's get home! I'm starving." He gave me a yip in response, curling himself into a fluff ball in the bottom of the large wicker basket.

Before pulling away, I shamelessly eyed the door of the guys' apartment. I hadn't seen any of them all day. Kai had told me earlier that he had to go out on a run to burn some energy. *Ugh*. I

THE MAGIC OF DISCOVERY

loathed running and did everything in my power to avoid it. Biking was as far as I went when it came to physical activity, aside from walking everywhere and doing hard labor on my land.

I had only made it about a quarter of the way back to my cottage when I felt the telltale signs of a flat tire. Shit. The squishing sound was just getting worse and worse, and there was no way I could finish the ride back. Dismounting, I leaned the bike seat against my hip and hastily gathered my long hair in a top knot and secured it with the elastic band I had around my wrist. *This is exactly why you should never be without one, ladies and gents.*

Sighing, I began pushing my now useless bicycle down the side of the road. By bike, I could make it back and forth in just over five minutes, but having to walk was going to really increase my time. My stomach was pissed, and I was getting hangry. Maven stalked me from a few paces behind, his mood matching my own if the scowl on his face was any indication. Then again, he scowled so often that who knew what the little beast was actually feeling.

"This is our life now, Mave. Flat tires, creepy prophecies, wonky magic, hot men we can't touch... yet, and ex-dicks who won't fuck off. It's just me and you, buddy," I mused, glancing down at the little fox. He yipped, whether in agreement or because he was tired of hearing me whine, who knows.

The roar of a motorcycle sounded in the distance, and I scoffed, "Show off." Turning around, I looked back just as the rider would have passed me, but instead of flying by, the rider slowed. *Cam.*

My eyes met his, and he slowed down even more, pulling up behind me. Fuck me, he looked edible. Like a big leather-wrapped present. *I know what I want for my birthday.* Swinging his leg over his Harley after kicking out his kickstand, he left his bike and started walking in my direction. His right hand came up under his chin as he unclipped his helmet, removing it from his golden head and tucking it against his side with his arm.

I'm not kidding you, this guy was sin personified. Big black boots, tight black leather pants... *Are you fucking shitting me?* A long-sleeved black shirt and a leather vest over that with various patches on it. I pinched my arm. Was I having another episode like I'd had at The Pig?

Please let this be real. Please let this be real, I pleaded with whatever deity in the universe would hear my prayer and make this leather daddy not disappear when I opened my eyes again. Cam's baritone chuckle made me snap my eyes open. I squealed, mentally fist pumping the sky.

"Please let what be real?" His velvety voice carried over to my ears, and goosebumps erupted on my skin. *Fuck, I must've said that out loud.* Heat enveloped my cheeks.

"Oh, you know. Just got a flat tire here, and I'm getting hangry. Still have about half an hour to walk back home since my bicycle's busted, so I was just happy to see a familiar face." I smiled big at him, hoping he bought that.

"Here, let me take a look." I held my hand out so I could hold his helmet, and he stepped up to the opposite side of my bike, kneeling down to investigate the tire. His big ass hand squeezed the rubber, looking for whatever might have caused this travesty. "Ah, here we go."

Holding his hand out to me as he stood, I took the nail he dropped into my palm.

"Great. Of course it's not the kind of nailing I'm interested in," I whined, stuffing the offensive object into my jean pocket. Its tire shredding days stopped with me!

Cam barked a laugh. *Shit, I said that out loud too. Focus, Saige.* Seeing Cam's face, I laughed along with him, trying to hide my embarrassment.

"Let me give you a lift home. I don't have anywhere urgent to be. I was just going out for a drive. No business, just pleasure." He winked. Mave snorted. I creamed. *Mother of the moon.* My jaw slammed shut before I embarrassed myself further by telling him my new fantasy of having him wink up at me from between my legs.

"Oh, no. I don't want to inconvenience you, Cam." My fingers twisted in the straps of his helmet, unintentionally drawing out our time together. I wanted to be on the back of that bike, but I didn't like putting people out. "It's not that much further; we'll be alright."

"No way, Saige." He stepped up right in front of me, reaching for the helmet. "It wasn't a question, so let me rephrase. I'm giving you a ride home. What kind of man would I be if I left a woman stranded on the side of the road at dusk?" Cam gestured to Maven. "Grab the furry little guy. I'll push your bike over against the fence here, and I can come back tomorrow with a fresh tire and change it out for you."

Wow, okay then, bossy leather pants. I *did* want a ride home. I *did* want to spend time with Cam, and now that I was being given the perfect opportunity, I was surprised by just how true that realization was. That helped calm the initial struggle I was having about being maneuvered into doing something I didn't want. My stomach jumped with joy as I scooped up Maven and turned to walk back to the stunning Harley. Spotless silver so shiny I could see my reflection in the metal and an impeccable paint job. Glittery purples, black, and blues swirled around each other, huge lightning streaks in whites and golds crackling against the dark backdrop. I let my fingers trail over one of the bolts, awed at how realistic it was.

Cam walked up beside me, and I flushed under the weight of his quizzical stare. "This is beautiful, Cam," I breathed.

"Custom paint job, worth every penny. I love this fucking bike. Have you ever ridden one?" He had his arms crossed across the broad expanse of his chest, his feet just as wide as his massive shoulders.

"No, so you'll have to tell me what to do. Maven can run home." My foxy friend growled in response, but he could get over it. *I'm riding this fucking bike!* I set him down, and he took off down the road before cutting right into the fields.

Jumping up and down a few times, I dropped my bag onto the pavement and went to throw my leg over the seat while grabbing the handlebars.

"Whoa, whoa, whoa. What are you doing?" A firm arm snaked around my waist, hoisting me right out of the damn air before I could sit. Cam pulled me against his front, and I spun around to look up at him, an innocent smile at the ready.

"I'm mounting this metal stallion! What's it look like?" Of course, I didn't think I was actually going to drive his bike, but he didn't know that. And he was so easy to fuck with.

Cam looked at me like he couldn't decide whether he liked my sass or wanted to squash it. *I kind of want to find out which one it is, though. I like teasing him.*

"Abso-fucking-lutely not. You're riding on the back. Where you'll be safe. You can't think I would actually fit on that seat. I can't even imagine how that would look." He shook his head, exasperated with me, but his eyes were glittering with amusement.

Glancing at the smaller seat in the back, I couldn't blame him. *I mean, he does have a point.*

"You think my ass is going to fit on that?" I raised an eyebrow at him, and he grinned as he secured his helmet. Safety first.

"I'm excited to see what your ass looks like hugging it." His eyes flashed at the thought, and I realized I was still pressed right up against his hard body. Releasing me reluctantly, Cam left me standing with my mouth gaping once again and headed for the back of the bike where he lifted one of the flaps on a saddlebag and produced a second helmet for me to wear.

"This crown won't fit right with that top knot, little witch," he teased. Fingers easily finding the elastic in my hair, he tugged on it gently so it didn't pull. My breathing hitched and his gaze heated when my hair spilled down around my shoulders and face. Tucking a few wayward strands behind my ears, Cam put the helmet on and buckled it, making some adjustments to be sure it was fitted correctly. Satisfied with his ministrations, he nodded once before turning me to face the Harley.

"Here, I'll get on first and stabilize it, then you can climb up once I'm on. Put your feet here," he directed, pointing to a small foot grip, "and keep your legs away from here. This gets really hot." He continued to direct me as he put the kickstand away, his strong arms pulling the bike upright. With zero effort on his part, Cam stepped over the seat of the bike like he was merely stepping over a pesky little mud puddle. Quickly snagging my bag and dusting the dirt and gravel from the bottom, I slung it over my back. When he was situated with both feet flat on the ground, he turned to me. "Go on, then. I got you."

For someone who'd been in a horrible relationship not long ago, it surprised me how naturally I trusted Cam. He made me feel safe, even from the first moment in The Pig, when he'd scolded Kai for possibly scaring me. The funny mage's face flashed in my mind, and my belly flipped when I thought about how I also had a date tomorrow with Fischer, yet here I was, about to saddle up against an absolutely massive mage who could crumple me up like a pretzel. *Not that I'd mind... Gran is going to flip her lid over this!*

Poly relationships were accepted in the magical community, but there just weren't any in Emerald Lakes, though not for Gran's lack of trying to score herself a harem with unlimited members. Honestly, I'd never considered it for myself, especially since the options in town were insanely limited.

I wiped my sweaty palms down my jeans a few times. Placing my hand on his forearm for balance, I swung my leg over and wiggled to get into position, my thighs effectively squeezing his hips from behind.

As he turned the key, the bike flared to life. Whooping my excitement to the sky, I could feel Cam's laughter, the vibration of his body adding to the bike's revving. The engine quieted down to a low rumble, and he turned his head back toward me. "Wrap your arms around me and hold on tight. If we take a corner or a turn, lean into the turn slowly. Let it flow naturally."

My arms snaked around his hard torso right where I could feel his abs rippling when he steadied the bike with his legs. He gave a little gas, and I held my breath in anticipation as he picked his feet up. We were doing it! *I'm riding this big ass Harley with this big ass mage.*

"Here we go!" he shouted, and we shot down the road, the bike's vibrations thrumming straight through my body. I was already so turned on, I knew I was going to be a fucking mess by the time we got to my place. The entire two minutes it took to get to my long driveway were filled with my shrieks and hollers of excitement. Cam was laughing so much, it just made me go even more wild.

"This is my driveway on the right," I shouted, tapping my right hand against his stomach. I swore I felt every rock in that one hundred foot driveway. *Mmmmm. I might need to buy a motorcycle.*

Cam pulled up to my garage next to the side door leading to the little mudroom off of the kitchen. Cutting the engine, he stood up and once again held the handlebars steady for me to dismount.

"That was so awesome!" I squealed once my feet hit the gravel.

After securing the kickstand, Cam turned to face me, and without thinking, I threw my arms around his neck and hugged him. "Thank you so much for that. I've always wanted to ride on a motorcycle. What a rush! Gah, I feel like I could do anything right now. I'm so pumped up!"

His arms engulfed my body, my cheek pressed against his chest, and I was *not* petite. A deep inhale brought his scent to the forefront of my mind. The leather from his clothes was prominent, but there was also another scent that was all Cam. Gods, he smelled delicious, like fresh rainfall.

"Well, that is one of the best perks of having your own motorcycle." A genuine smile lit up his face, his eyes crinkling slightly at the corners, and I wondered if he was hiding dimples under that burly beard. "Any time I need an adrenaline rush, I can just hop on and get energized," he explained. His tone was full of love talking about the open road, and I completely understood from just that two-minute ride.

We stepped apart from each other at the same time, awkward silence descending. I shifted from foot to foot as he stared at me, studying his features, examining his short well-kept beard. It was a dark shade of gold, a few shades darker than his hair. A colorful tattoo snuck up his neck to the base of his jaw. *Fuck, I bet that shit hurt.* His bottom lip was full, and his smile was rugged. Everything about Cam screamed 'The Boss.' If he walked into a room, you couldn't help but be drawn to him; he was captivating. I knew he had stories, I could feel it, and I wanted to know *all* of them.

"I better get going..." Cam trailed off as he took a step toward his bike.

"Stay for dinner? It's the least I can do since I interrupted your adventure, and I did make homemade potato soup." I rubbed my palms together in a completely dorky as fuck manner that was meant to be enticing. *This is why I'm single.*

He looked torn. Deciding to make it easier on him, I closed the short distance between us and grabbed his hand. Intertwining my fingers in his, I pulled him behind me as I made my way to the door.

"Are you sure? Do you have enough? I can always just head back to the apartment to eat. It's no big deal." His voice sounded the tiniest bit vulnerable, but despite that, he wasn't resisting my lead.

"Of course, I'm sure. I always make enough to have leftovers to freeze. Makes easy lunches when you're only cooking for one or two," I explained. "Gran eats over often, but on Thursday evenings she goes out with a few of her friends, so it'll just be us. It'll be nice to have the company," I told him, throwing a glance over my shoulder and smiling at him. I dropped his hand and muttered an unlocking spell to disarm the wards I set every time I left my house. Pulling open the screen door when I felt the magic dissipate, I waited, sensing Cam's hesitation. He was running his hand over the top of his head, flattening down some of the flyaways that had escaped the low messy bun he had his long golden hair twisted up in.

"Okay, I'll stay for dinner." He dropped his arms to his sides, a grin tugging at the corners of his mouth.

My inner witch was losing her shit, jumping up and down, spinning in circles, air humping... It was an episode, honestly.

He's coming in my house. Oh, fuck. I wish I could high five myself right now without that being weird.

Cam

Chapter Ten

Saige walked through the doorway, the smell of something delicious wafting through the entryway. Entering a small room that held her washer and dryer, a shoe rack, bench, and a sink, she kicked her shoes off onto the rug in front of the rack. Bending down, I loosened my boots enough to slip them off. I was used to this since both Kaito's and Fischer's families never wore shoes inside. A soft sound came from behind me, and I twisted my head just in time to see a flash of white dart around me and into the house, the small doggie door swinging slightly from Maven's arrival. Saige laughed and yelled out to her pet, getting a growl in response. Little jerk.

"So, welcome to my lovely cottage, Cam." She held her hands wide as she walked, her back still facing me. "Let me just throw up some locking spells." Hearing her murmured words, I knew she had put up a general sealing spell on the doors and windows, and I cocked an eyebrow when she also moved her hands and cast a motion detecting spell that would notify her immediately if a person got within a certain radius of the house. *I guess the little witch is pretty skilled.* While her back was to me, I reinforced her magic with my own. Fischer had filled us all in on her abusive shithead ex, and a surge of relief spilled through my chest, knowing she was capable of placing strong spells around her home in order to protect herself.

Satisfied that her magic was in place, she led me out of the mudroom and past a short set of stairs that brought us to a small landing. Sheer navy blue curtains draped down from a window that took up the main wall. Heading right, we passed a door which she pointed out as a bathroom. Continuing on our path, I let my eyes scan the walls, the operative in me pushing me to be aware of my surroundings at all times. *I can't protect people if I'm not prepared.*

The home was decorated heavily in mid-century modern furniture and decor, and it was totally Saige. I barely knew the woman, but the kitschy, vintage vibe she had going on in here reminded me of her personality. Quirky and over the top at times, but also strong enough to endure the test of life. In the moments between inspecting her home, my eyes kept dropping to her ass. I was trying really hard not to blatantly check her out, but shit. *That ass. So round, I wonder how much it would bounce if I were to fuck her from behind.*

Nearly plowing her over while my brain was held hostage by the ass-filled daydream, her palm hit the center of my chest hard enough to halt my progression. My eyes flicked down to hers, and she grinned, having caught me checking her out like a fucking perv.

"See something you like?"

Christ, the balls on this woman.

"I'll let you know if I do, have no doubt." She was smirking at me, and fuck if that didn't make me want to slap it off of her face with my rapidly growing cock.

Ignoring my response, she whirled back around and padded over to the kitchen island. The cabinets were also dated, painted white. There was a matching island in the middle of the workspace, with a sink in the center of the butcher block countertop.

"Smells good in here. Can I help you with anything?" Sliding beside her, I studied her from above. Her arm was extended to turn on the warm water, pumping the soap dispenser a few times into her small hand. Her hair was windblown from the ride, cheeks flushed... perfection.

"Behind me, in the drawer next to the fridge are spoons, and in the cupboard above are bowls. We'll sit in here. I rarely use the dining room," she said, inclining her head in the direction of the round table that had six chairs arranged around it.

Spinning around, I grabbed the items she requested and deposited them on the table before heading back over to where she was standing.

"I have lemonade, diet Dr. Pepper, beer, and tequila. Pick your poison, big guy." Her smile lit up her face as her green eyes twinkled. *She really is stunning.*

"Beer would be great. Here, let me carry this." Grabbing the two pot holders she had set out, I lifted the cauldron with ease and deposited it on the table.

She joined me a moment later with two beers in one hand and a ladle in the other. Once my beer was in hand and each of us in our seats, we served ourselves in comfortable silence.

"This smells so good. It's been years since I've had homemade potato soup. Kai is the chef in our group, but we rarely eat soup."

"I love soup. This is my gran's recipe." She smiled while she talked, the love for her grandma shining through her words.

"What about your parents?" I inquired, hoping it wasn't a sore subject.

"Not much to say. My mom had me when she was nineteen, and she wasn't ready to be a mother." A harsh laugh left her lips at that. "She still isn't ready to be a mother, for that matter. Thankfully, Gran stepped up and raised me while my mom went back to the city to continue developing her career. She's never been very talkative about her job, but she's an independent contractor for some kind of magical conglomerate. Similar to Radical, I think. I only see her a few times a year, but I never really saw her as my mom, so I don't miss that or anything. Gran filled that role completely." She lifted her drink to her lips, and I waited to see if she would continue. A look of acceptance flitted across her features, and she sighed.

"Honestly, my mom is really selfish. She's not kind, rarely has a nice thing to say about anybody. I'm still not convinced we're related. I have no clue who my dad is since my mom says she got pregnant from a one night stand at a party." She shrugged, lifting a spoonful of soup to her mouth and blowing on it gently before cautiously taking the bite. "Mmm. It's cooled down enough, finally."

Getting the sense that she was done talking about her family, I didn't push it. Instead, I dug into my own bowl.

"This is really good, little witch. You'll have to make it for the rest of the guys sometime. Kai will be impressed."

"Thanks." After another bite, she prompted, "Is your family close?"

Fuck. I set myself up for that one. I tried to hide the cringe that wanted to take over, but I must have failed because she quickly added, "You don't have to tell me anything you aren't comfortable with."

"Let's save that discussion for another day," I muttered, shamelessly taking the out. *I don't want to talk about that shit. Not today. Not any fucking day.* Lifting the cool bottle of beer to my lips, I quickly drained half of it.

"So you're the leader of your group." I raised my eyebrows at her statement because it *was* a statement. I didn't remember telling her that before. Reading me with ease, she added, "Oh, come on. It's freaking obvious. You exude BDE."

"Do I want to know what BDE stands for?"

"Big dick energy, of course." She grinned, and I threw my head back and laughed.

"Yes, little witch. I'm the leader. You're very observant, clearly."

"Did your boss put you in charge, or was that a decision your team made?" she questioned before taking a swig of her beer.

"Our boss made the final call, but the guys were in agreement. I've been the team lead since we started this job ten years ago."

THE MAGIC OF DISCOVERY

She nodded. "I can see why. You're pretty level headed, and you seem like you're the kind to think before you act."

"That is an accurate assessment." Unable to tell her much about my real job, a pang of guilt rose in my chest. "I love my career. Top of the line training. Endless resources to further my education and hone my abilities. Room for advancement— the list goes on and on."

"Sounds like a lot of responsibility, though. You must travel a lot scouting properties for Radical. They're a massive company. I mean, do you ever get a break?" Placing her elbow on the table, she rested her chin in the palm of her hand.

"Do you? You own a shop. Being a business owner is more than a full-time job." I hated doing it, but I had to deflect the question back at her. Telling the least amount of lies was always the best tactic, making it easier to keep up with the cover. Not discussing it at all would be even better.

"You got me there." A chuckle spilled from her lips, drawing my attention to them, and I couldn't look anywhere else until she continued talking. "After I worked myself into the ground a couple of years ago, Frank and Arlo insisted that they become my part-time helpers in addition to being our handymen here on the property and at The Pig. They've been true friends. We're also now closed on Sundays. Saturday, we're only open from ten until two, and we rotate those between us, so I do get a nice amount of time to relax over the weekend. I'm there Monday, Tuesday, and Wednesday from ten to five, and Frank and Arlo open and close on Thursdays and Fridays. Today I just popped by to drop some things off. And then there's Gran, who I'm very thankful I also have here to do things around the gardens while I'm in town."

Now that our bowls were empty, she made her way to the fridge, opening the door to look inside. "Another?" She held up a fresh beer in question, and I nodded. *First one went down so smooth. I'm going to have to call a Broom for a ride back to the apartment if I continue.*

The sound of glasses hit the table, shot glasses, to be exact. And a bottle of tequila.

"Oh, I don't know if I should get into liquor tonight. I'm already going to need to call a Broom for a lift..."

"You do know where we are, don't you? Emerald fucking Lakes. Broom doesn't run out here." Saige was laughing like this was the funniest shit in the world to her, and it was contagious.

"Well, fuck. Maybe I should stop drinking altogether, so I'll be able to drive back home in a bit." I pushed the beer away from me.

She batted her long dark eyelashes, giving me puppy dog eyes. "Aww, please? I never get to hang out. Stay and have fun with me? We can play twenty questions!"

I let out a groan as I swiped my hand down my face. She was temptation in its purest form. *If I stay here, there is a strong probability that I'm going to fuck her. My dick has been raging since she pressed her curvy body tight against mine on my bike. Her thick thighs squeezing my hips, tits pressing into my back...*

Clearing my throat, I began, "If I were to stay..." She let out a squeal, plopped down in her seat, and swiped the tequila bottle, popping the round cork top off before I could finish. In a flash, my hand snapped out, my fingers wrapping around her wrist that was holding the bottle.

Her eyes flew to mine, dancing with the promise of mischief and sassiness. *I cannot wait to spank her bratty ass. Fuck it, I'm staying.*

"Do you want me to stay tonight, Saige?" I knew I was growling at her again, but I also knew she fucking loved it. I just needed to hear it from her mouth. She was squirming in her seat so much I could only speculate how soon she would detonate when I finally touched her. "Say it." I commanded the last two words, my tone going into full alpha mode, and I could hear the lust dripping from those two words. Narrowing her eyes at me, I could tell she was warring internally with herself, but I saw the moment her resolve broke. Despite being a wildcat, she liked me bossing her around. Pulling her wrist from my grip, she poured two shots, sliding the glass closer with a wink.

"Yes, I want you to stay. I'm having fun, and so are you. I've seen you smile and laugh more in the past couple of hours than I have since I met you, and I want to know more about you." She was dancing in her seat victoriously, knowing she'd already won me over. "Come on, let's get drunk, you big ass caveman."

She was absolutely right though. I'd been using my facial muscles so much tonight that they were actually sore. *Worth it. We're safe here.* Eyeing the clear alcohol, I sighed and placed it in front of me, my middle finger running circles around the rim of the shot glass.

"Okay, so I'll ask you a question first. You can either answer or drink. Then you can ask me one," she explained like I didn't know how to play twenty questions. I let that slide, mostly because I definitely had questions I wanted to ask. To be honest, I was surprised by how *much* I actually wanted to know about her. Sure, this would be excellent information for our assignment— any information pertaining to this town could be a clue in finding Laura—but I genuinely wanted to know all about the witch before me.

"Let's do this one together first. Liquid courage to loosen the lips, yeah?" I winked at her, lifting the shot up. "To finally getting the night off we fucking deserve," I said before we clinked our glasses together then tossed the shots back. It was smooth, instantly warming me up. *These leather pants might have to fuck off sooner rather than later.*

"Whew! So good. I love tequila." Saige pulled my glass over to her again, refilling them both quickly. "I'll go first. How old are you?"

"I'm thirty-one," I answered without hesitation. I would have asked her the same one in response, but I already knew that thanks to Kai, and I didn't want to waste a question.

"Do you like living here?" She seemed to really enjoy this place, but then again, a lot of people could present themselves one way when actually, they felt completely different on the inside.

She paused for a moment, almost seeming surprised that was what I'd asked. "Yeah, I love it. I've lived here my entire life. I know everyone. It's comfortable. I have my shop, my customers, my friends... Well, actually, most of my friends have moved to other places in the past few years. I have my cottage and my gran though. Even if I wanted to try living somewhere else, I don't see how I could just abandon all of this. It's not everyone's cup of tea, but it's home."

"I respect that. You just have such a wild spirit I would have thought you had an itch to travel, you know? Don't you want to see everything that's out there?" Tapping my fingers on the table, I watched her face because she wore all of her thoughts right there for the world to see. I wasn't sure if she did that without knowing, or if it was just because she didn't have a fuck to give about it. I hoped it was the latter.

"That's another question, and now it's my turn. Does it bother you guys that I'm flirting with Kai, have a date with Fischer tomorrow, and I'm here with you tonight?" Her eyebrow cocked at that, her reddened cheeks deepening in color even further.

"Kaito is a free spirit. He sees something he wants, and he goes after it. He didn't hesitate when he laid eyes on you, did he?"

"No, you're right. He is very forward and hilarious, and I love texting him all day. He makes me laugh," she replied, and a shy smile sprang to life, causing her dimples to pop. "And Fischer? It doesn't bother him? I was worried after I agreed to the date because I didn't want to upset Kai. I genuinely like them both, and they're so different from each other."

"You have nothing to worry about. The four of us are rock solid. We grew up together, lived on the same street even. We're used to sharing our things." I said the last part and studied her closer to see her reaction, watching as the wheels turned in her pretty little head and leaning in closer when I could see she was starting to understand what I was hinting at. Her green eyes widened, and she grabbed her full shot glass, throwing it back so fast some of her hair got stuck to her mouth. A laugh bellowed out of my chest as she wiped the hair from her face.

"Sharing. You *share* women?" she asked quietly, before pulling her bottom lip between her teeth.

"Ah, ah, ah, little witch. It's my turn for a question," I reminded her as she refilled her glass.

"Fuck, you're right. Okay. Lay it on me."

I'll lay something on you...

"Does that turn you on? The thought of us sharing you?" *It fucking turns me on. I'm going to bust out of these damn pants if we stay on this line of questioning much longer.*

"I... uh, well..."

"Spit it out, Saige. Or drink. If you drink, I'll assume the answer is yes. I can see your nipples pebbling just thinking about it."

She sucked in a breath and dropped her hands to said pebbled nipples to cover them up, a motion that had me wanting to knock her hands away. The thought of her covering up, hiding from me... *absolutely not.* "You mean, like, group sex? Or like a poly relationship? I need more information and alcohol here. Drink that shot, big boy. This conversation definitely needs more tequila." Pulling the bottle of alcohol closer, she poured another and threw that one down the hatch. "I figured you guys must have been okay with things because Fish wouldn't have asked me out otherwise, right? He wouldn't do that to his friend."

Smirking, I raised my glass to my lips once again, letting the liquid slide down with no hesitation. I let her ramble. She was cute as fuck when she got fired up, and she was one hundred percent fired up right now. After downing another shot, she stood up and started pacing in front of the kitchen island. I set my glass down on the table with a small thud, smiling as I watched her. *Fuck, my cheeks hurt.*

"Is that something you guys do often? I mean, I know it's normal in some magic communities, but I've just never even met somebody who was poly before. Is it really *that* common? Oh my gods, are you guys in relationships like this all the time? Are you in one right now? Are you even single? I do *not* tolerate cheating!" She was going to wear a hole in the floor if she kept this up, but she was on one, and who was I to stop a fiery redhead? "But you'll only be here until you figure out what's going on with that property in Kingstown... Is this a test? You're fucking with me, aren't you?" She stomped over to me, a single finger raised in my direction. "I swear, Cam, if you're fucking with me, I'll—"

"What? You'll *what*, little witch?" *Enough of this shit. I need her on my lap.* I pushed my chair out and away from the table before I snatched the wrist that was attached to that damn finger she was shoving in my face. I tugged her down onto my thigh. She squealed, and fuck if it didn't go straight to my dick. My legs were spread wide, and her delicious ass felt better on me than I could've imagined. Saige was sitting level with my head now, and when she twisted around to look me in the eyes, I knew the heat I saw swirling there was a reflection of my own.

"That was eight questions, and you still didn't answer mine." I snaked my hand around her waist, my palm sliding down to cup the side of her hip where her skin was burning up. She was hot and bothered and liked what little she had heard. "But I think we're beyond the game now, so I'll answer your questions." I couldn't keep my hands off of her body. Her breath caught as I gripped her hip and she squirmed, brushing against my hardness with her thick thigh. Fuck, this woman was curvier than a back fuckin' road, and I desperately wanted to navigate each and every one.

"Group sex? If you're into it, sure. Kai is an animal, so he's down for anything. Fish usually doesn't join in if we pick someone up, but that's because of his issues with being smothered by emotions. Sloane is typically working too hard on his career to think about it much. As far as I go? I'd be game for anything you offer. You're so fucking sexy and just begging for my handprints on your ass." A soft moan escaped her lips as she wiggled on my thigh.

"A poly relationship? Well, we've never met anyone we wanted to be in an honest to the moon relationship with. We're often busy traveling and working, so I'm not sure how that would work. Usually, it's just a one night fling. We're not jealous of each other; I love seeing my men being taken care of, and they're good guys. They deserve a break whenever they can get it. So, no, baby girl. I'm not fucking with you, but if you want me to..." I shrugged my shoulder and flashed a smile at her while I squeezed her hip.

Saige tilted her head while she studied me, the red hairs around her face beginning to curl. Her breathing was shallow now. I held completely still, wanting her to process this information before I moved any further.

"You mean it? You're all okay with this?" She motioned between the two of us with her finger. "Because, if I'm honest, I really don't want a relationship right now. My last one was a shit show." At the mention of her bitch ass ex, I growled deep and low. Her palm pressed down on my pec, willing me to calm.

"Fischer told us about what happened in the store the other day. We'll be on the lookout for him, and if anything further happens, please tell me. I protect my crew, and seeing as how we're all kind of casually dating? Friends with benefits? Whatever you want to call it, you're part of my crew now. I won't stand for some limp dick little shit coming after the woman we're with. Please believe me when I tell you that we're *nothing* like him."

She smiled wickedly at my intensity, and that made me feel good. *What is she doing to me?*

"I love hanging out with you guys, and I'm willing to keep an open mind, but that's only if you are too. Same for Fischer and Kaito. I believe you when you say you're all on board. I'm not worried about Sloane because I'm pretty sure he can't stand me. And to answer your question, yes. It turns me on so much I can't stop imagining what it might be like." She leaned in so close to me that our mouths were a breath apart. Her tongue darted out, making her lips glisten, daring me to taste them. We were frozen in this intense fucking staredown, and I was just about to make the move myself when she closed the minuscule distance between us. *Oh, I am so ready for this. Those pillowy pink lips are going to feel-*

"Ouch! What the fuck?" I jerked my head back. *She fucking bit me.* A metallic tang spilled into my mouth. *She bit me so hard I'm bleeding. Unbelievable.*

Raising my hand from her hip, I grabbed her ponytail and stood up, bringing her with me.

"Hey! Let me go, asshole." *Fuck, did I hurt her?* Loosening my grip on her hair slightly, she giggled. *Ah, so this is the game she wants to play?* She clawed at my body and arms, so I wrapped my free arm around her, effectively securing her arms to her curvy body. Then I chuckled as I pulled her back against me so she could feel how fucking hot she was making me.

Dropping a chaste kiss on her neck, I ran my nose up to her ear and rumbled, "Do you want me to manhandle you, baby girl? Do you want me to toss you around and force you to comply with what I want?"

She stilled as I pressed my cock against her ass. Pulling her head back by her hair, I twisted my wrist so that she was looking up at me, flashing her a smile that would normally terrify its recipient. My teeth were bloodied, I had no doubt. Her eyes widened, knowing she'd fucked up. She wanted to play games with me, but I would always win.

"You bit me. You're such a brat, and little witches who are bratty suffer consequences, but I'll give you a free one-time pass for that since you clearly don't understand yet how this is going to go down." Releasing her arms and her hair, I turned her around to face me. My tongue swiped across the stinging little wound she'd marked me with, her eyes burning with pure heat, black eclipsing the green with her pupils blown. *She wants me. I know she does. My little witch just wants to tease... I'll just need to teach her right off the bat how I operate.* So, with a stern expression on my face, I leaned down to try this whole kissing thing again.

"Son of a BITCH!" *Again?* I kept my eyes closed and tried to gain some composure. *Fail.* A boom of thunder shook the house when I momentarily lost control of my power, which never fucking happened. Not since I was a shithead teenager with a huge ego and too small a dick to go with it. Lightning crackled along my fingertips, and I snapped my eyes open just in time to see her sprint down the hallway, laughing like hell.

"SAIGE!!!" I roared, my eyes narrowing on my target. I stalked forward, intent on finding her then spanking her ass and fucking her so hard she'd feel it throughout the weekend.

Tomorrow night when she's out with my best friend, I want her to feel the ghost of me between her legs, the soreness on her ass cheeks every time she sits down... and remember that I am in charge here.

The sound of her laughter was drifting through the hallway, and I heard her race up the steps. I kept a determined and purposeful walk behind her; she could run all she wanted, but I was going to catch her. Continuing my hunt, I walked back past the mudroom we had entered through earlier. My foot hit the first step, and it creaked under my weight, giving my location away. *I might as well let the little brat know I'm onto her...*

"I'm coming for you, you bad little witch. If you choose to be standing in my line of sight when I get to the top of these stairs, you'll get a more lenient punishment for biting me." I paused. "Or you can continue to try and hide. I will still find you, but there will be no mercy. You have about five seconds to decide."

"Fuck you!"

Another boom rocked the house, and I heard a scream come from behind the closed door to my left. *She's playing a dangerous game.* A dark smile took over my face. My dick was aching, and I felt a flash of surprise that I was actually really fucking turned on by her blatant brattiness.

Reaching out, I turned the door handle and pushed the door open slowly. This room had to be hers. Plants were everywhere, like walking into a miniature greenhouse. Flares of vibrant colors bled into my vision as my eyes swept the room.

I couldn't even focus; my sole mission was to find Saige and follow through on my threats. *I hope she can handle me.* Doubt left my mind as quickly as it entered. This woman was strong, and I knew damn well she could handle anything I decided to throw at her.

Saige

Chapter Eleven

I stood as still as I possibly could as the door to my bedroom swung open. My heart was dancing a frantic beat, and I could hear the blood rushing through my body in excitement.

Always being seen as a good girl, the sweet one who would drop anything for anyone, always forgiving... I was tired of that. I hadn't felt this alive in a long time. Possibly ever. These guys brought something out of me that was buried deep. I *wanted* Cam to chase me. I *wanted* Cam to find me and do whatever he wanted. Each time he used that bossy ass voice and commanded me to do things, the small whisper in the back of my mind grew louder and more persistent. Right now, it was screaming, "Make me!"

He wouldn't hurt me; I could see it in his eyes. Cam was a complete protector, and I felt safe playing this game with him. Knowing he would stop if I wanted to took away the fear that I would have felt if it were Bryce using that tone with me. Right now? I was the one in control, and I knew that. Cam was giving me a chance to be myself and enjoy what we were doing *because* it was my choice. Learning how to be assertive when I'd always been a people pleaser was hard fucking work, but seeing the way his body responded to my disobedience was such a turn on.

His large feet stalked across the hardwood floor until he neared my bed, the sound muffled thanks to the thick, vibrantly colored rug peeking out from the bottom. As he approached my nightstand, an idea formed that had me smiling. I held in a giggle as he leaned down to look at a photo of myself and Gran that I had proudly on display. It was from the day I took over ownership of The Mystical Piglet. We were both wearing our famous matching t-shirts that read 'If gardening was easy, it'd be called your mom.' The perk of living in a small town? Everyone knew and loved our humor, so we never had to censor ourselves. I'm not sure Gran could actually be censored, so we were really lucky.

Thank fuck she'd called me earlier and said she was staying over at her friend's place for the night. Something about a bonfire, dancing, and too much whiskey. Eyeing up the towering man in my bedroom right now made me extra thankful.

A large elephant ear plant sat in the corner where Cam was standing, the leaves massive and sturdy. *Perfect.* Calling on my magic, I let the power build in my fingertips, sparks of gold flitting to the ground as its intensity built. Flicking my wrist, gold wisps fired out of my hand and surrounded the plant. I pictured in my mind what I wanted to happen, and my magic did not disappoint. One of the largest leaves pulled back on its own and swung forward with impressive force, spanking Cam right on his cocky ass.

Jerking upright, he spun around so fast that I couldn't step back and hide behind the door. Flashes of lightning lit up the room, its flickering mirrored in his very eyes, his magic trying to take over. Rain began pelting the windows at a merciless rate. *Oh shit.*

I stopped laughing and took a step backward.

"Do. Not. Move." His voice was nothing but a rumble that matched the sounds coming from the sky. In giant strides, he ate up the distance between us in mere seconds, and my eyes widened as I tilted my head back to meet his intense gaze.

I think I've fucked with him enough. He looks like he wants to devour me, and I want him to.

He scratched his beard, staring at me down the length of his nose, his brain working so hard I could see the wheels turning. "You are something else. Biting me? *Twice*? Girl, I am going to fucking turn your ass red."

I opened my mouth to respond, but before I could, he leaned down and hoisted me up, throwing my body over his shoulder so that my head was right above his tight ass.

"Put me down! Ow!" Pain seared through my ass cheek as he spanked me, then a moan escaped my lips as the shock of the pain turned to pleasure. Despite his warning, I was stunned he had done it, and then he chuckled. *Chuckled*.

So I did what any self-respecting witch would do. I reached under the hem of his shirt and grabbed a hold of the waistband of his underwear. Then I yanked upward as hard as I could until he yelped. *Never underestimate the power of a well-timed wedgie, my friends.*

"You fucking brat," he spat out, and next thing I knew I was being catapulted forward onto my mattress. Crawling between my thighs, he ground his erection against me. My eyes closed involuntarily as a moan slipped through my lips.

"No. Open your eyes. We need to get a few things straight here, little witch." He ground against me again, and I forced my lids open. Gods, it had been too fucking long.

Strands of his golden hair had come loose from his bun, making him appear wild and fierce, and I couldn't look away from his gaze. The lightning had settled down, and his green was bleeding back through. Planting his left forearm down beside my head, he studied my face like I was a rare thing that he hadn't encountered before.

"When we fuck, I'm in charge. If I tell you to stop doing something, you had better damn well fucking freeze. If I tell you to be naked and waiting for me, there better not be a scrap of fucking clothing anywhere near your body. If I tell you to wrap your lips around my dick, you drop to your knees and suck like your life depends on it. And if you *ever* bite me like that again..." He closed his eyes and inhaled deeply through his nose. "I'll spank you, but that's a given. I might even get Kaito to help me. I will drive you insane with my tongue on your clit. You'll beg and beg for release that will never come, and I will lick up everything that leaks out of your sweet cunt. I'll drive you every bit as wild as you drive me, don't forget that. Do you understand?"

Fuck. Me. Silly. My stomach bottomed out, flipping and twisting like I'd just started speeding down a huge hill on a rollercoaster. The thought of him and Kai both... *Mercy.*

"Yes, Daddy." *Shit, I didn't mean for that to come out.* His cock hardened and twitched the moment the name left my lips. *Guess he likes it...*

"Daddy? Is that your kink?" He raised an eyebrow.

I shrugged. "I think with you it might be? I don't know where that came from, but it feels like you liked it. A lot." I couldn't resist lifting my hips to rub against him, seeking friction of any kind.

"I like your cunt rubbing against my dick," he grunted out through clenched teeth.

My hands ran down his huge arms. "We have too many clothes on. I need to feel you. Please, Daddy." My breathy voice was practically dripping with lust. *Who am I right now?*

Growling, he pushed upright and slipped his fingers into the waistband of my pants before wiggling them down and taking my panties with them. What a shame. The moment he tossed those items over his shoulder, I let my legs fall apart, baring myself to him completely. His emerald eyes locked on my pussy.

"Shit," he cursed when he saw exactly how much I wanted him. Slowly, he reached for me, his fingers swiping through my wetness, and when he pinned me with a hooded stare and popped those digits into his mouth, licking them clean...

Well, that's a wrap. My vagina is now dead. Cause of death? Drowning. The old gal creamed herself to an early grave. A deep groan

THE MAGIC OF DISCOVERY

reverberated through my room as his eyes closed. *Mother of the moon, he looks like he's tasting a fucking delicacy.*

He released his fingers with a pop and a wink. Damn him. He was still wearing those fucking leather pants, and I needed those off immediately. Realizing I was in a stare off with his now offensive apparel, he chuckled and fluidly rose from the bed. I leaned up on my elbows because no way in hell was I not going to watch this beautiful man strip in my freaking bedroom.

"You want to see me, little witch? Is that why you look like you're trying to burn my clothes off with your eyes?" He gave me an amused look, especially when I flipped him the bird in response... *Because umm, yes, I do want to fucking see him.* He reached back with one hand, grabbing the neck of his shirt before yanking it up and over his head. After dropping it onto the floor, he pulled out the elastic that was containing his hair, sending those glorious golden waves falling down to his collarbone. Every inch of his chest, arms, and neck were covered in ink; he was a walking piece of art. A smattering of light hair dusted down the center of his chest, making a glorious reappearance just underneath his belly button. *Fuck, he's pure sin. I can't wait to have a taste.*

"Do you want to see my cock?" He cupped his massive erection, drawing my eyes to where I could see the outline of his shaft, and I let out a mewl.

"Please," I breathed, bringing my thighs together to try and create any friction that could alleviate this red hot desire. He approached the bed, his long tattooed fingers deftly undoing the buckle on his belt.

"Arms up." I immediately sat up and put my arms in the air so he could lift my shirt off of my body. "Lean forward." Again, I obeyed. This was by far the most erotic thing I'd ever done. His arms enveloped me as he unclasped and removed my bra, tossing it onto the floor to join my other clothing items.

Sitting there, I realized this was not my most flattering position. Fighting the urge to cover up my soft stomach, I pushed my shoulders back and my breasts out toward him.

He stared at me, his face so intense that I felt like I was going to break if he didn't do something.

"Beautiful," he rasped, like he'd had trouble getting his throat to push the word out.

And fuck if that didn't do things for my confidence.

Cam pushed his pants down over his hips, his thick cock springing out of its leather prison like a jack-in-the-box, and I sucked in a breath. *It's pierced. And inked. He has a fancy peen. I've never seen one with accessories.*

I pointed my finger at the anaconda that was staring me down. "I don't think that's going to fit." He barked a laugh as he stepped out of his pants.

"Don't worry, little witch. By the time I'm ready to fuck you, you'll be begging for it, and you'll be so wet I'll slide right inside your sexy body. But first, there's the fact that you fucking bit me twice, then ran, and cussed at me," he reminded, a wicked smile on his face.

Scooting backward on the bed, I tried to retreat but failed as his hand encircled my ankle, stopping the movement. He pulled me toward him so fast my back hit the mattress, and I was suddenly on my stomach, draped across his lap. I'd never been manhandled in a fun sexual way like this before... *but I really fucking like it.*

The urge to fight against him rose up inside of me like a tidal wave. Attempting to squirm out of his grip, I realized it was no use. His cock was digging into my stomach, and the more I rubbed against it, the tighter his hold on my thighs and back became.

"Don't fight me. You knew there would be consequences, and I'm willing to bet that you wanted this to happen." His large hand smoothed down the curve of my ass and then snaked between my thighs on the way back up, smearing my wetness up the crack of my ass.

"So wet for me. I wonder how much wetter you'll be after I spank this delicious ass."

I want this. So much. This is uncharted waters for me, but one fact remains. I've never been this turned on in my fucking life. May as well rile him up a little bit more since I'm obviously crazed with lust right now. Poke the giant, Saige. Go on.

"Quit talking and find out then." I turned my head to look at his face for a split second before his palm cracked against my skin. My pussy clenched, and I moaned. That wasn't so bad.

The second slap echoed in the room, and I squealed like a baby pig.

"Fuck. Your skin is already turning red. I can see my handprint, baby. Your ass was made for these hands, I swear to Saturn." His palms were swirling over said handprints, and I was panting.

Thwack.

"Ow! Oh my gods, that one hurt!" I yelled out then quickly smashed my face into the comforter because two fingers pushed into my pussy.

"You are so tight, baby. Do you need me to loosen you up? Take care of you?" His voice was nothing more than a dark whisper, almost as if he were speaking his internal thoughts out loud.

"Please. Please, Daddy." I tried to buck my hips up, spread my thighs, *anything* to get more. His fingers withdrew, and I whined at the loss.

"Three more, little witch. Take them."

Before I could protest or blink my eyes, three slaps rained down on my ass in quick succession. Tears pricked my eyes, and my back bowed. I squeezed my eyes shut as I was pulled upright, my thighs spread to straddle his and my arms around his neck. Cam's chest was flush with mine.

"You did great, baby. That was the hottest thing I've ever seen."

If I were a peacock, I would've preened.

What the hell just happened? Yes, it had hurt like fuck, especially the ones at the end, but the heat that was spreading across my flesh had me breathing a sigh of contentment. Closing the distance between us, I kissed him like I was a starving tiger and he was some poor crazy bitch's husband that I was gonna eat the fuck out of. My hands threaded through his soft wavy hair. Increasing my hold, I slightly tugged the strands, breaking the kiss to look at him. His hands slid up from my hips, dipping in at my waist and then slipping to the front to palm my large breasts. Increasing my hold on his hair, I pushed my luck and pulled it a little more before I was quickly reminded that I was not the alpha in this bed. Yelping, I slapped his hands away from my hard nipples he had just squeezed.

Chuckling, he lowered us back to the bed. Grip firm on my hips, he ground me down on his dick, the cool metal of his piercing making me gasp.

"Climb up here and put that pretty pussy on my face." His tongue flicked out, and he licked my bottom lip.

I've never done that before either. I'm going to crush him. My ass will dwarf his head.

"I don't see how you'd be able to breathe. I'm more likely to smoth-" I was cut off abruptly when I felt his fingers stroking my clit.

"Do as I ask, little witch. I can't think of anything I want more right now. I need to lick that pussy; I had a taste earlier, and I want you to grind all over my mouth. Wrap those thick thighs around my head and mark me with your scent, baby."

Fucking hell. He has the filthiest mouth. Wetness slid down the inside of my thigh. *Guess I'm here for it.*

"Here, lift up a minute." Once I moved to his side, he slid so that instead of lying horizontally across the bed, his head was now on one of my pillows. "You can hold onto the headboard. Now get the fuck up here and let me worship you."

I clambered up his body, resting my knees on either side of his head. This felt awkward, and then it felt all kinds of fucking right. Keeping my body straight, he leaned up so that his lips could caress the inside of my thigh. His tongue worked in tandem with his soft lips, teasing me and making breathy gasps fall from my mouth. Feeling his head drop back down to the pillow, my body chased what he was offering. The moment my hips bent, his big hands gripped my ass and pulled me down firmly onto his mouth.

Oh, my merciful moon maidens.

Cam's tongue moved from my opening up to my clit and all around. My hands hit the headboard as a full body shiver worked its way through my lust-filled body.

"Fuck, Daddy! Oh, my gods. Yes. Yes." His arms wrapped around the backs of my thighs, locking me in place so that all I could do was grind. His deep growls and slurping sounds were nothing more than the equivalent of a cheering crowd, so I picked up my pace.

I threw my head back as his mouth sucked on my clit until a scream tore out of me as pure euphoria took over my senses. Stars danced behind my eyelids, and my muscles convulsed.

"I need your cock. Please, fuck me. Now," I begged as I dismounted, leaving his face glistening with my juices.

He followed me, twisting us around so that I was sprawled out beneath him. His mouth was on mine in a flash, our tongues dueling with each other as he rubbed himself against me. I could still smell a faint hint of leather and my own arousal. He moved his mouth to my neck, and my stomach flipped as he kissed his way down to my breasts, a smirk twisting his lips just before he closed his talented mouth around my peaked nipple. Groaning, I tried to use my legs to bring his cock back to where I needed it, but he didn't give in.

"Fuck!" I yelped when his teeth sank into my flesh, but the pain disappeared as he swirled his wicked tongue around the bite. "I need you inside of me."

He reared up and looked into my eyes. My hair had come loose of the elastic at some point during our fucking, and the long red strands were splayed out in all directions. He pushed some hair off of my forehead. "You look beautiful like this, Saige. Flushed, glistening, begging for my cock. Are you up to date with your spells?"

The magical community was lucky; we could spell ourselves each month to prevent pregnancy. It was ninety-nine percent effective, but as with any form of birth control, shit sometimes happened. I mean, exhibit A right here. Fortunately, human STDs didn't affect us at all.

"Yes, now get the fuck in me."

His eyes flashed with lightning, and he surged forward, impaling me to the hilt in one motion.

"Oh, my gods! Ah!" My thighs clenched, holding him in place, and I wrapped my arms around his neck to pull him down to me. His golden hair fell forward, creating a private little bubble, our noses touching while we let my body adjust to his size.

"You feel even better than I imagined. So tight, so perfect for me." He pulled back a little bit before thrusting forward again. "So responsive, baby. Take my cock." He pulled out completely before slamming back into me, causing us both to groan.

"Fuck me, Daddy. Make me scream."

Cam sat up on his knees, grabbing my thighs. He pulled my legs up to his shoulders and continued to fuck me without hesitation. My boobs were moving so fast I used my hands to keep those fuckers from knocking me out, playing with my nipples as I watched him own me. His abdominal muscles rippled, and a flash of silver drew my attention to his chest. *His nipples are pierced, too? Fuck. How had I not noticed that before?*

"Look at me." The command was more of a bark. Our gazes collided, and my thighs started trembling.

"Oh gods," I yelled out.

"Come around me, little witch. Squeeze the cum out of me." Cam's head tilted back, and he picked up his pace, fucking me relentlessly. The sounds of our bodies slapping together were loud, but my cries of pleasure were louder.

My orgasm hit me with the force of a speeding bullet. He slammed into me one, two, three times before he roared as his cock jerked inside of me. Cam fell forward as he let go of my legs ensuring that he stayed inside of me. My legs fell to the bed, useless jelly-filled extensions of my satisfied body. Continuing to thrust into me with slowing movements, the flutters of my waning orgasm guaranteed that I took in every drop of his cum.

After several moments, he dropped a kiss on my lips before rolling beside me, arms above his head.

"That was..." I began, unsure of how to finish that thought.

"Intense? Amazing? Best sex ever?" He chuckled as his eyebrow cocked in question.

"All of those." I smiled at him, loving that he looked so relaxed.

"Come here." He extended his arm to make room for me to crawl up beside him. "Let me hold you."

Big Daddy Cam is a cuddler? Eek!

I wiggled against him, resting my head on his shoulder. His arm pulled me in closer, palming my ass, and I sucked in a breath through my teeth.

"Sore?" I could hear the smile in his question.

"Just a little. Worth it."

A rumble from his chest confirmed his agreement. My eyes felt heavy, the endorphins leaving me now that the excitement was over. A yawn made an appearance, and Cam's arm tightened around me.

He whispered, "Sleep, little witch. You did good."

And I obeyed.

The sun's rays spilled into my room, and I sighed in disappointment when I realized the spot next to me was empty. I was hoping to talk to Cam over breakfast about what we had gotten up to last night. A moment later, the sound of a toilet flushing and running water had me sitting up in bed as my giant walked out of the bathroom.

"You are going to need to cover those beauties up if you want to get out of bed in the next hour." He eyed my breasts, a hungry look taking over his features.

Feeling a little shy, I covered myself and blurted the first thing that entered my brain. "Want some breakfast? I'm starving. Let me throw some clothes on, and I'll cook some pancakes and bacon." I swung my legs over the side of my bed, wrapping the sheet around myself more securely as I stood up and padded over to my dresser.

I was digging around in one of the drawers when I felt him behind me. He pushed my hair over my left shoulder before leaning down and pressing a kiss to the spot where my shoulder met my neck, drawing a shiver through me.

"As appetizing as breakfast sounds, I do need to get some work done today, so I can't stay too long. I *will* head downstairs and start making some coffee." Another kiss, a little higher.

"Okay," I breathed. A little breeze against my heated skin signaled his departure, and I took a deep breath.

Grabbing some fresh underwear and a bra, I walked over to my nightstand and picked up my cell phone. It was only 6:12 AM, but I was surprised at how well rested I felt. I was normally the kind of witch who stayed in bed as long as possible. Swiping my thumb up on the screen, I opened my messages and smiled when I saw what waited.

Kai: I hope you're having fun tonight with boss man. ;)

And an hour later...

Kai: Sounds like you're having a LOT of fun. Damn, Sprout. Scream the house down.

My eyes bugged out of my head, and heat warmed my cheeks. He had been here, too? I hastily tapped out a reply, my stomach growling in impatience.

Me: You mean you were here? Outside of my house at midnight? The hell, Kai?

I wasn't mad. Quite the opposite, actually. The thought of Kai hearing what Cam had been doing to me last night had my body warming up... *not* in embarrassment. But what the fuck was he doing outside of my house like that? And why hadn't my spells alerted me to... oh. Of course. Bagheera. Clearly, I need to tweak my spell to include sneaky, sneaky shifters.

Determined to get some answers, I quickly dressed and took care of some necessities. Untangling my hair with one hand and brushing my teeth with the other, my mind began its daily mental checklist of what I had to accomplish.

Coffee with Cam. Shower. Check the sick flowerbeds. See what Gran might have figured out yesterday. No work today, so I can dick around in the gardens.

Slipping my phone into my pocket, I left my room and jogged down the steps. Clanging dishes met my ears just as the sweet smell of coffee invaded my nose. *Ah, I need that.*

Seeing Cam in my kitchen had the corners of my mouth pulling into a smile, the way he moved, so graceful despite his size. His hair was loose, and he must have borrowed my brush when he used my bathroom earlier because smooth waves draped over his shoulders, not a tangle in sight. Those wicked black leather pants were squeezing his ass and thighs again, and he had on his black t-shirt from yesterday. Quietly approaching him, I trailed my fingers down his spine.

"Thanks for making coffee. I can't function until I get at least one cup into my system." I opened the fridge and snagged the creamer.

He waved me away when I tried to grab the handle of the mug. "I'm the exact same way, so I made a lot. I'll bring your cup over to the table." I stood in front of the sink and leaned up to look outside. *Might as well rip the band-aid off right now and see what it looks like this morning.*

"Oh my gods," I whispered.

"What? What is it?" Cam was all business as he slid beside me and looked outside. His finger pointed at the dying plants in two different beds. "Those weren't like that yesterday evening, were they?"

"No, they were completely fine. I don't know why this keeps happening." Anger accompanied the end of my response, but I couldn't help it. I was getting pissed. Turning my back on the shit I apparently had no control over, I trudged over to the table. Cam was right behind me, coffee in hand. Placing the steaming liquid in front of me, he took the seat beside mine.

"Tell me what's going on, Saige," he ordered, concern lacing his voice. "Maybe I can help."

Flicking the lid of the creamer, I dumped a generous portion into my coffee and stirred. After a careful mouthful, I word vomited everything that had been going on with my plants.

He listened attentively, absorbing everything I had to share. "Has your gran planted any of these gardens? Are any of hers affected?" he questioned, stirring his coffee with a small spoon.

I thought about that, my heart sinking. "Shit. It's only the ones I planted and used magic on." My eyes widened at that revelation. "Is there something wrong with my magic?" My voice sounded shrill even to my own ears, and I winced.

"I've never heard of a witch's magic being tainted unless

THE MAGIC OF DISCOVERY

someone was deliberately casting against them. Hexes or curses, but even then, this is extreme. I'd sooner think that someone was sabotaging your gardens naturally than something being wrong with your magic. Honestly, Sloane is actually the best with this shit; he excels at wards. I'll talk to him today and see if he can come out and put some protections in place. If anyone is directly sabotaging you, he'll find out."

"Really? That would be great. This is driving me crazy, and I need my plants for my business. I haven't even checked the moonstone beds or the crystal caverns. I'm scared to see if those have been tainted too." I really, *really* hoped they were fine. Gran never grew crystals; I'd started that project on my own after I finished my college courses. Running my fingers through my hair, anxiety swirled in my belly like a warning of things to come. Rocks and crystals were already a finicky bunch; the slightest misstep could ruin everything, and they were a huge source of my sales in the shop.

"Yeah, let us help you. It's the least we can do since you've been so helpful by showing us around town and introducing us to everybody. I'll see if he can come out later today or tomorrow. I know you have a hot date tonight." He winked at me and smiled, seeming genuinely happy for me. I guess between him and Kai, that made two who were jealousy-free.

"Kai texted me last night, and I only just saw it." I opened my phone and slid it across the table to him.

He chuckled. "Goddamn it, Kai."

"Explain," I said flatly.

"Kai was out last night letting Bagheera run. If he keeps the beast locked down for too long, he starts to lose it. My guess? He was running in the woods, and he picked up on our scents outside. Then his super hearing picked up on something more interesting than scent, and he's a dirty fuck, so it's not really a surprise he eavesdropped. What do you think about that?" he asked, leaning closer to me. Instead of the question possibly going the flirty route, it seemed like he was actually interested in my feelings. *What a novelty.*

"At first, I wanted to be upset, but it kind of makes me hot knowing he heard how you were making me scream, and he wasn't mad about it," I admitted, winding some of my hair around my finger.

"Kaito loves to watch, little witch. Don't get me wrong, he loves to participate, too, but he would *love* watching me work you over." Cam shifted in his seat, adjusting his most likely growing erection.

"You guys are surprising. You're all incredibly sexy alpha males, and you don't get jealous of each other. It's hard to believe this is real life." I shook my head, raising the mug to my lips to finish the little bit of coffee left in my cup.

"Refill?" Cam held his hand out for my mug, and I gave it to him with a nod. He rose from his seat and refilled both of our mugs to the brim before bringing them back over and sitting down.

"Like I said, we're close. We're more than a unit. Not brothers by blood, but I believe in my bones that we have a soul bond. I love them, and I want them to be happy. It works the same for them."

"But you've never done this before?" I needed clarification.

"Not this, *exactly*. Fischer is taking you on a date, and I don't think he's ever taken anybody on a date before. If it would make you more comfortable, you could stop by the apartment today, and we could all talk about it?" he offered.

I thought about that for a moment, but I trusted what Cam was telling me, and after getting the messages from Kai, I figured that conversation could come up when it needed to. "No, I'll just go out with Fischer and tell him what happened last night. Make sure he's okay with it. I don't want to be tied down, Cam. After escaping that douchebag, I felt so liberated. *Free*. I need more time to explore what I want and need."

"Take as much time as you need. We'd never try to cage you, little witch, but as for tying you down?" A wicked grin bloomed across his mouth, and I scolded my vagina when she gave a couple of squeezes. His grin widened, because of course, he knew exactly where my mind had gone. *Tying me up? Damn.* I hid my blushing cheeks behind my coffee mug as he added, "We'll be here working for the foreseeable future, and I just know that I enjoy hanging out with you. I feel like I can relax."

"I like hanging out with you too, big guy." I smiled widely at him, relief flooding my system because everything was cool between us, and now I had some more help to solve this fucking pain in my ass mystery.

A squeak came from the hall, and Maven sauntered into the kitchen, breaking our moment. He was filthy.

I slid off my chair and squatted down to look at his dirty little face. "What the hell happened to you?"

Mud and leaves were splattered all over his fur, but mixed in with that were black hairs. I plucked one from his coat and held it up for Cam to see.

Cam took the hair from my fingers and held it up to scrutinize. "Looks like he and Bagheera were up to no fucking good last night." I laughed, imagining Mave running around with a huge ass panther.

"Alright, little witch. I have to head back to the apartment, but I'll let you know what Sloane thinks about what's going on out here." Offering his hand to me once he straightened from his seat, I allowed him to pull me up from the floor and tight against his body. His arms wrapped around my waist, and I lifted up on my tiptoes to bury my face into his neck.

"Thank you, Cam. For last night, for everything." I pressed my lips to his neck, his pulse steady against my mouth.

His arms released me, big hands moving to capture my face as he bent down and kissed me.

Groaning, he stepped back. "If I don't leave now, I'm going to fuck you on that table."

Yeah, I don't see a problem with that.

"Don't get any ideas, little witch. I have work to take care of this morning." Snagging his leather vest off the back of his chair, he also picked up his coffee mug and walked over to deposit it in my sink. *Gran always says a mage who cleans up after himself is a mage worth keeping around...* I started toward him, but he held his hands up. "Nope. Stay right where you are. I'll see myself out. I don't trust myself with the temptation. Thank you for dinner, the coffee, and especially your body. Have fun tonight, baby."

With that, he spun on his heel and headed down the hallway to the mudroom, slipping into the vest as he walked away from me. I heard him putting on his boots before the screen door slammed just moments later. The roar of his bike flooded the air, and I smiled.

Cam is full of surprises. I'm one lucky witch.

Kai
Chapter Twelve

It was early. I flopped over onto my back, throwing my arms above my head and stretching out. It felt so damn good that a purr rumbled from my chest. The big cat was still snoring away in my mind, satisfied with the freedom he'd finally acquired last night. Shit, we must've run for thirty miles. I didn't think there was a trail we didn't track, a tree we didn't scale, a piss we didn't take. The entire town probably smelled like us... and Maven. *That little shithead.* He'd spotted us when we were slinking back into the woods about a mile away from the town center. Tiny thing was fast as hell and caught up in no time. I was surprised he wasn't scared of us, but he'd stayed out with us the entire night.

Surprisingly, Bagheera liked him. Except for every time we marked something, that bastard came up behind us and pissed all over our mark. When Bagheera snarled at him, he snarled right back and moved to lift his leg on us. Dude had some big balls. *Respect.* The two of them got along much better than Bagheera and I had at first, that was for sure.

When Bagheera awoke and we completed our first shift, it was a pure battle of the wills. We fought like the couple of teenage shitheads we were, so many arguments over what we were going to do and who was going to get to do it. Was I going to get to eat a regular dinner, or was it going to be in cat form and a bowl of whole fish and dead rabbits? Ugh. One day, I challenged his ass for alpha, wanting to settle this shit once and for all. The guys were there to intervene if things got ridiculous, and things definitely got ridiculous. We shifted back and forth probably a hundred times, me screaming at him, him roaring at me. Trying to physically fight yourself was impossible, so he called me a twinkle twat while I called him an overgrown ugly ass house cat, and then shit jumped off. Baggie had shifted out of my human form so fast I thought some of my hair blew off. He'd paced around in circles, snarling and growling low in his throat, hissing at anything that moved. Internally, he tried desperately to push me into a mental cage, but there was no fucking way that was happening.

Little shit thought he was stronger than I was, but that wasn't the case then or now or ever. Rising up out of his makeshift cage, I barked his name, breaking free from his hold, and he'd known he was beaten. He fell over on his side, showing his belly, and I forced the shift back to my form. From that day forward, we'd been in perfect sync, though at times he did like to get a random stick up his ass about being bossed around. Technically, I could force a shift, but out of respect for my friend, I never did. We had total trust in each other, and that day had been a turning point for our relationship. Now, the two of us could go on adventures together, usually peacefully. When Bagheera took over, my mind was still completely present unless I wanted to take a brain nap, and sometimes I did. I usually wasn't missing much while he was frolicking around the forest, doing crazy cat stunts and hunting. Last night, on the other hand, well, it was a good thing I hadn't taken a nap then.

We'd been sprinting through the woods, chasing a raccoon when a scent stopped us dead in our tracks. Boss. Lifting our head to scent the air more thoroughly, we found another scent. 'Mine,' Bagheera growled, his thought rumbling through our shared consciousness before forcing our body to move through the thick woods at a punishing speed. Small animals scampered to get out of our way, and for once, Bagheera had no interest in giving chase.

THE MAGIC OF DISCOVERY

Jumping out of the tree line, we stood at the back of a large property. Trees and flowerbeds were everywhere, a greenhouse and a barn mixed among the landscaping. A small cabin to the right, no lights on. Straining to listen, I didn't pick up on any sound inside the cabin. Empty.

Light spilled into the darkness from a house a little ways ahead. Padding silently across the lawn like a shadow given life, we rounded the corner around the backside of the house. Ivy was crawling up most of the brick building, and we almost ran right into Boss's motorcycle while observing the outside of this place.

What the fuck is Boss doing here? *Last he'd told us, he was heading out on the bike to ride for a while and see if he could find anything interesting along the town limit lines. This was clearly Saige's house. Her scent was everywhere.*

We paced up and down the gravel driveway, Bagheera growing increasingly agitated because he could smell our woman, but he couldn't see her. Had Saige been in trouble? A low growl pierced the silence of the night. Calm down, you big fucking jungle boy. She's fine! She's here with Boss, *I consoled the possessive cat.*

Bagheera wasn't acting jealous at all, which surprised me since he was all about Saige and claimed her every fucking chance he got. Shouting about mine, mine, mine like a two-year-old with a shiny new toy. But no, he was content. He was relieved that our woman was being taken care of, and I agreed wholeheartedly. Once the sounds stopped and the light turned off above us, we sniffed around the gardens. Now that we could focus without the distraction of what Boss was doing with Saige, we noticed something smelled... off. Tainted. Dark and unnatural.

We dug around in one of the large flowerbeds, looking for the source of this stink. Coming up empty, Bagheera whined low in his throat, nausea creeping into our belly. The big cat was sensitive to dark magic, and he was feeling it here, which in turn, meant I was as well. Whatever this was, we didn't want it anywhere near our woman. I had personally never encountered anything like this, and it didn't feel right. Unlike a mage's magic, which felt light and organic, this felt shadowed and tainted, forced. It almost felt like something demonic, but that wouldn't make any sense. I hadn't seen anything in Emerald Lakes that would make me think there was a demon lurking anywhere near. And yet... that smell. Rotting, decomposing, something was not right. We'll have to talk to the others about it tomorrow.

It took convincing, but eventually, I got the stubborn cat to head back to the apartment. It had taken a lengthy discussion and promises of us sleeping in cat form tonight, but whatever. It was already later than I'd wanted to stay out, and I was exhausted from the amount of physical activity we'd put ourselves through tonight. Sprinting through the quiet town, the only sounds were our breathing and the hum of air conditioners. When we approached the front of the magic store, a flash of darkness caught our attention as a shadow slipped around the corner. Sniffing the air, something that didn't belong lingered. Bagheera growled, and I sharpened my senses, listening intently. One word came through the bond: mage. *Not one of ours. Water mage. We could smell the crisp scent of fresh water and a hint of whatever soap this mage had used in the shower earlier.*

We could've chased him down, but I was ready for a damn shower, and whoever it was was probably just out for a walk. It was warm enough for it despite the oddity of the hour. We shifted quickly, and I grabbed the towel I had left folded on the stoop of the entrance to the apartment. Wrapping it around my waist, I pulled the door open and headed inside.

Shaking my head to clear away thoughts of last night, I hopped out of bed and tugged a pair of gray sweatpants up over my hips, listening for any movement in the apartment, but all was quiet. Sloane and Fischer had been asleep by the time I'd gotten in last night, and as I made my way out of my room, I stopped and pressed my ear to the door, hearing Fish snoring lightly and Sloane's even breathing. I smirked, guessing they'd had a session last night. *Good. They both fucking needed to loosen the hell up.*

Cam and I knew the arrangement those two had. I mean, it

wasn't exactly a mystery. They'd started hooking up back when we were still in high school. Sloane needed to dominate, and Fischer needed to submit. It was perfect for them and their needs. *Plus, it's pretty hot. Hell, I still think about the times I'd joined in...*

The morning light was shining in through the windows in the living room area, but the kitchen was still pretty dark. Flipping the light on, I replied to the message I'd gotten from Sprout and set my phone down with a smile. I didn't feel like making a big breakfast this morning, so the guys could fend for themselves while I made a bagel for myself. I did make a pot of communal coffee though. I wasn't *that* much of a dickhead.

As soon as the coffee started dripping, I heard the door open downstairs and then Cam's heavy footsteps. I leaned over the island with my chin propped up on my fist, a dazzling smile spread across my face. One look at me and he barked a laugh.

"Fucking quit, Kaito." He shook his head, but he was still smiling.

"So, should I still call you Boss, or would you prefer something a little... kinkier? Can I also call you Daddy?" I darted to the other side of the island, narrowly avoiding Cam's lunge for me, laughing outright as we circled the square countertop.

"You want to call me Daddy, Kaito? Maybe I should spank your bratty ass alongside hers next time." He chuckled and turned his back on me, choosing caffeine over our game of cat and mouse.

"Promise?" I held my fingers up and crossed them while squeezing my eyes shut.

"Shut the fuck up," he shot back, only amusement in his voice.

"Fine, fine. But for real, dude. How did you end up over at her place last night? I thought you were going riding."

He shrugged. "That was my plan, but I'll fill you in when the other guys get in here." *The lucky bastard.*

"I'm sure you were really upset about having to spend the night."

"It was a real inconvenience, but somebody needed to do it, and I was the man for the job." He winked at me before downing his coffee. *Must not have gotten much rest after I left.*

Creaking floorboards announced the arrival of our other two friends. Sloane slid onto one of the barstools, brushing his hand through his hair. "You got laid last night, bro? About time."

"Seems I wasn't the only one," Cam quipped back at him as he eyed the bite marks that thoroughly decorated Fish's chest and neck.

"Sure did. Fischer had a great time, didn't you?" Sloane turned on his alpha dickhead voice with no effort at all, Fish raising an eyebrow at him from where he stood beside him.

Instead of answering, Fish smashed his lips to Sloane's. Caught off guard, Sloane's eyes widened briefly before closing as he deepened the kiss, making my dick twitch in my sweats. *Fucking hot. I could watch them all day.*

Breaking apart, Fischer added, "It was alright." Cam bellowed a laugh as Sloane's face heated, who could say if it was in embarrassment or annoyance? Either way, it was funny as shit.

"So who did you get lucky with, Cam?" Fish asked while he walked over to get himself and Sloane some coffee.

"I was heading out of town on my bike last night when I came upon Saige with a flat tire about two miles out from her house. I gave her a ride home. We talked, ate dinner, drank a couple of beers, then we fucked," he filled us in, and equally satisfied grins grew on mine and Fischer's faces. Sloane, on the other hand, looked surprisingly intimidated. *The fuck is that all about?*

"Good for you, man. She's a firecracker." Fischer's fingers tapped against the counter at an increasingly faster pace, and we waited for him to continue. "... Is she still okay with going out with me tonight? Like, does last night change things for her?" he asked, uneasiness lacing his tone.

Cam chuckled. "Don't worry, brother. She is very excited about going out with you tonight. We discussed the situation, she asked questions, and I answered them openly. I think she was really shocked that we would all be willing to date her. Which we are, right?"

Just talking about sharing our girl was getting my blood pumping, and Bagheera's little face popped up every time her name was mentioned, flooding our bond with possessiveness and longing, and I laughed at him when he flashed me an image of Saige rubbing his big belly. Leaning down on the island, my forearms rested against the cool smooth surface, and the shocking difference in temperature between it and my heated skin felt amazing. The damn cat was always causing my temp to rise whenever he decided to force his awareness closer to the surface of my mind. "I am one hundred percent down with it." I grinned and wiggled my hips, dancing in place. Fish laughed at my antics, his own shoulders matching my movements, which caused Mr. Grouchface to scowl.

"Don't include me in that arrangement," Sloane mumbled.

"We didn't," Cam snapped, his eyes narrowing. "She thinks you hate her. She's been nothing but hospitable toward us all, and you've been an ass."

Sloane just shrugged like he couldn't give a shit less.

"Regardless of your feelings for her, I need you to go over there tonight. She's having problems with some of her flowers and gardens. The ones she's used her magic on are dying, but the ones her gran cultivated are fine. I'm thinking someone hexed them or something, and you're the best at detecting that shit."

Standing up straight and clearing my throat, I added, "About that... we went on a run last night, and when we were heading off Saige's property, we picked up on a weird energy tainting the gardens. It smelled terrible, like rotting food, and it reminded me of the scent rogue demons give off. Remember when we went to spy on The Exiled?"

The guys nodded. Yeah, they remembered. How could they forget? One of the most notorious gangs in the country had consisted of five really powerful and really fucking dangerous demons and last year we'd been assigned to go and see what they were up to. It wasn't the demons themselves that had this scent, but the remnants of their magic. The darker the magic, the worse the stench. I supposed there *could* be demons whose magic smelled "clean," but the likelihood of finding an uncorrupted demon was about the same as Sloane not being a dick. So, really fucking unlikely.

"You think there's a demon hiding out in this town?" Sloane asked eagerly. He loved torching those destructive creatures. I mean, really, he enjoyed a good fight of any kind but found it particularly fun to roast demons. Larson almost exclusively used our team to dispatch the hellspawns when they got too murderous and troublesome. During our training, we'd been taught that there was a demon realm, but sometimes the creatures slipped through a barrier and snuck into our world. Sometimes, they'd go back willingly, but if not, well, it was the end of the road for them and torch time for Sloane.

"I haven't picked up on any demonic indicators," Fischer added, taking a swig of his coffee, his brow furrowed in thought. "Granted, they're pretty similar to humans or witches when they're wearing a glamour. Sometimes the aura can be a giveaway since demons' have a heaviness and radiate black and red, but humans can show those colors, too, especially if they're abusive or destructive in some way."

"I think we might have just found our first solid lead about whatever is off around here," Cam said, cracking his knuckles, the tattoos on his hands stretching out with the movement.

"I'll head there tonight when she's out with Fish and see if it's a curse or hex. Maybe that jerk ex is behind this. If it's something else, I'll know." Excitement was sparkling in Sloane's icy blue eyes. Even more than torching demons, he loved a good mystery.

THE MAGIC OF DISCOVERY

He was worse than a hound dog with the scent of a raccoon; once he had a mission, he was relentless.

"Alright, I'm going to shower and then call Larson to update him. I'll wait until tomorrow to tell him about the possible lead with the gardens since we'll hopefully know more then." Cam looked to Sloane before addressing the rest of us. "I like Saige. I'm going to be honest about that right now. I don't have any issues with the three of us dating her, but our mission still comes first. Our goal is to find Laura, but we also want to try and keep Saige and the rest of this town as safe as possible. I'm going to go down to the bank where Laura was last seen on the surveillance camera, and I might do some asking around to see if anyone knows her. I don't want to raise too much suspicion and have word get back to her, but so far, no one has given us a solid lead."

Cam liked Saige? Interesting. He was usually a love them, leave them kind of guy. She must have really gotten underneath his skin. I smiled. Boss was a good man. I knew he loved each of us, and I was happy he had found a connection with someone outside of our group. He needed a good woman to love on, and Saige was looking more and more perfect with each passing day. What he really needed was a partner, aside from us, that he could depend on, that he could trust implicitly, someone he could show his scars.

"I'm going to pick her up tonight at six. Should I take the rental, you think?" Fischer asked the room, but it was Cam who responded.

"That girl loves to ride. Take your bike. Have fun." A smile took over his normally stoic face as he clearly remembered something from the previous night. I didn't think I'd ever seen him look so... dreamy.

"For the love of Jupiter's cock," Sloane cursed, standing up and walking out of the room.

"Don't be salty, Sloaney Baloney!" I yelled at his retreating back, receiving double birds in answer as he stormed out of the kitchen and down the hallway.

"I thought he would have mellowed out considering what the two of you got up to last night," I directed at Fish.

"He could fuck me every day and still be a crabby bastard," Fish laughed, and it was the truth. Clearing his throat, he continued, "I'll talk to him if his shitty attitude toward Saige continues, but we all know how he is."

Cam and I glanced at each other briefly before agreeing that that would probably be the best route.

"Alright, shower time." Cam pushed off the island and disappeared into the bathroom, leaving Fish and me behind.

"Do you know what you're going to do with our girl tonight?" I inquired as Fischer got up and took everyone's mugs to the sink.

"I want to take her somewhere private, so I can get to know her without anybody else's emotions mucking up our date. She's a blank slate, K. I've never met another woman like her, and I just... I can't help but hope that maybe this could really be something. Maybe a picnic?" His fingers were tapping again, this time on his knees, his legs bouncing. He was nervous. *Aww, how fucking sweet.*

"I'll whip up some subs and stuff for you to take. Wine?" The relief on his face was instant, and I slung an arm around his shoulder. "Don't worry, bro. I got you. A successful date means our woman is having a great time, and that makes me and Bagheera very happy."

"Thanks, Kai." His arm wrapped around my waist as he leaned his head against my shoulder, squeezing me with a half hug. I took the opportunity and mussed up his thick hair with my hand before he pushed me away, laughing.

Even Fischer, the cold interrogator, was thawing out here in Emerald Lakes. Saige was quickly turning into someone that I didn't want to have to give up when our time on this assignment was over. Two of my best friends were laughing more in the six days that we'd been here than I'd seen them do in the past several years. Speaking for myself, I loved the rush I got when my phone pinged. My Sprout almost never responded in a way I thought she would, and I lived for that surprise. She was by far the most positive thing that had entered our lives to date. *Now, if only she could work some magic on Sloane...*

Sliding across the vinyl wood flooring on my socks, I stopped in front of the drawer that held sticky notes and pens. I wanted to make the best picnic for Fish and Saige, and the first step was a grocery list.

About half an hour later, I made my way around the store, grabbing the items on my list and some of those random extras you always grab 'just because.' Just as I was heading to the checkout, a familiar scent hit my nose, a growl nearly escaping as Bagheera pushed to the front of my mind when a man walked out of an aisle to my right. *The water mage from The Pig.* He was shorter than me, probably five foot ten, and built like a bear. His blond hair was buzzed, and I noticed a yellowish purple bruise around his eye and swelling on his cheekbone.

This must be the douchebag that thought he could lay hands on our woman. *Why was he skulking around Saige's shop?* Bagheera was snarling at the realization that this bastard was standing right here, so close, and my own lip lifted, but I managed to keep the sound inside. He wanted to tear his throat out, and I had to push his predatory ass down so I didn't shift and trash the place.

Bryce. I snarled his name in my mind. As if he'd heard my thoughts, he crossed his arms over his chest and locked eyes with me.

"Nice shiner," I growled.

"Yeah? You like this?" He raised his hand and let his fingers trail over the raised skin. "Some little asshole who doesn't know how things work in this town thought he'd get stupidly brave." He smiled darkly at me, not knowing when to back down. "Looks like he's not the only one since you're still walking around *my* town too."

"Do little assholes make you piss your pants, then? That's what I heard happened." I shrugged as I started putting my items on the conveyor belt, unafraid to turn my back to this douchebag.

He laughed. *Son of a bitch must have a death wish.*

"Do me a favor, tell that little slut that her pussy belongs to me. I don't care how many of you fuck her. In fact, it'll just make punishing her all the sweeter. Maybe I'll just have to fuck her tight ass and remind her—"

My eyes flashed to pure animal as my fist shot out and smashed his throat. The cashier screamed, and I knew this would be the talk of the town, but I'd be fucking damned if this piece of shit was going to talk about our woman like that. Douchebag was bent over, holding his throat and gasping for air as Bagheera called for *blood*.

Dude, we're in a grocery store for fuck's sake, I thought, trying to make my cat see reason.

I turned my attention to the cashier, my eyes landing on her name tag. "Joanne, I apologize for scaring you. However, I do not apologize for making him shut his filthy mouth. Nobody should talk about *any* woman like that."

She nodded, her permed hair bouncing in agreement. "It's about time somebody did it," she whispered under her breath. "Why don't you get out of here before the manager stops by? It's a shame that I saw a spider and screamed," she finished with a wink.

Douche-mage left his basket and slunk off like the bitch ass coward he was, not knowing how lucky he was that I'd run into him today and not Fischer. I couldn't inflict pain on someone without witnesses noticing, but Fish would've slipped right into his brain and scrambled it like a goddamned omelette.

I smiled as I handed over the money for the groceries. "Glad to be of service, then. Keep the change. Have a wonderful day, Joanne."

Picking up the paper grocery bag, I saluted her with my free hand and waltzed out of the store. *Damn, that felt good.*

HAVING PACKED THE FOOD AWAY IN FISH'S BACKPACK, I THREW IN A bottle of wine and a corkscrew. *They'll just have to drink it out of the bottle.* Tossing some napkins and a couple of bottles of water in the bag, I sat down on one of the barstools, satisfaction flowing through me as I scrolled through my phone to kill some time. At four, Fischer walked into the kitchen.

"You look nice, brother," I told him as I took in his black button-down long-sleeved shirt. His deeply bronzed skin practically shimmered as it met the dark fabric. He'd rolled the arms up to his elbows and tucked the shirt into a nice pair of dark wash jeans. His thick black curls were styled back, out of his face, with the help of some product.

"Thanks." He shook his arms out. "Fuck. I'm nervous, Kai. I can't get a read on her at all. How will I know how it's going? I've never had this problem before."

I walked up to him and put my arms on his shoulders. "You've got this, dude. She's into you. She wouldn't have agreed to go out with you if she wasn't."

"Maybe she felt obligated after I knocked that asshole on his ass," he worried, voicing his doubt at my statement.

"Then I'll ask her out next because I throat punched that little bitch in the grocery store earlier."

"You did what?" He laughed as his eyes flashed with darkness, making me shiver. *Dude is a scary motherfucker when he wants to be.*

"Yeah, he came up behind me in line at the checkout, unwisely cocky. I didn't like the shit he was spewing, so I jabbed him right in the throat."

Fischer threw his head back and laughed like hell.

"When we got back from our run last night, I smelled a water mage, but I didn't realize it was him until we ran into him at the store. I don't know what the fuck he was up to over here, but he was just leaving when we bounded up. We're all going to have to watch him. He said some really fucked up shit about our girl, and the piece of shit definitely doesn't realize who he's messing with."

Sloane had just walked into the kitchen, chiming in after hearing my last comment. "Fucking abusive meathead. If he comes at her again, I'll burn his balls off with my bare hands." He opened the fridge door and bent over to look inside. Pulling out a beer, he held it up with an eyebrow raised in question. I nodded and he grabbed another.

Nothing got Sloane quite so heated as men who beat on women. His father had been a master of all forms of abuse, and after nearly beating Sloane's mother to death, he'd been locked up in prison where he couldn't hurt her anymore. Unfortunately, Sloane's mom wasn't the only victim in the house. Eyeing the fire mage, I could practically see the heat billowing off him from merely thinking about a woman suffering at the hands of a man. The water mage would get more than a throat jab if he so much as looked at Saige wrong in Sloane's presence. Dude might be an asshole to her, but he would torch any bastard who tried to hurt her. *See? He's just a big ol' sweetie, my Sloaney Baloney.*

"Want me to come with you tonight to check out the property at Sprout's?" I had nothing else going on, and I was curious to see those plants again. If there was something evil targeting her, I wanted it banished as soon as possible.

"Sounds good. I'm going to head out at eight." Rummaging around in the utensil drawer, he pulled out a bottle opener and popped the lids off the two drinks. "Here." We clanked our bottles together, each taking a healthy swig.

Leaning against the counter, he surveyed Fischer. "You never dress up for me."

"I'm never dressed long, so what's the point?" he fired right back at Sloane, and I laughed.

"I can't argue with that. For what it's worth, you clean up nice... pet." Sloane winked, and Fischer's cheeks flamed. *Fucking hell,* the chemistry between the two of them was insane, and I was sporting a damn semi.

"Quit fucking with me. I'm nervous enough as it is without the two of you adding to it. I'm leaving before you get ideas or offer any shitty advice. I need to scope out a few potential locations, anyway."

"Here, don't forget the fucking food! What a disaster that would be." I sped over to him and put the backpack on him like a proud papa sending his kid off to the first day of school. "Now, get the fuck out of here and have fun." I slapped his ass, and he grumbled out a fuck you that held zero heat.

When the door slammed shut, Sloane and I stood there with our thumbs up our asses for a few moments before I couldn't take the idle silence. "Well, Sloaney Baloney, our boy's all grown up. What are we going to do with ourselves?" I asked dramatically.

"I'm gonna sit and watch TV until it's time to go investigate. Did you hear about that show that everyone's talking about? Something about a gay redneck who owns a tiger farm?"

My eyes flashed, and Bagheera growled. *Big cats are not meant to be confined. Fucking humans.* "Show me." With a smug smile, Sloane led me into the living room.

Saige

Chapter Thirteen

I'd spent the morning relaxing with Maven and daydreaming about last night's surprise encounter with Cam. When I finally came back down to Earth and realized it was already two in the afternoon, I got my ass into gear and hopped in the shower, pushing all thoughts of the guys from my mind.

Fifteen hurried minutes later, I shut the water off and grabbed my towel. Opening my eyes, I yelped and almost fell on my ass. All bright colors had been leached from my vision, leaving behind only shades of green, gray, and black. *What the hell is going on?*

"Sssssaige." The whispered voice came from my bedroom, the hiss seeming to wrap around my body until I froze, my heart beating so hard I thought I might have a heart attack at any moment. *I must be losing my mind.*

"Indespectus," I breathed, invoking the spell that could hide a witch from someone meaning to do them harm. I'd gotten well acquainted with the spell after dating Bryce for so long. Not hearing any more sounds, I dared a peek through the crack in the door. My vision was still fucked as I braved a look into my bedroom, sucking in a breath of surprise.

What are they doing? From what I could tell, the same two figures that I'd seen in the shop were moving around my bedroom, looking at everything they could. More whispers filled the air, but I wasn't close enough to make out what they were saying.

"Saige, where are you, child?" Gran's voice called out from downstairs, and the shadows shrieked and dissipated, the lingering hiss of 'ssssoon' causing my body to tremble as my vision returned to normal. I walked to my bed and dropped down on the mattress in a heap, taking a shuddering breath. During the short walk from the bathroom to my bed, my body had felt like it was wading through molasses, and I didn't know if that was from the fear coursing through my system or some lingering effect of the shadow creatures.

My door creaked as it opened, and then Gran was there, concern on her face. Her hands gripped my upper arms as she asked, "What's happened? Saige, talk to me."

Sitting up, I threw my arms around her and pulled her to me, tears filling my eyes as the adrenaline began leaving my body. She rubbed my back, shushing me in a soothing way.

"Gran," I croaked out, "we need to talk."

Pulling away from me, she nodded. "Get dressed, I'll be downstairs in the kitchen."

She quietly left, and I quickly threw on some clothes and ran a brush through my hair, feeling guilty that I hadn't confided in her yet about the 'prophecy' or those shadow things. I'd gotten so wrapped up in Cam that I'd forgotten to give her a call. Now these creatures were showing up again, and they not only knew my name, but where I lived, and from the sounds of it, they were interested in learning more.

Moving down the steps at a swift pace, I headed for the one woman who I knew would always help me, guide me, and love me, no questions asked. She was sitting at the table, a fresh pot of coffee beside our already full mugs.

"Talk to me, child. When I entered the house, I had this sick feeling in my stomach and felt unnatural energy. I need to know everything so that we can protect the house from further invasion."

Slipping into the chair beside her, I ran my hands down my face. "Gran, I don't even know where to begin. So many weird things have been happening, so at first, I thought it was all just a fluke. The flowers dying? It's only the beds I tend to. Did you notice that? Yours are completely fine. Yesterday, Matilda and Roberta showed up at the shop. They were waiting for me when I got there, going on and on about a prophecy and how important it was."

After a deep breath, I took a sip of my coffee. Gran's face had this serious expression I hadn't seen since my lovely mother decided to pay a visit when I was a kid. When she didn't speak, I continued, sparing her no detail. As I shared the part about the seers' eyes turning black and the power that had moved through me when they grasped my hands, Gran's face began to lose its rosy coloring. *Well, that's not fucking good. Keep going, Saige. Get it all out.*

With a deep breath to stall the questions running through my mind, I finished describing my change in vision, the shadow creatures, the prophecy, all of it. Still nervous, a tiny undercurrent of relief ran through me at having confided in Gran. Together, we could figure this out.

"And that was the first time you saw these beings?" Gran questioned, lifting her mug to take a sip, her face not quite so pale, though the stern expression remained.

"Yes. But just now when I finished with my shower, my vision went all weird again, and I heard one of those things whisper my name, Gran. They were creeping around my room and looking at all of my shit. What the fuck are they? Do you know?" I asked, my eyes pleading with her to say yes. Gran reached out and took my hand in her own, searching my face before she released a deep sigh and averted her gaze to the wall. Acceptance and sadness flickered in her expression, and I squeezed her hand in support.

"They're astral projections, child. They cannot harm you while they're in that form, thank the gods. It would appear to me that they're on a fact finding mission for their master, this 'king' they spoke about," Gran informed me, fiddling with the hem of her shirt. That had always been one of her tells. Ever since I was a little girl, she'd fiddle with her clothes when she had something big and uncomfortable to talk to me about.

"But what are they really? If they're projections, then they must have a physical body, right? Where the hell is their physical body?" *Am I going to be freaking abducted?*

"They're demons, Saige." Gran exhaled, leaning back into her seat.

"Demons. Like, from Hell? I didn't even think Hell was a real thing."

"Not Hell. They're from Besmet, the demon realm," Gran stated, matter of factly.

"Gran, how much did you drink last night? Have you eaten breakfast?" Putting my hands on my thighs, I went to stand up, but her little hand shot out, signaling for me to stay seated.

"It's true, child. Demons are real. They're not talked about in the magical community because they don't mix well with others. It was only by chance that I learned about them, and I wish I hadn't. They are supposed to stay in their realm, while we stay in ours."

My head is spinning.

"Why are they in my freaking bedroom then?" My voice raised to a shrill on the tail end of that question, but shit, I was starting to panic. "And how do you know about them?"

"I'm not sure why they were in your bedroom, child. But I know that we need to put protections in place, and I will get started on those right away." She stood immediately. "We can tend to the gardens after I get these items prepared. This takes precedence," she said with a parting worried glance before turning and walking away from me.

"Gran, wait. How do you know about them?" I called out, needing some answers.

Turning back to me, her eyes softened. A split second later, they hardened as she spat out, "Your mother."

"My moth-"

"Later. I must get these protections in place. They're crucial. We'll talk once I'm done." My playful, man-obsessed Gran was gone, her tone telling me how serious she was, so I bit my tongue.

Now I had more questions than ever.

Not really knowing what the hell to do with myself, I figured I might as well get started in my gardens. Throwing a quick spell up for protection, just to be safe, I stepped out onto the still wet grass. Mist was rising off of the ground like the sky was calling it back home, the sun peeking through the wooded forest, projecting golden rays across the yard.

The sound of birds singing was calming enough to let me feel some peace, and I twisted my damp hair up onto the top of my head. I freaking hated getting my hair in my face when I was trying to garden. Trudging across the property, I headed to the back corner where the moonstone beds were. *Ugh, please let these be okay.* I kept my eyes on anything I could except for my destination, dreading what I might find.

Throwing up one last *praise be to the stars*, I looked down and exhaled the breath I'd been holding. *They look fantastic.* They were slightly glowing, still charged up from the night, and I couldn't find anything to even hint at a problem. Well, thank the gods that these weren't affected by this fuckery. After a few moments, my happiness started to give way to a niggling in the back of my head, reminding me of the fact that while I did tend to these stones, my actual *magic* had no part in their success. That was all on the moon. Different moon cycles provided different types of properties, so it was really just a matter of time and dedication on my end to keep up with tracking which stones had been out for what cycles.

Anger suddenly charged to the forefront of my mind. Who was doing this to me? Was this connected to the demons? I wasn't going to take this lying down. Storming back across the property, I approached my gardens. The once beautiful spring flowers were completely dead. My plants hadn't even broken the soil yet, long overdue. Pissed off, I knelt down and shoved my hands into the dirt. The more I looked around me at the destruction, the more furious I felt. My magic was churning inside of my body, begging for release.

Deciding that I was in charge of my own shit, I sent out a wave of energy, picturing the seeds sprouting underground and pushing upward through the dirt, climbing to the sun. Opening my eyes, I gasped and yanked my hands out of the soil, falling back on my ass.

Gnarled, black sprigs had erupted from the earth where there should've been perfect green seedlings, all in a row. Wide-eyed, I watched in disbelief as some of them actually broke off and turned to ash. Tears welled in my eyes.

No. Not my power. I don't kill things! I give life. What's happening to me, and why do I have such a horrible feeling that this is going to get worse before it gets better?

Reaching into my pocket, I pulled out my phone and fired off a text to Cam. If Sloane hadn't agreed to come over tonight, I was fully prepared to beg.

Me: Did you get a chance to talk to Sloane yet? Things are worse than I thought.

I'd barely put the phone down before it pinged.

Cam: Are you safe? Sloane, Kai, and I are planning to come by

tonight to see if we can find anything when you're out with Fish.

Cam's message helped to dry my tears, and a small grin broke through at the thought that they were all coming over to help me. *They'll be here in less than four hours*, I reassured myself with a sigh. I typed out a response, holding back the extent of my distress so as not to worry him. The big protective mage would be over here in a heartbeat if he felt I was in danger.

Me: I'm safe. I just wanted to make sure that someone was willing to help. This is beyond my witch level.

"Saige, come meet me in the kitchen. Let's get started," Gran yelled out to me from the house, closing the window in the kitchen after I acknowledged her. I headed for the house, reading another text while I walked.

Cam: Yes, little witch. We'll do everything we can to help you figure this out. It'll be okay. Enjoy your afternoon. I might need a nap later. I didn't get a whole lot of sleep last night.

Cheeks on fire, I tucked my phone into my pants and headed for the kitchen. *Let's get this over with.*

"What is all of this stuff, Gran?" I questioned, taking in everything she had spread out across the entire table.

"Stuff that's going to keep you safe. Sit down. You can help out, and then I will tell you a little story." The last part of her statement was weighed down with a hint of sadness. Lifting up a bracelet that had several crystals in it, she motioned for my wrist, securing the dainty gold chain around it when I held out my arm.

"This will give you strength from the stars and protect you from any possession, although I'm not convinced that is their objective. Seems to me they would've done it already if that was the plan. It will also allow you to have increased awareness so that you'll feel when a demon is near. Most describe it as a tingly sensation at the base of the neck or goosebumps, that kind of thing."

Picking up a mortar and pestle, she pushed them into my hands. "Sit, grind this up to a fine dust. We will place it at all of the windowsills, doorways, and around the entire perimeter of the property. While you grind, I'll cleanse each room with sage sticks and cast protection spells and wards."

Lifting a small basket that held her tools, she sped out of the kitchen, the sound of her chanting and the smell of smoke reaching my nose within thirty seconds.

Gran was quirky, but this was beyond anything I'd ever seen from her. Yeah, she was always determined to protect me, but I could see something else in her eyes that was an even larger driving force— *Fear.*

That scared the shit out of me. I'd never seen anything close to fear cross her face. Happiness, amusement, longing, annoyance... absolutely. *Never* fear. Hell, I'd just discovered that demons - *demons* - were an actual thing. Sitting at the table, I ground the ingredients into a dust, questions racing through my head as I worked. *What in the world would demons want with me? And what connection does Laurie have to them? Ugh.* Feeling pissed off again, I put some extra elbow grease into the motions and pulled back when the pestle went through the bottom of the mortar.

By the moon, I'd just ground through the damn thing. *How is that even possible?* Picking up the pestle that was now a good inch shorter than when I started, I stared down in shock at the hole in the bottom of the stone basin. Lifting it up, the powder I had been grinding spilled out onto the table. Gran had just hustled back into the room, and I turned to her with wide eyes as she looked from my face to the destroyed items in my hands.

"What in the name of Saturn's balls happened to it?" Taking them from my hands, she peered at me through the hole.

"Uh... I put my back into it and broke it?"

"This has been in my family for generations; it's made from enchanted rose granite. This shouldn't be possible." Gran slumped down into her chair and tossed the now useless heirloom onto the table.

"Yeah, well, seems to be a lot of impossible shit going on right now. I need some answers, Gran." I tossed my hands up in exasperation, needing her to know I was on the verge of flipping out.

"Scoop that powder into two bowls, and we can quickly place it. I'll answer all of your questions as soon as that's complete."

Rising from my chair, I padded over to the cupboard that had some paper bowls inside and snatched two of them. Gran took one, and we each pushed half the powder into each of our bowls.

"I'll take the perimeter and the doorways; you can go around and do all of the windows," she ordered, placing her bowl into her basket and heading out of the house through the back porch.

"Sure thing," I muttered under my breath. *Blah, what is going on with me?* Now that I thought about it, I'd been on edge the past several weeks, quicker to anger than normal, and now getting frustrated with Gran? That was really not like me, and I was starting to get unsettled.

Moving quickly through the house, I made sure to hit every single window, even the tiny ones in the attic. The last thing I needed was any more freaking visitors. *Well, unwanted visitors, that is.* Remembering my date, I pulled out my cell to check the time. *Wow*, it was already after three. The afternoon was getting away from me fast. Heading down the steps, I made a beeline for the sink in the kitchen so I could wash the dust off of my hands.

Not seeing Gran anywhere, I went ahead and pulled out the container with last night's leftover soup and popped it into the microwave. Just as it started beeping, she bustled in and collapsed into her chair at the table.

"Are you okay?" I rushed to her side, taking her hand in mine.

Waving me off, she replied, "Yes, yes. I'm fine. Just takes some extra power and exertion that I'm not used to using anymore. Something smells good. Can you get me a glass of water, child?"

Now I felt like a dick for being frustrated with her lack of answers when she was clearly putting forth a lot of effort to lock my house down like a bunker. Filling up a large glass with ice water, I brought it over and set it down in front of her.

"Let me grab the soup. Drink that water, Gran. I don't need you passing out on me. This day has already been eventful enough for my liking." I turned and headed for the counter. Spooning the soup into two bowls, I carried those over and sat down beside her. She looked a little better, some color returning to her face. "How do you feel now? Do you need anything else?"

"The water is fine. Thank you. I'm better now that I know those creatures can't get in here. Later this evening, I'll go into town and put the same protections over the shop. Now, I know you're dying of curiosity, so how about I tell you what I know first. We'll see what questions you have afterward." I smiled as best I could, dipping my head in response.

"Back when your mother was a teenager, she went away to New York City for a weekend with some classmates to tour a couple of magical museums. The first evening they were there, she and a few of her friends thought they'd give the teachers the slip and sneak into some bars, ending up at a club that catered to the magical community..." Gran looked away, closing her eyes as she took a deep breath. My own breathing nearly sped up, nervous for what she was about to say.

"From what I was able to squeeze out of her, she'd gone outside with a guy she'd picked up, and they were making out in the alley beside the club until a fight broke out between him and another guy who'd been checking her out. The attacker had lost control, talking about how she was his, and the two men started growling and sprouted horns, their eyes turning completely black. Laurie had no idea what she was looking at, but the two demons were fighting to the death over her, a potential mate. In the end, the demon who had been kissing her beat the other to death. She stood frozen to the spot while the monster stalked over to her and caged her against the wall. He spouted all kinds of nonsense about mating with her, producing healthy babies, and being a savior." Her voice caught on the last part, but I wasn't sure what emotion was overtaking her. This time, it seemed like Gran might be reliving the fear she'd had for her daughter. Though they didn't have a relationship now, I knew Gran had loved her, still did.

"A couple of bouncers from the club had raced into the alley, taking in the dead man and the horned creature who was hovering over a teenage witch. One of them pulled out a gun, shooting the demon with a strong tranquilizer, while the two mages pulled Laurie out of the dark alley, kicking and screaming. She'd wanted to stay with that *beast*." I opened my mouth to ask what had happened to the demon, but she raised her hand, shushing me.

"Typically, demons do not live in our realm. They stay in Besmet unless they're sent here by their rulers for either a mission or sometimes punishment. There are rogues, that's what they call them, who somehow gain access to a portal, and they come here to do what demons do best. Taint, ruin, corrupt, tempt... and we are the perfect victims for such desires. Too trusting, too soft, too pure.

I had no idea of their existence until Laurie returned home. After that, she was never the same. We both know how much your mother loves attention, and this was better than a strong batch of drugs to her system. Sure, she had always been a selfish girl, but most teens are. Now obsessed with knowledge and power, the demon had completely invaded her mind. Her grades started to suffer, and nothing held her focus besides her studies into *Demonology*, she called it. At first, I thought she had made the whole thing up, but after doing some research of my own, I discovered that they are indeed real."

THE MAGIC OF DISCOVERY

At that point, she reached out and took one of my hands in her own, her eyes pleading with me as though I could provide some kind of comfort or forgiveness for what she was about to say.

"I tried my damnedest to rid her of her obsession. We fought so much, and all she would talk about was leaving Emerald Lakes after graduation so she could get the answers that she needed. She wanted to go to Besmet, driven mad with the idea of a whole other world being just beyond her fingertips. As far as I know, the only ones capable of summoning a portal to get there are actual demons, though I'm sure she gave it every ounce of magic she had to try and get it to work. Then, after she graduated, she was gone.

I was so angry with her, and in a way, I still am. She was a brilliant witch, one of the strongest I have ever known, but her addiction to power was stronger." Gran paused, releasing my hand and lifting her water to her lips.

How was this the first time I was hearing this story? Taking a couple bites of my lunch, I waited patiently for her to continue, afraid she'd never start again if I interrupted.

"I didn't hear from her again until she showed up on my doorstep claiming to be three months pregnant. She only seemed upset that she was going to have to hang around here for six months until you were born. I knew she didn't want to be a mother; the girl never had a motherly bone in her body. She needed to explore, run, do whatever she wanted. Offering her an out, I told her that I would raise you." Gran's voice grew sharply bitter, and even I felt the sting of the animosity she felt toward Laurie's selfishness. But I didn't question for one second that she resented *me* for this situation, no, that was all on her daughter.

"You could stay with me for as long as you'd like, and I would teach you about green witchcraft. I would be the one to provide for you, care for you. Obviously, she accepted that, and you know the rest." Gran's eyes hardened, and she looked like she'd tasted something horrible.

How different would my life be right now if she had never gone on that weekend trip with her school friends? Shaking my head, I dumped that thought right in the mental trash can in my brain. My life was amazing. I had everything I could ever want, and most importantly, I was happy.

I'd always wondered why Laurie hadn't stepped up. Why she didn't *want* me. And now I knew, the answer was so simple it almost seemed unreal: she was just too selfish to care for anything besides herself.

"I'm so sorry, Gran." Reaching out, I grabbed her hand and gave it a squeeze.

"I try not to think of it because I still get so angry. It was a long time ago, and I can't even wish it had been different because everything happened the way it should. It got me you, after all." Squeezing my hand back in response, she pulled back and started to dig into her lunch.

"Why do you think they're coming around now? Do you think they're looking for her and got confused by me?"

Raising an eyebrow in thought, she swallowed her bite and snorted. "That would make sense. Of course the stupid girl would lead the damn things right to our home, even unintentionally. They won't be getting in here again, though. I'll sleep easy tonight and even better after I put the protections around The Pig as well."

"Did you put the same protections around your place? If you need me to help do that, I can cancel my date tonight and help you," I offered. *Oh, shit. My date! What time is it?*

She held up a hand to wave me off. "No worries, dear. My tiny house doesn't need anywhere near the level of work this one did. I'll take care of it after a nap. Roxanne and I were out shaking our asses under the moon last night well into the morning hours, and the whiskey was flowing like a waterfall. This shit sobered me right up, but it's taking its toll now that I'm sitting down for a moment." The last part was said around a yawn that had broken free.

"But before I nap, I do have a few questions of my own." My gaze snapped to hers, and she blurted out, "When were you going to tell me about the man that slept here last night? And what's this *date* that you're definitely not canceling?"

"Gran! How do you know there was a man here? Do I even want to know the answer to that?" I studied her amused face and smiled.

"First of all, the whole place stinks of leather and sweat. I've always appreciated a man who could rock some leather. Your grandfather—"

"No. Absolutely not. Do *not* finish that sentence," I sternly told her, miming zipping my lips.

Laughing, she added, "Second of all, your bed was a hot mess. One does not cause that type of disarray without just cause. Third, you are radiant, the look of a satisfied woman. Fourth, you're sitting kind of gingerly on that chair, so I'm going to go out on a limb here and guess that he's into span—"

"For the love of the moooooon. We're done. No more. Yes, there was a man here, and his name is Cam. He's one of the mages who lives above The Pig," I supplied as quickly as I could.

"Ah ha! I knew there was something to those tarot cards you chose the morning they moved into town. But if that were true, then..." Her eyes sparkled as her brain worked, and then she whooped, causing me to jump in my seat. "He's not the only one vying for your affections."

Sighing, I fessed up because she would find out soon regardless.

"No, he isn't the only one. I'm actually kind of casually dating three of the four. In fact, I have a date tonight. He's picking me up here at six, so I probably need to get a move on if I want to look like a real human before he gets here." Checking the time, I gasped. "In an hour and a half!" I stood up, frantically grabbing our bowls and tossing them into the sink as gingerly as a panicked person could.

"Three men. You went from zero to three men in what? Ten days? That's impressive. Reminds me of the time I once went from zero to five in sixty seconds, but that wasn't a relationship. Strictly sexual. Hell of a wicked time." A smile lit up Gran's face as she lived out her glory days in her mind while mine cried out for her to stop.

Busting up laughing, I winked at her. "I'd never dare try to outdo you, Gran. I don't believe it's something that's possible... though if I'm even going to try, I *really* need to get ready for this date."

"Okay, I get it. My bed is calling my name. I'll let you get all dolled up. I won't come out to meet this boy tonight, but I make no promises that I won't be spying from my windows to sneak a peek," she teased, waggling her eyebrows at me as she stood and sauntered out of the kitchen.

What a freaking day.

Fischer
Chapter Fourteen

I was nervous. When was the last time I had felt nervous? Sifting through my memories as I drove out of town toward Saige's cottage, I honestly couldn't recall. I could read people and manipulate their minds; that typically made me the most powerful man in the room. The only reason I was able to put a name to the fluttering feeling in my stomach was from dealing with this particular emotion so often from other people.

Feeling out of control and out of character, I tried to take some deep breaths. That's what they told people to do when they were anxious, right? Yeah, it wasn't really working. Her driveway came up on the right quicker than I would've liked despite having ridden around for a couple of hours, scoping out the perfect picnic spot, and trying to calm my nerves.

Turning onto the gravel path, I studied her cottage. Cozy and lived in. Those were the first words that I'd use to describe this place. A lot of it was covered in vines, and hanging baskets were suspended along the covered front porch. The siding was whitewashed, and the paint was chipping in spots. Maven came darting out from behind the house, yipping at my bike, so I slowed down, worried I'd hit her beloved fox. He sure didn't give a shit, keeping pace with me the rest of the way to the house, snapping at my tires. *Ballsy little devil.* I laughed at his antics, only seeming to piss him off further. There was a garage on the side, so I pulled up there and cut the engine so that I could check my phone. There were a few messages from the guys, but I ignored those and opened up the newest one.

Saige: Come on in through the side door by the garage. I'm almost ready.

Those freaking butterflies were back as I pulled open the screen door and stepped inside. I'd made it to the hallway when the sound of someone coming down the steps pulled my attention to the left.

"Hey, you found the place!" Saige jumped down the last two steps and slid across the hardwood floors on her socks, wrapping her arms around me in an embrace as she collided with an *oof*. The nerves dissipated immediately as I reciprocated her hug.

"Yeah, the directions were pretty easy," I replied. *The directions were pretty easy? What the hell kind of response is that?*

Giggling, she stepped back and smiled up at me. "I'm so excited to hang out with you tonight."

I couldn't read her emotions, but I could read her face, and she meant it. Joy and excitement were simply radiating from her body. She'd put on some light make-up, but her lips were painted a deep red. She was wearing a pair of ripped black skinny jeans and a dark green tank top that was more lace than anything else. Her breasts were pushed up, a necklace with a crescent moon hanging precariously close to the dip between those beauties.

"You look beautiful," I breathed, my voice raspy as hell.

Pink bloomed on her cheeks, and she gave me a beautiful smile.

"You look good, too. I just need to grab my sweater. It's still pretty warm out, but just in case I need it for later..." Stepping around me, she walked over to the hooks that lined the wall in the mudroom. Plucking a dark gray cardigan off one of the pegs, she draped it over her arm and turned to face me. "I'm ready when you are."

"Right. Okay, let's go." Motioning for her to lead the way, she stepped outside and squealed when she saw my bike, the sound sending a wave of desire through my body. *The sounds she makes... stars give me strength. Thanks for the tip, Cam.*

"You brought your bike? Okay, this is already officially the best date I have ever been on." She bounced up and down on the balls of her feet, her contagious excitement bringing a smile to my face.

"And to think, I was so nervous to take you out this whole time. All I had to do was bring the bike, and I'd be the winner of 'best date ever'?" I teased, and she laughed along.

"What can I say? I think they're sexy, but the men who ride them are even sexier." She winked at me, and I groaned internally. *Thank god she'll be sitting behind me. I can regain some self-control then.* "Well, hop on behind me, and we'll see if I can continue to impress you tonight, sweetheart."

Her eyes twinkled at the nickname that had tumbled from my mouth without my permission. She was the sweetest person I had ever met, so at least it was fitting. Pulling the bike upright, I swung my leg over and held it steady, pointing out the footrest for her.

"Oh wait, can you put this on your back? It's not heavy. I just want you to be able to hold on safely," I asked, slipping the backpack off of my shoulders. Nodding, she reached out and took it from me, sliding it on her curvy body and tightening the straps a bit before holding my arm and hopping on the seat behind me.

"This feels different from Cam's," she nearly whispered, uneasiness lacing her voice.

"Well, this bike was built for speed. You have to lean forward instead of sitting upright. Press your chest completely flush against my body and give me your hands," I directed, taking hold of her wrists and pulling her closer. Her arms wound around my waist, her breasts pressing tightly against my back. Now I was pretty sure the guys told me to bring the bike because they knew

I'd blow my nuts off in my jeans before we even made it to dinner. *Bastards*.

"Like this?" she breathed, her cheek resting on my shoulder blade.

"Perfect. Let's do this," I grunted, needing to move so I could focus on something other than the goddess wrapped around me.

I pressed the ignition button, and the engine roared to life, causing her thighs to tighten as her heartbeat raced. Just as I pushed the bike backward, I finally picked up on a single emotion, and although it was small, I breathed a sigh of relief. *Desire*. Red hot. Dropping a hand to her knee, I gave it a squeeze.

Preparing to head out, I looked around to make sure Maven wasn't lurking somewhere. There was a tiny cottage along the back of the property, and my eyes widened when I saw a woman standing in the front window, the curtain pulled back. *I'm such a fucking idiot.*

The desire I'd picked up on hadn't been from my goddess. No, it was coming off of this witch like flames. Her eyes widened when she saw me, and the desire quickly changed to amusement. The curtain closed, and I gunned it down the driveway. *Is her beloved grandma a pervy old witch?*

I'd scoped out the area for a nice place to take her. I didn't want any distractions, just the two of us getting to know each other. Feeling giddy, *again,* I drove us about ten minutes outside of town where there were some small mountain ranges. It was pure luck that I'd found it, the perfect place.

At the base of this mountain, there was a small river with a couple of little waterfalls. Hoping she hadn't seen it before, I pulled the bike off the side of the road, steering it down a dirt path that led to the forest that expanded before us. The path narrowed once we hit the trees, a bit overgrown from lack of use. Letting the bike roll slowly to a stop, I killed the engine, and the sounds of nature took over.

She slipped off the seat behind me, and I turned around to

find her gazing up at the mountain. Hooking my fingers through the strap at the top of the backpack, I lifted it off her back and slid it on my own.

"I could've carried that," she told me, eyes still locked on our surroundings.

"I'll be damned if the woman I'm taking out is going to lift a finger. I already feel shitty that you had to wear it on the way out here."

Tearing her eyes away from the view, she looked up at me and reached out to intertwine our fingers together.

"Who knew you were so romantic?" she murmured.

Well, I sure as hell didn't, but it seemed like Saige liked my romantic side, and that thought had a surge of warmth spreading through my chest, so I hoped I kept it up. Her smiles, her happiness, her laughter, I wanted all of that tonight. All of this was all new to me. I'd never had an official relationship; the closest thing would be my arrangement with Sloane. I did love him, and I'd do anything for him, but he'd never expressed a desire to take our casual relationship to the next level, which was why his recent mixed feelings had been confusing as hell to me. He was jealous, extremely so, and that was an emotion I had never picked up on from him. I wasn't sure how to process that, and I was willing to bet that he wasn't either.

My mind was turning into a little bit of a battlefield because I was struggling with the fact that Sloane didn't seem to be a fan of Saige, and for whatever reason, that hurt me. There was just something about her that pulled me in and refused to let me go, and Sloane was deluded if he didn't think that I felt the same way about him. I couldn't give him up; I would never want that. I needed to talk to him sooner rather than later because I wanted them both, and I would find a way to get what I wanted.

Shaking off those thoughts, I brought myself back to the glorious woman who was here with me now instead of dwelling on the grumpy bastard I had waiting at home. Rubbing my thumb over the top of her hand, I smiled at her. "We have to walk for about five minutes, and then we can eat."

"It's beautiful out here. There's a state park about ten more minutes down the road. I've been there a few times, but I never thought to just park on the side of the road and go scouting on my own." Saige laughed at the end of that thought, and I glanced at her from the corner of my eye as she took in everything with her big green eyes, not paying attention to where she was walking. She struck me as the kind of woman who would rather experience the journey versus sticking to a map or any sort of plan.

"I wanted to find the perfect place. I like finding things that nobody else pays attention to, places that haven't been trampled by thousands of feet. There's something calming about a spot that you can be alone in, the view unseen by others. I spend a lot of time looking for quiet, and I've gotten pretty good at finding it, at least in nature."

Squeezing my hand, she seemed lost in thought for a moment.

"Thank you for sharing this with me, Fischer. From what you've told me, I know that you don't get much alone time. I'm happy you decided to share some time with me tonight."

Flicking my gaze to her again, her eyes were now locked on the ground in front of her, a shy smile gracing her mouth, and my blood warmed at her declaration. Little did she know, when I was with her, it felt like I was alone, but not in a shitty way. In a way, being here with her allowed me to be *me*. To feel what I wanted to, knowing that my emotions weren't being manipulated by anyone else's. She made me feel normal, and it was quickly becoming addicting.

The sound of rushing water drifting through the pine forest caught my attention. "Ah, here we go. I'll get everything set up!" I announced, dropping her hand and striding over to a large open spot just off of the water.

Opening my bag, I pulled out the large quilt I'd packed and laid it out on the grass while Saige grabbed one of the corners and helped me to lay it flat. "This place is amazing, Fish. I can't believe this is here, so close to everyone, yet nobody knows about it. The water is so clear, too," she observed as she leaned forward and dipped her fingers into it.

"Uh huh," I mumbled. I wasn't looking at the water; my gaze was locked onto her ass as it stuck up in the air. *By the moon, I can only imagine how glorious it looks naked.*

She pushed herself back and sat down with her legs crossed. A grimace flitted across her features, and concern struck me as I reached for her. "Are you hurt?"

"No," she squeaked, a blush tinting her cheeks, "just a little, um, sore."

Sore? From the ride here? I watched as she fiddled with the hem of her shirt, and realization dawned on me. Barking out a laugh, I startled her accidentally.

"Oh, yeah. Cam didn't give details, he would never do something like that, but I do know he spent last night with you," I confessed, raising an eyebrow to see how she would react to that information. My own ass was a little tender if I was being honest, so who was I to judge?

"And you're okay with that?" She dropped her eyes to the blanket, cheeks tinting with a slight blush that made her all the more adorable.

"Sweetheart, look at me, please." Her beautiful green eyes lifted, and I continued, "Cam is my best friend. All of the guys are. I love them all equally. They're great men, and they deserve to be happy. You do, too. If we can all make each other happy, why wouldn't I be okay with that?" Based on her nervousness about dating multiple guys, I had to admit I was slightly worried about what her reaction would be when I told her about Sloane and me. Would that be the bit of information that sends her into overload? Knowing I would tell her tonight before this went any further, I decided to wait a little longer, ensuring first that she was comfortable.

"I guess I just never thought that anything like this was possible or that it could actually work. What are the odds of a group of hot guys moving into my small town, then three out of four of them wanting to not only date me but being okay with all of this? It's like a hot fantasy come true," she laughed, shaking her head in disbelief.

Moving across the small distance between us, I picked up her hand and pressed a kiss to her fingertips.

"What are the odds that we would come here for a job and find a gorgeous, sweet witch who wants to put up with all of us? I think we're the ones living out a fantasy. I had hoped that one day we might find someone who would be willing to accept our team." We shared a look and a shy smile, and I could feel the heat of a blush spreading across my cheeks this time. *Christ, I feel like I'm thirteen years old again.*

"Thank you, Fischer. You're so sweet." Her voice was soft as she stared at me. *Stars, if she only knew just how not sweet I truly am.*

Clearing my throat, I turned to my bag and pulled out the foil-wrapped sandwiches and the container of homemade chips.

"Aww, did you actually make this for tonight? That is so cute, Fish," she gushed as she grabbed the container and flipped the lid before popping one of the chips into her mouth. Groaning, she closed her eyes as she savored the taste. *Why is she so damn sexy when she's eating? For fuck's sake.*

"Actually, I can't take credit. Kai's the chef of our group, so he offered to make us dinner," I confessed.

Swallowing her bite, she giggled. "Gods, he is too much. So are you, by the way, and these chips are the bomb. I need to get the recipe." She leaned in and kissed my cheek, and an emotion that I wasn't familiar with bubbled to the surface of my mind: contentedness.

Using our foil as makeshift plates, we poured out the chips and continued eating together, the moment peacefully quiet.

After a few moments, I pulled out the bottle of wine and held it up in question.

"Wine sounds great, thanks." The date suddenly felt much more 'date-like' if I was judging by what I'd seen others do. Food, check. Alcohol, check. Sexy as sin witch, check.

"Yeah, we didn't have any unbreakable glasses so... we'll have to drink it from the bottle. I apologize," I explained with a frown. What if she wasn't the kind of girl who would just throw back a bottle of wine? I'd been watching her intensely the whole night, not wanting to miss a reaction since I had to scrutinize each one to figure out how I was doing with this whole date experience. Searching her expression for any sign of disappointment, I released a breath I hadn't realized I'd been holding when a brilliant smile lit up her features. *Shit.* When she smiled at me like that, it made me feel like *I'd* genuinely pleased her, not my magic, but me, Fischer Bahri. It was addictive, and I wanted to see that brilliance every moment I could.

I'd never been a lazy man or a slacker. Bored was often the best word to describe me. It might sound arrogant, but I couldn't remember ever really having to work hard to win someone over. Look at that real estate agent last night. Initially drawn in by my looks, all it took was a slight push of magic to snare her in my trap. Saige was an enigma though, and she captivated me. I found myself wanting to know everything about her so that I could earn her happiness and affection, not manipulate it. I welcomed the challenge. To be fair, I was downright fucking excited about finding out all the things I could do to get her to smile at me, the words I could say to get her to swoon in my arms, the delicious things I could do to her body in order for her to give herself to me completely. Yeah, I was going to implant myself in this woman's mind, in her gods damn body, and I was going to do it organically as *myself*.

"This will be perfect as long as you don't mind getting my cooties," she teased, taking the uncorked bottle from me. Raising it to her plump red lips, she took a drink, a drop of wine dripping from her chin when she pulled the bottle away. I found myself reaching out and swiping it with my thumb. I popped it into my mouth, and her pupils dilated at the action.

"I'd be honored to have your cooties, sweetheart." I flirted and she blushed.

She passed the bottle back to me, and we ate while we made small talk about the quirks of the town, how good the food was, and stories about her gran. *Yes, that pervy old lady was indeed her gran.* We finished eating and drained the bottle of wine, the time having passed quickly.

"Oh my stars, I am so full," she groaned, laying down across the blanket on her back. Rubbing her hand over her belly, she draped her other arm over her eyes. A breeze whipped through the trees, my hair tousling with the force of it.

"Are you getting cold? I have your sweater here in my bag..."

"I'm okay right now. Come down here and talk to me," she murmured, keeping her arm over her eyes. I scooted over to where she was and laid down next to her, on my side. Propping my head up on my hand, I couldn't look away from her. Red waves splayed out around her head, her pearly skin nearly glowing in the dusky lighting.

"Fischer?" My name on her lips was like a prayer.

"Yes, sweetheart?" I answered, heart racing with anticipation of what she might say next.

"For someone who can read emotions, I thought you might have kissed me by now," she nearly whispered, lifting her arm off of her eyes and giving me a cheeky grin.

A genuine laugh spilled out of my mouth, surprising me when it filled the air around us. I wasn't used to a partner who made me laugh and smile like this; I was used to one who fulfilled every dark fantasy and had very different noises coming from my mouth. My heart sped up at the thought of having them both and how well they complemented each other.

"Is that what you want? A kiss?" I moved closer to her now, my body pressed up against hers.

"For starters," she quipped back with zero hesitation. Throwing my arm over her waist, I leaned away so that I could look down at her beautiful face. She blinked slowly, her eyes drinking in my features just as greedily. The soft touch of her hand warmed my cheek, her fingers running through the dark stubble that was always there.

Lowering my lips to hers, I brushed them lightly with my own, a shiver working its way down my spine. *So soft.* Breaking away, I looked down at her to see if that was okay. I didn't want to push or take advantage of her.

The next thing I knew, I was the one on my back, and she was leaning over me, her hair falling around us, blocking out everything else. I ran my hand up the back of her thigh and hooked it over my hip, grabbing a handful of that amazing ass. Groaning, she took my mouth and ran her tongue over the seam of my lips, wanting entry. Opening for her, she dipped into my mouth and teased my tongue, deepening the kiss as my hands ran along her back. I pulled her closer to me, the sudden, hungry movement throwing her off balance until her thighs straddled me, moans escaping us both when she settled and sank her hands into my dark curls.

"Gods, I have wanted to do that since the freaking cookout at the lake," she panted above me. I pushed my hips up against her core, the movement blessing me with a small whimper.

"The sounds that you make would bring any man to his knees before you," I gritted out between clenched teeth.

Carefully pushing myself upright since she was still wrapped around me like a monkey, I held her tighter, loving the feeling of her curves against me. I tucked a strand of hair behind her ear then gathered the rest into one hand behind her back. Tugging gently, her neck stretched, and I buried my face into the nook between her shoulder and throat, inhaling. I ran my nose up her neck, peppering her jawline with kisses while I held her hair tightly to keep her locked in place.

"Fish!" The breathy sigh that slipped from her lips had my cock jumping, and I was ready to hear it again and again.

"Sweetheart," I growled, "you are something else, but as badly as I want to take this further, I can't. I want to romance you and win your affections, learn everything there is to know about Saige Wildes. I have never been so captivated by a person in my life."

Leaning back, I dropped her hair so that she could look into my eyes. I felt exposed, and for the first time in my life, truly seen.

"You're a good man, Fischer Bahri. I didn't peg you as being such a romantic, but I guess I just got lucky." She slid off my lap and put some distance between us.

"I don't know about all of that, but I do have something to confess. A couple of things, actually..." I trailed off, swiping my palms down my thighs, hoping to dry some of the moisture that had come out of nowhere. Raising her eyebrows, she nodded and waited. I wasn't a good man, and I'd done some really dark and disturbing shit in the name of my job. The underground criminal networks all knew who I was, shit, they knew my entire team. If they got stuck in a room or cell, and I walked in, *I* was the one who struck fear into the hearts of our enemies. I'd seen some of the most ruthless and depraved men shit their pants when they realized I was going to be doing an interrogation.

Feelings of guilt rose up inside me. I was already beginning to hate having to lie to her about who I really was, who we all really were, but that was the job, and the job always had to come first. Before *everything*. We were all in our thirties, or close to, and only one of us had ever had a serious relationship. I'd never given a shit about that since Sloane always took care of my sexual desires and a relationship always just seemed like too much work for someone with my affinity.

Deciding that I wanted to be a little more honest with Saige, I started, "So, I wasn't being completely honest at the cookout; I can't actually read you. At all. You don't give off any readable emotions or feelings." Her brow furrowed, a flash of alarm spiking in her eyes.

"Really? Is that... normal?" I could hear the concern in her voice, so I took her hand in my own.

"I'm not sure if it's normal or not, but it *is* very rare. There has only ever been one, maybe two peopleI can think of that I couldn't get a read on. Some witches and mages are better than others at mentally shielding themselves from cogs, but I don't think that's what you're doing, especially since it's not conscious on your part. It would be incredibly hard to keep that up for longer than a few minutes," I surmised, thinking out loud.

"No, I'm just being my regular self. That's so weird." She bit her bottom lip, and I could almost see how hard she was thinking by the little crease that showed up between her eyes.

"It's not a bad thing; it's one of the things I enjoy most about you. Since I was a teenager and all of this started, I don't feel like I've been able to just be myself. The guys are all great with shielding their minds around me; they've done it so often that it's second nature to them," I reassured her. Running a hand through my hair, I stared at her through my dark eyelashes.

"So that's why you're so attracted to me? Because I'm the first person you've been with who you have to actually interact with? You know, the peasant method of dating."

I blanched, but amusement danced across her face.

"Are you... teasing me right now?" I asked her, letting false disbelief filter through my tone.

Giggling, she shrugged. "I think it's cute. You're learning what it's like to read body language for the first time. I just thought you were studying me so intently because you liked my face."

"Oh, sweetheart, I *do* like your face, and the rest of you for that matter. But yes, you do show what you're thinking through your facial expressions, and this is all new to me. You're the first person I've taken on a date. Just never saw the point before. Sometimes, my affinity is more of a damn curse. When it comes to the mind, sometimes the less you know, the better," I explained.

"I'm glad you asked me out. I'm having a great time, and you deserve a break from your powers." Her hand squeezed mine, and she was handling this first hurdle so well that I was just so tempted to skip the next for now.

"We should head back to the bike before it gets dark," I thought out loud, looking up at the darkening sky.

"You said there was something else you wanted to say?" She tilted her head to the side and reached over to grab her sweater. Slipping her arms through, she pulled it tight around herself.

Fuck. I hope this isn't a deal breaker for her.

"Yeah, so I told you before about how it's hard for me to get out of my own mind. When I was seventeen, I kind of found a way to achieve that even though it doesn't last for long," I explained, wringing my hands together.

"That's great! I'm sure any break, even a small one, probably feels so freeing." She smiled, that small reassurance giving me the push to just fucking tell her.

"Sloane and I, we have a little more than a traditional friendship..." I cleared my throat as she gave me a puzzled look. "He likes to be in control, and I like to completely let go."

"You mean, what? Like BDSM?"

"That's part of it, yes."

"You two..." She paused, her cheeks turning the reddest I'd seen. "Have sex?" She squeaked the last part out, but it wasn't in disgust. More like... curious and slightly confused interest.

"We do."

"Shit, that's so hot," she breathed. I barked a laugh, but then she stiffened and narrowed her eyes on me, a quick but righteous fury already building. "Does he know you're here? You aren't like, cheating on him? I am *so* not meant to be the other woman."

"By the moon, I swear he knows we're seeing each other. It's not like we're exclusive or anything. It's really an exchange of needs when we hook up, and I love him just like I love all of the guys." *Kind of.* I shrugged my shoulders, trying to portray the casualness of our arrangement.

"I'm sure he's thrilled you're out with me of all people," she muttered, her gaze now locked on the water, and she sounded almost... sad?

"Sloane likes you. I know he's abrasive and rough, but deep down he is one of the best men I know. He just doesn't trust easily and is very career-driven. He'll come around. He wasn't bothered at all, and even if he were," I shook my head, "it wouldn't have stopped me from pursuing you. Does this change things for you? I can't give him up, Saige." I held my breath, hoping like hell that it wouldn't.

"Do you want a relationship with him? A real one?" she questioned, tilting her head and searching my face for the truth.

I opened my mouth to respond and then shut it again quickly because I had no idea how to respond to that. Seemed ridiculous, but the possibility of officially locking down Sloane was always so fucking slim that I'd never allowed my mind to venture down that route. Maybe it was from fear of ruining our dynamic that already worked so well, or maybe fear of rejection, but I simply hadn't let myself consider it.

"Would it be crappy to say that I don't know? Believe me when I say that this is the first time I've ever thought about it. It has always been purely sexual, each of us chasing a release that the other knows how to perfectly provide. I don't know what a relationship with him would look like, but what I do know is that I want to explore things with you. So, does it change things for you?" I asked again, feeling shy and vulnerable.

Her focus stayed on the rushing water for several moments,

and I thought my heart was surely going to beat right out of my chest. Just as I was about to open my mouth and fill the silence, she spoke. "Thank you for being honest about it. I know that we're also not exclusive. I mean, I'm dating two of your friends, so it would be very hypocritical of me to be jealous. The fact that it's Sloane and not another woman makes me feel better about it somehow. So, no. It changes nothing for me. I still want to get to know you better, and this was a good start," she told me honestly before she leaned forward and pressed a slow kiss to my lips.

Thank the freaking moons. Relief flooded my system, and I enjoyed taking her mouth, licking her tongue with promises of what mine was capable of. Maybe, just maybe, I could keep her... and my fiery pyro. Gods, I could only hope. Stepping back from her, I tucked a strand of hair behind her ear, and she smiled up at me.

"Come on, sweetheart, let's get out of the woods."

Standing, I pulled her up to me, and together we folded up the blanket before putting everything back in my bag, linking hands, and trekking back to the bike. Glancing down at her, the setting sun lit up her hair like shimmering fire. Her whole body glowed with the setting rays, and I swallowed roughly. Emerald Lakes was shaping up to be the best assignment I'd ever been on.

THE SUN HAD SET COMPLETELY BY THE TIME WE PULLED BACK INTO Saige's driveway, my headlights illuminating the tall figures of my brothers standing by the damaged gardens. All three of them turned their heads when we approached, so I cut the lights as I pulled into the open spot in front of the garage and killed the engine.

Kai had already bounded over and was lifting Saige off of the seat, squeezing her in his arms, straight up *sniffing* her hair. Instead of being creeped out, she just laughed and called him a weirdo, slapping his shoulders in an effort to get him to put her down.

Cam and Sloane shuffled up behind Kai, and I gave them a smile. Cam gave me the bro nod, but Sloane just stared at me with an expression that had me on edge. *That's definitely jealousy.*

"Do you mind if I go inside and use the restroom before we head out, Saige?" Sloane asked, but still, his eyes didn't leave my face.

"Oh, yeah, of course." Saige tossed the keys to him. "Just go in through the mudroom and take a right. It's the first door on the right," she explained as Cam reached out, pulling her to him and I watched Sloane stomp off into the house. She smiled up at him, and the big man stared at her like she was something precious to protect. I could feel his happiness and arousal, and once he had her firmly in his grasp, relief. He was *relieved* he had his large hands on her hips, feeling her body pressed against his to confirm that she was safe. *He's got it bad.*

Kai slid up beside me. "How'd it go, man?"

"It was great. Thanks for the help with the food. She loved it, and I definitely owe you." A grin broke out over my face, the feeling of it welcome but almost unfamiliar. *When was the last time I smiled like this?*

"Is it weird that I don't find *this* weird at all?" He gestured to Cam who was depositing kisses up and down Saige's neck, small, dark chuckles rumbling from his chest as she squealed.

"Then I'm also weird because I think it's hot as hell," I confessed. "Cam deserves something good, and I'm glad she's breaking through his tough exterior."

The screen door swinging shut had our heads snapping over to where Sloane had just walked out of the house. Never one for chit chat or social niceties, he stalked over to me, and didn't waste any time.

"So, this shit over here," he abruptly said, gesturing with his arm to indicate the dead gardens, "is fucked."

Saige snorted in disbelief. "No way."

His eyes narrowed on her as he crossed his arms over his chest. For the love of the stars, I hoped he was only at a level five or six on the Sloane Sullivan scale, not a ten or eleven. *Yes, it's a ten-point scale*. I held my breath.

"Red, this property is tainted with the dark magic exhibited by only one race: demons. I have zero doubt about it. But my question is, what would demons achieve by fucking with your little plant paradise, hmm?"

I see we're closing in on a level seven, and if she sasses him, this could escalate quickly.

"Quit being a dick," Kai whispered like Saige couldn't hear him. Sloane definitely did, judging by his eye roll.

"There's been some... strange things going on. It's a really long story, but I do feel better having confirmation as to what's causing this. I was really scared, it was like my magic was fucking up. Can you imagine? A green witch who kills everything she touches?"

Saige was trying to remain calm, but I could see the rapid rise and fall of her chest. She was spooked. Cam noticed and put his hands on her shoulders and began rubbing them for a few moments before moving to stand before her in line with the rest of us. He spoke in a low voice, attempting to soothe her nerves.

"Now that we know what the cause is, we can figure the rest out. It's getting late now, but I'm sure I can speak for the rest of the guys when I say that we want to hear about what else has been happening. There's just one question that I need you to answer before we get out of here, and I need you to be honest. Your safety is my number one priority, little witch. Are you safe?"

"Yes, I'm safe. Gran and I put some wards and protections around the cottage earlier today. Nothing will be able to harm me there." She pulled her sweater around herself as the wind picked up, hugging herself.

"Well then, you better get in there, Sprout," Kai ordered with a fake sternness to his voice, earning a mocking salute and sarcastic 'yes, sir' in response.

Hearing a noise to my left, I looked at Sloane. Could've sworn he groaned at her use of those two words. *Interesting.* But he was studying her with curiosity, not lust. A hint of suspicion slipped through his shield, and that had me wondering what the hell was going through the pyro mage's dark mind.

"We should let Fish end his date. Let's get out of here. Text me later, little witch." Cam darted forward and kissed her lips in goodbye, heading to his Harley with a wink as her cheeks heated.

"Come here, Sprout." Kai opened his arms, and Saige melted into him. He dropped a kiss to the top of her head and mumbled little compliments about how pretty she looked. Begrudgingly, Kai released my date and hopped on his bike.

Saige looked at Sloane, the brave girl. "Thank you so much for your help. Cam told me this was kind of your specialty. I can't tell you how much it means to me."

Giving her a curt nod, he turned and grabbed the helmet off of his vintage Indian before climbing onto his bike, the three of them firing up and taking off down the drive at the same time. Inhaling, I turned to where Saige was last standing and startled when I found she was right beside me.

"We'll get this figured out," I breathed, wanting to reassure her.

"I know. I'm freaked out, but right now? I'm mostly happy. I had a wonderful night with you. Thank you, Fischer." Her arms snaked around my waist, and she laid her head on my chest.

"Thank you for coming out with me, sweetheart." With a lift of her chin, I lowered my mouth to hers. She tasted like perfection, a balm of normalcy for my fucked up soul. I swallowed a moan that slipped out of her throat, and groaned as she pushed her tongue against mine. *Gods, this woman.*

Saige pulled back, panting. Fire flared in her eyes, and she sucked her bottom lip between her teeth.

"Don't look at me like that. Deep down, I'm a weak man who is hanging onto my earlier declarations by a fucking thread." Closing my eyes to block out her face and heated gaze, I took a couple of deep breaths to get a hold of my damn self.

Her laugh carried on the wind that was picking up by the minute; rain was on the way.

"Okay, okay. I'm going inside, but I was thinking that on Sunday you guys could all come over. Meet Gran, eat, drink, and we can discuss all of the crap going on so everyone is on the same page? Can you ask the others if that will work with their schedules?"

Grabbing her hand, I walked her over to the side/front door. "I'll ask as soon as I get back. I'm sure it'll be fine, though. I'll shoot you a message and let you know for sure."

"Goodnight, guppy." She lifted up on her tiptoes and gave me a quick peck on the lips before slipping into her house.

"Goodnight, sweetheart— Wait, did you just call me guppy?" I asked, sure I'd misheard that.

Laughing, she gazed at me through the mesh of the screen and blew me a kiss. Dropping her hand, she proclaimed, "What? You're my sweet cutie guppy."

My mouth fell open as she turned and walked away, giggling. *I'm a goddamned stone cold killer, and she just called me a guppy? I know that's some kind of fish, but I can't picture what it looks like. I'm going to google that when I get home, and it better be the size of a shark or some shit.* Smiling to myself, I strutted over to my bike. *Badass guppy. That's me.*

The sound of the door closing and the light in the mudroom shutting off sent a wave of calm through my body. My girl was safe, she'd had a great night, and she liked me. *The real me.*

Saige

Chapter Fifteen

Stone walls and high ceilings with domed entryways greeted my eyes as awareness crept into my mind. *This room looked like something from a fairy tale, complete with a throne sitting at the far end, white and red banners decorating the entire room, billowing sashes cascading down from the ceilings.*

My bare feet had carried me forward, curiosity overriding all other emotions, to investigate the enormous throne when a man entered at a fast clip from a door to the left. I was so startled I squeaked, and his head snapped around to see who had made such a sound. He was gorgeous in an other-worldly kind of way. Freckles covered most of his face, his deep red facial hair kept short and trimmed.

"I'm so sorry. I didn't mean to scare you," he said, walking toward me. I could tell he was trying to figure out who I was and what I was doing standing in this castle in a silk nightie. "Who are you? Are you here to see my father? I'm not sure where he is. I just popped in myself from the other realm. I haven't been home in a couple of years," he rambled, lifting a finger to slide his black-rimmed glasses up on his nose then pushing back some of his hair that had fallen into his eyes.

"I-I'm not sure. I think I'm dreaming," I said, motioning to the nightgown and bare feet I was sporting. "Where are we?"

"Well, we're in Naryan, the capital city. This is the king's castle, his home," he answered slowly, studying my face as I took in that information.

"Naryan. Right," I muttered, running a hand down my face. I'm definitely dreaming.

"Can I get you something, anything to drink? A robe?" he offered, his eyes trailing down my body. Swallowing, he held up a finger and stalked over to the side of the room where a massive wardrobe was standing. I watched with interest as he flung open the doors and snatched something made of dark green velvet.

"Here, let me help you slip this on. You must be cold. This is not the warmest time of year for a visit." He held up the robe, its wide sleeves and deep hood inviting me to burrow inside. It was beautiful.

Turning, I extended my arms back, and he slipped the long sleeves on me, pulling it up around my neck. Glancing to my feet, the soft material pooled around the floor and would trail behind me when I walked.

"There, that should help with the chill," he assured, moving in front of me. I pulled the robe closed, feeling more secure now that I wasn't in danger of giving this sweet man an unexpected nip slip.

"Thank you." I smiled. Unsure what to do next, I shifted my weight back and forth from leg to leg. Freckle cutie was just standing there. Hmm, this is awkward. *He must've realized it because he jerked himself straight and started rambling again.*

"It's just about dinner time. If you're hungry, you can join us. Do you need to see a healer, though? I'm concerned that you don't recall why you're here or even where you are. Are you injured?" His eyes widened at the thought that I might be, and he stepped forward quickly, reaching for my hands. "Did a rogue hurt you, my lady?"

The moment our hands touched, I sucked in a breath, both of us freezing, his amber eyes searching the depths of my green ones. Fire raced through my veins, and I whimpered at the same time a groan reverberated from his chest.

"It can't be," he breathed.

I didn't know what the fuck that meant, but I couldn't drop my hands from his. We were two magnets slamming together, and the force of that vibrated through my bones right down to my soul. Suddenly, the vision before me started rippling like the waves on a lake. This dream was about to be over.

THE MAGIC OF DISCOVERY

"Don't go, please," he begged, his eyes pained. I didn't want to leave him, and that was the strangest damn thing, especially considering I had three men in the real world.

"I'm sorry," I whispered, though I doubted he'd heard it...

My eyes snapped open, and I flew upright in bed, my heart racing. Patting down my arms and chest, there was no green velvet robe. Maven did not appreciate being jostled from his slumber, and he growled, also needing a moment to take in his surroundings. I searched my room, but I didn't see any sign of the beautiful man with the pained amber eyes even though I could still feel the whisper of his warm skin against mine. Throwing myself back on my pillow, I stared up at the ceiling. The dream had felt so damn real, and as much as that was screwing with my head right now, I'd take that over those creepy ass shadow demons any day. Luckily, I hadn't been visited by them since they'd shown up in my room on Friday morning.

It was Sunday, and the guys were coming over this afternoon to hang out. Not in the mood to analyze my bizarre dream, I pushed thoughts of the red-haired dream man away and focused on my mages. The real, flesh and blood ones that looked at me with heat every time we were in the same room. The very ones who would be here soon. My inner witch gave me a mental high-five before she strutted around like a model on the catwalk. *Dating three hot as sin dudes will do wonders for your self-esteem, in case any of you are needing a boost.*

All three of them had been texting me since Friday night. Kai with his usual flirty banter that I lived for and Cam being a total Daddy, inquiring about my wellbeing every chance he got while promising sweet, sweet punishments when I got sassy with him. Fischer, my sweet guppy, had video called me last night, and we talked about anything and everything. Favorite books, foods, television shows. His smiles were addictive, and as much as he was enjoying trying to win me over without his powers, I was getting just as much out of seeing the stress and weight he carried vanish when we were talking.

Kai had told me that yesterday they'd been doing some work during the day, checking out that warehouse that was for sale again. *Maybe if Radical purchases it, the guys could relocate here?* I tried not to go down that rabbit hole, but it was hard not to. The thought of them leaving had my stomach feeling like I'd swallowed a pile of rocks, so I was content to just pretend that it wasn't something that would ever happen. As Gran always said, "She who looks at the world with the eye of a newt will see a newt-like world." *Yeah, I don't know what the fuck that means either, but this seems like the first appropriate situation I've had to use it.*

It was still hard to believe it had only been just over a week since they'd blown into town and my very normal and uneventful life. Funny how you got so used to your life that you didn't realize what you were missing until the stars smacked you in the head with four hotties. Suddenly, your old life seemed monotonous in comparison.

Hauling myself up and out of bed, Mave jumped down with me, his feet padding softly behind. Opening my bedroom door, he flew past me down the steps. *Good morning to you too, dude.* Scrolling through my phone as I moseyed my way into the bathroom, I read a few messages from Miranda. I'd been making an effort to talk to her daily to see how she was holding up; it seemed the moonstone she'd gotten was helping. We hadn't gotten the chance to have our hangout yet, but she was living vicariously through my dating life and was one hundred percent supportive of my unconventional relationship.

While she was all for this arrangement, we lived in a little blip of a town, and there was no telling how the members of my community would react to such a thing. *Ha. Yeah, right.* As soon as Roberta and Matilda got their hands on this information, it would be all over town. I mean, the whole town was still talking about that time Mr. Peterson cheated on his wife with another teacher. Imagine the splash a quad relationship would cause! It was likely to wind up in the town history books to live on forever, shocking future generations to come.

I refused to be ashamed or embarrassed, though. My guys were good, and it was like Gran always told me: "You don't let the good ones get away, especially if they're romantic and know how to wield their magic sticks." Direct quote. She had a point. Dressing quickly, I bounded down the steps, heading for my beloved coffee and finding Gran ready and waiting.

"Morning, Gran," I said, enveloping her in a hug as she filled our coffee mugs to the brim. My heart squeezed looking at her. She was too good to me. Some people my age might not appreciate their grandmother being around pretty much all the time, but I did. She was my best friend, my mentor, and I was pumped that my guys were going to be here in a few hours to meet her.

Gran and I had talked in detail yesterday about what Sloane had discovered during his investigation, and I was hoping that today wouldn't turn into an interrogation, but one never knew what was up Gran's sleeves.

Gran returned my hug, her grip surprisingly strong. "Morning, did you sleep well?"

"Decent. I had some dreams though," I confessed, popping a shoulder.

"Not about those beasts, I hope?"

"No, thank the gods. Nothing demon-related, no need to worry," I assured her, attempting to keep her calm. Warm amber eyes flashed in my mind, and my skin warmed when I recalled the connection I'd felt when our skin touched.

We fell into a comfortable silence, sipping our coffees, and scrolling through our phones. Mornings like this were perfect, and I enjoyed the peace. The way my life had been going lately, they'd become a rarity. Determined to savor it, I created a group text with the guys, except Sloane. He hadn't asked for my number again since the first time when I'd told him to eat a bag of dicks. One of the others could fill him in on the details for the day.

Me: Let's plan on one for today. It's going to be hot, but I'm hoping Kai might spoil me with some more of his grilling talents? We have steaks in the freezer that I can get out.

I added the fingers crossed emoji and hit send. Gran and I both laughed when my phone started pinging out of control.

Kai: Sprout, I will spoil you with anything you desire. Just tell me your wishes and I will grant them.

Cam: You are nothing but a butt kisser, K.

Kai: Okay, but have you seen her butt?

Fish: He's got a point. It's a really, reallllly nice butt.

My face went up in flames, and Gran gave me a knowing smirk before she tsked and lifted her mug like she was the Queen of fucking England, pinky finger out, and took a small sip before placing it back on the table and using her hand to fan her face.

"Oh my gods, stop it. I can't deal with their shit and yours all at once," I laughed, which was quickly smothered by the thought that in a little bit, I was going to be surrounded by them with no escape. "You all are going to kill me later." I sighed, not hating it in the least.

Gran cackled, her face lighting up with excitement. "You already know this will be a memorable evening. Best to embrace it, child. I'm going to go do some stuff at my house for now, but I'll make my way back over here at some point. Probably when all the fresh mage meat arrives." She stood and practically skipped her way to the back porch. "No need to call me when they get here. Sensing hot men is my second affinity!"

May the moon have mercy.

Cam: It is the best butt. You do have a point, Kai.

Kai: Thank you. I love being right all the time.

Fish: You wish, furry fucker.

Me: You guys are killing me. Kai, if you grill for me I'll let you feel both butt cheeks.

Cam: Hey, that's not fair. What can I do to get the same reward?

Fish: * eyes emoji *

Cam: FYI, Kai just jumped up, muttering something about needing to go to the store for spices and other essentials. In his excitement for potential ass pats, he forgot his phone.

Fish: I think it's safe to assume we're grilling, sweetheart.

Me: Yay! I'll think about what you can do to earn... rewards. ;) Oh, and someone tell Sloane about when to be here.

Fish: I'll tell him... for a kiss.

Me: Guess we'll see...

Standing up, I slipped my phone into the pocket of my yoga pants and prepped some food for later. It didn't take long to wrap the potatoes in foil and put them in the cauldron pot to slow cook for a few hours. Deciding it would be best to just get as much done as possible now, I pulled out a large bowl and cut up ingredients for a fresh salad. Steak, potatoes, and salad, my absolute favorite meal.

A small sneeze from the direction of the mudroom alerted me to Maven's arrival. He made a beeline for me, plopping his ass down on the floor with a huff of indignation.

"What's that attitude about, mister?" I narrowed my eyes at him, our sassiness equally matched.

He snort-sneezed at me again before turning his back and heading toward his empty food bowl. No, it was more like he *stormed* across the kitchen to his bowl and used his paw to flip it over before turning his head back to me, eyes narrowed to slits.

"Do not act like you didn't eat last night before bed, you chunky animal," I scolded him... but I was actually a softie, so I flipped his bowl upright and gave him a hefty scoop of food.

He didn't spare me a second thought, munching to his grouchy heart's desire. Whatever, I knew he loved me deep down in his tiny black heart. He'd softened a lot toward me in the four years we'd been together. After seeing him sneaking around the property for a couple of weeks, I finally let him in the house one night during a storm, and he just never left.

My body was a live wire, so amped up that sitting still was basically impossible. After pacing around the kitchen, making sure everything was clean and tidy, I headed for the linen closet in the hallway to snag some fresh sheets for my bed, and towels for the bathrooms.

As I stacked my arm with towels, something fluttered to the floor. Bending down to grab it, I realized it was a picture of Gran, Laurie, and myself from the grand opening of The Pig. Laurie had blown into town in her usual shit storm fashion, trying to make my successes somehow a product of the blood we shared.

The photo had been hanging on the fridge for a couple of years, for Gran's sake, not mine, until one visit in particular when she'd gotten really mouthy with Gran. It had pissed me off so badly that I'd taken down every picture of her in my home, forgetting I'd even stuck this one in here. I was in the middle, Laurie off to the side. Smiling, I ripped the photo so that she was removed and stuffed her fake ass smirk into my back pocket, leaving Gran and me smiling at the camera with The Pig in the background. It was like she was never there at all. *How fitting.*

I snatched the dirty hand towel from the bathroom and hung up the new one before going back out to the kitchen to stick the picture on the fridge. Laurie didn't get to steal away all of my proud moments just because she was a jerk. No, I'd worked my ass off, gotten through college, and put so much work into my store. Wiping my forehead after my eye stung from an unexpected droplet, I realized I'd started to sweat, my heart rate steadily picking up. Anger was rising like a high tide inside my body, and I was beginning to feel like I would burn up from the inside out.

Who the hell does that to their own child? Rains on their parade, and belittles them? With a huff, I turned and ran up the steps, ignoring the little part of me that whispered I might be reacting a bit irrationally. I needed a cold shower. *Stat.* Once I got in the bathroom, I peeled my damp shirt off, followed by the soaked sports bra I'd been wearing. *Why am I sweating like a sinner in church?* I was practically panting by the time I got naked and stumbled into the shower's icy cold spray. The water pounded against my fiery pale skin, and it might have been my imagination, but I could have sworn I heard a sizzle as steam rose off of my flesh.

Practicing deep breathing, I tried to rein in my temper. *Focus, Saige. Today is a good day. Don't let that witch bitch ruin this for you.* Shaking my head as if that could banish her from my mind and my veins, I put all thoughts of Laurie in a metaphorical box and slammed it shut. All of these changes my body was going through were starting to become worrisome, the increased heat, moodiness, restless sleep, the magic shit show, and the list went on. The only thing staving off my anxiety at this point was knowing that I had Gran and my guys behind me, and I trusted them all. Even Sloane.

I'd finally begun to cool down as I soaped my body up, thoughts of Kai, Cam, and Fish filling my head as my hands trailed down my breasts. My nipples popped their rosy little heads up at the attention, so I tweaked them a little bit because I figured it'd be a jerk move to not reward them for being so responsive.

Ever since that night with Cam, my libido had been awakened like a bear that had been hibernating for months and was now starving. One hand trailed further south while the other reached out to turn the handle, making the water warmer. *Maybe I could convince one of them to sleep over tonight... or more than one.* With that thought, I slipped my hand between my legs and felt how wet I was just from the thought of them.

Would Kai and Cam be willing to share me at the same time? I could only imagine how that would play out. Visions danced through my brain as I brought myself to climax. It didn't take long, and I could bet it wouldn't in real life either. My mind was already sifting through ways to get them to agree to sleeping over. With a grin on my face, I hopped out of the shower and spent about an hour getting ready. Curling my long red hair so that it fell around my shoulders in big waves, I went for a natural look with my make-up.

There was a dress I'd been dying to wear but hadn't had the opportunity. Pulling it from my closet, I ran my hand down the soft white cotton material, loving its cheery pattern of yellow lemons with green leaves. In pure mid-century fashion, the dress fit snugly like a corset until it met my waist where it flared out slightly, hitting about mid-calf. Slipping it over my head, I shimmied it down and whispered a spell, the dress squeezing closed around my chest as the zipper was pulled upward. I couldn't imagine how human women must struggle without magic.

Fluffing up my boobs, I studied myself in the full-length mirror that hung on the wall, a dark smile spreading across my face. I felt *amazing*. My self-esteem had never been low, despite Bryce trying very hard to that effect, but lately, I felt like I'd been given an extra boost. *Doesn't take a seer to figure out why that was.* Before I could get lost in another fun round of thinking about my mages, a rumble in the distance had me jumping. *Oh shit, what time is it?* Spinning around, I glanced at the alarm clock, and sure enough, it was two minutes to one. *Fuck.*

Swiping on some tinted lip gloss, the menacing roar of approaching bad boys caused my stomach to flip, and I darted out of my room, flying down the steps just in time for the sound of crunching gravel to hit my ears. Swiping my hands down my dress, I inhaled, trying to calm my wild heart. Forcing myself to walk like a normal person and not a five year old all sauced up on sugar, I made my way to the door just as Kai bounded into my field of vision with a wolfish smile lighting up his beautiful face. The screen door flew open as he used his magic to remove the barrier between us, reaching for me with his free arm and making me giggle when he wrapped his arms around my waist and squeezed. And then he just *had* to start sniffing my head again.

"Hi, Sprout. Hope you're ready for the best meat of your life," he said, stepping back with a wink.

Fucking hell.

Before I could sputter a response to that, Sloane's voice broke through the moment.

"Keep moving, fluffy boy. My arms are full here."

"Lead me to my creation station, Sprout." Kai grabbed my hand, and I laughed as I pulled him through the house, the rest of the guys following behind us.

"This is my kitchen, feel free to make yourselves at home. You can put your stuff down on the table for now if you want," I offered, turning around to look at everyone. Damn, my house suddenly felt a whole lot smaller with these four in here.

Sloane walked over to the counter, starting to empty his arms. My eyes tracked his movement, and I was about to go help him put whatever it was away when a huge shadow fell over me. *Daddy's home.* Hahaha, I'm losing my mind. But, no, for real. He's here.

"Little witch, you look good enough to eat." Cam's deep timbre caused me to instantly squeeze my thighs together. He spun me around, resting his hands on my hips as he ran his eyes down my figure while I peeked up at him from under my eyelashes and smirked. Since we were blatantly checking each other out, I took my time ogling him. A red and black buffalo plaid buttoned-down shirt hugged his chest and shoulders, sleeves rolled up to his elbows, leaving his painted forearms on display, and what a sight they were. Black jeans completed his outfit, and fuck, he looked good. Bringing my attention back up to his face with a clearing of his throat, he smiled smugly. He knew he was hot shit. *He's a good Daddy, I shouldn't antagonize him. Pfft.*

"You look alright," I deadpanned, turning for a split second before his hand circled my wrist and I was spun back against his chest. His eyes glittered with unspoken promises, and I swore to the moon I wanted to find out what each entailed. Naked.

Dropping his head to my ear, he whispered, "Playing games already, baby? We have a long afternoon ahead of us, but don't think I won't put you over my knee in front of everyone in this room if you continue being a brat and trying to get a rise out of me. That dress will flip up real nice and easy."

Damn near took all of my strength but I suppressed the shiver that wanted to claim my body at his threat. My inner witch was pushing real hard for me to say something bratty, and my ass cheeks were begging for his hands, but no. *As much as I want to play with him, I want to do it later when we won't have to stop.*

Releasing me, he stepped back, holding his hands out in challenge, a wide smile spreading across his handsome face. Narrowing my eyes at him, I blew him a kiss, but Fischer snatched the invisible gesture out of the air, pretending to eat it.

Rubbing his belly after his obviously filling snack, Fish shoved Cam in the pec. "My turn, BFG. Go pillage some townspeople or something."

Shocked for a moment, I stood there with everyone else before we all lost it.

"Oh, you're suddenly a comedian?" Cam choked out between laughs, Kai and Sloane cracking up along with us, the argument they'd been having over which spices to use ending in favor of a good burn. Judging by how stunned everyone was at first, I had to guess my guppy didn't usually crack jokes. That made me sad but also happy that he felt comfortable enough around me to let loose a little.

"But BFG doesn't pillage! He's friendly. That's what the F stands for, bro," Kai called out, taking it upon himself to educate his friend.

Fischer pulled out a chair at the table, motioning for me to sit. Obliging, I dropped into my seat, and he sat down beside me.

"Ah, well, in *his* case," he shot back, pointing at Cam, "the F stands for fuckin'. Big fuckin' giant. Suits him better." Even when the laughter started again, his eyes stayed locked on mine, and I smiled at him as he ran a hand through his thick curly hair. "Hi, sweetheart," he whispered with a blush, the words just for me. Gods, he was the cutest.

"Hi, guppy," I replied, and his blush deepened. Not giving it any thought, I grabbed his hand and locked our fingers together. "I'm glad you're here," I confessed. Leaning over, I pressed a kiss to the corner of his mouth. As I started to lean back, he moved forward and wrapped his free hand around the nape of my neck, pulling me in again.

Kissing Fischer was sensual. His kisses, although intense, were thorough and slow. He never rushed, his tongue dipping in and out and pressing up against mine in a dance that told me when we did get more physical with each other, it was going to be like a bomb detonating. He swallowed the moan he'd coaxed out, his oak-colored eyes sparkling as he pulled back, biting down on his bottom lip.

A throat clearing had me turning my head to look at the men behind us, and it seemed the three of them had gotten just as caught up in the moment as we had. Now I was the one with red cheeks, and *that* was the moment my Gran decided to make her entrance. *Of course.*

"Sorry, I'm a little late. I just had to finish up a call with my dance instructor," she called from the back porch, and my brows furrowed. *What dance instructor?*

Gran sashayed into the kitchen, and I almost choked. What in creation was she wearing? Skin tight black booty shorts and a hot pink sequined tank top that had been cut to ribbons from the waist up to her tits.

"Gran," I croaked as I stood up so fast the chair almost toppled behind me.

She ignored me as her eyes flitted around the room, no doubt taking in the fine specimens before her. I just stood there like an asshole, my mouth opening and closing like a fish out of water.

"Greetings, boys. I'm Saige's grandmother, but feel free to call me Bette," she announced, strutting over to where I was standing. Fischer stood up, wide-eyed and just as stunned as I was. Luckily, there was a casanova amongst us, and Kai strode toward Gran with no hesitation.

"It's a pleasure to meet you, Bette. My name is Kai. You look fantastic, by the way," he told her, lifting her hand and dropping a kiss on the top.

"I know. Thanks," she said, giggling.

Cam let out a deep laugh, coming over to introduce himself.

"I'm Cam, thank you for sharing Saige with us today." He smiled, extending his hand.

Gran shook his hand, and quick as a whip, she replied, "Nice to meet you, Cam, but I think we all know I'm not the one doing the sharing around these parts."

I swore to the stars that Sloane was choking.

"Gran," I scolded, but she just waved me off.

"And who do we have here?" she asked, her focus was solely on the man at my side.

"Fischer, ma'am," he replied, seeming to have regained his composure while she'd harassed Cam and Kai. Gran nodded and looked to the corner where Sloane was still rooted in place by the fridge.

I swore to all that was cosmic, if he was a dick to her, I'd kick him right in the nuts.

Sloane moved across the kitchen, flashing Gran a roguish smile that pulled a laugh from Kai and an eye roll from Fish. *Great, this is probably going to be eventful.*

"I'm Sloane, and I thought I had already met all of the women in this town. You've clearly been hiding because I definitely would've remembered someone so beautiful. I can see where Saige gets her looks," he schmoozed as he pulled her in for a *hug*. A motherfucking hug. I didn't miss the way Cam's eyes widened or the gasp that fell from Fischer's lips. My eyebrows lifted to my hairline as I observed this bizarre behavior, and I had to wonder if perhaps he was drunk or had gotten a personality transplant in the past two minutes.

"Ah, yes. Sloane, the boy who has been running around town the past week flattering all of the old women. Tell me, my boy, is that why you're not included in this... harem of my granddaughter's? You have a fetish for old ladies?" she asked, holding both of his hands as she pulled away from him.

Kai doubled over in laughter, his arms wrapped around his trim torso, while Fischer had a look of pure amusement painting his features. I choked when I saw Cam nodding enthusiastically, his top knot bobbing with the over the top motion.

"Yes, that's exactly what his fetish is, Bette. Do you know of any single ladies who might like their own personal boy toy?" Cam lifted an eyebrow, trying to fight the smile that was threatening to break free.

Sloane dropped Gran's hands and opened his mouth to say something, but it appeared that the wily Bette Wildes had stunned him speechless. Laughter tumbled out of me as I watched him struggle.

"I-you-no. I do *not* have an old woman fetish." He turned and glared at Cam, Kai taking that opportunity to nod vigorously behind Sloane's back, indicating that *that* was a bunch of bullshit.

"My boy Roger has told me all about your little warfare, by the way," Gran divulged.

Sloane's brow furrowed. "Who the fuck is Roger?"

"Roger," Gran repeated, flicking her wrists like she was talking to a dumbass, "'about yay tall, looks like he hasn't bought clothes since nineteen seventy six?"

"Oh, you mean Randy! Yeah, uh, I've met him," Sloane said sheepishly, his cheeks starting to turn red.

"No, his name is Roger. Randy Roger. I gave him the name Randy because he's got some grabby fucking hands, and everyone knows it, too," Gran explained while all of the guys laughed. "But Sloane, I wanted to let you know that I heard about the Battle of Thyme. Witnesses are calling it The Calamitous Cucumber Carnage of twenty-twenty, and I've heard there's video footage. I can't wait 'til I lay eyes on that!" She threw her head back and laughed and laughed.

"What in the hell is she talking about right now?" Fischer whisper yelled at Sloane and me, but I was clueless, so I focused my attention on the blushing mage.

"Shhh. I'll tell you guys later," Sloane gritted out.

Gran lifted her arm to Sloane's shoulder. "Come now, boy. Don't be shy! You've been promoted to Captain Cuke-zuke. This calls for a celebration!"

A wheezing sound came from the kitchen island where Kai looked like he was going to pass out, clearly enjoying seeing big tough Sloane get his balls handed to him by a scantily clad old witch. *Not gonna lie, I'm loving it, too. And I* will *get my hands on this cucumber war video.*

"Okay, now that we're all introduced, can I get anyone a drink? We can hang out on the patio while Kai grills and talk about all of the craziness that's been going on?" I suggested, and everyone agreed, Sloane more eagerly than the rest.

Kai headed to the fridge and pulled out the steaks I'd put in there earlier then passed out beers to everyone. Gran asked for a glass of red wine, so I opened a bottle and poured her a glass that she floated toward the back porch, sequins and tassels just a shimmerin' and a shakin'.

"This way, boys," she called out, not turning to see if they were following. *She marches to the beat of her own drum, always has and always will.*

"Well, that was interesting," Fischer blurted, and the rest of us laughed.

"Yeah, she can be intense. She's the best person I know, though, and you will always know where you stand with her. She couldn't sugarcoat anything even if she was holding a five-pound bag of sugar." I mean, I had warned them, and explained how eccentric she was. But explaining Bette Wildes and *experiencing* Bette Wildes were two very, very different things.

"She's freaking awesome, Sprout. My kind of people," Kai declared as he began working his magic on the steak. "I'll just get these spiced up, and then I'll join you guys outside. If you could light the grill, that would be perfect," he said to me, before dropping a kiss on my cheek.

I nodded uselessly, Kai already too in the zone to notice.

"Yeah, she's a real gem," Sloane muttered under his breath, back to being the resident grump.

"Shut up, Captain Cuke-zuke," Cam teased as he slipped his hand into mine. "Come on, little witch. Let's not keep your gran waiting."

I allowed him to pull me in the direction that she had disappeared, Sloane and Fish following behind us. *Overall, I think that went better than I could've hoped.* I mean, I didn't expect her to show up dressed like that, but I shouldn't have been surprised. Gran was savage. *Let's just hope we all make it through this little gathering without anything too crazy happening.*

Even with that last thought, my inner witch was already laughing at me. She knew just as well as I did that the chances of that happening were slim to none.

Sloane

Chapter Sixteen

My brothers had all lost their nuts, and I'd bet I'd find them if I checked Red's pockets. She was smooth, I'd give her that. That woman had infiltrated my group in a little over a week. She'd embedded herself so deeply that she could honestly have a job at Radical if Larson ever needed an undercover agent. Even I was starting to warm up to her. The guys were happy; Fischer particularly had a lighthearted look in his eyes that I had rarely seen. It was obvious we all needed a break from work, and I was willing to take the load so that they could spend time with their girl. Blow off some steam, fuck her out of their systems, and then we would move on again. Women never lasted long around us. We never stuck around long enough for that to happen, and even if we did, there had never been anyone who we came close to considering, and there was no reason to think that this time would be different. That was the nature of who we were and what we did.

It was luck, I realized, that we were here for work because something was definitely up with this witch and her property, and I had *a lot* of questions. On Friday, when Fish had brought her home from their date, I had dipped inside to use the bathroom.

My mind was moving a mile a minute, trying to put this puzzle together. Why the fuck would demons be messing with someone as sweet and innocent as Red? Yeah, I'd been suspicious of her, but I was suspicious of everyone. Even that fat ass pug Baked Potato who strutted around in a CovenFit tank top. But I just couldn't see Red as being malicious, no matter how I tried to make that work in my mind.

After I got done pissing, I washed my hands and looked in the mirror, giving myself a pep talk. Do not be a dickhead to your brothers' girl. *Groaning, I looked for a towel to dry my hands but came up short. The hook where one should be hanging was bare. Not seeing anywhere extras might be stored, I headed into the hallway.* Bingo. *Opening up the built-in closet across the hall, I snatched a gray towel, a photo fluttering to the floor and landing on my boot.* What? Why the fuck would that be in there? *Drying my hands, I bent down to retrieve it, freezing in place when I registered who was in the picture.*

Laura. The woman we were searching for was standing right next to Red in front of the magic shop, her gran taking up her other side. What the fuck? *My eyes bounced from Laura to Saige to Gran and back. Sweat rolled down my spine as my body processed what my brain already knew to be true.* Laura is Saige's mother. *Flipping the picture over, the year 2010 was written and underneath that, 'Bette, Saige, and Laurie.' I quickly snapped a couple of pictures of the front and the back and then returned the damning photo to its place. Spinning on my heel, I tossed the clean towel on the hook in the bathroom and walked out of her house.* Holy shit.

Of course, I'd texted Larson the moment we'd gotten back to the apartment. If Red could lead us to wherever her mother was, this assignment would be over real fucking quick. Larson had called me immediately, sounding excited about this discovery, but I detected a hint of wariness in his deep voice. After filling him in on the guys and the relationships they'd built with Saige, he ordered me not to tell them what I'd found. Since they were now emotionally involved with Red, their professionalism could be compromised. Being so close to the mark, he couldn't expect them to do what might need to be done.

I kept my mouth shut about what I'd discovered, promising my loyalty and silence to our boss. A little voice in the back of my head tried to protest, but when the time came to leave this place, they'd thank me for protecting them. This was definitely for the best. Now I just had to keep the mission moving forward so we could get this wrapped up. Larson asked me to retrieve one of Red's hairs so that he could run a test to verify her relationship to Laura, and that was what led me to this moment.

Cam and Red were hand in hand, heading outside, her head tilted up as she laughed at whatever he was saying. *Ugh, when this goes south, my brother is going to be fucking wrecked.* My hand landed on Fischer's shoulder, his stride coming to a stop as he looked at me in question.

"I'm gonna take a piss. I'll be out in a few," I told him, running my hand down his muscular arm and giving a gentle squeeze.

"Sure. Bring out a few more beers when you come." He pulled away, heading after the others.

Backtracking to the kitchen, Kai was bent over, sprinkling all kinds of bullshit over the meat. He looked like a fucking flavor fairy, coating his meal in fairy dust with a dramatic flick of his fingers. Shaking my head, I strolled right past him without him even noticing. *Now, where would the princess sleep?* Spotting the stairs straight ahead, I bounded up. One door at the top of the landing was cracked, and I poked my head inside. *Oh yes, this is definitely her bedroom.*

So many goddamn plants filled the green witch's space, I felt like I'd fallen into *The Jungle Book*, but when I looked closer, many of the green leaves were turning brown. I was about to check her pillow for loose hair, but then I noticed the en-suite. Perfect. On the counter sat a brush, and I quickly stuffed a clump of her hair in the zip-lock baggie I'd stored in my back pocket. She'd never even know. After the bag was tucked away in my pocket, I took care of the last step: notifying Larson.

Larson: Good work, son. Now, I want you to earn this woman's trust. Work your way into a relationship with her just like the others.

My eyes flew over that text message several times, my body stiffening as his words infiltrated my brain. He wants me to *date* her? That little voice was back again, telling me all of the ways that this was despicable, especially because of the way my brothers felt about her.

Me: Sir, with all due respect, I don't exactly think that's a great idea. When the guys find out about all of this, I think they're going to be really upset. I don't need to be romantic with her in order to make this assignment a success.

Larson: It's a direct order. While you may be able to get the job done otherwise, it's not something I'm comfortable risking. Not being this close.

Fuuuuuck. This wasn't good. They would probably be able to forgive me for keeping my particular orders a secret since that was just the nature of our careers. We took orders, then we executed them. An operative was worthless if he broke his boss' explicit directives.They'd be heartbroken and pissed when they discovered I'd known about Laura being Saige's mother, but there was just no fucking way they'd be able to avoid raising suspicion if I told them. That would put the whole assignment at risk, and I wasn't willing to do that. Larson was right; they were too invested now to be able to hide their feelings.

Groaning, I ran my hand through my hair, swiping the strands out of my eyes. Knowing that Larson wanted this mission to be a success, I decided that this could be an opportunity to push and get something that we wanted in return.

Me: They are taken with her, sir. If I do this, I'd like to request permission for a personal assignment. One that helps Cam finally get some answers, sir. The opportunity could go a ways toward mending the bridges that will be damaged by this.

I held my breath as sweat broke out across my forehead. *Damn, I probably overstepped.* Just as I was about to pocket my phone, Larson began typing his response.

Larson: Fine. I will grant you and the team leave to pursue whatever you need to. They won't harbor any ill feelings toward you. You're doing this for them. For him.

Me: I'll get it done. Expect the hair to be delivered on Tuesday. I'll send it first thing tomorrow morning and overnight it.

Stuffing the phone back into my pocket, I slipped back down the stairs and stopped at the fridge to get some more drinks. I nearly dropped them a moment later when I saw the picture from the other night stuck on the freezer door with a magnet, Laura ripped clean out of the frame. *Appears to be some family drama. Fuck, I love drama. Not in my personal life, but in my work? Fuck yeah, keeps my blood pumping and my brain working.*

Kai was gone, so he must've finished his marinating meat masterpiece. Passing through the kitchen, I made my way outside, nearly dropping the beers for a second time when I found Saige's Gran practically grinding up on K as he laid the steaks on the grill. Cam was losing it, and Red was perched on Fish's lap, his arms wrapped around her hips, matching smiles on their faces while they watched Kai as he soaked up all of Bette's attention. He shook his ass right up against hers and spun her under his arm before dipping her in a dramatic move that had her hooting. *Dude loves attention, doesn't matter who it's from. Dicks, chicks, or old ladies in this case.*

Fischer's eyes locked on mine as I sank into my seat, my eyes flicking to where Red's hands were running through his dark, thick curls, and I *might* have put the beer down on the table with a little more force than necessary. *Fuck. I'm feeling out of control, and I need to process. Does it bother me that Fischer is seeing Red and cuddling up with her like a puppy? No.* But shit, even as I thought that my stomach rolled uncomfortably. *What is going on with me? I don't get jealous.* Did it bother me that I saw this ending only one way, with all of my brothers being heartbroken? Yes, yes, it fucking did. Maybe Saige had nothing to do with her mother? I'd never heard her mention her. We had only been invited to meet Gran, and I wondered if one of the others had any insight to that.

Everyone was laughing and joking back and forth while I sat and stewed over the best way to handle everything. She owed us an explanation, and I was tired of waiting. Patient, I was not. Taking a deep breath, I mentally practiced what I wanted to say, so it hopefully wouldn't come out wrong. I needed to win her over, so I willed myself to tame the monster who lurked beneath my skin. *Yeah, that'll work.*

The words burst from my mouth without permission, interrupting the conversation. "This is fun and all, but let's talk about the fact that demons have it out for Red."

Everyone's eyes zeroed in on me, most of them narrowed glares. *Well, shit sticks. I guess I need to try harder next time.* Holding both hands up in a placating manner, I continued, "Look, I'm not trying to be an ass, but I think we all need to get on the same page here about what's going on."

Cam opened his mouth to scold me, no doubt, but I was surprised when Red cut him off.

"No, he's right." She looked from Cam to me. "There have been strange things happening over the past week, too many to be coincidence or ignored. I'd be lying if I said I wasn't scared, because I am."

Kai growled low in his chest over her admission, and a spark flew from Cam's fingertips. *Damn, their feelings are running deeper than I thought.*

Red glanced at her gran, and the woman gave a slight nod. Saige took a deep breath, Fish's thumb rubbing over the top of her hand in small, reassuring circles. I hadn't missed the way his hold had tightened on her when she admitted she was scared.

"I've seen demons, first at the shop last week and then in my bedroom on Friday morning," she said, suddenly standing up. Fish reluctantly released her from his arms, his focus solely on the witch who'd captivated him so thoroughly.

Suddenly, everyone was talking except for myself and Bette. Leaning back into my chair, I observed Red as she paced back and forth across the paved patio, her worry shining clearly through her gaze that landed on mine every so often. Catching a glimpse of pink sequins, my eyes flicked to her gran, wanting to see her reaction to everyone losing their shit. I kept my features flat when I found myself suddenly staring into her cornflower blue eyes. Bette's eyebrow raised, acknowledging she'd caught me studying her granddaughter. A slow smirk appeared, and I returned the expression, earning me a subtle nod of... understanding? Something that felt vaguely reminiscent of approval. Uncomfortable with that thought, I focused on the group again, the guys having finally settled down enough for Saige to continue explaining.

"I didn't realize what was happening when it first started. The town seers showed up at the shop on Wednesday, talking a bunch of nonsense about a prophecy they had been blessed with, and it involved all of us," she said, looking to Cam, Kai, and then Fischer before her gaze landed on mine. *The fuck do I have to do with anything?* "I saw the demons while they were in their trance, saying things I didn't understand. Then I saw them a second time in my bedroom, but Gran interrupted, and they disappeared. I was scared shitless, so I confessed everything to her despite the fact that I thought I was going crazy. I had no clue that demons were real. Apparently, they were just projections, but that doesn't change the fact that I'm the only one who's seen them."

Everyone was shifting uncomfortably as she paused, looking vulnerable and lost. Now knowing that she'd thought she was losing it, the urge to get her out of her head bloomed in my mind, shocking the hell out of me. Fischer had always told me I enjoyed the role of provider, which I shot down immediately every time he brought it up. Now, though? I was wondering if he might be onto something there. *Ugh, my head is a fucking mess, and I'm giving myself whiplash.*

Red cleared her throat, her face projecting the worry in her heart. "That's not all, unfortunately. I've noticed some changes with myself. Using my magic has taken on an almost euphoric reaction, like I'd imagine taking a hit of drugs would. When I get upset about something, my anger flares instantaneously, and I've *never* been quick to anger. Hell, I never even get full blown pissed off! Today, I started sweating moments after feeling angry, and a cold shower was the only thing that helped," she huffed, clearly frustrated with the mountain of shit that was piling up in her life.

"Tell us what the prophecy says, little witch," Cam said encouragingly, giving Red a little boost.

She sighed, and we all held our breath as she recited the words:

> "A witch, a mix of green and red,
> Save a race before they're dead.
> Hurry, witch, find your five,
> If there is hope to survive.
>
> Change, rise, manifest,
> A soul so pure, soon possessed.
> Before the year of two and eight
> The chosen one must find her mates.
>
> If she should fail to meet her task,
> To another the role will pass.
> Evil will consume her heart,
> Her soul captured by the dark."

The silence was deafening, everyone's minds likely running a hundred miles a second trying to work that puzzle out.

"Did the demons say anything to you?" Kai questioned seriously, his usual joking tone long gone.

"There were two of them, and they were talking to each other, something about finding me, how their master would be pleased, my name, and the word 'soon.'" I studied her as a visible shudder took over her body.

Cam walked up behind her and pulled her back against his front, his huge arms encasing her waist. She dropped her head back against his chest, the quick rise and fall of her chest abating almost immediately. His presence alone was enough to calm her. That was Cam, though. Everyone felt safe with him around; he made sure of it. He was one of the best men I had ever known, and he'd been dealt a really shit hand with his past. We were similar in that regard, but while there was hope for closure with Cam, there was no fixing my past. Having grown up with a piece of shit father who beat my mother almost daily until I was old enough to handle an ass whooping, I suppose a rough around the edges exterior was just bred into who I was.

Anger issues were common among Pyros. Fuckin' cliche, but true nonetheless. My picture was probably in the dictionary next to the term 'hot head.' I'd die before I'd ever raise a hand to a woman, though. The thought of it alone had my skin heating, and I took several deep breaths to stave off the oncoming flare of anger.

Fischer must've picked up on some of my emotions because he started tapping his fingers on the table, drawing my attention to him and out of my own head. I flashed a cocky smile and ran my hand through my dark hair, swiping it out of my eyes.

"There are a lot of things in there that line up, Sprout, as well as a lot of things that don't. That's the joy of prophecies; you can interpret them so many different ways, not knowing how things will turn out exactly," Kai told her, turning his back to the grill and crossing his arms across his chest.

"He's right. I can definitely draw some hypotheses, but it talks about five mates, change, manifestation? I have no idea what that means..." Fish trailed off, focusing on something in the distance, probably sorting through his thoughts.

"When's your birthday?" I asked despite already knowing that information.

"June twenty-fourth, in like three weeks."

"Okay, so on the off chance that this is actually about us," I contemplated aloud, circling my finger around, including myself and my brothers, "there are only four of us. Who's the fifth?" A growl tumbled from Kai's mouth as he snatched the meat off the grill and slapped it down on a plate, his lip lifted in a snarl when he turned back to face us. No doubt Bagheera didn't want to hear shit about another possible boyfriend.

"Kai, it's okay," Saige cooed, stepping away from Cam and moving to the snarling shifter then wrapping her arms around his waist and laying her cheek against his chest. The aggressive sounds slowly turned into purrs, both the man and the beast settling down. *For the love of Jupiter's cock, these whipped assholes...*

"Let's move this inside, boys. Everyone can process this information overload once we refresh our drinks. Plus, I'm starving, and I do love a big hunk of meat," Bette purred, trailing her fingers over Fish's arm as she swept past him with a surprising amount of grace.

"For the love of the moon," Red groaned as she checked to make sure Fish wasn't offended.

"She's fine, sweetheart. Honestly, she's hysterical," he assured her, pushing to his feet. Red reached out for his hand, and they laughed together as they walked inside, leaving Cam, K, and I alone. *Okay, now that Red's gone, let's take care of this.*

Holding off to speak until the door closed behind them, I just had to ask, "I mean, does anybody else think it's weird that

THE MAGIC OF DISCOVERY

the ground is tainted with demon magic, Red is seeing demons, the seers had a vision involving the five of us, and all of this starts happening right when we show up to town? What about the fact that she's showing some telltale demon qualities?" I threw it all out there, leaning back in my chair with my knees splayed wide.

Growling came from K, low and menacing, again.

"Dude, get your shit together! Your panther is in a fucking tizzy over this witch, and you need to settle the fuck down!"

We stared each other down, not like a dominance thing, but in a 'come on, you stubborn fuck, get a grip' kind of way.

Cam grunted, breaking the tension and leveling me with a glare that said he was clearly done with my shit. "She's not a demon. That's not even possible. We've seen her cast magic, and I've never heard of a mixing of the two races before. Maybe a possession of some type? That was mentioned in the prophecy, wasn't it?" He crossed his arms over his wide chest, pausing for a moment. "What I find bizarre is that Larson's been looking for this witch Laura, and she happens to pop up here of all places, then we arrive, and shit starts jumping off. It's too weird to be a coincidence. She's gotta have something to do with all this fuckery."

Oh, brother. If only you knew how much she had to do with your woman. I expected guilt to hit me, but it didn't come. Instead, sadness did. When all of this turned to shit, these guys were going to be downright miserable to be around, and oh my gods, the feelings. So many fucking feelings. I might have to live in a hole for a while or something.

"Let's get inside and eat. We can discuss it further tonight after we leave. I just want to make sure that Sprout has a nice evening with her *boyfriends* and her gran," Kai chuckled. Having finally snapped out of that growly shit, he carried the tray of steaks toward the sliding doors, a smile on his face. "That old witch is next level nuts. My only wish is to be the male version of her when I'm her age. In fact, I'm going to make it my personal mission."

Following K inside, we walked in to see Fish helping Red carry stuff to the table and Bette laying down the final place setting. Dropping down into a chair, I watched as Cam and Kai went to help gather up the rest of the food, Cam begging him not to become the male Gran. *He's already at least sixty-five percent on the gran scale. It's too late to stop that train.* Awareness prickled along the back of my neck, the sensation of being watched. I flicked my gaze over to the older Wildes witch and raised a brow. Beckoning me closer with a dramatic flick of her hand, I leaned in to see what fresh hell would come from her mouth this time.

Whispering so that only I could hear, she said, "There's darkness inside of you, child."

I scoffed, "Ya don't say?"

Her face remained serious, a no-nonsense set to her previously smiling face. "So tell me why, when you focus on Saige, does the turbulence in your eyes fade away? Why are you fighting against what you need?"

"I'm not. I don't know what you think you've seen, but I have everything I want," I whispered harshly, not dropping eye contact. Why did that feel like a lie, though?

"Need and want are two very different things, but it's not only you who will suffer if you continue to lie to yourself. She needs you, too. Something is brewing, and you're all supposed to be there with her. Get your head out of your ass," she bit out. Pulling away from her, I slumped back against the chair.

"Everything okay?" Looking up, Red was standing between us, taking in both of our faces, and I hadn't even heard her approach. *Damn it, Sloane. Keep your head in the game.*

"I was just getting to know Mr. Sullivan a little better, child. Let's eat."

Slicing and dicing my steak, I silently listened while the guys asked questions about the visions and changes that she'd been experiencing, Red answering each one. When Cam demanded to know what security precautions were in place around her house, Gran explained everything in detail. Everyone seemed satisfied with her explanation, especially when she informed them that she'd given The Pig the same treatment.

Remaining quiet through dinner, Bette's words ran through my mind in a loop. Why did I feel so unsettled, like she'd seen a piece of me that I wasn't comfortable sharing? Did I need Red? No, this was a fucking mission. I needed to keep my head and focus. Though it was good to know that her gran wouldn't suspect a thing when I made moves on Red. *I have to. I'm doing it for Cam.* Now that Larson had granted permission for a personal assignment, that was my goal. It didn't hurt that my career would also be getting a boost, but the difference was that now it wasn't my main motivation.

Once dinner was over, Bette addressed everyone. "Boys, it has been a lovely evening. I'm happy I finally got to meet the men who were exceptional enough to catch Saige's attention. With everything going on, I think we all need to be diligent and aware at all times. Keep communication open so that nothing falls between the cracks. For now, let's keep everything we discussed within this circle. The last thing we need is for this to leak to the town. It'll be chaos, especially since most don't know demons exist. How did you know about them, anyway?" She raised an eyebrow and crossed her arms on the table.

"We learned about demons in our schooling, ma'am," Fish smoothly provided.

"Trust us when we say we can, and will, do everything in our power to protect your granddaughter," Cam promised, the sincerity in his tone causing my heart to skip a few beats. K and Fish were nodding in agreement. Lifting an arm, I ran my fingers through my hair until I felt eyes on me once more. Red was studying me from across the table, an indecipherable look on her face, like she was once again trying to figure me out but coming up short. The corner of my mouth lifted in a smirk, and I winked at her. She narrowed her eyes at me and brought her hand up to her face, propping her chin on her palm then tucking every finger down into her fist except the middle one.

Without thought, a bark of laughter escaped me. Everyone looked at me to see what was so funny during such a serious conversation, and Red put her middle finger away, feigning innocence with a shrug when their gazes landed on her. Damn if that didn't ignite some fire in my bones.

"Sorry, didn't mean to interrupt," I apologized, unfazed by Fischer's stare that told me he knew I was full of shit.

"How about you three help me clean this stuff up, and Sloane and Saige can go out to the gardens to see if he can figure out anything with her magic?" Gran suggested, and when my eyes snapped to hers, she feigned her innocence even more successfully than her granddaughter. She didn't blink, but I could see the mischief dancing there. With agreement from the group and a pat on the back from Kai, my fate was sealed. Son of a bitch.

"Oh, I don't know if tha-" Red started, but I cut her off, rising out of my chair and glowering down at her until her face pinched at my expression. *Shit, happy face, man, happy face.*

"Let's do this, Red. Come on," I ordered, spinning on my heel and walking away from the table toward the patio. A resigned sigh and the sound of a chair sliding across the floor reached my ears, and I grinned. So, she *is* capable of following commands. My dick perked up at that idea, the sick fuck.

Trudging across the yard, Red didn't ask me to wait up or slow down. She just ran up beside me, breathing a little heavier than normal.

"For fuck's sake, Sloane. I didn't know we were racing," she huffed.

Tossing her a side eye, I didn't respond, continuing at my fast pace until we reached the pathways that led into the gardens.

There must've been over twenty different beds, and over half of them were being affected by whatever this demonic bullshit was.

"Show me your magic. Make shit bloom or anything else you want to try. I'll feel it out with my magic and see if I can detect anything. It'll confirm whether it's the grounds that are the problem, or if it's... well, you." I shrugged, not knowing another way to say it.

"Why are you even helping me, Sloane? I know you don't like me. And now probably less than you originally did since I started seeing Fischer..." She kept pace beside me as I stalked across the pea gravel paths that wove between the gardens. I had no idea where I was headed, but I didn't want to stop moving.

"Ah, so he told you about us?" I glanced down at her face, noticing it was beginning to turn a nice shade of crimson. *Christ, I bet her ass lights up like a stop light after one solid slap.*

"Yes. He did. Are you okay with it? He told me you weren't exclusive, but I still want to know that you're comfortable," she murmured, wringing her hands.

Stopping suddenly, I spun her toward me and looked down at her. *Why does she give a shit if I'm comfortable?*

"Red, if I weren't okay with it, it wouldn't be happening. We're here for a job, a job I thought would've been done and over with by now." Her face displayed shock at that statement, so I guessed the guys hadn't emphasized the finite aspect of their relationships. "Yeah, it's been just over a week, but I truly didn't expect to be here for more than a few days. We've had some... issues with the real estate we were looking into," I explained, sticking to our cover.

"Well, okay then. The last thing I want is to cause any issues and make you dislike me even more. You four are so close, and I wish I had friends like that. Or family."

"Where are your parents?" I asked gently. She was the one who'd brought up family; she wouldn't have done that had she not been willing to talk about it.

She shrugged. "Who knows where my dad is, never met him and never will. I'm the product of a one night stand with way too much alcohol and too little common sense."

"And your mom?" I pushed softly.

"Probably in some big city doing gods know what with her job. She's a consultant for magical businesses. At least, that's what I heard last."

"You don't have a relationship with her then?"

I kept my reactions to her words neutral, knowing this was the best chance I had at getting information on Laura without raising any suspicion. *She's the one who brought her up, not me. I'm just showing interest.*

Sighing, she looked out past my tall body, eyes trailing along the tree line that bordered the back of her property.

"No. Not a good one, anyway. She pops up randomly, stays a couple of days. Says shitty things, and then she's gone again. I don't hear from her while she's away, and that's perfectly fine. She's toxic. A black hole of negativity. Gran raised me, and she's all the mom I need," Saige elaborated.

Nodding in understanding, I opened my mouth. "Sounds like you're better off. If I've learned anything in my thirty years on this shit hole, it's that family is what you make it. Cut out the blackened, energy sucking parts and fill the holes with the people who deserve to share your life. Blood doesn't mean shit, Red."

Her right foot swept back and forth over the small rocks as she nearly whispered, "I really like them, Sloane."

The setting sun illuminated the red gold strands in her hair, calling to the fire god who lurked beneath my skin.

"They really like you too, Red. And I don't dislike you. Spoiler alert, I'm not the best with people." I grinned, and she shook her head as a giggle slipped out of her plump red lips. My eyes dropped to the source of the sweet sound and then back to her eyes. Reaching out, I tucked a strand of her glittering hair behind her ear. She swallowed at my touch and shifted her weight to her other leg. Nervous, perhaps?

"Why would I try to get involved with somebody when I didn't expect to be here long-term? Seems like a lot of work to me, so yeah, I held back. I'm not blind. I see the way you care about my brothers and the way they look at you. I'm not a good guy, Red. My heart pumps blackness through these tainted veins. You're too pure for me. I'd corrupt your sweet mind with a whisper of the wicked things I'd like to do to your sexy body." I leaned down, dropping my mouth to her smooth neck, a whisper away from making contact, "I'd torment your bright soul with a single brush of my depraved lips against your ivory skin."

Her hands came up, and she pressed against my chest, her eyes wide. "I'm not some porcelain princess, Sloane. I'm not as good as you seem to think, and I'm willing to bet you aren't as bad as you think, either. Sometimes we have to take a risk and let people in. It's good to let someone see all the sides of yourself. I know what I see when I look at you," she murmured, her grassy green eyes lost in my icy blues. It felt like this woman was stripping back my layers and seeing what my poor shriveled up soul looked like, and my heart sped up at the thought. I wanted to storm away from her, break this moment. I felt exposed, and the hairs on the back of my neck started tingling, but I couldn't move, and I wanted to know what she saw.

"What's that, then?" I breathed, putting my hands on her hips, pulling her closer. *What the fuck is going on?*

"I see a man who loves fiercely. Protects his brothers at all costs. I see a man who works hard to be the best he can be at his career. I see someone who is strong and dominating. I see a powerful mage who has more in common with me than he thinks, a man who I'd like to get to know. I also see the pain that flickers in your eyes from time to time. We all hurt sometimes, Sloane."

Trying to hide my reaction to her spot-on analysis of me, I

brought my hand up to her chin and tilted her head up. I followed her gaze as she looked at my lips, running the tip of her tongue out over her full bottom lip.

"I'm tired of hurting, Red."

Where in the hell did that come from? As much as I want it to be, that didn't feel like a line.

"I'm tired of being good," she whispered, her arms wrapping around my neck. She pushed up onto her tiptoes and pressed her mouth against mine. It was soft and sweet, just like her. My head was spinning; this was *not* what I'd intended when we walked out here together. Confusion over what I was actually experiencing cycled through my body, and it was too much. *She's gorgeous.* I knew that from the moment I first laid eyes on her. Right now, though, I felt vulnerable, like she was peering into my soul, seeing all my scars and deciding if I was still worth something. One kiss and I swore to the moon I heard a crack in my armor, the first one that anyone besides my brothers had ever caused.

Saige

Chapter Seventeen

I pressed my lips against Sloane's, sighing at the contact, and his body froze, not responding in the slightest. Maybe I'd misread the moment, but it had felt like we'd had a breakthrough. He'd been honest with me; there was no faking the way his eyes had flashed with hurt and then the confession of how exhausting it was. He'd stood before me, looking floored that someone had paid close enough attention to see what was really beneath the asshole persona that he executed perfectly.

Feeling like an idiot, I pulled back and sheepishly looked up to see how pissed he was going to be. It seemed like such a contradiction that his eyes were so light blue they nearly glowed white, yet his affinity was red hot. Sloane studied my face, the wheels in his brain clearly at work. His stare was piercing and intense, and I felt warmth spreading from my chest, up my neck, and settling on my round cheeks. Dropping my eyes from his to stare at the ground, I yelped when my body was pulled flush against his seconds later. His hands were cupping my ass, the hard as steel evidence of his arousal pressing into my stomach.

Gasping when he brought one of those hands up and tangled it in my hair, my gaze met his before he sharply pulled my head back. *Shit, shit, shit,* I cursed internally as the ice gave way to flames, oranges and reds flickering across his eyes, his power given life. Dark eyebrows furrowed, and a sharp exhale from his nose had my pulse racing when the heat of his breath hit my face.

Opening my mouth, to say... what? I didn't have a fucking

clue. Anything to break the intensity, for fuck's sake, I was both terrified and turned on.

No sooner had my bottom lip parted from the top when he pounced with a growl. His tongue swept into my mouth, dominating mine, and my stomach bottomed out. His grip on my ass tightened as he pulled me against his erection, kissing me like he lived his life: silently commanding and not giving a fuck what anyone thought. My lips would be bruised, but surprisingly, the thought didn't upset me. I was too far gone in the moment to think further on it.

Sloane dragged his lips down my jaw, biting my neck and pulling a mewl from my throat.

"Mmm, you sound like a little kitten when you make that sound, Red. Let's see if I can get you to do it again," he murmured against the fluttering pulse in my neck.

Wetness flooded my core, and when his teeth sank into my skin a second time, I released a louder mewl than the first, earning a chuckle from him. I had never made a noise like that in my life, but I'd also never had Sloane Sullivan marking me up like I was his to claim.

"I've had so many daydreams about this ass, kitten." He squeezed sharply, and I groaned. Barely a second later, the sounds of gravel crunching underfoot had my pulse skyrocketing. We were about to be caught. Trying to pull back, I was firmly stopped by Sloane tightening his hold.

"Don't move. I want him to see," he growled in my ear. Fisting a handful of my hair once again, he turned my head to where the sound was coming from.

Fischer came to an abrupt halt when he saw us standing there, hands tucked into the pockets of his jeans. His gaze darted between our faces before dropping down to Sloane's hand gripping my butt. Fish's eyes darkened to pitch black, but he didn't approach further.

Sloane released a dark chuckle. "You see, kitten... when we

play, he's mine to command, and I'm his to please. That's why he waits; he needs me to tell him what to do. I wonder, would he follow your orders the way he does mine? Or would he like to be the one to boss you around? So many choices..."

Fish heard every word that dripped from Sloane's seductive tone, the bulge in his jeans signifying that the pyro had told no lies. Fish got off on this, and I could see why. Fuck, I was pretty amped up myself.

"Come here, pet." Sloane smirked, and seconds later, Fischer materialized behind me, his hard cock pressed against my ass and the back of Sloane's hand. He placed a feather soft kiss on my exposed shoulder, and I closed my eyes, taking my fingers and reaching back to sink them into his soft curly hair. Sloane still had a vise grip on my long tresses, turning my head in Fischer's direction.

"Kiss your witch, pet. She's panting for it," Sloane ordered, his voice taking on a domineering quality that had the both of us snapping to attention, the desire to obey him driving our actions.

Fischer's hand trailed up my arm, his fingertips dancing over my shoulder, before his hand spread over my throat as he leaned down and smashed his lips against mine. Gone was the unsure man from our date the other night, and in his place was a guy who was going to do everything in his power to make his lovers happy. He didn't hesitate, nipping at my lips and licking my tongue. Fuck, he was talented with his tongue. My thighs clenched at the thoughts that it brought to the forefront of my lust-filled brain.

Breaking the kiss, I searched Fischer's eyes, needing to know that he was okay with this turn of events, not only the fact that he'd caught me making out with his... dom? But that he was okay with engaging in sexual stuff despite the fact that he'd said he'd wanted to wait. He must've seen the question in my gaze because he leaned down to whisper into my ear. "Don't overthink it, sweetheart. Sharing you with him right now is everything."

A moan slipped out when his lips found my throat. "Or are *we* sharing *you*, Fischer?'" I questioned, that thought sending me into a tailspin.

My nipples hardened, and a moment later, I felt a sharp sting. Instinctively, my eyes flew open as Sloane toyed with my breasts through my dress, my head dizzy with so many sensations I was going to melt. Fischer's hand moved up to my cheek, drawing me back into the kiss and away from Sloane's wandering hands.

"Very good, pet. You've always had a wicked mouth, though I much prefer when it's wrapped around my cock." Sloane smiled smugly, and I moaned. Legit *moaned* at the thought of watching them together.

Their attention shifted to me, the heat of it causing my body to tremor.

"Kitten likes that idea, pet. Maybe you should drop down to your knees and show her how much you enjoy pleasing me?"

Fischer ground his dick into my ass, a groan vibrating against my back.

"Turn around to face Fischer and tell him what you want, kitten."

Quickly, I was spun around, gasping when Sloane's length settled against my lower back. His teeth dug into the skin where my shoulder met my neck, and Fish trailed his fingers down my chest and over the swell of my breasts that were still hidden underneath my clothing.

"Tell me what you need, sweetheart. Do you want to watch us?" He studied my face, and I knew he was trying to read my feelings.

"Yes," I breathed. *Fuck, I want that.*

"Tell him what to do, kitten. Make him yours," Sloane encouraged, his voice husky with desire.

Fischer wanted this, no, he *needed* this. This was their dynamic, and they were sharing it with me. I'd never been a dominant person, but the idea of being in control of this powerful man had adrenaline firing through my brain at a rapid fire pace. Plus, there was a part of me that was reveling in the fact that *I* could possibly give Fish what he needed sexually.

"Open his pants," I whispered, eyes locked on Fish's face. The side of his mouth lifted in a small grin as he pulled Sloane around so that they were both standing before me. He didn't look away from me as he easily undid the button on Sloane's jeans. The sound of his zipper lowering was loud in my ears, but my heartbeat was thunderous.

"Take my cock out, pet. Show her what owns you."

Fuuuuck.

Fischer's skin looked even darker in the dusky lighting. He dipped his hand into Sloane's pants, the latter pulling up the hem of his black band t-shirt to mid-chest. His stomach was a work of art. Intricate flames wrapped up the entire left side of his torso, disappearing into his waistband. *I wonder if it goes down his leg?* Transfixed by the sight before me, I was completely frozen. Only my chest moved, its rapid rise and fall the sole clue I hadn't spontaneously combusted. "Commando, Master?" Fish shook his head, a laugh leaving his mouth.

"Show her." An order.

Inhaling sharply, I dared to drop my eyes to where he wanted them, nearly gasping when Fish pushed down Sloane's jeans and I got my first good look. His dick was as beautiful as the rest of him. Not as big as Cam, but he was still thick and solid. Black hair was neatly trimmed, running from his belly button down.

"Kitten," Sloane rumbled, and my eyes snapped up to his, "come here."

I floated the few steps it took me to reach him.

"Fischer's gonna be a good boy and swallow me like I know he's dying to, and we're going to watch the show," he commanded, every bit of his alpha personality coming to the surface. Swallowing, I nodded.

"Begin, pet."

Fascinated, I stared as Fish dropped to his knees, his hand wrapping around the wide base of Sloane's cock. The tip of it was glistening with pre-cum, and Fischer groaned as he leaned forward and swiped his tongue over it. *Oh my stars, I've never seen anything this erotic.*

Sloane hissed when Fischer took him into his mouth, bobbing his head back and forth. I must have made some kind of noise because Fish's eyes locked on mine, and he popped Sloane's dick out of his mouth, swirling his tongue around like he was licking his favorite ice cream cone. A warm hand gripped the back of my neck, and I tilted my head up to look at Sloane. His lips crashed against mine, his mouth warm. Actually, really fucking *hot*!

Whimpering, I pulled back, and he grinned down at me wolfishly.

"Sex heats me up, kitten, and it seems it does the same to you. You're almost as hot as I am. Now, be a doll and grab his hair. Hold him there while I fuck his face," Sloane directed, leisurely pumping his hips back and forth. *Oh, my gods.*

Glancing down to Fish, looking for some kind of consent, he grabbed ahold of Sloane, pausing his movements.

"Do it, sweetheart. I want it."

Deciding it wasn't my place to stand between my man and... his... *our?*... man's cock, I stepped next to my sexy submissive mage and snatched a handful of his hair. Sloane didn't waste any time before picking up his pace, his dick completely disappearing, over and over again.

"Kitten. Eyes up here."

Forcing myself to look away from the hottest shit I'd ever seen, Sloane lifted my hand to his mouth, sucking on two of my fingers. His eyes were ablaze, and I clenched my thighs, seeking friction. If I didn't come soon, I was positive I was going to die.

The way his tongue flicked over my fingers had me wishing it was between my thighs instead. He tugged my fingers out, groaning as his head fell back.

"Like that, take it. Fuck," Sloane's gravelly voice gritted out between clenched teeth.

Fischer sped up, bringing his hand up to squeeze his balls. With a growl, Sloane slammed his hips forward and spilled himself down his throat.

Stepping back until his still hard cock popped out of Fischer's mouth, Sloane pulled his pants back up but left them undone and low around his hips. Fish stood, swiping the back of his hand across his lips and smiling at me as I tugged him over and kissed him. Sloane's taste lingered, but I didn't find it unpleasant.

"That was-"

"Not over, kitten. It's your turn. What kind of men would we be if we left you wet and wanting?"

"I don't exactly have a dick I can just whip out all nimbly bimbly," I exclaimed, and they both chuckled.

"No, but you do have a dress one can easily ruck up around your waist. What do you say, kitten? Something tells me it won't take long with how flushed you are," Sloane observed, Fish nodding in agreement.

"Let us, sweetheart. I want to see your face when you shatter." Fish stepped up to me, his eyes searching for permission. After nodding my consent, his hand lifted my skirt, exposing my lacy red panties.

"How wet are you, kitten?" Sloane asked, invading my personal space. His hand dipped into my underwear, swiping two fingers right up the center of me. My eyes squeezed shut when I realized I was drenched.

"She's soaked, Fish. Taste her." Sloane removed his hand and pushed his fingers into Fischer's mouth, both men groaning as Sloane's eyes shut and my legs shook.

"Sweet, just like I expected," Fish teased, smiling at me, and my cheeks flamed.

Four hands moved to pull my panties down, and I stepped out of them quickly. I'd never done anything like this before, and the thrill of it was almost enough to have me orgasm on the spot. Sloane moved behind me, his hands pulling my hair, winding it around his fist before jerking my head to the side and sinking his teeth into my neck. All rational thought had abandoned me, and the only thing that mattered was getting the release I desperately needed.

Fischer smiled at me, leaning down to press kisses along my jaw. "Lift your leg, sweetheart. Let Sloane give you what you need. Let us take care of you."

Even though he'd just sucked cock like a champ and was now persuading me to spread my legs for his dom, he was still incredibly gentle with me. My knee bent and a moan left my mouth as Sloane toyed with my nipples, Fish hooking my leg around his waist so that Sloane had a direct path to my cunt.

"Fish," I said with a breathy sigh, "kiss me."

His lips pressed against mine, soft and full, savoring me. The breeze to Sloane's hurricane, they complemented each other perfectly, especially when Sloane's fingers moved through my pussy, circling my clit in time with the presses of Fish's lips.

"Oh, my gods, yes," I moaned into Fish's mouth just before two thick fingers pushed inside my wetness, and I clenched around them like a greedy sex-crazed witch.

Fischer gripped the inside of my knee, pulling my leg up even higher, allowing Sloane to torture me with three fingers now instead of two, his merciless ministrations driving me higher and higher.

"I'm going to make you come, kitten. I can already feel it running down your thigh. Perhaps I'll have our boy clean you up with his tongue," Sloane promised darkly, and I whimpered.

"I'm so close, *please*," I begged as I reached for Fischer's face again. "Come with me, Fischer, I need you to-" My request was cut off by a deep moan when Sloane curled his fingers inside of me.

Fischer made quick work of slipping his cock out, Sloane

using his hand to coat his lover's dick in my cream before sinking his fingers back inside of me.

"Fuck, I could come just from watching this. Sweetheart, you're so beautiful."

In the end, Sloane was right. It didn't take long. The two men worked me over with their lips, hands, and fucking filthy words, bringing me to detonation in record time. When his thumb pressed hard on my clit as he curled his fingers inside of me, a strangled cry started to rip out of my lips before Sloane turned my face toward him and swallowed it with his mouth. My walls fluttered around his hand, and I broke the kiss when I heard Fischer grunting his release, ropes of hot cum hitting my thigh.

"Pet, you've made a mess on my kitten, and she's made a mess of herself," Sloane's deep voice rumbled against my ear.

"It's okay," I breathed, my head lolling back against Sloane's chest.

"We might fuck like beasts, kitten, but we're not going to let you walk around with cum slipping and sliding between your thighs." Sloane informed me just as Fischer dropped down to his knees, once again.

Surely he's not... oh fuck, he is.

Lifting my leg under my knee, Fischer's tongue licked a long path from the inside of my knee clear up to the apex of my thigh and I couldn't do a damn thing but watch as he cleaned his desire from my leg.

"That's it, that's a good pet. Taste yourself on her skin," Sloane encouraged and I swear to Jupiter that when his hand shot out and grabbed a handful of Fischer's hair, guiding his face up to clean my cunt, I felt more wetness flood down my leg.

"Gods, sweetheart. Tasting us together..." He growled before running his tongue up my center, not in a way to get the party started again, but gently, like a caress. Once he was satisfied that he'd efficiently devoured every last drop, he peppered my skin with soft, thorough kisses.

My body deflated, melting against Sloane in sated relief. *By the stars, they're going to ruin me.* Sighing, my eyes slowly opened, peering right into Fish's. His appeared to be glowing now, black pupils still blown with the lingering lust that we were all coming down from, the iris a vibrant honey color that popped against his thick dark eyelashes. He was absolutely beautiful.

Dropping my leg to the ground, my dress fluttered back around my legs like nothing had happened. The small grin on my sweet mage's face had me giving one in return, and he gently pressed both of his large palms against my face before dropping a sensual kiss on my lips.

The sudden loss of heat at my back made me twist my body to see where Sloane had gone, but I didn't get far.

"Kitten," he rasped in a deep, soothing balm that calmed my still racing heart.

Turning the other way, I found that my fire god had his arm wrapped around Fischer's waist. I'd expected him to walk away from us, and the thought stung somewhere deep inside. But he hadn't; he was here, and the relief I felt that he was still with us was surprising.

"You did so well, both of you. You pleased me tonight," he praised, and pride swelled in my chest. *Why do I care so much?* His posture was lighter, the strain between his eyes gone. He was smiling right now, a genuine smile. Not the dark slash of a smirk that he usually walked around with, the one that screamed *bad boy* and combusted the underwear of men and women alike. *And oh my moons, I want to see that every day.*

Sloane pulled me into them, both men engulfing me in their arms, taking turns planting small kisses on my lips, my face, my neck. They kissed each other languidly, a slow dance that they'd perfected the steps to long ago. Hands and fingertips ran up and down my back in slow, soothing motions. These touches, they weren't meant to arouse; they were meant to express gratitude and to bring all of us back down from the impossible heights we'd just reached together. My heart slowed, returning to normal within a few minutes.

"Of all the sights I expected to see when I strolled out here, finding you in his arms was probably at the absolute bottom of the list," Fischer chuckled, crossing his arms over his chest when we broke apart.

"I think it was at the bottom of our list of possibilities when we walked out here, too," I confessed, shrugging.

"She fell victim to my sex appeal. Are you really that surprised, Fish?" Sloane questioned, and I whipped my face over to glare at him, but he was grinning. *What a shithead.*

"Hmm, you sure it wasn't the other way around? She's quite appealing." Fischer sucked his bottom lip into his mouth and then smirked when my cheeks flamed with the realization that he was still tasting me.

Bending down to snatch up my discarded panties, Sloane hummed in agreement. "She is, indeed, but I still need to see her cast some magic, so let's get to it. This puzzle is pissing me off."

The red lace disappeared into Sloane's pocket as he looked at me expectantly. "Hey! Those are a matching set. Give those back!"

Fischer shook his head with amusement when Sloane promised he'd return them after he got to see the other half of the set. Turning from us, he strode away like a slightly brighter little storm cloud. *Damn pervert.* We followed him down the path, moving out of the cover of the rows of saplings that had hidden us during our moment.

"So you left Kaito and Cam in there with Gran?" I asked with mock horror.

"Dude, she's showing them her dance moves. She's using Cam as a stand-in pole, claimed he was a little thicker than what she was used to working with, but she could make do."

My mouth dropped open, and all three of us laughed like hell.

"That woman is savage. She called Cam thick? I wish I

could've seen his face." Sloane wiped his eyes, and his deep laughter got us all going again. This was the first time I'd seen him let loose more than a chuckle, and the sound was like music to my ears.

"Honestly, she's not fit for public consumption. I'm going to have to apologize to them," I wheezed, short of breath after laughing so intensely.

My bright mood dampened slightly as I led the guys to a garden that looked particularly terrible. All of my beautiful plants were dry as a fucking tumbleweed, and damn, if that sight didn't send a wave of fury through me.

"Fix them, and then I'll see if I can sense anything that feels off in your magic," Sloane instructed.

Suddenly, I felt anxious. What if it *was* me? Maybe I was sick or cursed, and this would keep happening for the remainder of my life. *What would I do if I didn't have my green magic? I love my affinity. Watching life erupt from my palms, creating beauty, connecting to the earth when my hands plunge into the soil, I need that. Damn these demons who have caused such a clusterfuck in my life. I've never even gone further than a few miles outside of town. I have done nothing to deserve this bullshit.* White hot energy rolled through my body, my skin prickling with each second that passed, rage building inside of me so fast I felt like my skin would split if I didn't release it.

I vaguely registered hearing my name being said, but it was overpowered by heat and fury. *Blink.* I was on my knees. *Blink.* Hands in the cool dirt, searching, seeking. *Blink.* Magic was pouring out of me. *Blink.* Can't stop. *Blink.* So much power. *Blink.* Fix it, fix it, fix it. *Blink.* On my back, looking up at the sky. *Blink.*

Not moving, I sucked in deep lungfuls of air. I felt like I'd just broken through the surface of the lake, seeking oxygen like a flower sought the sunlight.

"Sweetheart, can you hear me? Fuck, Sloane. She's just staring.

THE MAGIC OF DISCOVERY

What the fuck was that?!" my reserved mage barked, his distress clear in the way he raked both hands through his hair.

"Fine... I'm fine," I nearly whispered, my voice shaking. The statement didn't sound believable, even to my own ears.

Sloane scoffed, his voice full of ice shards and then a dose of wonder. "Like fuck you're fine, Red. Look at what you've done."

His stern face came into view, hands reaching for my arms, and then I was standing. The world spun, and I squeezed my eyes shut, trying to get my bearings.

"Holy. Shit." Fischer's whispered words had my eyes snapping open.

"What the hell is all of this?" I shrieked, spinning in a circle, eyes widening to take in the state of my garden.

Cam, Kaito, and Gran's concerned voices carried to us on the wind, but we couldn't see them. We couldn't see shit. Every single plant within one hundred yards had exploded to triple its starting size, including the grass and trees. The dried up plants I'd set out to repair had been a mix of summer flowers, and not only had they been restored to health, but they were also exploding with blooms.

Fish called out to the others, telling them we were all okay. He grabbed my hand just as Sloane claimed my other.

"Well, Red. Doesn't look like your magic is failing you, but it *is* changing. Growing, becoming much more powerful. It's still carrying your specific signature, but darker. I don't know what those fucking beasts are up to, but they've done something to you," Sloane explained, searching my face. I'd never seen him look anything other than pissed off or indifferent before tonight. Right now? Wonder, curiosity, and alarm were cycling on repeat, and an alarmed Sloane was something that scared me to death.

Cam
Chapter Eighteen

The sound of glass shattering had the three of us freezing and looking to the window in the kitchen. A thick ivy vine had broken the glass and was continuing to grow at an unnatural rate, wrapping itself around any and every surface it could find.

"Saige," Bette breathed.

I exploded from the house, Kai hot on my heels. *She's okay*, I tried to tell myself. *She has to be.* But my brain wasn't functioning correctly; something was wrong, and I wasn't there to protect my woman. Fuck. I snarled and sprinted through the grass that was up to my knees. Everything was overgrown and wild, greens and a spectrum of bright colors bleeding into my periphery, but all I knew was that this wasn't normal, and I couldn't see my little witch.

Darkness flashed beside me, along with a deep growl. *Bagheera.* Good, the big cat would be able to sniff her out, and he'd lead me right to her. A blip of white darted past me with another growl, this one much softer. *Maven.*

Lightning lit up the sky with every step I took. "Saige!" I roared, needing to hear that she was alright. *Please.*

Bagheera and Maven disappeared into the wild growth while I followed, stomping through the damn foliage. Vaguely registering the voices of my brothers calling out that everyone was alright, I changed my direction. My heart didn't calm at their declarations though; I needed to see for myself, take her in my arms and feel her heartbeat pounding in her chest.

Pushing through a wall of pines, I froze. Her back was to me, Kai's arms wrapped around her. Red hair whipped through the wind that was picking up, matching my erratic pulse.

"Little witch," I rasped.

Seeing her big green eyes and flushed cheeks did something to me. I never wanted to see that look on her beautiful face again. Her dress was filthy, and dirt was covering up to her elbows, as well as smeared across her forehead. Tears welled in her eyes as I closed the distance between us.

"Cam," she sobbed, collapsing against my chest.

"Baby, are you hurt? I'm so sorry," I grumbled against her neck. The intensity of my feelings for her hit me like a freight train, and the thought of losing her had a crack of thunder exploding from the heavens so loud Maven started snarling.

"I'm not hurt, Daddy," she whispered in my ear. "I'm okay. Just... freaked out and exhausted."

Scooping her up into my arms, she protested, but I narrowed my eyes as more lightning crackled, illuminating our faces. She didn't argue when I turned from the others and stomped through the gardens, not giving a fuck what I was crushing under my boots. The paths were completely hidden from view, so it wasn't like I could've taken more care.

Bette was standing on the back patio, her coppery head barely peeking over the tips of the grass. Relief flooded her face, and her body deflated, adrenaline no doubt draining away. I nodded toward the door, signaling I was carrying Saige directly inside. Sloane and Fischer materialized out of the jungle behind me, Fish wrapping an arm around Bette and guiding her to follow us. I assumed Kai was probably getting some clothes out of his backpack in the mudroom before joining us. Even Maven, the little grump, was on high alert, his hackles raised as he patrolled through the house, ears flicking with every sound he detected.

"You can put me down, Cam."

"I'll put you down when I'm good and fucking ready. Living room in here?" I nodded to the entryway that was off of the kitchen, and she confirmed. Scowling, I carried her into the room and sat down at the end of a large navy blue sectional, positioning her in my lap so that my arms could wrap around her waist. She pulled my head against her shoulder, as if sensing I needed the connection, and began running her fingers through my hair.

Kai darted into the room, eyes wild before they landed on our girl. Sometimes it took him a few minutes to shake off Bagheera's energy after a quick shift between forms. It definitely hadn't helped that even though we had Saige, she didn't look her best. Not wasting a moment, he lifted her feet and dropped down right beside me, his hands running up and down her legs while tense growls slipped through his lips.

Once everyone was seated, Kai couldn't hold it in any longer. "What the hell happened?"

"Red got a power boost somehow," Sloane recounted. "I asked her to fix some dead plants and the next thing we knew she was in la la land, completely zoned out and dropping a metric fuck ton of magic into the earth. She didn't respond to us, and it wasn't until I yanked her back, physically severing the connection with the dirt, that she snapped out of it." I studied his face while we listened. His mask of not giving a shit was in place, but his eyes told a different story. He was flustered, and Sloane Sullivan didn't do flustered.

"How do you feel, child?" The older witch sat in a chair and rocked back and forth, drawing everyone's attention, like she was going to pull out a bedtime story and read to all of us crazy kids.

Before my little witch could respond, a huge yawn broke free, earning a chuckle from Fischer.

"Like I ran a marathon after being awake for twenty-four hours. My whole body aches," Saige confessed, sighing.

"Let me make you some tea, Sprout. It'll help with the muscles and lure you to a peaceful sleep. You should rest," Kai told her, but the last part of that was more of a message to everyone; now was not the time to push. With one last look of warning, he stood and prowled out of the room.

"Perhaps I shouldn't do any magic for a while, just until we see what happens over the next week or so. The rush, it felt... addictive. I've never felt more powerful in my life, and honestly? It scared me. Who knows what I'm capable of, and I don't want anything bad to happen to anyone because I can't control myself," Saige sniffed, her sadness seeping from her body into my own.

Bette's gaze softened on her granddaughter. "Perhaps that is for the best, child. This won't last forever, and we'll figure it out, together. Your men are intelligent, and the knowledge from their training will prove incredibly useful. Plus, I don't think the big man is going to let you out of his sight."

Slipping back into the room on silent feet, Kai pressed the mug of tea into Saige's hands before reclaiming his seat underneath her legs. A small contented sigh escaped her as she sipped the calming brew, her body growing pliant in my hold.

"I do believe I will take my leave now," Bette announced, having taken in the desperate looks we'd all focused on our girl.

"Let me make sure you get to your place without trouble?" Fischer offered, but she waved him off.

"There's nothing out there that my magic can't handle, boy. Stay here where you're needed. It was a pleasure to meet everyone. I have no doubt we'll be seeing more of each other now. You're all welcome to help as much as you'd like; we need all hands on deck," she told us as she approached Saige, holding her hand when she got close enough. "Call me if you need anything."

My little witch squeezed her grandmother's hand and nodded. "I will, Gran. Goodnight."

The rest of the guys called out goodnights and farewells, and I think I grumbled some sort of noise, but I couldn't do much of anything at the moment besides squeeze Saige and run my nose up and down her neck.

"Boss, how about we get her upstairs so she can shower and relax?" Kai questioned, but it was more of a statement seeing as how he was already rising from the couch.

"That sounds great," my little witch mumbled around another yawn.

Sloane and Fischer hopped up, eager to help wherever they'd be needed. Good guys, the both of them.

"Whatever you did out there was next level, Red. I'll continue doing some digging and see if I can find anything that relates to the signatures I saw in your magic. Fischer, see what you can find in the magical archives database tomorrow. There's got to be something that we're missing," Sloane grumbled. He never could stand not knowing all of the facts. At least he was being more cordial to her, so that was a win. She must have really impressed him out there, but that wasn't surprising to me in the least because I'd known she'd win him over, just like she'd done with the rest of us.

"Let's get you to bed, Sprout." Kai bent down and lifted her into his arms, and I had to fight the urge to clamp my arms around her and refuse to let him take her. She wasn't only mine, and satisfaction thrummed through my veins at the thought of all of us protecting her. It was enough to finally return my heart to a normal rhythm.

Fish stepped up to them, running a hand down her mud-speckled cheek. Leaning in, he kissed her gently and whispered something in her ear that in turn produced a sleepy smile on her face. When Fischer stepped back, Saige's eyes searched the room, and I was about to step forward to see what she needed, but then her body relaxed. Curious, I followed her line of sight, shocked that she was staring at Sloane. His blue eyes studied her face in return, his features softening. Realization crept down my spine, my eyes flicking between Sloane and Saige. *Holy shit.*

"Oh, fuck it," Sloane huffed, dropping his arms and closing the small distance. I swore on Jupiter's cock my mouth fell open when he grabbed the back of her head and crashed his lips against hers. This was no gentle kiss like she'd just received; oh no, he was *devouring* her. Lifting my gaze up to Kai, shock was evident from his raised eyebrows and widened eyes. Guess he didn't know about this new development either.

A movement to my right pulled my attention, and I caught Fish adjusting his obvious hard on while he watched them kiss. Well, he wasn't shocked in the fuckin' least. Guess there was more going on out in the gardens than magic. Sloane broke away, winking before letting us know he was heading back to the apartment. Fischer followed him out of the room after his own farewells

"Well, I'll be a son of a bitch, Sprout. That was like, the fourth hottest thing I've ever seen. When did that happen? Damn, I love plot twists. Totally did not see *that* one coming."

They were already heading up the stairs, Saige laughing at his antics before she paused. The creaking steps silenced, and I was about to charge up there to see what the hell was going on when her smooth, sweet voice carried to me.

"Cam?"

I swallowed. "Yeah, baby?"

"Are you coming up? I, uh... need you tonight." Her vulnerability was clear as day, but did she really think I would leave her alone, especially after earlier's shit show?

"Be right there, little witch. I'll clean up down here, and then I'll be up. K will help you get ready for bed."

A moment later, the sound of them climbing the stairs resumed, and I quickly made my way to the kitchen to make sure everything was put away. We'd done most of the cleanup duty while she'd been out with Sloane and Fish, but when I walked into the kitchen, a pair of blue eyes narrowed. Maven was sitting beside his empty bowl, so I gave him a couple of scoops of food and freshened up his water bowl.

Pulling out the trash can and a small handheld broom, I swept the glass that had fallen from the cracked window. The damn vine had stopped growing, but it was wound tightly around the curtain rod, so I decided to leave that to the older green witch to deal with in the morning. *What a weird fucking day.*

The raw power that Saige had blasted through the landscape was astounding. I mean, my brothers and I were all powerful, thanks to years of training and honing our affinities, but Saige had no such training, and when we used our magic, it didn't own us. Being in control of your abilities was crucial in the field. The thought of any one of us losing that hold was sobering; the results would be devastating. Leaning over the kitchen island, my thick golden hair fell forward, and I took a deep breath. We were no closer to getting any leads on Laura, but I had a feeling that she would somehow be connected to what was happening. A sleepy town didn't go from predictable and tranquil to chaotic and wicked overnight. Not knowing who all the players were in this game had me growling low in my throat. *Fuck!*

The little witch had infiltrated my mind, body, and heart. When I wasn't with her, I was thinking about her, wondering if she was smiling or how I could ensure that she would be. There had never been a shortage of women for myself and my brothers, but it was a cold day in hell if I ever slept with one more than once. Being constantly on the move contributed, I mean, fucking of course it did. Nikki, the one official girlfriend that I'd ever had, was responsible for her share of my emotional damage too. She'd cheated on me after claiming I was incapable of letting my walls down to let her in. When she'd first brought that up, I remember feeling blindsided. I'd opened myself up more with her than any other person aside from my crew. To hear that wasn't enough, when it had been so painstakingly difficult for me to tear down the barriers that locked my heart safely inside my chest, felt like getting kicked right in the dick.

Throwing rock salt into the wound, she'd sought out another mage's cock to ride while still hounding me about showing her *more*, being *more*, giving *more*. And fuck if I didn't try. When the cheating bitch was exposed, every little crumble and stone that had come down went right back where they belonged, and I mentally solidified that bitch in cement and mortar.

So when my little witch showed up with sticks of dynamite and started demolishing that wall around my heart, and I let her, I knew she was different, I knew she was mine.

The fear I'd felt earlier at the prospect of her being hurt... Christ, I'd barely registered the trek through the yard, all of the grass and plants brushing against my legs causing me to push harder, the invisible tether that bound my soul to hers pulling me along like a fish on a line. I knew then, I'd never give her up, I couldn't.

Standing up, I stretched and pulled my hair up into a knot on the top of my head. Sounds of movement from upstairs put my feet into motion, and I drifted through the house like an apparition finally being called to the light. That light being a curvy, strong, and bratty goddess, and I wanted nothing more than to bask in her brightness, hoping that it might purge some of the darkness hidden inside me so that I could be worthy of her.

Pushing open her bedroom door, my eyes landed on Kai's. His tall body looked ridiculous on the hot pink loveseat in the corner. The sound of running water had me assuming our girl was still in the shower.

"What in the fresh fuck was all of that? One minute, you're getting grinded on by a mini Magic Mike-grandma, and the next, someone started playing gods damn Jumanji! And then Sloane is making out with our girl? My brain feels like someone reached inside my skull with spirit fingers and wiggled them around just enough to slightly fuck me up," Kai blurted. When he was on a rant, it was really just best to let the man do his thing. Just as I was about to respond, the water in the bathroom shut off, and my brother and I froze, looking at each other.

Shaking myself, I had to ask, "How is she?"

Running a hand through his jet black hair, he sighed. "She's tired, man. Took a lot of energy to raise a rainforest like that in North America. A shower will do her good, though. Either she'll be a whole new witch with a second wind when she emerges, or she's going to pass out within minutes. Guess we'll see."

And see, we did.

The bathroom door flew open, and a towel-wrapped Saige strutted into the room, steam billowing out of the open doorway. She was a sight to see, damp hair, not an ounce of makeup on her perfect face, her radiant skin glowing faintly.

"Oh good, you're both here. Thank you guys so much for everything," she said over her shoulder while digging around in her dresser for a moment before tossing a pair of panties on the bed behind her. "That was some weird shit earlier, huh?"

"Huh?" I mocked, not believing the lightness in her voice.

Kai stood and walked over to stand beside me. "Yeah, Cam, pretty weird shit, huh?" He raised both eyebrows at me, his signature shocked look almost shaking loose a laugh. Saige shot us both a look over her shoulder and smiled.

"Well, what else am I supposed to do? Cry about it? Not much I can do, is there? So I've decided I'm not going to let it get me down. Super strong magic or not, I'm still just me."

Stubborn as fuck was what she still was. The image of her bent over my knee flashed behind my eyes, and I tried to shut that shit down. *She needs to rest.*

"What do you want to do, Sprout? Do you want us to go downstairs so you can get some sleep? We could watch a movie if you don't feel like sleeping?" Kai proposed, moving toward her and placing his hands on her shoulders. Her head fell back in order to peer up at him, damp hair dangling nearly down to the curve of her delectable ass.

She's sex on legs. Mother of the moon, sink this boner before I come across like a total fuck. Her palms ran up Kai's chest, and I watched the grin on his face grow. Aw, shit.

"Yeah, I don't think I feel like watching a movie. And sleeping right now..." She actually pretended to think before she continued. "I'm too amped up, Kai. It's like I got a second wind after the adrenaline crash wore off. I'd likely just flop around the bed for hours," she whined, not looking away from his face.

"Sounds like our girl has a real problem, Boss. Do you have any suggestions on how we could possibly help her burn this excess adrenaline and energy?" he questioned, but his eyes stayed locked on the little brat in his arms.

We shouldn't indulge her; that was what my brain was telling me. My dick, on the other hand, he had several ideas. Yep, my dick was going to win.

Prowling across the room, I pressed myself up against my little witch's back and enjoyed the way her breathing hitched as my cock made itself known. Meeting my eyes above her head, Kai gave me a lopsided grin, and I nodded.

Gathering her hair in my hand, I exposed her neck before dropping a kiss right behind her ear. "What do you think, baby? Should we show Kai how we like to play? Maybe he should make sure you're wet enough for us." Tugging on the towel, it dropped to our feet.

"I think you're both overdressed for the occasion," she sassed, popping one of her hips out. Not being able to see her face, I could only imagine the look she was giving Kai, especially when he chuckled darkly and lifted his shirt up over his head.

"Kiss me, Kaito."

Yellow flashed in his eyes as he tugged her into his body, bending to meet her lips in a harsh claiming. Rumbling blanketed the space around us, Kai's primal instincts in full swing. Lust zipped along my nerve endings, firing sparks down my spine, and a moan from my little witch had my cock hardening like steel. Fighting the need to squeeze her deliciously round ass, my feet held steady and my gaze locked in on Kai's hands sliding down her back and over the cheeks I wanted to bury my face into.

Suddenly, grassy green eyes were burning into mine as Kai spun her so his front was pressed to her back. Hips grinding forward, my baby's eyes rolled back in her head with the silent promise of what my brother would give to her soon. *Fuck me.*

His hand disappeared between her legs. "Mmm, Boss. She's soaked for us." Leaning down to her neck, he growled when she began to squirm in his hold, his forearm flexing with the motions his fingers were making. Goosebumps erupted on her pale skin as she wiggled her hips against his palm. *Enough, I can't stand it another minute.*

"Get over here."

Her mouth parted, and a moment later, she sank her teeth into her bottom lip. *By the stars...* Kai removed his hand, and Saige stiffened as her eyes narrowed in challenge. Excitement flooded my system because I knew that look. *Little witch wants to play. So be it.*

"K, let's strip down and make ourselves comfortable on the bed. If the little brat wants to be stubborn, we can show her what she's missing out on." My voice was a low grumble, and Kai chuckled as he shucked his jeans and boxers in one fell swoop. Turning his back to her, he prowled to the bed, and my little witch's pupils blew out into a sea of black as her gaze zeroed in on his bare ass.

"You can be such an ass, Cam."

Shuffling and creaking came from my back, and I stripped off my clothes as her eyes flicked back and forth from the shifter who was no doubt sprawled out across her sheets to my bare skin. Smirking, I fisted my cock and slowly moved backward before dropping my ass down and leaning back against her headboard.

"Sprout, is this when you call him Daddy? Because I've been hard as a goddamn rock since that night. I gotta hear you say it," Kai pleaded, and Saige threw her head back, laughing loudly.

"Goddammit, Kai," I exhaled without any force behind the statement. In fact, my mind was tossing up all kinds of wicked scenarios about how to make this memorable for everyone involved.

"I'm not fucking around, Boss. I've jacked off at least twice a day thinking about this," he groaned, his long cock twitching against his flat stomach. I couldn't even scold the man since I'd done the same fuckin' thing. We were all under her spell, and I wasn't going to fight any of it. There was no doubt in my mind that this beautiful woman had bewitched each of us. She'd unwittingly shone a light on the shadows that lurked in each of our souls, her very presence causing the darkness to recede. She was made for us, and damn them to hell if anyone tried to take her. In the end, I could only hope that when we were able to reveal the truth about our careers, she would be understanding and know that we'd only omitted the truth because we had to.

Light flashed, illuminating the dimly lit room, quickly followed by a roll of thunder.

"Come on, baby girl, let us take care of you."

Saige

Chapter Nineteen

First thing, there were two deliciously big mages in my bed right now.

Second thing, now that both dicks were out and at full mast, I had a deep and newfound respect for the women who partook in porn. *You're the real MVPs, do you hear me? Fucking fearless.*

Third thing, Kai kissed like a wild animal. I could only speculate as to what would happen when he finally got me underneath him. Or on top of him. Either way.

Fourth thing, Cam was eyeing me like he'd been deprived of food and water for days and I was some juicy steak cooked to perfection just for him. He wasn't wrong.

Fifth thing, I really, *really* wanted to try-

"Fuck's sake, woman. You're torturing me here. Quit thinking and bring that sexy as hell body over here. I need my hands on your ivory skin and my face buried between your legs."

Yeah, my stomach did a somersault down low, and I all but speed walked and dove onto the bed, rolling over Kai and squeezing myself between the two. We all laughed, but those noises quickly died out in favor of more breathy moans and sighs.

"See, Boss? Just mention going down on her and she'll bend to your will with zero hesitation. She's a greedy, greedy little thing… but I'm no liar."

Kai slid down the mattress, positioning himself between my thighs that were already falling open, ready to welcome him home. His eyes slid down my naked body, darkening when Cam rolled onto his side and cupped my breast in his large hand, a sigh breaking the silence when my stormy protector sucked my nipple into his warm mouth. My eyelids fluttered, and my back arched when I felt soft lips press on the inside of my knee before continuing down my inner thigh.

"Oh gods, you're killing me," I breathed as two mouths worked in tandem to set my entire being ablaze.

"Open your eyes, baby." Cam's voice rumbled in my ear, my eyes snapping open just in time to see Kai run his nose down my thigh while he inhaled deeply. Was he... smelling me? "Look at him, at what you do to him. He's scenting you." A growl came from Kai, low and deep, as Cam explained what was happening. "He's scenting his woman, so it's best to just let him do whatever the animalistic urges are driving him to right now."

Was this just a shifter thing? I had so many questions, but my brain fucking melted when Kai leaned in, shoved his face into my pussy, and inhaled so deeply I swore a part of my soul left my body via my vagina. Mouth hanging open, I couldn't look away, and when he lifted his head, his eyes glowing yellow, a whimper escaped my mouth.

"Mine," he said, his deep growl raising the hair on the back of my neck and pebbling my nipples. *Fucking right, I am.* When he dropped his head once more and slid his tongue from my ass to my clit, my back arched, one hand clutching the sheet and the other sinking into Cam's thigh. Shit, I was going to come fast and hard, already sensing the building of endorphins as that wicked tongue swirled, slurped, and sucked in all the right blessed places.

"Fuuuuuck, Kai, don't stop," I begged, and my head thrashed from side to side.

"Never."

My eyes were squeezed shut, but I needed more. Blindly reaching for Cam, his huge palm cradled my cheek as he turned my head and pressed his mouth to mine. Their tongues were moving in tandem, ramping my desire to new heights, while Kai pushed two fingers inside of me with ease. "You're going to come for us, baby. Give it to him." Cam barked the order like the alpha he was, and I was more than happy to obey. Especially as I felt pressure against my ass seconds before Kai sank his finger deep inside.

That. Was. It.

Boom. Bang. Fireworks. Happy Fourth of July. Merry Christmas. My body was spasming so intensely I hadn't registered Cam rising to his knees before I was flipped over. Suddenly, my hips were pulled up, ass smacked, and hair wrapped around his fist tightly enough to sting. I screamed when Kai buried his cock deep inside me. I hadn't even finished my first orgasm! My scream was cut off when a thick, pierced, steel pipe slid inside my mouth.

They were merciless. This was a possession, a claiming, an exorcism, and a damning. If I hadn't known it before, I knew it now: these men were mine, and I was theirs. Each one of them had staked a claim on my heart, my body, and my soul. The fire we created when we came together ruined me for any other men, not that I could even imagine needing to look, but there was no going back now. Having two of them use my body like this, hearing the grunts and filthy words they exchanged about how my pussy and mouth felt, how I was made to be shared between them, always, I'd never felt more powerful. Even earlier, when magic poured out of me like a volcano, that power didn't hold a candle to this.

Kai had really hit his gods damn stride, every thrust propelling me toward Cam, my moaning becoming nothing more than a humming around his shaft. Just as I felt Cam starting to harden to impossible limits, both men withdrew and Kai pulled me up so Cam could lay on his back. His massive body overtook the space, and four hands guided me to straddle his hips in reverse.

"You taste like sunshine and flower petals," Kai whispered in my ear.

"Let me taste you, Kai. I want my lips wrapped around your dick."

A palm landed hard on my ass, and I yelped in surprise. Turning my head back to glare at the smug mage beneath me, I sassed, "What the hell was that for?"

"Because I felt like it, baby. Now, impale yourself on my cock. I need to feel your walls squeeze me when I spank you next," Cam grunted between clenched teeth as I ground down against him, coating him in my cream.

I brought my face back to Kai, the sexy shifter grinning before reaching down between my legs and grabbing Cam's dick. Holding it straight up, he pushed down on my shoulder, slowly connecting our bodies. Once I was fully seated, everyone sighed. Languidly rocking my hips, Kai and I kissed each other at the same pace, exploring more thoroughly than our previous kisses. Sliding my fingers through his black hair, I really began to work my hips as Cam started moving with me.

"Bend forward, I want to watch myself disappear inside of you, see how much your ass shakes when we really get going. Suck his dick, baby. You want his cum, don't you?"

Oh gods, I didn't think I'd ever wanted anything as much as I wanted that in this moment.

"Yes," I moaned.

Spank.

"Yes, what?" Cam rumbled, freezing my movements with his massive hands.

Kai stiffened and sucked in a breath. I smiled, knowing this might just make him explode all on his own.

"Yes, Daddy." Damn, that sounded hot as hell even to my own ears. I'd made sure to lace that with a double dose of sexy, just for my shifter.

"Sonofabitch," Kai groaned, his hand squeezing his cock as he jerked himself in a steady rhythm, "that was a million times hotter than hearing it from outside."

I giggled, but that was short lived. Cam began thrusting up into me, hitting so deeply I could already feel the build of another orgasm barreling toward me.

"Gotta feel your mouth, Sprout. I'm not gonna last." Kai sounded pained, clearly holding back his release with all the will power he embodied.

After dropping forward onto my palms, Kai immediately moved in, and I licked the tip of his cock. The noise that left his throat was all animal, and he began moving his hips back and forth, chasing the pleasure that was so damn close.

"Like the way he tastes? Gonna swallow that cum like a good girl?" Cam sounded dark, his voice gravelly and promising. A finger pressing against my ass caused my pussy to clamp around him in warning; if you stick that inside of me, this shit will be done real fast.

Sliding backward slightly, just enough to free my mouth, I answered. Like a good fucking girl.

"Yes, Daddy."

All bets were off. Kai's fingers sank through my hair, firmly holding me in place as he pushed back in and fucked my mouth, my hand clapping around his ass cheek and pulling him in as far as he could go. He pulsed, spilling hot cum down the back of my throat as my name was ripped from his lips. He collapsed sideways, breathing heavily, eyes closed in post orgasmic bliss.

I gasped as Cam grabbed my hips and tossed me beside him, barely giving me a moment to get my bearings before he settled between my wet thighs and slammed into me.

"Ah, fuck me good, Daddy, make me come."

His hips pistoned like a machine, the speed punishing as his balls slapped against my ass with every wild thrust. Continuous commentary fell from our lips, a mix of sounds and filthy encouragements, and then we were soaring. Stars exploded

THE MAGIC OF DISCOVERY

behind my eyelids as my back arched, my entire body feeling like it had exploded, and I had no idea how I'd ever be whole again. Cam filled me up, his pumping slowing down as he completely emptied himself inside me. Fuck, I felt incredibly sexy right now.

When Cam flopped over next to me, attempting to catch his breath, I felt all of our combined juices trickling out of me, and I smiled. With a wink, he rolled off the bed and sauntered to the bathroom like the sex god he was. By the stars, he was a massive man, and he was mine.

Kai pulled me over so my head was resting on his chest as he said, "Sprout. You are perfection. I must've imagined a thousand different ways that it would go down when we finally gave in, but that surpassed every single one. There's just something about you, Sprout. You wear your heart on your sleeve and your selflessness shines through in everything you do. There was no anticipating you, not when it came to sex, and certainly not when it came to you completely ensnaring me from the first moment I laid eyes on you. " Every word came from his heart, and my eyes got a little misty.

His cheek was warm as I pressed my lips against it, his slight stubble prickling my skin. My fingertip ran across his full bottom lip. "Kai, I had no idea that this was where we were headed when your head popped over my sales counter, but I knew there was something *special*, something *different*, about you. The way your magic called to mine, the way you completely invaded my thoughts from day one... you captured me, Kaito."

Gently pushing me onto my back, he propped himself up on his forearm, his other hand gripping my hip as he stared down into my eyes with so much emotion swirling in their inky depths.

"I thank the stars every morning, Sprout. I thank them for bringing us here, bringing us to you, and I'll never be able to get enough," he breathed, leaning down to kiss me thoroughly.

Using our mouths and hands, we spent several moments expressing our feelings in a language that was exclusive to us. Kai dropped down beside me and tugged me against his body, once more resting my head on his shoulder in comfortable silence. My eyes were growing heavy, and I must have closed them briefly because something warm and soft sliding up my inner thigh startled me.

"Shh, little witch. Just cleaning you up."

Cam wiped me gently with the wet cloth, cleaning away the culmination of our pleasure, as Kai took his turn in the bathroom.

"You always take good care of me," I whispered, sleep trying desperately to pull me under its call.

A grunt came, then, "Always will. Scoot up here, let's get some sleep."

Cam shifted me toward the headboard, and I nestled down into the pillows. Slipping in beside me, he pulled the blankets up and over both of us. Cuddling up against him in the same way I had the last time he slept over felt right; I felt safe and cherished. The door to the bathroom opened, spilling light into the room, but darkness fell soon after with the soft flick of a switch. Only a moment later, the mattress dipped and Kai pressed himself along my back, wrapping an arm around my waist.

Sleep claimed me instantly.

WALKING THROUGH THE STONE CASTLE, *I FELT THE PULL TO THE throne room, just as before. Silent and swift, my bare feet carried me through the eerily quiet hallway. Glancing at the mirror to my right as I passed, I continued a few paces before stopping.*

Pump the brakes. Pump all the motherfucking brakes!

Moving backward, I nearly screeched when my body came into view. Butt ass naked. What if I run into someone? Oh gods, it would probably be that sexy red-haired man from before with my luck. Dream or not, strangers had no business seeing this bod. *The massive ornate double doors loomed ahead of me, so at least I knew there was a wardrobe in there with more of those robes. I just needed to be quick.*

Sprinting down the hall... okay, I mean, really, it was more like a brisk walk. I don't sprint. Especially not without serious boob support, I'm not a masochist. My hand wrapped around the iron handle, and I pulled the door open just enough to peek inside. Coast is clear. *Darting along the shadows against the walls, I was just about to pull out a deep purple robe when the sounds of voices carried through the gigantic room. Fuck, fuck, fuck.*

The talking grew louder, so I got inside the damn wardrobe and pulled the door shut. Heart pounding in my chest, I realized the heavy footfalls were heading my way. A voice I recognized, the man from before, was talking with another man. Willing my body to chill the hell out, I tried to calm my breathing so I could hear what they were saying.

"We've lost another twenty-six. That makes four hundred, thir—" Dream boy was cut off with a snarl.

"I know the numbers!" the other man bellowed before pausing and continuing in a more acceptable volume. "You don't need to remind me every time you pop in for a visit." Not being able to see them couldn't disguise the sneer I was sure was on his face.

"I'm sorry, Father. We're trying everything we can think of in the human realm, but it's just not working," the dream man sighed.

"It hasn't worked for over one hundred years. Asrael and the other three have failed, and time is almost up."

"We just need a little longer. The seers have seen a woman, and she is the one. We're close, so close. I can fucking feel it," dream boy insisted, but his father was done with the conversation.

"I have a meeting. Go back to your other life. Leave the running of the kingdom to the man who actually has the fucking title."

One set of footsteps pounded against the stones, moving away from my hiding spot, and dream boy cursed under his breath, "Asshole."

A chuckle. That's what blew my cover. Damnit, Saige.

Hearing him approaching, I hastily threw the robe on to cover my body, cinching the tie around the waist just as the doors opened wide. Holding my palms up, biting down on my lips, eyes rolling from side to side, yeah, I probably looked like an idiot, but I was going for innocent and an 'oops, my bad' kind of vibe. It didn't land.

Dream boy's amber eyes widened. "What the hell are you doing in the wardrobe, and are you having some kind of episode? What's wrong with your eyes?"

"Oh! Sorry, I um, have this thing sometimes, but it's no big deal. Anyway, I'll go now, see ya."

Turning my back to him, I walked a couple of steps to the back of the wardrobe. This was a dream, right? I should be able to do whatever I wanted. Picturing a snow-covered pine forest and a single lamppost, I didn't slow my gait, and my forehead slammed into a very solid piece of wood, knocking me backward.

"Holy shit, are you okay?" *He caught me under the arms before I fell out of the furniture that* did not *have my back.*

"Yeah, just a little collision, no big deal," *I told him, trying to play it cool while I brushed my hands down the robe as I stood up.*

Amber eyes were staring at me like I was a lunatic, and I didn't blame him.

"I really think you might need to sit down. Let me get you some water. Where were you trying to escape to through the back of the wardrobe?"

"Hmm?" *Lifting a hand to my head, my fingers gently traced the lovely goose egg that was growing by the second.* "Oh, just figured I might finally get to Narnia, so it was worth a try. Anything's possible in a dream, right? Sucks that your dad's a dick, though."

Suddenly, he was in my personal space, leaning down to my ear, whispering, "Do not insult the king in his own castle. Death has been issued for far less transgressions." *His tone wasn't threatening, he was warning me, and the flash of fear that had flickered across his face was enough to make me listen.*

A cold tendril of fear zipped through my body; this guy was dead serious. Inhaling, trying to steel myself, his scent invaded my nose, and I had to suppress a sigh. He smelled like a bookstore, and that was my all time favorite scent. Book bindings and old pages perfuming the air with their words, drawing you in, daring you to pick them up and give them a chance... freshly brewed coffee and warm baked goods.

"By the stars, you smell like heaven. Are you a hugger?"

Rising back to his over six foot height, he peered down at me, a smile tugging at his mouth. "It's been quite some time since I've partaken in the act."

I mean, he didn't say no. Leaping forward, I wrapped my arms around him and buried my face into his chest. I'd never smelled a man this intoxicating before, and my men in back in the real world smelled fucking delicious. This was next level, though.

"How do you smell so good?" I groaned. Honestly, I was starting to feel drunk. My head was swimming, and I wanted nothing more than to just lay down here and use this man-candle as a pillow.

He patted my back awkwardly, as if he was unpracticed in the simple act of a hug, but I could feel his nose burying into my hair. He was sniffing me just as much as I was him. "I could ask you the same question; you smell irresistible."

Giggling, I stepped back and grinned at him. "The smell kind of makes sense; you do have kind of an awkward sexy nerd thing going on."

"I am not a nerd!" he exclaimed, his eyes narrowed.

"Not gonna dispute the other two words?"

Brow cocked, he shrugged. "Awkward sexy kind of describes me perfectly." He gave me a slanted grin, dimples popping on his cheeks. Ohhh, boy's got game, huh? *"Now, what are you doing here? Where did you come from, and who keeps letting you in? And are you staying this time?" The hope in his voice tugged at my heart for some fucked up reason. He was like a puppy, and how do you tell a puppy no?* Just avoid that question. That's what I'll do.

"I told you, I'm dreaming. This time I gained consciousness while walking in the hallway outside of this room completely naked, so I

rushed in here to find a robe. When I heard voices, I hopped inside. You know the rest."

His eyes flicked down my body, his neck blushing. Cutie.

"Well, as entertaining as I find you, the others here won't give a shit about that. Trust me when I tell you that you don't want to be caught sneaking around. It's not safe, especially not for a woman of another race."

"I'm. Not. Sneaking! Wait, what do you mean another race? How am I so different from you? And I know you don't mean my gingerness because so are you!"

Shaking his head at me, the long strands of his red hair spilling into his eyes, he sighed as he pushed them back to their rightful location. "You really don't know where you are, do you? We're in Besmet, the demon realm."

My heart jumped into my throat, and it became increasingly harder to inflate my lungs with the precious oxygen they were demanding. I'm in the demon realm with the demons who are fucking up my magic and life, the demons who want to do gods know what with me? Nope. Time to wake up from this nightmare.

"Just try to calm down. Focus on your breathing."

He reached out to touch my arm, but when I flinched, he froze.

"I'm not going to hurt you."

My vision was tunneling, and all I could see were his beautiful eyes filling with concern. But he would hurt me... his people were trying to do exactly that. He probably just didn't realize who I was. Maybe I could get some information out of him before I got sucked back to reality? Focusing on my breathing and trying to take deep breaths, dream boy stepped closer, encouraging me by jumping into the exercise with me. Slowly, the panic that was desperately trying to seize my body receded, and I stabilized. Lifting my eyes, I saw how unsure he was now that I'd flinched when he'd tried to comfort me.

"I'm sorry. I know you won't hurt me, just an involuntary response," I murmured, wrapping my arms around myself.

He cocked his head to the side, studying my face, and whatever he saw there had his gaze darkening. His voice was deep and laced with fury when he stepped toward me, two horns rising out of the top of his forehead. I squeaked, but that didn't deter this demon. "Someone's hurt you? Tell me where the miscreant dwells, and I'll snap his fucking neck with my bare hands and bring his severed cock back to you as a trophy."

Whoa. Holy mother of moons and maidens, Mr. Awkward Sexy is no longer in the building, people. His alter-ego, Mr. Horned and Murderous has taken the wheel.

Giggling nervously, I put my hands on his chest. I needed to match his crazy in order to defuse this madness. "Oh no, that won't be necessary. I've already ripped off the shriveled up snail and coated it in... iron. Yeah, sometimes I wear it as a necklace, and it works wonders to let fuck boys know what I'm about."

An appreciative and devilish smile spread across his mouth. "Can I see it? Are you wearing it now?" *He raked both hands behind his horns, through his hair, leaving it wild and untamed.* "Fuck, that is the most arousing story I've ever heard; you're a warrior." *His mouth-watering scent slammed into me so hard I almost dropped to my knees, a soft moan slipping out before I could stop it, his pupils dilating. He was aroused, and I could scent it.* What the fuck is happening!?

"Tell me your name, warrior woman."

His form rippled, signaling I was about to lose the connection. That was okay with me, though. The guys and Gran needed to hear about this shit as soon as possible.

"Maybe next time, dream demon," *I called out as everything went black.*

So warm.

Lying on my side, Kai's head was buried between my boobs, his long leg curled around my hip and legs. Cam was pressed up against my back and ass, a huge arm thrown over both myself and the snoring, motorboating son of a beast.

"Guys," I groaned, attempting to wiggle my way out of their clutches. Sexy and strong clutches, but still... I had to tell them what I'd just dreamed... or whatever that was.

They both woke up immediately. Flying upright and off the bed, they fell into fighting stances, their eyes scanning the room.

"Since when are you guys ninjas? That was some serious spy shit right there," I laughed, but for real, that didn't look like some basic gym self-defense training.

Cam's gaze locked on Kai, and something passed between them silently. *Hmm, what's that about?*

"We've all taken martial arts classes, Sprout. All the better to protect you with. You scared us. I thought there was a break in or something. Shit," Kai breathed, pressing a palm to his heart, probably trying to get the hyped up organ to chill out.

Before I could respond, Cam's eyes narrowed as he questioned, "What the hell are you wearing, little witch?"

"Noth-" I inhaled sharply when I dropped my chin and saw the deep purple velvet robe I'd put on in my... dream. "Oh shit. Ohhhh shit."

Both men rushed to me, climbing back on the bed and each taking a hand. "Oh shit, what? What's wrong, Sprout?"

"There was a man—"

Cut off again, they demanded, "What man? Where is he? What did he look like?"

I held up my hand to silence them, emphasizing, "In what I *thought* was a dream."

Damn, my voice sounded strained and wobbly even to my own ears. Waking up wearing this robe was really messing with my strength. My head was pounding fiercely, too. Ugh, yep, still had the bump from my attempt to join forces with Aslan. Growls vibrated through the air when they saw the injury, and Cam was already flickering like a faulty set of Christmas lights.

"He didn't hurt me; this was embarrassingly self-inflicted," I reassured, pointing to my forehead, "but it was the strangest thing because this was the second time I've seen this man! Before you jump me for not telling you until now, I legit thought it was a dream! I overheard a conversation between him and his father this time, talking about their race being in danger." I grabbed my forehead with a moan. "Shit, that hurts," I whimpered.

"Are you okay? Do you need some water?" I felt Kai slide off the bed at Cam's question, probably going to fetch me a drink. "Lay down, little witch. You might have a concussion. Just... take it easy," he soothed, helping me to slowly lower my head down to the pillows once more.

"It's just getting worse, Cam. It feels like my skull is trying to crack." Tears leaked from my eyes, but my hands were still covering the majority of my face.

"I've got water if you want it, Sprout. Boss, do you think we should call a doc to come and check her out?" Kai was pacing beside the bed; I couldn't see him, but I could hear his movements.

"Water," I croaked, leaning up slightly as a straw found my lips and greedily downing half of the glass.

"Call someone, and the other guys, K. Now."

A scream ripped through the room, and I felt something wet running down the sides of my neck and nose, my muscles spasming as the horrible noise continued. People were yelling my name, cursing and crying frantically, and then roars and barking pierced through the blinding, most excruciating pain I had ever felt.

Oh gods, I'm dying.

Blackness and silence welcomed me like a warm, comforting blanket, and I drifted into nothingness.

Epilogue
Khol Larson

I'd just finished reading a slew of messages from both Cam and Sloane, each of them recounting the events of the past couple of days when a knocking pulled me out of my head. While their stories were vastly similar, Cam was still in the dark about the photograph his brother had uncovered.

Fuck, from the moment I laid eyes on that image, it had taken everything in me not to charge into that shithole town and tear it apart until the red-haired bitch showed herself, wards be damned. It wasn't the fact that Sullivan had found proof of her being connected to Emerald Lakes; I had known that already. The heavy magic keeping me away from the place was enough of a red flag that even a human child could've figured out that Laura was responsible. *Did the witch forget who she'd fucked with? I can't wait to remind her.*

A grin tugged at my lips, and I called out, "Come in, Bram."

I knew it was my number two, likely bringing the information that I had been waiting for. Results of a test that would confirm what I already knew to be true. Leaning back in my large, dark leather desk chair, I watched as one of the double doors swung in, the man I'd trusted with my most valuable secrets sliding through the opening. Sharply dressed in a gray suit with a dark blue dress shirt, arms rolled to the elbows, Bram crossed the room with an envelope clutched between his fingers. His dark red hair was neatly pulled back, leaving a clear view of his heavily freckled face adorned with a well-kept beard that matched his hair color.

EPILOGUE - KHOL

Amber eyes locked on mine, excitement churning in their depths. I'd confided in Bram about Laura years ago, and he was the only one that knew the extent of her treachery. Bram and I had the same goals and fought on the same side for the same race. Too fucking long we'd searched and experimented in the name of Asrael.

Skilled beyond belief, Bram would've fit right into Cam's unit, but I needed him behind the scenes. Instead, I appointed him as their handler, and with his ability to shapeshift, the guys knew him as Johnny. He frequently joined their foursome when they were stateside. He'd work out with them, discussing new developments in the magical world and what Radical had been working on in their absence.

Handing me the envelope, Bram stood straight and clasped his hands behind his back. "It's done, sir. The results are inside."

Turning the white rectangular enclosure in my hands, I broke the seal on the back flap and closed my eyes. I had waited; *we* had all waited centuries for this moment.

"Do you want me to leave?"

My eyes snapped open, meeting his. "No, you've also been waiting for this, and we'll learn the truth together."

He swallowed and gave me a sharp nod. Dropping my eyes to the piece of paper that was sticking out, my long fingers grabbed a hold of it and removed it from the envelope. My heart was racing; the implications of these results would change everything. *Everything*.

Unfolding the white sheet, I scanned the document for the information. When my eyes took in the data, I simply sat there, seconds ticking by. I couldn't stop re-reading, processing.

Bram cleared his throat, and I lifted my gaze to his as he wiped a hand down his face. The boy was nervous.

"Well? You're killing me. I can't wait any longer." He began bouncing on the balls of his feet in an uncharacteristic show of nerves.

EPILOGUE - KHOL

A sinister smile crept up, overtaking my mouth as I stood behind my desk. Holding up the document, I read the results aloud. "Saige Wildes and alleged father, ninety-nine point nine percent match. She's my daughter," I announced, and we shared a conspiratorial grin. "And she's fifty-one percent demon."

WANT MORE?

Check out book 2, now: The Magic of Betrayal.

So, how are we feeling? Hopefully you didn't throw your kindle or anything wild like that! We need that intact for the next journey to Emerald Lakes, which hopefully, won't be too long of a wait!

You, beautiful reader, I cannot tell you how much I appreciate YOU taking a chance and diving into this wonderful world. If someone had told me six months ago that I'd be writing this author note, days away from ARCs of my debut novel releasing, I would have laughed like hell. Why? Because writing is always something I'd wanted to do, but I always came up with excuses about how I couldn't possibly pull it off. Not enough time, not creative enough, my ADHD brain won't ever focus long enough to write a full length novel, and the list goes on and on.

Turns out, I COULD write a novel, and I COULD stay focused, I just needed the right characters and a story that sucked me in and wouldn't release my brain until the words were all out on paper. I really, really hope that you love the characters as much as I do. When I set out to write a reverse harem novel, I made it my personal goal to make each harem member unique and likable by at least one reader. If you have had a hard time choosing ONE, I achieved my goal. As an RH reader I always felt bad for the least fave guys of the group, I want everyone to get equal love.

If you could please leave a review, that would help me out immensely, seeing as how this is a debut novel. Hopefully more readers will take a chance on my book when they see that others already have.

ACKNOWLEDGMENTS

So here comes the thank you portion of this exciting little note!

Suki motherfucking Williams. You've probably heard of her, but if not, she's an absolutely brilliant and talented author. Her debut novel, The Beauty of Corruption, was what led me to attempting to try writing. Once I finished that book I was so damn inspired, I tracked her down on Facebook, infiltrated her beta team, became friends with her, and then she pushed me to try a solo writing project. She told me, "I think you'd be really good." Six words, guys. Six words that sent me down a rabbit hole of late nights, ample caffeine, copious amounts of alcohol, lots of middle fingers to my computer screen, and a friendship that I'm so lucky to have. Thank you, my friend. You're so special to me, and I'm forever in your debt.

To my P.A. Nicole Babinsack, thank you for your love and hardwork in getting my name out there and being my hype chick. You rock, and to Nicole's other merauthors, your support and help has been a gift from the gods. Thank you so much.

My beta team, editor, proofreader.... Could not have done this without you ladies. I'd be lost without you! And all of the other author friends, bookish friends, anyone who has supported me through this journey, you fucking ROCK and I'm so grateful for everything.

And last but certainly not least, my husband. Thank you for bringing me all the drinks and snacks while I was sprinting, for taking the kids to the park so I could write or edit, for celebrating every little milestone with me, and just for being your supportive self. Love you.

STALK ME! It'll be fun.

Come join the reader group to talk about The Magic of Discovery and for all kinds of other filthy shenanigans! Gran makes regular appearances:

Britt Andrews' Magical Misfits
    https://www.facebook.com/groups/187380059350040

Join my newsletter, here!
    https://mailchi.mp/c95f361e79a2/britt-andrews-newsletter

Find me on goodreads: here!
    https://www.goodreads.com/author/show/20607704.Britt_Andrews

- facebook.com/authorbrittandrews
- instagram.com/authorbrittandrews
- bookbub.com/profile/britt-andrews

Printed in Great Britain
by Amazon